©

D0051072

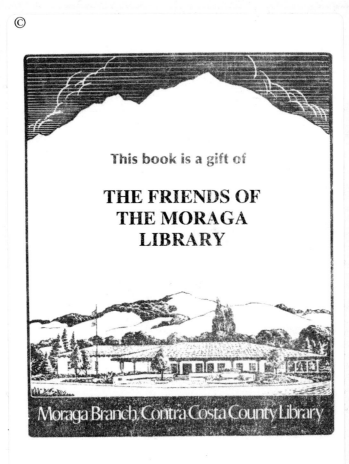

This book is a gift of

THE FRIENDS OF
THE MORAGA
LIBRARY

Moraga Branch, Contra Costa County Library

BUYING
TIME

Also by Pamela Samuels Young

Vernetta Henderson Mysteries

Every Reasonable Doubt (first in series)

In Firm Pursuit (second in series)

Murder on the Down Low (third in series)

Buying Time

Pamela Samuels Young

Buying Time

Goldman House Publishing

ISBN 9780981562711

© 2009 by Pamela Samuels Young

All rights reserved. No part of this book may be reproduced, transmitted or used in whole or in part in any form by any electronic, mechanical or other means now known or hereafter invented, including, but not limited to, xerography, photocopying and recording, or by any information storage or retrieval system, without the express written permission of Goldman House Publishing.

This book is a work of fiction. The names, characters, dialogue, incidents and places, except for incidental references to public figures, products or services, are the product of the author's imagination and are not to be construed as real. No character in this book is based on an actual person. Any resemblance to actual events, locales or persons living or dead is entirely coincidental and unintentional. The author and publisher have made every effort to ensure the accuracy and completeness of the information contained in this book and assume no responsibility for any errors, inaccuracies, omissions, or inconsistencies contained herein.

For information about special discounts for bulk purchases, please contact the author or Goldman House Publishing.

Goldman House Publishing
P.O. Box 6029-117
Artesia, CA 90702
www.goldmanhousepublishing.com
www.pamelasamuelsyoung.com

Cover design by Marion Designs

Printed in U.S.A.

For Ellen Farrell,

Thanks for being such a great
colleague, supporter and friend.

BUYING TIME

PROLOGUE

Veronika Myers tried to convince them, but no one would listen. Her suspicions, they said, were simply a byproduct of her grief.

Each time she broached the subject with her brother, Jason, he walked out of the room. Darlene, her best friend, suggested a girls' night out with some heavy drinking. Aunt Flo urged her to spend more time in prayer.

Veronika knew she was wasting her time with this woman, too, but couldn't help herself.

"My mother was murdered," Veronika told the funeral home attendant. "But nobody believes it."

The plump redhead with too much eye shadow glanced down at the papers on her desk, then looked up. "It says here that your mother died in the hospital. From brain cancer."

"That's not true," Veronika snapped, her response a little too sharp and a tad too loud.

Yes, her mother had brain cancer, but she wasn't on her deathbed. Not yet. They had just spent a long afternoon together, laughing and talking and watching *All My Children*. Veronika could not, and would not accept that the most important person in her life had suddenly died. She knew what everyone else refused to believe. Her mother had been murdered.

"Did they conduct an autopsy?" the woman asked.

Veronika sighed and looked away. There had been no autopsy because everyone dismissed her as a grief-stricken lunatic. When she reported the murder to the police, a disinterested cop dutifully took her statement, but she could tell that nothing would come of it. Without any solid evidence, she was wasting everyone's time, including her own.

"No," Veronika said. "There wasn't an autopsy."

The funeral home attendant smiled sympathetically.

Veronika let out a long, exasperated breath, overwhelmed by the futility of what she was trying to prove. "Never mind," she said. "What else do you need me to sign?"

Later that night, Veronika lay in bed, drained from another marathon crying session. She rummaged through the nightstand, retrieved a bottle of sleeping pills and popped two into her mouth. She tried to swallow them dry, but her throat was too sore from all the crying.

Tears pooled in her eyes as she headed to the kitchen for a glass of water. "Don't worry, Mama," Veronika sniffed. "I won't let them get away with it."

Just as she reached the end of the hallway, a heavy gloved hand clamped down hard across her mouth as her arms were pinned behind her back. Panic instantly hurled her into action. Veronika tried to scream, but the big hand reduced her shriek to a mere muffle. She frantically kicked and wrestled and twisted her body, but her attacker's grip would not yield.

When she felt her body being lifted off the ground and carried back down the hallway, she realized there were two of them and her terror level intensified. But so did her survival instinct. She continued to wildly swing her legs backward and forward, up and down, right and left, eventually striking what felt like a leg, then a stomach.

As they crossed the threshold of her bedroom, she heard a loud, painful moan that told her she had likely connected with the groin of one of her assailants.

"Cut it out!" said a husky, male voice. "Grab her legs!" he ordered his partner. "Hurry up!"

The men dumped her face down onto the bed, her arms still restrained behind her back. The big hand slipped from her mouth and Veronika's first cry escaped, but was quickly muted when a much heavier hand gripped the back of her neck and pressed her face into the comforter.

Fearing her attackers were going to rape, then kill her, Veronika defiantly arched her back and tried to roll her body into a tight ball. At only 130 pounds, she was no physical match for her assailants. They easily overpowered her, forcing her back into a prone position. As one man sat on her upper legs, strapping her left arm to her side, the other man bent her right arm at the elbow and guided her hand up toward her forehead.

During the deepest period of her grief, Veronika had longed to join her mother. But now that she was face-to-face with the possibility of death, she fought valiantly for life.

That changed, however, the second Veronika felt something cold and hard connect with her right temple. She stiffened as one of the men grabbed her fingers and wrapped them around the butt of a gun. At that precise instant, Veronika knew with certainty that her suspicions were indeed fact. Her mother had been murdered and now the same killers had come to silence her before she could expose the truth. And just like her mother's death, her own murder would go undetected, dismissed as the suicide of a grieving daughter. A conclusion no one would question.

As the man placed his hand on top of hers and prepared to pull the trigger, a miraculous, power-infused sensation snuffed out what was left of Veronika's fear, causing her body to go limp. The heavy pounding of her heart slowed and she felt light enough to float away.

Completely relaxed now, Veronika closed her eyes, said a short prayer, and waited for a glorious reunion with her mother.

PART ONE

When All You Have Is Hope

CHAPTER 1

Lawyers get a bad rap. Strip away the arrogance, the greed and the half-truths, and you'll find a decent human being underneath. That's exactly how Waverly Sloan saw himself. A decent guy who'd screwed up.

Waverly pulled his battered BMW into the parking stall outside his Culver City townhouse and turned off the engine. He dreaded going inside. All the way home, he imagined his wife's face contorting in horror in reaction to the news he was about to deliver.

He closed his eyes and rehearsed the spiel in his head. *I'm about to be disbarred*, he would tell her. *So you'll have to stop teaching Pilates three days a week and get a real job.*

Waverly exited the car and climbed the short flight of stairs to their unit. He was a large, solidly built man with skin the color of honey. Borderline handsome, his lopsided smile was the primary source of his appeal. It compelled people to like him.

"You're home early," Deidra called out the second he opened the front door.

Waverly found her in the kitchen, poised over a cutting board chopping carrots and bell peppers. He dumped his keys on the counter, walked up behind her and swallowed her up in a bear hug. "I'm home early because I couldn't stand being away from you for another second."

Deidra reared back to peck him on the lips, then returned to her chopping.

Resting against the center island, Waverly folded his arms and stared at his wife. At thirty-seven—five years his junior—Deidra had the firm, voluptuous body of a highly compensated stripper. Her long, auburn hair fell past her shoulders, perfectly accentuating her barely brown skin. After two years of marriage, Waverly still had no idea what her real hair looked like underneath the five-hundred dollar weave.

"Is everything okay?" Deidra glanced back at him over her shoulder.

His wife had good instincts, at least about him. Waverly eyed the knife in her hand. He had a mental image of Deidra accidentally chopping off a finger when she heard what he had to say.

"I love you," Waverly said, not in an effort to sidestep her question, but because it was how he truly felt.

"Ditto." She smiled, then waited.

Waverly had wanted Deidra from the second he spotted her walking out of a store on pricey Rodeo Drive weighed down with shopping bags. Instinct told him there was little chance that a woman like her would give a guy like him a second glance. He had only been in Beverly Hills for a meeting with an opposing counsel. Risktaker that he was, Waverly turned on his charm and, to his surprise, it worked. Too bad that same skill couldn't get him out of his current fix.

He took a bottle of Chardonnay from the refrigerator and poured a glass for each of them. "What if I decided not to practice law anymore?" he began.

The pace of Deidra's chopping slowed. "I thought you liked being a lawyer." She placed the knife on the counter and turned to face him. "What would you do instead?"

He shrugged and cleared his throat. "I've been thinking about insurance investments."

Deidra put a hand on her left hip. "Insurance? That doesn't

sound very exciting. Can you make any real money from that?"

Waverly shrugged again. "I hope to find out."

According to a guy he'd met at a legal conference, he could make a bundle in the viatical business. Waverly had no idea what a viatical was, only that it had something to do with insurance. He had an appointment to talk with the guy in a couple of days.

He could tell that his wife wasn't happy about his possible change of professions. The men in Deidra's life before him had given her whatever she wanted, whenever she wanted it. Waverly now worked hard to do the same, often placating her with promises of better things to come. Deidra enjoyed the prestige of being a lawyer's wife and was banking on Waverly eventually landing a case that propelled them to the big leagues.

"This doesn't mean we'll have to put off moving, does it?" Deidra asked.

Waverly had agreed that she could start house shopping as soon as his next case settled. But even if he saved every dime he made for the next thirty years, he still wouldn't be able to afford the gated communities where Deidra wanted to relocate.

"Maybe," he said.

She was about to complain, but apparently noticed the angst on his face and retreated.

Waverly took a sip of wine and debated delaying his planned conversation with Deidra until he was absolutely certain about his situation. The written decision from the State Bar Court could arrive any day now. There was a slim chance that he might be hit with a suspension rather than disbarment. He'd hired Kitty Mancuso, a sixty-plus, powerhouse mouthpiece whose client base consisted exclusively of rich, white-collar criminals and lawyers who'd screwed up. If anybody could save the day, it was Kitty.

"I'm going to put on my sweats," Waverly said, wimping out. "How long before dinner's ready?"

"Not sweats," Deidra replied. "Find some nice slacks. They'll be here at six."

"They who?"

Deidra smiled sheepishly. "Mom, Dad, and Rachel. Didn't I tell you?"

No, because if she had, he would have faked a migraine. "Uh, I just remembered a motion I forgot to file."

Deidra squinted and playfully pointed the knife inches from his nose. "Don't even think about it."

By the time their dinner guests arrived, Waverly was seated in the den, insufficiently buzzed and ready for the show. Watching his wife's dysfunctional family was better than reality TV.

Leon Barrett, Deidra's pint-size father, strutted in and gave her a kiss on the cheek. He waited all of three beats, then started boasting about his new sixty-inch flat screen. Rachel, Deidra's older sister, showed off a diamond bracelet a new boyfriend supposedly gave her.

Leon spotted Waverly sitting in the den and made a beeline in his direction.

"How's the law business these days, counselor?" Leon's thumbs hung from his belt loops like a cowboy and he rocked back and forth from heel to toe.

Waverly didn't bother to stand. "I'm making it."

Leon walked over to the sliding glass door and surveyed their small patio. Waverly wondered what he would criticize first.

"So when are you two going to give up this place for a real home?" Leon joked.

Instead of answering, Waverly reached for his wineglass and took another sip. The thought of Leon Barrett finding out that he'd been disbarred made him want to puke.

"They're building some new homes in The Estates," Leon continued. He always referred to Palos Verdes Estates as *The Estates*. Waverly figured he'd moved there just so people would think he lived on an estate.

"If you'd bought over there when I told you to, you'd have nothing but money in the bank." Leon owned a small construction firm that had done well, in part, because he was a major tightwad.

The wine was doing nothing to reduce Waverly's irritation level. Too bad his own father was dead and gone. Henry Sloan wouldn't have just thought about telling Leon Barrett to kiss his ass, he would have done it.

The evening plodded painfully along as it always did. Deidra's father and sister talked nonstop about themselves while Deidra's mother Myrtle, smiled and nodded like a big bobble head.

"I have to go to Paris at the end of the week to interview a bunch of obnoxious designers," Rachel said, feigning annoyance. She was a fashion editor for *Vogue*. Like her sister, Rachel was a good-looking woman, but she lacked Deidra's talent for capitalizing on her beauty.

"I hate you," Deidra exclaimed. "I've been dying to go back to Paris."

"Why don't you come with me?" Rachel prodded. "I'll be there three weeks. It'll be fun."

Deidra gave Waverly a hopeful look.

Having Deidra out of town for a few weeks would give him time to get a backup plan in place. But the funds for a ticket to Paris didn't exist. His face must've conveyed that.

"If you can't afford it," Leon said facetiously. "I'd be glad to pick up the tab."

Waverly smiled across the table at his father-in-law. "That's a very generous offer." He paused to take a sip of wine. "And we'd love to take you up on it."

A razor-sharp silence whipped around the table. No one was more dazed than his blowhard father-in-law. Leon Barrett frequently offered to share his money, but never actually parted with any. Waverly thought the man might actually choke on his toothpick. Deidra shot Waverly a look hot enough to scorch his eyeballs, but he pretended not to notice.

Pleased with what he had just pulled off, Waverly got up and retrieved another bottle of wine from the wine rack.

The minute her family walked out of the door, Deidra went off.

"What in the hell was that about?" she shouted. "How dare you let Daddy pay for my trip?"

Waverly headed back to the den with Deidra on his heels. "Well, he *did* offer."

"He's offered to pay for a lot of things, but you've always refused. Are we having money problems? Because if we are, I need to know."

"Cases have been a little slow coming in, that's all."

"So slow that you can't come up with four or five grand for a trip to Paris?"

Four or five grand? He wanted to laugh. "Look, I'm working everything out. Just give me some time."

"Well, you better figure something out fast because this is not what I signed up for. We were only supposed to be living here for a few months and it's been two years. I've never lived in a place this small before, but I did it for you."

Small? Their townhouse was more than two thousand square feet.

"And now you're telling me that we're basically bankrupt."

"We're not bankrupt." *Not yet.*

"If we can't blow a few grand on a vacation, that's bankruptcy as far as I'm concerned," Deidra barked. "And please don't embarrass me in front of my family like that ever again. If we're having money problems, I should know about it before they do." Deidra stalked out of the kitchen.

Waverly opened the cabinet over the bar, grabbed a fifth of brandy and took a gulp straight from the bottle. His wife's little tantrum was really uncalled for. *But what the hell?* He had never expected to keep a woman like Deidra happy forever.

Too bad he hadn't listened to his father. After divorcing his third wife, Henry Sloan swore off pretty women. *Way too much work*, he'd told his son. *Find yourself a basic broad and she'll ride with you until the wheels fall off.*

Waverly chuckled to himself. Right now he could use a woman who could hang, because the ride was about to get rocky.

CHAPTER 2

Assistant U.S. Attorney Angela Evans entered a conference room on the eleventh floor of the federal courthouse on Spring Street and slapped a thick stack of papers on the table. The rest of the newly formed task force was already assembled.

"Hey, Angela, what are you trying to do, blind us?" Zack Hargrove, another AUSA, shielded his eyes with his forearm. "How about turning down the wattage on your ring finger?"

The entire team—Zack, a paralegal, two case agents, and a junior attorney—erupted in laughter.

"Alright everybody, that's enough." Angela pretended to chuckle along with them. "This is really getting old." Her three-carat, princess-cut diamond was still the butt of jokes even though she'd been wearing it for almost six months. *Would it ever stop?*

She actually considered the ring embarrassingly pretentious, but her fiancé, Judge Cornell L. Waters, III, was all about the show. So she quietly concealed her disdain and responded to his proposal with a soft *yes*, when she was actually thinking, *I'm not so sure.*

"So where's my wedding invitation?" Zack asked, refusing to lay off.

A pretty boy with blue-green eyes and well-moussed blonde hair, Zack enjoyed being the center of attention. As usual, his Ralph Lauren suit and Italian shoes made him look more like a big firm partner than a government lawyer.

Angela winked at him. "Your invitation's in the mail."

She took a seat at the head of the table with a confidence gained from nearly a decade of putting criminals behind bars. First as a deputy district attorney and now with the U.S. Attorney's office. Tough, smart and passionate in her professional life, her personal life was another story.

"Let's get started." Angela's hair was a crinkly mass of natural curls that resembled a limp afro from a distance. Her narrow face and wide brown eyes were striking enough to grace the cover of a fashion magazine.

She eyed the box of Krispy Kreme donuts in the center of the table. It wasn't even two o'clock yet and she only had nine Weight Watcher points left for the day. One donut would wipe out seven of them. Maybe stuffing her face with donuts was the easiest way out. *Sorry. Couldn't shed the twenty pounds. Have to call off the wedding since I can't find a dress that fits.*

Angela directed her attention to Tyler Chen, who'd just joined the U.S. Attorney's Office after three years at Gibson, Dunn & Crutcher. "Tell us what you found out."

"The U.S. Attorney's Offices in Las Vegas, New York and Miami are close to returning indictments against a company called The Tustin Group," Tyler began. "The company is pressuring terminally ill people to sell their insurance policies."

"Sell them?" asked Salina Melendez, a paralegal who was attending Southwestern Law School at night. "Who would buy somebody's insurance policy?"

"An investor," Tyler said. "It's called a viatical settlement and it's sort of like a reverse mortgage. Except these companies trade in people, not property."

Angela nodded. "Say, for example, you're dying and you've got a policy worth a hundred grand," she explained. "A viatical broker will go out and find somebody willing to pay you a portion of the face value. All you have to do is name the investor as your beneficiary. After you die, the investor collects the full value."

"Six months ago," Tyler continued, "one of The Tustin Group's principals began operating in California under the name Live Now, Inc. It stands to reason that if they're pressuring people in the other states, they're probably doing the same thing here. Main Justice wants to make this a multi-district indictment."

"Sounds like a sad way to make a buck," said Jon Rossi, a case agent with the U.S. Postal Inspection Service. He was a forty-plus, rail thin, vintage car enthusiast. The AUSAs always worked their cases with agents from one of the federal law enforcement agencies, such as the FBI or DEA. "But then again, if the people are dying and need the money, maybe it's a good thing."

"It would be if Live Now was playing it by the book," Angela replied. "But they're targeting people too sick to know what they're signing and convincing them to take peanuts for their insurance policies. Once we catch them in the act, it won't be hard to get an indictment."

Criminals didn't realize that no matter what the offense, the feds could usually nail them on mail, wire and internet fraud charges since they routinely used these methods of communication to further their fraudulent operations.

"I wish this case had more pizzazz," Zack sulked.

Angela ignored the comment. Zack was still put out that she had been selected to head up the task force even though he had a few more years of practice.

"Any complaints filed yet against Live Now?" asked Jon.

"Just one." Angela pulled a document from the stack of papers in front of her. "It's actually a little strange. The daughter of a woman who sold her policy through Live Now claims her mother was murdered and thinks the viatical broker or the investor are responsible. Says they killed her to get a faster return on their investment."

Zack had been staring off into space, but immediately perked up. "How did the woman die?"

Angela perused the complaint. "She had brain cancer. The hospital where she died found no evidence of foul play."

"It wouldn't be in the hospital's interest to find any," Salina said.

Zack's face blazed with interest. "That would certainly be a clever racket," he mused. "Invest in the policy, then kill the policyholder. The police wouldn't waste much time looking into the death of somebody who was already dying. Are we investigating that angle, too?"

Zack the Hack, as everyone called him behind his back, was always on the hunt for a high-profile case that might evolve into a highly paid talking-head job. He actually told people he was going to be the next Anderson Cooper.

"Murder is the D.A.'s jurisdiction, not ours," Angela said. "Besides, the police don't buy the daughter's theory and there's been no evidence of anything like that going on in the other states."

"It might not hurt to talk to the woman," Zack pushed. "We may find some information that could strengthen our case."

Angela pursed her lips in frustration. Maybe appeasing Zack on this would make him more cooperative down the line.

"Salina, why don't you talk to the woman over the phone? See if you think there's anything to her allegations. If there is, I'd like you and Jon to interview her in person." Angela slid a folder across the table. "Her name is Veronika Myers. Here's a copy of her complaint."

"I'm on it," Salina said.

Angela handed out a three-page document to the team. "We have a lot of work to do over the next few weeks. This memo lays out everyone's role. We received the go-ahead to stage a sting operation."

"How's the sting going to work?" Salina asked. "Is somebody going to go undercover as a terminally ill patient and see if they get the screws put to 'em?"

"That's exactly how it's going to work," Angela said.

Jon smiled. "Sounds like fun."

"Glad you feel that way because I think you'd be the perfect undercover patient."

"Hold on." Zack turned to Rob, the case agent sitting to his left. "I think Rob could also do a pretty good job."

A smile masked Angela's true feelings. The ultimate designation of their undercover patient would be made by the Postal Inspection Service. Still, Angela planned to lobby hard for Jon. Rob was way too passive for a case like this. He hadn't even opened his mouth during the entire meeting. On top of that, he was basically Zack's puppet. With Rob as the undercover plant, Zack would effectively control the investigation.

"Jon has more experience doing undercover work than anybody else in this room," Angela said. "He just helped snag two big-time drug dealers."

"Rob's had his share of undercover cases, too." Zack gave him a fatherly pat on the back.

Rob, in turn, looked admiringly at Jon. "Not nearly as many as Jon."

Zack's face reddened and he glared at Rob.

"Then it's settled," Angela replied with glee. "Jon's our choice. Now we need a name for our task force. Any ideas?"

"I'm way ahead of you." Jon paused for dramatic effect. "Operation Death Scam."

They all groaned in unison.

"Too depressing," Angela said.

"It should be depressing," Jon protested. "It's a depressing business."

"How about Operation Buying Time?" Tyler offered. "That's really what these people are trying to do. Many of them use the money for experimental medical treatments in hopes of extending their lives."

They all paused to mull over the suggestion.

"Too bland," Zack said. "We need something with some real punch to it."

"I like it," Angela said, overruling him. "Operation Buying Time it is."

Zack muttered something under his breath as Angela dismissed the team.

"Who wants to join my pool?" Zack asked, as everyone headed out. "I'm taking bets on who the President's going to name as our new boss."

Six weeks ago, U.S. Attorney General Stanley Harrison was caught leaving a penthouse suite on the Vegas strip with a high-priced call girl. If he hadn't paid for the room with his government credit card, he might still have a job.

"I'm going to pretend I didn't hear you propose illegal betting in the workplace," Angela chided him.

"Aw, lighten up," Zack replied. "You can be such a killjoy sometimes."

Angela gathered the rest of her papers and headed back to her office. While Zack's bravado often got on her nerves, she otherwise liked working with him. He was smart, tenacious and had good instincts. But as the lead attorney, she'd probably have to spend as much time containing Zack's ego as she did managing the case.

Considering the fragile state of her personal life, she didn't need the added hassle of any headaches from Zack Hargrove.

CHAPTER 3

Y es, Mr. President. Of course, Mr. President. Thank you, Mr. President."

Lawrence Erickson squeezed the telephone receiver and struggled to keep his emotions in check. A tall, athletic man in his late fifties, Erickson's light blue eyes accented sandy hair badly thinning near the crown.

As he stood behind his desk, talking to the President—the President of the friggin' United States of America—he grinned down at his law partner Roland Becker, seated in front of him. President Richard Bancroft had just informed Erickson that he was among the final candidates being considered to fill the recently vacated job of U.S. Attorney General. Was he interested?

Hell yes, Erickson had wanted to say. After a few more *thank yous*, he hung up the phone.

"You knew I was getting that call!" Erickson sputtered, grinning down at his friend. "Why didn't you tell me?"

"And miss that shit-eating grin on your face. No way." Becker stood and gave his friend and mentor a hug. "Anyway, I was sworn to secrecy. If I told you, I would've had to kill you."

Becker and President Bancroft's Chief of Staff had shared an apartment in law school. That long-time friendship occasionally gave Becker access to inside information.

Shortly after the debacle that led to Attorney General Stanley

Harrison's resignation, a White House staffer notified Erickson that he was being considered for the job. Erickson had assumed, however, that his selection was a long shot.

A former assistant U.S. attorney in the Southern District of New York, Erickson had gained a name for himself by prosecuting high-stakes corporate fraud cases. After joining Jankowski, Parkins, Gregorio & Hall, one of the most powerful law firms in the country, Erickson limited his practice to complex contract disputes. His multimillion-dollar verdicts were a testament to his excellent litigation skills. Few knew, however, that this hugely successful lawyer harbored deep personal insecurities.

"According to the President, I'm on the short list." Erickson was literally beaming.

"Screw the short list," Becker said. "I know for a fact that you're their number one candidate. The job is yours. So we have to start thinking ahead." Becker returned to his seat. He excelled at expecting the unexpected and preparing accordingly, skills he perfected as a Navy SEAL. Though he had only twenty years of legal practice under his belt compared to Erickson's thirty, Becker was clearly the more strategic of the two.

"What about your situation?" Becker said. "Once the vetting process gets underway, they'll be digging deep. Has anything changed?"

Becker's question cast a somber cloud over their celebration. Erickson slumped into the leather chair behind his desk and studied the ceiling for several seconds. His *situation* was his wife, Claire Erickson. His confidante turned enemy who was dying of pancreatic cancer.

A fiercely private man, Erickson had shared only limited details of his failing marriage with his best friend. Claire had been threatening to file for divorce and to make the split as public as possible. But there was more, a lot more, that neither Becker nor anyone else needed to know. That's how people screwed up. They talked too much to too many.

Erickson rocked back in his chair. "Claire's pretty unpredictable these days. I'm just trying to play the dutiful husband in hopes of keeping things under wraps."

"Is it the cancer?" Becker asked. His hard looks—pockmarked skin, sunken cheeks, and dark wavy hair—matched his aggressive litigator's demeanor. "Is that what turned her into such a bitch?"

Erickson flinched. While the description fit, he did not like hearing his wife disparaged by somebody else. Even someone as close as Becker.

Erickson massaged the back of his neck. He wished he could blame everything on the cancer, but Claire's actions could not be attributed to her physical condition. Though she was not of sound body, her mind was another matter.

"Our marriage was strained long before her diagnosis," Erickson said wearily.

Becker shrugged. "These days, divorce isn't the end of the world."

"True," Erickson said. "But like I said, this won't be a quiet split. If Claire decided to call the *L.A. Times* and spread the lies she's been threatening me with, Stanley Harrison and his hooker girlfriend would be reduced to a one-inch story on page twenty in comparison."

Becker's eyes expanded in surprise.

"Hey, hold on a minute." Erickson moved quickly to correct any misconceptions. "I'm not screwing around. The only mistress I have is my career and that's the one Claire wants to destroy."

"As we've discussed before, there *are* ways to keep her quiet." Becker fired a sinister look across the desk. "Permanently."

The room fell strangely silent.

During a recent dinner consisting of more drinking than eating, Erickson had spoken in jest of wanting to *dispose of* his wife. *Was Becker serious?* "What do you mean?" he asked cautiously.

"You know exactly what I mean." Becker's face showed no emotion as the silence in the room rose to flood level.

Erickson swiveled his chair and gazed out of his office window. His friend's words did not shock him. Becker had never liked Claire. Disloyalty among wives, Becker had said more than once, constituted grounds for the death penalty. Becker still bore battle scars from a bitter divorce in his late twenties.

Erickson tried to laugh off what his law partner seemed to be suggesting. "You know all about my fantasies, but—"

Becker's phone vibrated. He eased it from the inside pocket of his jacket, glanced down and smiled. "Katy's getting pretty good at texting. She just sent me a riddle."

Erickson watched as Becker's large fingers awkwardly maneuvered over the tiny buttons. It confounded Erickson that a hardcore litigator like Becker could turn so spineless when it came to his family. Who in the world had five kids under the age of ten in this day and age? Becker needed a vasectomy and his wife needed her tubes tied, then ripped out as an added safety precaution.

"Sorry about that." Becker slipped the phone back into his pocket. "I get such a kick out of my kids."

Too bad I don't, Erickson thought. Becker had named him godfather of his oldest daughter, a title Erickson despised as much as the demands of the job.

"Look," Becker continued, "we just can't sit back and let Claire destroy this once in a lifetime opportunity."

We. Erickson liked Becker's word choice. The man was fiercely loyal. But Erickson needed time to fully evaluate Becker's proposal.

"If I get the nomination," Erickson said, changing the subject, "I guess you know what that means for you?"

Becker gripped the arms of his chair and a big grin splashed across his face. "Wow. You don't think it's too soon?"

Erickson was perplexed. "*Too soon?* Too soon for what?"

"I assumed you were talking about my replacing you as chairman of the firm."

Erickson laughed off the idea. "Yes, it's way too early for that," he said dismissively. "I was talking about your coming to Washington with me. If I'm nominated, I want you to be my Deputy Attorney General."

Becker's face flat-lined and it took a few seconds for him to respond. "I'm flattered," he said finally. "But, honestly, I'm not sure I could afford the pay cut. Do you know what it costs to send five kids to private school?"

"It's only a short-term job. Think about all the national exposure."

Becker hunched his shoulders. "For you, maybe. Name me five Deputy AGs."

"C'mon," Erickson pushed. "We can both take a leave of absence. Your chances of succeeding me once we return will be a lot better after all the connections you'll make in Washington."

Becker ran his fingers through his hair. "I'll give it some thought. When the time is right, I'll need to discuss it with Staci. She may not want to uproot the kids."

"I understand," Erickson said, though he didn't.

In Erickson's world, a wife's sole responsibility was to serve in whatever capacity requested by the breadwinner. Children had no role, which was why he'd never fathered any. Claire's disaster of a daughter had proven that decision to be a sound one. If they hadn't shipped her off to boarding school at the age of twelve, their marriage never would have survived as long as it had.

After Becker left his office, Erickson's thoughts drifted back to his marital problems. He didn't just want this job, he deserved it. There was no way he was going to let some vindictive little bitch stand in his way.

Even if she happened to be his dying wife.

CHAPTER 4

Waverly lumbered into the State Bar Court on Hill Street, his heart thudding with apprehension.

He'd received a call from Kitty Mancuso's assistant an hour earlier. Mancuso was handling a suspension hearing and wanted to meet with him during a break. Waverly figured the court's decision had arrived and Mancuso preferred to deliver the bad news in person. Or maybe, he prayed, the news was good and Mancuso wanted to see the ecstatic smile on his face when she told him he'd received the luckiest break of his life.

His BlackBerry vibrated as he waited for an elevator. Waverly winced when he saw his brother's number. He only picked up to prevent Quincy from leaving a long, rambling message on his voicemail.

"What up, bruh?" Quincy said.

"Nothing much." Waverly hoped his brother could sense that he wasn't in the mood for pleasantries. "I'm on my way to court so we have to make this quick."

Quincy responded with a long, practiced sigh that Waverly had heard hundreds of times before. "I'm in a jam, bruh."

Waverly waited.

"I need a small loan."

This was usually when Waverly complained and asked how much. This time he didn't.

"Just five hundred. I swear I'll pay you back. I need it to—"

"I don't have it," Waverly said, cutting off his brother's pitch. *And if I did, you'd only use it to gamble away or score some crack.*

"C'mon, bruh, I—"

"I said I don't have it."

Waverly thought about telling Quincy that he was about to be disbarred, but couldn't face letting him down. Quincy didn't have the same concern. "I'm having my own financial problems at the moment."

He could almost see his brother's stunned expression.

"It's Deidra, ain't it?" Quincy charged. "C'mon, bruh. Don't let your wife get between us. We're blood."

"I love you, man, but I'm broke." Waverly abruptly turned off his BlackBerry.

He stepped onto a waiting elevator and exited on the fifth floor. As he proceeded through the security checkpoint, he examined the forlorn-looking faces all around him. A thin woman in a pastel suit walked by and Waverly detected the faint scent of alcohol. At least he'd been smart enough not to show up to court buzzed.

Waverly spotted Kitty Mancuso prancing toward him. She was a short, feisty dishwater blonde who favored pink. Pink lipstick, pink nail polish, even pink pearls around her neck.

"Well," he said, as she walked up, "what's the verdict?" Although anxiety threatened to explode from his chest, he tried to sound upbeat.

Mancuso's solemn demeanor told Waverly everything he needed to know. "Let's go in here." She pointed in the direction of a small conference room.

As they both took seats, Mancuso pulled a document from her satchel and handed it to him. "The court ruled as we expected."

Although Waverly had anticipated as much, the news still hit him like a jolt from a stun gun. He scanned the judge's ruling.

*The evidence shows that Mr. Sloan improperly retained thirty thou-
sand dollars in settlement payments from two clients and converted
the funds to his own personal use. His conduct breached the oath he
took to act ethically toward his clients at all times.*

Waverly briefly glanced up at Mancuso, who gave him a look
that said she wished there was something she could do. His eyes
went back to the ruling.

*Mr. Sloan has been disciplined in the past for failing to comply with
his obligations as a member of the Bar. In the first instance, he failed
to timely pay a fine after the court sanctioned him in a discovery dispute. Six months later, he neglected to file a complaint after accepting
a nine-thousand-dollar retainer from a client. He also failed to timely
notify a client of the receipt of a settlement check and subsequently
did so only after the client complained to the Bar. Mr. Sloan's long
record of misconduct cannot be excused.*

Maybe the result would have been different had he begged for
the mercy of the court. *I only borrowed the money, Your Honor. To pay
my mortgage, the note on my wife's Lexus and a few other household bills. I
always intended to pay it back.*

He turned the document face down on the table. There was
no need to read more. "So what's next?"

"That's only the court's tentative ruling. It has to be formally
approved by the state Supreme Court before you're actually
disbarred. But that could take several weeks. So you'll have some
time to transfer your existing cases to other counsel."

Waverly needed minutes, not weeks to wrap up his personal
injury practice. He only had two active cases: a man injured in a bad
motorcycle accident and a slip-and-fall in a grocery store that was
about to be dismissed because his client lied during her deposition.

Waverly stood up.

"I'm sorry," Mancuso said, sounding as if she really meant it.

Waverly thought about thanking her for her help, but changed his mind since he hadn't really gotten any.

After leaving court, Waverly spent the next hour sulking at Nick's, a dive with decent food and strong drinks not far from the courthouse.

It was over. After all the effort he had expended getting into Hastings Law School and staying there, he was no longer a lawyer.

Waverly pulled a note pad from his inside breast pocket and looked at the figures. He had tried to calculate how long he could pay the bills with his dwindling savings. He was already facing eviction from his office space. He could pay the mortgage on the townhouse, two maybe three months if they drastically cut back. Every drop of equity had already been squeezed out of it. Short of pawning Deidra's jewelry, he knew of no other quick fixes.

Deidra would be leaving for Paris at the end of the week. Having her out of the way would be a big help. He'd been down before and had managed to climb out of whatever hellhole he had dug himself into. He would just climb out again.

Waverly glanced at his watch. Vincent Rivera, the guy who'd been trying to sell him on the viatical business, had called earlier to say he was running late. Seconds after Waverly asked the waitress to bring him his third brandy, Vincent slid into the booth across from him.

"Get rid of that long face," Vincent ordered, "because I'm about to change your life. Your days of chasing ambulances are over." Vincent's dark suit was practically molded to his muscular frame. He had a hint of an accent, but Waverly wasn't sure whether he was Italian or Hispanic.

Waverly made a loud slurping noise as he sucked on a piece of ice. "Okay, let's hear it. What's the scam?"

"No scam at all." Vincent popped open his briefcase. "A company called Live Now is going to make you very, very rich, very, very fast. Did you get a chance to read that brochure I sent you?"

Waverly had only perused it minutes ago while waiting for the buzz from his first drink to kick in. "Yep. You want me to go out and find a bunch of dying people with hefty life insurance policies and convince them to name somebody else as their sole beneficiary in exchange for some upfront cash."

Vincent looked as if he was offended. "Don't make it sound so cold. Live Now is running a humanitarian business. Viatical brokers are like real estate brokers. Except they don't sell homes, they sell hope."

Waverly chuckled. "Now hope is something I could definitely use." He was anxious to hear the get rich part. "Exactly how does the broker make money?"

"The policies are purchased through a trust. As soon as the parties sign on the dotted line, the broker gets ten percent of the face value of the policy, paid by the investor," Victor explained. "The investor has to wait until the insured dies to get paid, but not the broker."

Waverly took a sip of his drink. "And this is actually legit?"

"One hundred percent. Viatical settlements are actually similar to securities like stocks. I'm telling you, man, this is a goldmine. If you come up with just five clients with two-hundred-thousand-dollar insurance policies, your ten percent cut is a clean one hundred grand. Most of our brokers are pulling in seven figures a year in commissions." Vincent slid a book and a folder to Waverly's side of the table.

Waverly picked up the book, *Viatical Settlements, An Investor's Guide,* and thumbed through it. He opened the folder to find articles from the *Wall Street Journal, Newsweek, The American Cancer Society,* and *AARP,* plus a copy of *Out* magazine.

"Wait a minute." Waverly glanced up. "To make any money, I'd have to find a boatload of dying folks *and* a bunch of rich investors. That doesn't sound all that easy."

"Wrong again. Live Now has investors who are itching to part with their cash and lots of leads to help you find terminally ill people." Vincent handed him a sheet of paper.

The left side listed churches, AIDS organizations, cancer support groups, hospice facilities and senior citizen groups. Waverly pointed to a column on the right. "Who're these people?"

"Doctors, ministers, financial planners, hospice operators and human resources managers. People who might know someone who's terminally ill. The ten doctors listed there are cancer specialists. They'll be your best source for referrals."

"And why would they be willing to do that?"

Vincent winked. "A small under-the-table finder's fee. A thousand bucks a head. We can't solicit people directly, but there's no problem with someone referring a client to us."

Waverly sat more erect in his seat. This stuff was actually beginning to make sense to him. The feeling of despair that he hadn't been able to shake for weeks suddenly started to dissipate.

"What are the requirements for becoming a broker?"

"You have to be licensed by the California Department of Insurance. They're looking for ethical people. You won't have a problem. You've already passed the State Bar's ethics requirements."

Waverly stared down into his drink, then briefly looked up. "There's something you should know." He paused and took a quick sip. "I was disbarred today."

Vincent slumped back in the booth. "Aw, man, that's a real problem. They don't even want to see a blemish in your background. What happened?"

"A little misunderstanding with a client over some funds." Waverly could tell that Vincent didn't buy his simple explanation.

After brooding for a minute, Vincent leaned in over the table and lowered his voice. "I'm going to share something with you. As a recruiter for Live Now, I get three percent of every deal, so I'm looking for guys who're hungry. It's been my experience that the hungriest people have the toughest past. A guy I recruited with a fraud conviction in the Las Vegas area is my top broker in the state."

"How did he get licensed?" Waverly asked.

"In Vegas, if you know people who know people, you can get practically anything done."

"If it helps, it could be weeks before my disbarment shows up in the system. Couldn't we just rush my application through?"

Vincent stroked his chin. "We do have an inside contact at the Department of Insurance who might be able to help you out." He seemed far less enthusiastic than he'd been just a few minutes ago. "It's worth a try, but I can't guarantee anything."

Waverly opened the *Out* magazine to a page flagged with a Post-it Note. The Live Now ad showed a brawny, bare-chested generation Xer walking along the beach, a grave look on his face. Bright yellow text read: *HIV doesn't have to be a death sentence. Get thousands for your life insurance policy. Quick and strictly confidential.*

Waverly wished he hadn't drank so much. The wheels of possibility were turning so fast he felt woozy.

"You know what investors call viatical settlements?" Vincent asked.

Waverly waited without responding.

"Death Futures."

Waverly cringed as a surge of excitement shot through him. If he could get past the licensing process, he could easily transition into this business.

"I want to make a toast." Waverly smiled and raised his empty glass in the air. "To you. Thanks for giving me hope."

CHAPTER 5

Angela studied Cornell's face as he slept. Her husband-to-be snored lightly, his mouth agape, a sliver of the whites of his eyes fully visible.

In the beginning, it bothered her that Cornell slept with his eyes open. But later on, it made complete sense. Cornell thrived on order and control. Closing his eyes, even in sleep, might cause him to miss out on something.

The orange glow from the clock radio on the nightstand read 6:29. In less than a minute, Cornell would climb from bed, exercise, shower, shave, peruse the *L.A. Times* online, then watch a snippet of CNN. Only then would he acknowledge her presence in his world. Cornell demanded total silence for the first forty minutes of the day. Every day.

The alarm jangled and Cornell's hand reached out like a claw to quiet it. On autopilot now, he hurled his legs over the side of the bed and lowered himself to the floor. His fifty push-ups would be followed by three hundred sit-ups.

She watched as Cornell lowered and raised his body in perfect push-up formation, grunting with each repetition. If he could grunt, she should at least be able to say *good morning*.

Angela repositioned her head on the pillow and glanced down at her ring. She wished she could quiet the persistent voice in her head. *Stop procrastinating. Call off the wedding.*

Each time she was finally ready to back out, indecision resurfaced. An African-American woman of thirty-four didn't have a multitude of marital options, particularly in L.A. To be honest, she liked the idea of being married to a judge. Especially one who was smart, handsome, and wanted children. For Angela, motherhood was a must. She had watched too many of her friends wait and hope until it was too late, then run off to adoption agencies or sperm banks and struggle as a single parent. Angela wanted nothing less than the traditional family unit. Two parents, two kids, a minivan and a vacation home.

She ambled out of bed and made her way to her private bathroom as Cornell plodded into his on the opposite side of the room. For Cornell, the twin master baths had been the top selling point of his loft condo in Playa Vista. Angela hated the forced separation the two rooms created.

Staring at her reflection in the mirror, Angela ran her fingers through her unruly curls. Cornell's suggestion that she straighten it was a concession she had refused to make. With her schedule, she needed a no-fuss do.

Her relationship with Cornell had begun three years earlier, following a painful breakup with an ambitious MBA. After Angela made it clear that her career would not take a backseat to his, he dumped her for a younger, thinner woman who couldn't do long division without a calculator. Months later, Cornell—her first older man—had stormed into her life and taken charge. In the beginning, Cornell had been fun, charming and attentive, causing Angela's concerns about their ten-year age difference to eventually disappear. Over time, however, he'd become inflexible and condescending. Before she'd realized it, his subtle, but stinging critiques had slowly chipped away at her self-esteem.

When she heard Cornell reenter the bedroom, she calculated that their adult time-out was almost over. She jumped into the shower and was dressed in minutes.

She found Cornell in the kitchen, engaged in another morning ritual. He laid out a multiple vitamin, along with one vitamin E, two Cs and a B-12. He repeated the same lineup for her, adding a calcium tablet and a birth control pill. Cornell wanted children, but only when *he* was ready for them.

"Morning," he said, brushing his lips against hers.

He smelled fresh and clean and looked striking in his black suit and burgundy tie. His lean frame, closely cropped hair and wire-rimmed glasses gave him a professorial look. He tossed the pills into his mouth all at once, followed by a swig of orange juice.

Angela took a cinnamon raisin bagel from the breadbox on the counter, sliced it down the middle and dropped it into the toaster.

"How many points is that?" Cornell asked, placing his glass on the counter.

Angela tensed. She did not need a points monitor and had told Cornell as much. More than once.

"I'm using fat-free cream cheese," she said curtly.

"But how many points is it?" Cornell always demanded straight answers. Whether in his courtroom or at home.

Angela slapped the eject button on the toaster and the bagel sprang up.

"I was just trying to help," he said.

Cornell's own success had been fueled by a childhood of constant criticism, so he knew no other way to motivate anyone else. He bent to peck her on the cheek, then headed for the door.

As soon as he was gone, Angela pressed the toaster button again, then peered into the refrigerator. She was about to reach for the fat-free cream cheese, but grabbed the raspberry jam instead.

Zack and Jon convened in Angela's office to discuss Jon's new identity as a terminally ill businessman.

Angela handed him a thick manila envelope. "That file contains your life story, so memorize it. Your name is Jerry Billington and you have lung cancer. We're working on finding an actual doctor who can pose as your personal physician just in case they ever want to talk to someone."

Jon pulled a medical file from the envelope. "Looks like you're pretty screwed up," Zack said, peering over his shoulder.

"That's the point," Angela noted. "You're selling your policy to fulfill your lifelong dream of sailing around the world before you die."

Zack offered only lukewarm approval. "I guess that's a plausible story."

Just then, Salina burst into the room, her face brimming with excitement.

"You know that woman you wanted me to interview who filed the report with the Department of Insurance claiming her mother was murdered?"

Angela nodded.

"She's dead," Salina said. "The police think she may've been murdered and so do I."

All three of them gave Salina their full attention.

"The woman was shot at home in bed," she continued. "Whoever did it, set it up to look like she committed suicide, but the police aren't buying it."

Salina went on to explain that Veronika Myers supposedly shot herself with her right hand, but was actually left-handed. "Someone broke a window latch to get in. It looks like they tried to fix it on the way out."

"That's not exactly proof of murder," Jon replied.

"There was also evidence of a struggle," Salina added. "A table was knocked over in the hallway and the comforter on her bed was all twisted up, which could mean she'd been trying to fight off an attacker."

"This might turn out to be a decent case after all." Zack was close to salivating now. "Sounds like something we should definitely check out."

Angela gave him a dismissive look, then turned to Salina. "Is the D.A.'s Office looking into her death?"

"They're all over it."

Zack looked crushed. "It won't hurt if we just—"

"No," Angela said, raising her hand. "We don't have the resources. Let's wait and see what the D.A.'s Office finds out. If the police conclude that the woman and her mother really were homicide victims and find a connection to Live Now, then we'll take a closer look."

Angela left the office just before seven, stopped off for a quick weigh-in at Weight Watchers, then headed for the Spectrum Club in Westchester.

She had been wanting to try out the cycling class and decided that tonight would be the night. After changing into her workout gear, she hurried upstairs and awkwardly climbed aboard a bike on the second row, only because the bikes in the back of the room were all taken. Within five minutes of the start of the blaring hip-hop music, Angela was ready to bail. She repeatedly had to stop to catch her breath and mop the sweat from her eyes.

During her fifth rest break, she locked eyes with a man riding a bike at the end of her row. This wasn't the first time she had noticed him. She sensed that he was nothing like Cornell. There was something about his shaved head, neatly trimmed goatee and hazel eyes that made him both fascinating and sexy.

He leaned forward and smiled, revealing deep-set dimples. Angela couldn't help but smile back.

By the time the music stopped, Angela was huffing and puffing so hard she was sure she had sweated off at least ten pounds. When she climbed off the bike, every muscle in her body quivered in pain. As she reached out to open the door, someone on the other side opened it for her.

"Your first time?" It was the man on the bike. He was even more handsome up close.

"Yep." Angela could barely speak. "Was it that obvious?"

"Naw. You rode like a pro."

"Yeah, right."

"No, really, you did. Most people quit after five or ten minutes." He extended his hand. "I'm Andre. People call me Dre."

"Angela," she said, still winded.

As they headed downstairs to the locker rooms, Angela quietly moaned with each painful step.

"You okay?" Dre gently took her upper arm and guided her down the last few steps.

To her surprise, his touch shot a flutter of arousal through her body.

"They should tell you how much this hurts *before* you go through the first class."

Dre laughed. "No pain, no gain."

They had reached the bottom of the stairs and were about to depart.

Dre slung his towel across his left shoulder. "You comin' back for more?"

"Ask me that when I wake up in the morning."

Dre cocked his head and narrowed his eyes. "I wish I could."

Angela blushed. *I wish you could, too*, she thought, then caught herself. What was she thinking? She was an almost-married woman. She slipped the workout glove from her left hand so Dre would see her engagement ring. If he noticed, he didn't let on.

"Thanks for helping me down the stairs."

"Anytime," Dre said.

As she walked away, Angela could still feel his eyes on her.

"You should come back tomorrow night," Dre called after her. "I'll save a bike for you."

Angela smiled back at him. "You do that."

CHAPTER 6

The pretending was what Erickson hated the most. Had his wife been healthy, he would've packed up a long time ago. But no decent man ups and leaves a dying woman.

Erickson sat next to Claire in the waiting room of her doctor's office. He thought about putting his arm around her shoulders or trying to make conversation, but every time he tried to be a caring, attentive husband, she rebuffed him.

"How about lunch in the Marina when we're done?" he asked, hoping she said no.

"Let's see how I'm feeling later."

Great. That was as good as *no.*

Erickson studied Claire as she flipped through a magazine. Her naturally blonde hair was covered by a pricey wig that actually resembled her own golden locks. Her skin was pale and paper-thin. The yellowish tint to her brown eyes bothered him the most. They had already died.

A nurse showed them into the office of Claire's oncologist, Dr. Lisa Cranston. The doctor was warm and funny and not bad looking if you liked women in the fifty-plus range. Erickson didn't. He wondered why she chose such a depressing specialty.

"I have your most recent test results," Dr. Cranston said, once they were seated. "There's been no change."

You're still going to die is how Erickson interpreted her words.

He reached over and caressed Claire's forearm. She stiffened, but he pretended not to notice. His display of affection was more for the doctor than for Claire. Erickson mentally checked out as the conversation went from blood counts to medication to chemotherapy.

"How much time does she have?" Erickson suddenly blurted out. He realized too late that his tone was all wrong.

Dr. Cranston's nervous glance in Claire's direction seemed to convey some private message that only the two of them could interpret. "Time estimates are just that," she said. "I've seen some of my patients with pancreatic cancer live for a few weeks or months, and others miraculously last another two or three years."

Erickson nodded solemnly, then looked away. It had already been a year since Claire's diagnosis. He needed this problem resolved in days or weeks, not months or years.

He gripped his wife's hand. "Well, whatever time we have left, we're going to make the most of it."

They were both seated in his Mercedes before Claire spoke again. "That was quite some performance you put on for Dr. Cranston." Her eyes sizzled with suspicion.

Erickson turned on the ignition and released the parking brake. "I don't know what you mean."

A dubious smile spread across Claire's thin, dark lips. "You're hoping I change my mind about going public. Is that it?"

"No matter what you think, Claire, I still love you."

For an instant, her eyes softened, but just as quickly, they turned callous again.

"You're not fooling anyone," Claire snarled. "You're only doing all this because you want me to give you that DVD."

You're absolutely right. That's exactly what I want. "And you said you would," he reminded her.

"Well, I've changed my mind. I'm still thinking about it."

Erickson put the car in reverse and backed out of the parking stall. He marveled at the once beautiful, but not particularly bright, single mother he'd rescued at the age of twenty-nine. In the beginning, Claire had a feisty, independent nature, which had taken tremendous effort on Erickson's part to corral.

Her life following their marriage had basically been his life. At Erickson's insistence, Claire had abandoned her aspirations of a career in interior design and devoted all of her time to planning his parties, entertaining his guests, shopping for his clothes. Her needs were dictated by his needs. After thirteen years of marriage, he now despised the reemergence of her rebellious spirit.

Erickson was determined to recreate the dependent little flower he had so carefully planted, pruned and nourished.

At least until he got his hands on that DVD.

"So how'd Claire's doctor visit go?"

Becker had just walked into Erickson's office at Jankowski, Parkins and closed the door behind him.

"Pretty much the same," Erickson said. "She's doped up on pain medication most of the time."

Becker remained standing and rested his arm on the middle shelf of the bookcase behind him. "As we discussed before, you can't have this thing hanging over your head."

Becker had just stated the obvious. That his problem must disappear was something he already knew.

"I don't mean to sound crass," Becker said. "But how much time does Claire actually have?"

"I wish I knew. According to her doctor, it could be three weeks or three years."

Becker glanced over his shoulder as if to confirm that the door was still shut. "If I could make the problem go away, would you be amenable?"

Erickson let a long beat pass. "Very."

Becker spoke often of his days as a Navy SEAL, admitting with pride that he'd done his share of killing for his country. Over the years, Erickson had watched his law partner ruthlessly defend his corporate clients, sometimes crossing ethical lines Erickson wouldn't dare to. But this was different. They were talking about offing his wife.

"The prisons are full of people who thought they could commit the perfect crime," Erickson said.

"And none of them possess our level of intellect," Becker retorted with unapologetic arrogance. "And frankly, I don't view what I have in mind as murder. Claire's going to die. We're just going to speed the process along. Anyway, you haven't heard my plan yet."

Plan? Erickson was happy to know that Becker had given it that much thought. "I'm listening."

"What if you convinced Claire to undergo an experimental surgery and what if it didn't work?"

Erickson's forehead creased. "You want me to pay some doctor to botch a surgery?"

"No, I—"

Becker pulled his ringing phone from his breast pocket and glanced down. "Kaylee had a big game today. I gotta take this." He pressed a button and walked over to the spacious window. "Hey, sweetie, how'd it go?"

Erickson sat there for three full minutes listening to Becker tell his daughter how proud he was of her performance on the soccer field. *How ridiculous.* They were plotting a murder, for Christ's sake. The kid could wait.

"I'm sitting here with your godfather." Becker turned and winked at Erickson. "He wants to tell you how proud he is, too."

Becker stalked back across the room and shoved his phone into Erickson's face. Erickson grudgingly took it.

"Congratulations, Kaylee," he said stiffly. "Sounds like you had a great game."

Erickson was relieved that the child did not attempt to prolong the conversation. He handed the phone back as if he feared it might be radioactive.

"Sorry about that," Becker said, stuffing it into his pocket. "I really hate missing her games. So where were we?"

"You tell me," Erickson said, not hiding his annoyance.

"The surgery I'm talking about is completely above board," Becker continued. "UCLA Medical Center is one of only two hospitals in the country performing the procedure."

"So how would Claire be—" Erickson could not bring himself to say the word. "How would her demise occur?"

"After the procedure, there would be unexpected complications." Becker took a seat and expanded upon his plan. When he finished, there was a glint in Erickson's eyes. The plan, like Becker, was brilliant.

"It won't be cheap," Becker continued. "As a matter of fact, much of it won't be covered by insurance. You'll have to shell out at least a quarter of a million dollars of your own money."

That number was daunting. Erickson had invested well, but blowing two-fifty on an operation he really didn't want to work wasn't a sound financial move.

Becker must've read his mind. "Don't worry, it won't cost you a dime. You told me years ago that you insured Claire for five hundred thousand. You still have the policy, right?"

Erickson nodded.

"You're going to sell it."

"Sell it? To who?"

"I'm amazed that people don't know about this." Becker quickly explained how viatical settlements worked.

The more Erickson listened, the more he liked what he was hearing.

"The fact that you encouraged Claire to sell the policy removes financial gain as a motive," Becker said. "Not only are you taking extreme measures to save your wife's life, you're giving up hundreds of thousands of dollars in insurance proceeds in the hope of keeping her alive. No one would ever suspect you of killing her."

"Becker," Erickson said, grinning, "you're amazing."

"Thank you, Mr. Attorney General." He stood up. "And before you ask, I'll take care of everything."

Erickson's eyes held his friend's. He quickly interpreted that everything meant *everything*. His law partner was a gift from God.

"You ever consider putting Claire in a hospice?" Becker asked. "Those places have way too many people to really keep a close eye on anyone. There would be easier access that way."

"That might not be a bad idea," Erickson said, mulling over the suggestion. "I'd have to sell Sophia, Claire's sister, on it first. Caring for Claire around the clock is really wearing her down. I can't guarantee she'll agree to it, though."

"If you can make that happen, great, but even if you can't, things will still be taken care of. I promise you that."

Becker stood up and pulled an envelope from his breast pocket and slapped it on Erickson's desk.

"What's that?"

"Information about the surgery. Give me some time to check around for a referral to a viatical broker. It'll be several weeks before the White House announces their selection for AG, so we have plenty of time to plan everything to prevent any screw ups."

Erickson smiled. Becker was a detail man. Nothing would be left to chance.

"Now go home," Becker ordered, "and convince your wife how much you want to save her life."

CHAPTER 7

J oanna Richardson sat at the Formica table in the kitchen of her
Leimert Park home. Early afternoon was her favorite time of
the day. She enjoyed sipping herbal tea and soaking up the
glorious sunrays that seeped through her kitchen window.

She was feeling particularly strong today. No nausea and her
appetite was back. When you were fifty-six and dying of kidney
disease, a day like today was a reason for celebration.

A copy of *Our Weekly* newspaper was open on the table in
front of her. She had circled three items on the Events Calendar.
There was a flower show at Exposition Park, a Walter Mosley
signing at Eso Won Books, and a Farmer's Market on King
Boulevard. Too bad she couldn't make all three. But it wouldn't
make sense to tire herself out.

Though her doctor was constantly sugarcoating her prognosis,
Joanna had thoroughly researched acute renal failure on the
Internet for the real story. Her one good kidney wouldn't hold
out much longer.

At least she could take comfort in the money sitting in her
bank account. Thank God for the nice man from Live Now who
had helped her sell her insurance policy. After paying off some
bills and buying a new bedroom set, a nice burgundy casket, and a
spacious plot with a marble headstone, Joanna still had thirty-four
thousand dollars left.

The phone rang and she let the answering machine pick up.

"Hey, Mama, I'm just checking on you. Hit me back."

Her son, Damien, called from time to time, but rarely dropped by to see her. Young people today didn't have time for anybody but themselves. Joanna blamed herself, not Damien, for the way he'd turned out. She raised him wrong. Gave him too much.

Other than her son, she was pretty much alone in the world. The Sick and Shut-in volunteers from Faithful Central checked on her from time to time, but friends could never replace family.

Joanna thought about the will she'd just revised and chuckled to herself. Damien would be shocked to learn that she'd only left him five thousand dollars. The boy just wasn't responsible enough to handle any more than that. The money probably wouldn't last him a month as it was. He'd also be upset to find out she'd gotten a reverse mortgage on the house. Damien could barely pay the rent on his studio apartment in Gardena. Why leave him the house and let it end up in foreclosure? Joanna's will left the rest of her money to the church.

After finishing her tea, she walked into the bedroom. She planned to take a short walk before commencing her day. Slipping into a pair of yellow sweat pants and a T-shirt, Joanna went looking for her iPod. She selected the playlist with her favorite gospel songs, plugged in the earphones and headed out of the house.

Joanna hummed along with Kirk Franklin as she headed north on Roxton Avenue toward 39th Street, thankful to be able to put one foot in front of the other. Some people her age didn't like all that finger-snapping gospel music, but Joanna would rather see young people praising God than singing that rap mess.

A blue truck crossed her path just as she turned right onto 39th Street. She'd finally made up her mind to check out the flower show. After a nap, she might just have the energy to attend the book signing, too.

As she strolled and hummed, she spotted the blue truck again. There were two men inside. The driver sidled alongside her and rolled down the window. She saw frustration on his face.

"Ma'am, can you tell us where Mountain Street is?"

Joanna stopped, always willing to help a stranger. "I don't think there's any Mountain Street in this neighborhood."

The man looked down at a piece of paper in his hand. "They told us it was south of Rodeo."

"I don't think so. I've lived in this neighborhood for fifteen years. Somebody steered you wrong."

"Thank you, ma'am." The man frowned and rolled up the window.

Joanna continued her walk, finally reaching 2nd Avenue. Before her illness, she could make it past Arlington. She turned back and marched toward home. She was surprised to see the blue truck again. It had slowed to ten or fifteen miles an hour now and seemed to be trailing her.

Joanna snatched the earphones from her ears. Were the men out to harm her? She picked up her pace, but quickly became winded.

As she approached the intersection at 3rd Avenue and 39th Street, her throat suddenly felt dry and scratchy and she began to wheeze. For the first time, she took note of her tranquil surroundings. Should she run up and bang on somebody's door? Or at least scream to alert someone? It was just after two o'clock on a Thursday. Most people were at work. Where were all the nosey neighbors when you needed them? She couldn't believe that not even one retiree was outside tending to a garden or sweeping a porch.

She glanced back at the truck, which was still meandering along behind her. Maybe she was overreacting. Nobody would try to snatch her off the street in a nice neighborhood like this. Anyway, that only happened to kids. Who would mess with a sickly, middle-aged woman like her?

Still, her heart would not stop pounding. She looked over her shoulder a second time and saw that the men were half a block behind her now. At the next intersection, Joanna stepped off the curb, desperate to reach the safety of her home. She was halfway across the street when she heard the gunning of the truck's engine. It picked up speed and seemed to be heading straight for her.

Instead of running, Joanna froze. She tried to move, but fear molded her feet to the asphalt right there in the middle of the intersection.

She watched in horror as the truck barreled toward her at full speed. The impact of the bumper against her left hip hurled her high into the air. The pain was so intense it seemed that every bone in her body had shattered all at once. Joanna flailed in midair like a wounded bird. Then, the pavement began careening toward her.

Good God! This was not how she wanted to die!

CHAPTER 8

I t was almost nine on Saturday morning and Waverly was sitting in his home office in a pair of silk pajamas, punching numbers into a calculator. He purposely set his sights low. If he sold just three policies a month with a face value of one hundred thousand dollars, his ten percent cut would mean thirty grand in commissions. Finding a few dying people in need of cash couldn't be *that* hard.

He leaned back in his chair as a feeling of hope washed over him. Getting disbarred might actually turn out to be a good thing.

Deidra appeared in the doorway carrying two cups of coffee. "What's that big smile all about?" She handed him a cup and took a seat across from him on a small couch.

Since she was leaving for Paris later that evening, they planned to spend the day together. Their tiff earlier in the week had been forgotten after Waverly brought home roses and a new Prada purse.

"Remember that career switch I mentioned a few days ago?" he said, taking a sip of coffee. "Well, I've been looking into some things."

Waverly watched Deidra's hands tighten around the coffee cup.

He was about to repeat the same spiel Vincent had given him, but stopped. Selling the insurance policies of dying people sounded too morbid. He wanted to give his new venture a positive spin.

"It looks like this insurance investment business might be pretty lucrative, which means we should be able to buy our dream house sooner rather than later."

Deidra set down her coffee and jumped into his lap. "You're amazing and that's why I love you!" She planted a wet kiss on his lips. "When can we start looking?"

"Hold on a minute," Waverly said. "Let me get my feet wet first." He immediately regretted his exuberance. *What if I can't get licensed?*

"Okay, okay," she said. "But you better keep your promise."

Waverly didn't recall making a promise. Rather than point that out, he kissed her.

He knew Deidra wouldn't demand any specifics about his new business venture. In that respect, she was her mother's daughter. As long as the bills were paid and she had an American Express card with no spending limit, Deidra wasn't concerned about the particulars of how he earned his living. He just prayed everything worked out.

"You going to miss me while I'm strolling the streets of Paris for three weeks?" she asked.

Waverly buried his face in the crook of her neck and kissed her. Her skin was always soft and warm to the touch. "You have no idea."

He had wanted to make love to her last night, but Deidra was already asleep when he climbed into bed. He felt the urge coming on now and kissed her again, more deeply this time.

Deidra slipped off his lap, crouched next to the chair and eased her hand past the elastic of his pajamas. Waverly immediately swelled in anticipation of what was to come. She gently took him in her paraffin-softened hand and slowly moved up and down.

Lately, Deidra had resorted to jacking him off. Her body, she said, could not tolerate the heavy pounding of sexual intercourse on a regular basis. She typically reserved blowjobs for special occasions, like Christmas or his birthday. If he could swing that new house, he'd probably get head every night for a week.

Waverly rocked back in his chair, closed his eyes and smiled. He'd take it any way he could get it.

Hours later, when Waverly pulled their BMW to a stop in front of Bradley International Terminal at LAX, he spotted Deidra's father two cars away hoisting Rachel's luggage from the trunk of his Lincoln.

"Perfect timing," Leon said, walking up to them. "I don't know why you didn't let us pick you up."

Waverly wrapped a protective arm around Deidra. "I wanted my wife all to myself for these last few hours. We've never been apart for more than a couple of days. This is going to be rough."

They said their good-byes and Leon and Waverly watched as the two sisters disappeared inside the airport terminal.

"You're welcome to join us for dinner tonight," Leon offered.

"Can't," Waverly said. "Got a business meeting."

"On a Saturday evening?" Leon sounded skeptical.

Actually, he was scheduled to meet two executives from Live Now for drinks. Instead of elaborating, Waverly jumped into his car and drove off.

Waverly sat at the bar near the lobby of the Luxe Hotel on Sunset Boulevard nursing a beer.

Vincent was late. He had promised to make some calls to gauge Waverly's chances of getting through the licensing process. Waverly wanted to know the results of his efforts before the executives arrived. If he couldn't get licensed, why waste everyone's time?

Finally, he spotted Vincent walking into the hotel.

"So?" Waverly said, as soon as Vincent reached him. "Am I in?"

Vincent smiled, but didn't answer. He hopped onto the stool next to Waverly, flagged the bartender and ordered a beer. "I can get your license," he began, "but it's going to cost you five grand."

Waverly's shoulders sagged. "I don't have—"

"Don't worry about it," Vincent interrupted. "I'll front the money and we can take it out of your first commission payment. I have faith in you."

"So is this a payoff?" Waverly asked.

"That's exactly what it is and the guys we're about to meet know nothing about it. So keep it to yourself. Are you in?"

Yet again, Waverly found himself faced with the option of doing the wrong thing for the right reasons. He had bills to pay and a wife to support. The decision was a no brainer. "I'm in."

Seconds later, two men, both casually dressed, approached from the rear. Vincent stood and introduced them. "This is Tom Bellamy, the CEO of Live Now," he said, pointing to the taller man. "And this is his business partner and Vice President of the company, Jonathan Cartwright."

Cartwright was toned and tanned and looked affluent even in khakis and a golf shirt. Bellamy, older and not nearly as fit, had bushy black hair and a thick paunch around his midsection. He wore a bland, beige leisure suit.

They moved to a comfy seating area on the nearby patio.

"I hope Vincent's done a good job of selling you on our business," Cartwright said, after a waiter delivered two more beers.

"He has indeed," Waverly replied.

Cartwright picked up his beer. "We just lost our only L.A. broker. He made so much money that he retired to Jamaica. We'd like to replace him right away. You'd be covering all of the metro L.A. area. It's great that you've got office space you can use."

Waverly swallowed hard. He would worry about his impending office eviction later. "Where else does Live Now operate?"

"Through our parent company, The Tustin Group, we're in three other states right now, New York, Nevada and Florida. If things go well here, we'll be expanding to Texas by the end of the year."

"How do you decide where to set up your operation?"

"We're starting to focus more on the elderly, so we're looking at states with the largest elderly populations. New York, Florida, California and Texas are all in the top ten. Many people don't adequately prepare for retirement and others, frankly, didn't expect to live as long as they have. So in their seventies or eighties, they decide to sell their insurance policies because they need the cash. Those are called life settlements."

Waverly was astounded. "You do this for people who aren't dying, too?"

"Absolutely. The investors may have to wait a little longer to cash in, but it's still a great investment. More and more people are choosing to retire in the Las Vegas area, so we're expecting the elderly population there to have a big growth spurt. But don't worry about that side of the business. We want you to concentrate on the terminally ill for now."

During the next twenty minutes, Cartwright confirmed everything Vincent had told him about the business, but Waverly still had more questions. "How do you prevent somebody from taking a payout and disappearing? You might never know they died."

"They're required to send us a postcard with their signature by the fifth of every month," Cartwright explained. "In almost twenty years, only one person tried to skip. It took just six days for our investigator to track him down."

"What happens if the policy lapses?" Waverly asked.

Cartwright smiled. "You must be a damn good lawyer because you're asking all the right questions. It's the investor's obligation to continue paying the premiums. For that reason, they aren't too happy when a policyholder lives longer than we estimated."

"How do you even know the person is really dying?"

"We have a team of doctors who review their medical records," Cartwright said. "We're looking for people with a life expectancy of six months to a year max. It's really amazing, but most of the time, our doctors' estimates are right on the money."

This was actually sounding too good to be true. "Are most of your investors individuals?"

Bellamy finally entered the conversation. "About fifty percent, and they're mainly doctors. Physicians are used to dealing with death and don't have any ethical concerns with this type of investment. The remaining investors are small companies, even some insurance companies. They're all looking for a safe investment with a solid rate of return." Bellamy took a sip of his drink and grinned. "Nothing is guaranteed but death, taxes and a big 'ole return on your viatical investment."

They all laughed.

"Can I get started before I get my license?" Waverly needed money yesterday.

Vincent slapped him on the back. "See what I told you. This guy's a real go-getter."

Cartwright nodded approvingly. "I like your enthusiasm. "You can start making presentations now, but you'll need to have your license before you can actually ink a deal."

"Sounds like you're sold," Bellamy said.

Waverly took a big swig of his beer. "Bought *and* sold."

CHAPTER 9

Angela speed walked into the lobby of the Biltmore Hotel. She spotted Cornell seated at the bar. She could tell before she reached him that he was fuming.

"Sorry, I'm late," she said, panting. "We were discussing this case and—"

"I don't understand why you can never be on time, Angela," Cornell scolded. "You were supposed to be here twenty-six minutes ago. This is unacceptable. And I specifically asked you to wear the red St. John suit that I bought you. Why aren't you wearing it?"

Because I didn't feel like dressing like my mother.

"It's in the cleaners," she lied. "What's wrong with the suit I have on?"

Cornell looked her up and down. "I guess it's fine." He drained his glass and hopped off the barstool. "Can you believe the Court of Appeal reversed my summary judgment decision in the Banker case today? Just wait until one of those arrogant assholes from Latham & Watkins comes into my courtroom again. I'll show them who's in charge."

Angela put a hand on Cornell's arm. "What are you saying? You're going to retaliate against the whole firm because you got reversed?" He still hadn't gotten over being rejected by the firm for a summer associate position more than twenty years ago.

"C'mon, you know I was just mouthing off." His lips angled into a diabolical smile. "I'd never do anything like that. That would be unethical."

Cornell took off down a hotel corridor wider than most city streets. Angela had to practically jog to catch up with him.

"Tell me again," she said, "what's going on tonight?"

"Bar Association fundraiser. Paul Streeter, who's on the Federal Judicial Nomination Advisory Committee, is supposed to be here tonight. This'll be a good opportunity for me to meet him."

After ten years as a superior court judge, Cornell now aspired to a seat on the more prestigious federal court bench. He was already lobbying his political contacts in hopes of being considered for the next district court appointment. Meeting Streeter, he assumed, could only help.

They picked up their dinner tickets at the registration table and entered a ballroom filled with business types. Cornell scanned the room. "I think I see him over there." He grabbed her hand and they began winding their way through the crowd.

Cornell stopped just short of a small circle of men who seemed to be in the midst of a serious debate. "That's Streeter right there," Cornell whispered, indicating a lanky, bearded guy with salt and pepper hair.

Angela hoped Cornell wouldn't be bold enough to interrupt. She was about to caution him not to, when she felt a tap on her shoulder.

Angela looked back and found Rick McCarthy standing behind her.

"Saw your closing in the Pell case last month. Nice job." McCarthy was a well-connected assistant U.S. attorney who still enjoyed trying cases after nearly thirty years on the job.

"Thanks," Angela beamed. She linked her arm through Cornell's. "This is my fiancé, Judge Cornell Waters. He's on the superior court bench downtown."

They shook hands, then Cornell rudely turned his attention

back to the group of dark suited-men surrounding Streeter.

"You ever think about the bench, Angela?" McCarthy asked.

Cornell abruptly spun around.

"No way," Angela laughed. "I don't think I'm judge material."

"I disagree. We need sharp young lawyers like you on the bench. And needless to say, the federal courts could certainly use some diversity. Let me introduce you to a friend of mine." McCarthy tapped Paul Streeter on the shoulder. "Hey, Paul, I have a future judicial candidate I'd like you to meet."

Out of the corner of her eye, Angela could see Cornell's jaws expand into a pout. McCarthy spent the next few minutes bombarding Angela with accolades. She wished he would stop talking so she could introduce Cornell.

Streeter removed a card from his inside breast pocket. "Can't beat a recommendation like that," he said with a warm smile. "Let's stay in touch."

"I'd like to introduce my fiancé," Angela began, "Judge Cornell Waters. He's—"

The lights began to flicker, signaling that everyone should proceed to their tables. Streeter acknowledged Cornell with a curt nod, then walked off.

Angela glanced down at her ticket to check their table number. When she looked up, Cornell had walked off.

When she finally caught up with him, he was already seated. "What are you doing here?" he snickered. "I figured there'd be a seat for you at Streeter's table."

Cornell could be such a baby, Angela thought. She pulled out the chair next to him and was about to sit down, but changed her mind. "I'm going to the ladies' room."

Angela walked out of the ballroom and into the restroom, where she touched up her lipstick and fluffed her hair. She tried to ignore her nagging doubts. Did she really want to be a mother bad enough to endure a life sentence with Cornell? *Maybe.*

A feeling of dread consumed her as she trudged back toward

the ballroom. Halfway there, she pulled her BlackBerry from her purse and fired off a short text to Cornell: *Not feeling well. Going home.*

As she headed for the valet stand, the tension she'd felt only seconds ago had magically disappeared.

CHAPTER 10

Erickson had not expected his first visit to the White House to affect him this way. As he sat waiting in a reception area outside the Oval Office, he was practically giddy.

Hold it together, buddy. It's show time.

He looked up to see the President's executive assistant, a petite, stylishly dressed woman with a practiced smile, approaching from a long hallway. She stopped just in front of him, appropriately respectful of his personal space. "Mr. Erickson, the President will see you now."

Gripping both sides of the chair, he easily hoisted himself upward.

Erickson felt a sense of power like nothing he'd ever experienced before. Being chairman of a preeminent law firm was one thing, but he was about to meet the freakin' President.

He followed the President's assistant, easily matching her steady stride. She slowed, opened a tall door, then stepped aside so that he could enter.

President Richard Bancroft and his Chief of Staff, Mark Wrigley, both stood up.

"Good to see you, Lawrence." The President greeted him with a strong, two-handed grip.

"Good to meet *you*, Mr. President," Erickson replied.

He shook Wrigley's hand next and tried to get a handle on his excitement.

The majesty of the room overwhelmed him. It suddenly hit him that the place was called the Oval Office because it actually was. He glanced down at the Presidential seal on the rug in front of President Bancroft's desk.

"Let's have a seat over here." Bancroft pointed to a seating area in the middle of the room. "First things, first. How's your wife?"

Erickson lowered his eyes in what he hoped was an appropriate display of distress. "As well as can be expected. But she's a trooper."

The President responded with a look of grave concern.

Erickson seriously doubted that Bancroft had any genuine interest in the state of his wife's health. At dinner the night before, one of Wrigley's assistants, relaxed from too much vodka, let it slip that his wife's illness might help him edge out the other candidates. At least two of the President's advisors felt the press might cut Erickson some slack since he was about to become a widower.

As the President made small talk, Erickson struggled to stay focused. Here he was, Lawrence Adolphus Erickson, son of a steelworker, grandson of a corn farmer, sitting in the Oval Office. He wished his whack job of a father, who constantly told him he'd never be worth a damn, could see him shooting the breeze with the President of the United States. *This* would've killed him. Not sclerosis of the liver.

"Mark would like a few minutes alone with you," the President said. He stood and exited through a side door that Erickson hadn't noticed until now.

"You ready to roll?" Wrigley asked, as soon as the President was gone.

"All set," Erickson said.

"It's extremely important that the media doesn't get wind of our slate of candidates," Wrigley said. "So other than Becker, you should not share this with anyone. You can tell your wife, but only if you can guarantee confidentiality. A leak could threaten your candidacy."

Erickson had no intention of sharing his great news with Claire. "That won't be a problem."

Wrigley leaned back, crossed his legs, and extended his arm along the back of the couch. "As you know, we have a pretty thorough vetting process, but things can still slip through the cracks. You easily cleared the first round of vetting. Some other good candidates didn't. Now we go a whole lot deeper."

Erickson was dying to know who else was on the list, but such an inquiry would be out of line.

Wrigley fixed Erickson with a steely gaze. "There's a question I need to ask, and you're probably going to hear it a few more times before this is all said and done. Is there anything we don't know about you, your family or your background that might cause embarrassment for the President?"

Erickson chuckled as if the question was absurd. "Absolutely not." The lie rolled so effortlessly off his lips that he almost believed it himself.

Wrigley held Erickson's gaze for a few more beats, as if giving him time to retract his answer. "That's exactly what I wanted to hear." Wrigley rubbed his hands together, then bounced off the couch. "Then let's get to it."

The Chief of Staff led the way out. Walking two abreast in soldier-like formation, they made their way to a conference room, not far from the Oval Office. Already seated around a circular table were two men and a woman. All three looked to be in their late thirties. Too young, Erickson thought, to have presidential ties.

"This is your team," Wrigley said. "They will be your primary contact throughout this process. And if you are indeed the nominee, they'll be preparing you for your Senate confirmation hearing."

Erickson walked around the table and greeted each person,

only half-listening as Wrigley made the introductions.

His mind had wandered back to Wrigley's pointed question in the Oval Office. *Is there anything we don't know about you, your family or your background that might cause embarrassment for the President?*

Yes there is, Erickson answered in thought only. *But don't worry. I'm about to take care of it.*

CHAPTER 11

There could only be one explanation for the incredible turn of events in Waverly Sloan's life. God loved him.

In three short weeks, Waverly had successfully completed the registration process and had a nice, new viatical broker's license, complete with the official seal of the state of California. To top that off, the State Bar website still had him listed as an attorney in good standing. Thank goodness the wheels of justice turned at a snail's pace.

Waverly spent the bulk of his days glued to the telephone, scouring his personal contacts and making presentations to the ones supplied by Vincent. Only two days after getting his license, he was having lunch with an old friend who mentioned that his sister was in the latter stages of breast cancer. By seven that night, Waverly was at her house signing her up. Her policy was only worth ninety thousand, but his nine grand off the top wasn't a bad take for a few hours' work. After paying Vincent back, he still pocketed four grand.

Just days after that, a bigger payoff literally fell into his lap. Lawrence Erickson, a hotshot partner from Jankowski, Parkins, contacted him about selling his wife's policy. The referral came from a prominent probate attorney who handled the estate of one of Waverly's clients who'd died days after he'd settled her case. Waverly had mailed the lawyer a slick-looking Live Now brochure, but never dreamed the guy would actually refer someone so quickly.

Erickson's wife was dying of pancreatic cancer and the couple wanted to sell her five hundred thousand dollar insurance policy to pay for an experimental operation. Erickson was deeply concerned about keeping the transaction confidential. Waverly assured him that wouldn't be a problem. Not with a fifty grand commission coming his way.

Waverly actually whistled as he walked up the driveway to Erickson's stately Hancock Park home. Erickson greeted him at the door and led him inside.

Claire Erickson appeared to be minutes, not months away from death. She sat quietly in a pink dress, her hands clasped in her lap, her eyes downcast. Waverly gathered that something more than her illness lay behind her defeated demeanor. She reminded him of Deidra's mother. A woman who obediently bowed to her husband's every command.

"Why don't you explain to Claire how this all works?" Erickson began.

They were seated in the family room around a massive oak table that looked out on a colorful garden.

"It's actually pretty simple," Waverly said. "We find an investor who's willing to pay you a portion of the face value of your policy. The investor then becomes the beneficiary."

Claire turned to face her husband. "Sounds like a strange way to make money. But, of course, you know all about making money."

Waverly wasn't exactly sure what was going on between the pair and didn't know how to respond. As an uncomfortable hush fell over the room, he continued his presentation, meticulously explaining each step of the process, emphasizing the importance of obtaining Mrs. Erickson's medical records as soon as possible.

When Erickson reached over and stroked his wife's forearm, Waverly was certain he saw Claire recoil.

"We've completed the paperwork you sent over," Erickson said, handing him a folder.

Erickson didn't seem the least bit broken up over his wife's impending death. Considering the circumstances, he was far too businesslike.

Waverly browsed the papers Erickson had given him. "Are there any questions I can answer for you?" He directed his question to Mrs. Erickson.

She wrung her hands, then quietly shook her head.

Erickson took both of Claire's hands in his. "This is your decision, honey. Are you sure there's nothing you want to ask?"

"No," Claire said, her voice both softer and kinder than before. "Everything sounds fine."

"What's the next step?" Erickson was really rushing things along. He had explained on the phone that Claire's sister and daughter hadn't been told about the surgery yet. It was imperative that Waverly be gone by the time they returned from dinner and a movie.

"I have a few more documents for you to sign," Waverly said. "Some of them need to be notarized."

"We'll get them done right away. Here's the name of my wife's oncologist." He handed Waverly a business card. "I've let Claire's doctors know you'll be requesting her medical records. How long will it take before we get the payout? We really want to move forward with the surgery as soon as possible."

"Six to eight weeks is typical, but I've cleared the way to expedite processing since I understand time is of the essence. If there's no delay in getting the medical records, I think we may be able to complete the entire process in three to four weeks, maybe less."

Erickson smiled as if Waverly had just told him he'd won SuperLotto. Mrs. Erickson stared off toward the garden.

Something isn't right here, Waverly thought. Whatever it was, he hoped it didn't derail his forthcoming commission.

"Thank you," Erickson said, reaching out to shake his hand.

No, Waverly thought, as he envisioned his biggest commission check yet, *thank you.*

CHAPTER 12

Angela eased off the exercise bike, wiped her forehead with a towel and tried to pretend she wasn't aching all over.

"Good job," Dre said, walking up to her. "You kept up for almost the whole class."

Angela pressed the towel to her face again. "Let's just hope I've lost a pound or two."

"Exactly how much you tryin' to lose?"

"Twenty pounds would about do it."

"That's way too much. I like women with—" Dre stopped, then smiled. "A woman needs to have a little meat on her bones."

Dre's slip of the tongue intrigued her. Maybe he was feeling the same attraction she was trying to deny. When she'd pulled into the parking structure earlier, she'd found herself excited about the prospect of seeing him.

Angela chuckled and slapped the side of her thigh. "I assure you, there will still be plenty of meat left to spare."

They both headed into the workout room next door and grabbed floor mats to stretch. As she crouched next to him, Angela noticed a horseshoe symbol branded on his upper right arm.

"So you're a Q-dog?" she asked, referring to the fraternity, Omega Psi Phi.

Dre glanced down at his arm. "Yep."

"Where'd you pledge?"

"Long Beach State," Dre replied. "What about you? Delta or AKA?"

"Neither. Too busy studying. I regret not pledging, though."

Dre leaned forward, grabbed his toes and held the pose for way longer than Angela could have. "Where'd you go to college?" he asked.

"Stanford."

Dre arched a brow, obviously impressed.

"So what do you do for fun?" Angela asked.

"I read a lot, work out, hang out with my son. He's seven. That's about it. My regular gig is fixin' up foreclosures and flippin' 'em.

So he had a son. Angela wondered if that also meant he had a wife. A lot of men didn't wear wedding rings.

"And what's *your* gig?" Dre asked.

"I'm a government lawyer," she said, trying to sound matter of fact. Many men wilted with intimidation the minute they heard the word lawyer. She saw no need to add that she was a federal prosecutor.

"That's tight," he said.

"What do you like to read?" Angela asked.

"Mostly business books, biographies and political stuff. If I read any fiction, it's usually street lit. Lately, I've been readin' some interesting psychology books."

"Yeah, right," Angela said teasingly. "Name the last psychology book you read."

Dre cocked his head and stroked his goatee. "I can't believe you're dissin' me. I just finished *Blink: The Power of Thinking Without Thinking* by Malcolm Gladwell. You read it?"

"No, I haven't."

"You should check it out. He talks about how people make decisions and judgments in the blink of an eye. It's pretty heavy."

"How long have you been married?" The question was out before Angela could assess the propriety of asking it.

"Who said I was married?" Dre stroked his goatee again.

He had the cutest dimples. "Well, are you?"

"You must be pretty good in court 'cuz you sure know how to jam a brother up. No, I'm not married." Dre leaned forward for a final stretch, then stood.

He extended his hand and helped Angela to her feet. They walked downstairs and just as they were about to part, Dre slowed. "Since you've been all up in my Kool-Aid, can I ask you something?"

"Sure," Angela said.

"Where's the dude who gave you that big ass rock? Why don't he ever work out with you?"

Angela made an exaggerated show of glancing at the clock on the wall behind them. "Let's see, eight-thirty on a weeknight? Unfortunately, my fiancé is probably still at work. And he doesn't like gyms. Too many germs."

"Tell him I said he needs to keep closer tabs on his woman." Dre treated her to his killer smile. "Somebody might move in on him."

Angela smiled back. "I'll be sure to give him the message."

The next morning, Dre stood shirtless in front of his bathroom mirror, his head lathered with foam, carefully shaving his scalp with a razor. The daily task was a hassle, but the look worked for him.

After leaving the gym the night before, Dre found himself thinking about Angela. He really liked her vibe. It was strange how you could tell so much about a woman from the way she carried herself. Not only was she fine as hell, the sistah had class. Normally, a ring on a woman's finger would have detoured him, especially the kind of bling Angela was rockin'. This time, it didn't.

Dre threw on some jeans and a T-shirt and made a call to make sure the contractors rehabbing a duplex he'd just bought off Western Avenue were on the job. He'd drive by later to check things out.

For his primary source of income, Dre had the luxury of working from home, a one-bedroom apartment behind the Arco station on the corner of La Brea and Slauson. As he made his way to the kitchen, he had to step over stacks of books scattered about the living room floor.

In the last month, he'd read *The Covenant with Black America* by Tavis Smiley, *True to the Game* by Teri Woods, and *The Essays of Warren Buffet*.

Dre's body tensed in anticipation of the long, tedious day ahead of him. He filled a six-quart pot with water, set it on the stove and turned the burner up high. Once the water came to a boil, he retrieved a kilo of cocaine from a duffel bag stashed in a hidden compartment underneath the sink. He carefully measured two ounces of the powder and dumped it into a glass beaker. To that, he added boiling water and baking soda. Using a butter knife, he rapidly stirred the concoction until the liquid began to crystallize, ultimately crumbling and separating into rocks.

For most people in his profession, this was the end of the process. But Dre always took the time to re-rock his product. He placed the beaker inside the microwave and let it cook for one minute, which transformed the rocks into a liquid the consistency of vegetable oil. Next, he held the base of the beaker underneath a stream of cold water, swirling it around, allowing a few drops of water to get inside.

Dre watched with pride as the concoction hardened into a flat, solid cookie. He removed the cookie from the bottom of the beaker, set it aside and started the process all over again.

At eleven, Dre took a break to make himself a turkey sandwich and watch *The Young and the Restless*, which he TiVo'd every day. Dre identified with Victor, the Newman family patriarch. Victor didn't take shit from nobody.

Like Victor, Dre prided himself on always taking care of business. He didn't indulge in drugs—not even weed—rarely drank anything other than wine or beer and didn't see a need to floss.

His ride was a beat-up Volkswagen Jetta and he didn't have or need an entourage. He owned a .38 revolver, but had never fired it.

Dre had done prison time, but only once. His two-year sentence for possession with intent to sell was reduced to eight months of actual time, thanks to prison overcrowding. For Dre, prison time was simply a cost of doing business. Losing a kilo and thirty grand in cash had pissed him off way more than being on lockdown.

After finishing his sandwich, Dre returned to work. His next break wasn't until four, when he stopped to watch Dr. Phil, one of the few cats on TV with something to say. Dre had a whole list of Dr. Phil-isms. His favorite: *You can either wallow in your history or you can walk out of it.* Dre was just months away from walking out of his.

Once the entire kilo had been converted into cookies, Dre cut them into pieces with a razorblade and put them into plastic bags after weighing them on a digital scale. A rock weighing 0.1 grams would sell for five dollars, 0.3 grams for ten dollars. He'd collect twenty bucks for a rock weighing 0.6 grams, while an eight ball— 3.5 grams—went for a hundred and twenty-five dollars. A kilo cost him twenty-three grand and he made a profit of just over five thousand dollars on each one.

Dre pulled out his cell and called his son's mother. When Little Dre answered, his jaw tightened. "Why aren't you at school?"

"Uh . . ." Dre could always tell when his son was about to tell a lie. "Mama didn't feel good today."

"Put your mama on the phone."

"Uh . . . she's next door at Ray-Ray's house," his son said timidly.

"Go get her," Dre demanded.

The minute Shawntay picked up, Dre exploded. "You too goddamn lazy to drive him two fuckin' miles to school?"

"Don't be cussin' at me," Shawntay grumbled. "You know my

blood pressure's been up. I wasn't feeling good when I woke up this morning."

"I don't see why? You don't do shit all day," Dre shouted. "And you can't be feeling too bad if you hangin' out next door. The next time you can't take him to school, you call me. Put Little Dre back on the phone."

"I'll be over there in a couple of hours," Dre said, when his son came back on the line. "You and me gonna have school today."

"Aw, Dad."

"Just get your books out and be ready."

Dre hung up and massaged his temples. Only six more months and he'd be out of the game for good. Then Little Dre was coming to live with him. By then, he'd have one million dollars. From the start, that had been his only goal. To stash away one million dollars.

As soon as he went legit, he was going to find himself a classy lady and have a couple more kids. A white picket fence, too.

He thought about Angela again. Even though the sistah was nosey as hell, there was something about her that he really dug. Dre wondered what she was really all about. Maybe he would invest the time to find out.

CHAPTER 13

Erickson enjoyed spending time in his garden. He was busy pruning his rose bushes when the sound of his stepdaughter's shrill voice shattered what had been a pleasant afternoon.

"Aunt Sophia?" Ashley called out as she stepped onto the patio.

Erickson instinctively braced for the confrontation that was sure to follow. He turned to see Ashley scowling at him from across the yard. Corky, their Yorkshire Terrier, was tucked underneath her right arm.

"Sophia left to check on her place," Erickson said. "She should be back in an hour or so."

"Wow, the great leader of Jankowski, Parkins, Gregorio & Hall actually found time to come home before sundown on a weekday. Why aren't you sitting with Mommy?"

Erickson survived their volatile relationship by never taking Ashley's bait. He removed several dead petals from his English roses. "Your mother's sleeping," he said without turning to face her.

"She's dying. I'd think you'd want to spend all the time you could with her."

"I don't want to do this right now. Frankly, I'm tired of it."

"Oh, yes, it is all about you." She set Corky free to run about the yard.

Erickson reached behind him for the beer bottle he'd set inches away on the grass. He tried to put himself in Ashley's shoes. She was twenty-four years old, not particularly bright, not particularly attractive. She'd never had a relationship with her father and her mother was on her deathbed. She had no siblings, no cousins, no grandparents and no close friends. After Claire's death, she'd have no one except her Aunt Sophia. She had a right to be an angry young woman. He would let her be.

"I guess I shouldn't ask how Mommy's doing. You probably wouldn't know."

When Corky barked and ran off toward the kitchen door, Erickson flushed with relief. Sophia was back to referee. Ashley usually behaved more civilly toward him in the presence of her aunt. He continued to ignore her and she finally went back inside.

Erickson took longer than necessary to finish his gardening, dreading going into his own house. Just as he was done, Sophia called out to him. "We need your help getting Claire to the bathroom."

Tossing his gardening gloves to the ground, he reluctantly headed for the bedroom he no longer slept in. The place smelled and looked like a hospital room.

Claire was sitting on the edge of the bed when he entered.

"I told you, I can make it," Claire insisted.

Lately, Claire was showing more independence. Erickson hoped that didn't mean she was getting better. He took a step toward her, but she waved him away. She easily walked the short distance to their master bathroom. Erickson followed close behind, just in case she lost her footing.

He stepped aside as Sophia assisted her behind closed doors. When he turned around, he found himself face-to-face with Ashley. Her scornful eyes burned into his. She seemed to get off on staring him down. Erickson was relieved when the bathroom door finally reopened.

After helping Claire back to bed, Erickson asked Ashley and Sophia to join him in the den.

"We need to talk about Claire's care," he said, once they were seated before him. "I think we need to consider putting her in a hospice."

"No way!" Ashley bellowed. "I won't let you stash my mother away to die with a bunch of strangers!"

"Well, we can't continue to take care of her here," Erickson said. "It's—"

"*We*? You don't do a damn thing," Ashley fired back. "*We* take care of her. Is it getting to be too much trouble for you to escort her to the bathroom on the rare occasion you're even here? I bet you can't wait for her to die."

"Stop it right now!" Sophia scolded them both. "Claire's going to hear you." She turned to Erickson. "Have you discussed this with Claire?"

"I wanted to talk to the two of you first." Erickson had figured there was only a slim chance that they would agree, but had decided to give it a shot anyway.

"I agree with Ashley," Sophia said. "I can't see putting Claire in a hospice. We'll manage."

"It's going to get worse," Erickson said.

"And we'll handle it," Sophia replied. "If we have to, we can hire a nurse to help out. I owe it to my sister."

Erickson heard Sophia's unspoken words. *And you owe it to her, too.*

He did not like having someone else make decisions for *his* wife and run things in *his* home. He just wanted it to all be over.

Very soon, it would be.

CHAPTER 14

At three in the afternoon, Dre dumped his duffel bag in the trunk of his Volkswagen Jetta and climbed into the driver's seat. The car had 107,000 miles on it and had never once let him down.

As he backed out of the parking stall, headed for the city of Hawthorne, Dre smiled in anticipation of the ten grand he was about to collect.

Twenty-five minutes later, he pulled up in front of a well-kept house in a working-class neighborhood near 120th and Crenshaw. As he prepared to exit the car, his heart raced. You never knew when things could go awry, so he always braced for the unexpected. His eyes cruised the street ahead, then checked his rear.

Most of Dre's clients were small-time dope dealers who didn't want to hassle with the manufacturing part of the crack business, even though it would mean a bigger profit. Most dope dealers, Dre quickly learned, were not business oriented.

The marketing classes he'd taken at Long Beach State taught Dre the principles of supply and demand: make the best product, never run low and treat people fairly. That would keep them coming back for more. Dre also never stretched his product by adding cornstarch, B12 or any other crap. Everybody knew his product was pure.

Dre purchased his coke exclusively from the Mexicans. His black brothers were way too scandalous. They would sell you three kilos, then have one of their boys jack you on the way home. But the Mexicans were all about business. They operated by a code, probably because they had somebody above them calling the shots.

He pulled the duffel bag from a floorboard underneath the backseat and trotted up the driveway. Dre stared with disapproval as he walked past Lonnie's Benz sitting on twenty-twos. Flossin' in a ride with flashy rims like that was like begging the cops to hassle you.

"S'up, Biznessman?" Lonnie said, as he opened the door.

Dre's nickname on the street was actually a source of pride. He returned the greeting and stepped inside. Dre wasn't big on chitchat, preferring to get in and out without wasting time. The terms of their deal had already been worked out earlier in the day via phone. *Eight pizzas and nine hot links.* Their private code for eight balls and ounces.

He pulled a large paper bag from his duffel bag and handed it to Lonnie. In exchange, Lonnie passed him four neatly stacked wads of cash wrapped in rubber bands. Dre could hear kids laughing in a back room.

Dre quickly counted the cash, then looked up at Lonnie. "Dude, I think you miscounted."

Lonnie's chest swelled with indignation. "It's all there, man. I counted it three times."

"Well, you counted wrong." Dre extended his hand. "You gave me a hundred dollars too much."

Lonnie froze for a second before reaching for the bill. "Man, you're alright."

Dre stuffed the money in the inside pocket of his jacket and headed back to his car, smiling all the way. Lonnie would be telling that story for weeks. Dre's rep on the street would go up tenfold. Dre was a good businessman and good businessmen treated people right.

Not until he crossed Manchester did Dre finally relax. Since he wasn't driving an expensive car, there was only a slim chance that a cop would stop him. He was always careful to drive the speed limit and never even rolled through a stop sign. If he got stopped, it would be very hard to explain why he was carrying ten grand in cash.

Dre had been having a tough time keeping his mind off Angela. He couldn't remember the last time a female affected him that way. They had gotten into the habit of hanging around to talk after their cycling class. The more time he spent with her, the more he dug her.

Though she claimed to be a few months away from getting married, something definitely wasn't right in paradise. But Dre wasn't one to ask a lot of questions. If homeboy wasn't handling his business, that was on him.

Dre pulled into a parking stall in back of an apartment building off Florence. Little Dre waved from the balcony of the second floor and dashed down the stairs.

"Hey, Dad!" His son jumped into his arms before he was barely out of the car.

"Hey, dude. Ready to go?"

"Yep. Gotta go get my stuff."

Shawntay stepped out of her apartment, leaned over the railing and smiled seductively. "Hey, Dre."

He winced as soon as he saw her.

Shawntay's hair was freshly done and she was wearing enough makeup to scrape off and paint the side of a barn. Her shiny satin top was all cleavage and nipples. Dre had made the mistake of screwing her several weeks ago, simply to blow off some steam. He'd left as soon as he busted a nut.

Since then, he could tell that Shawntay assumed the encounter meant they might start kickin' it again. But that wasn't going to happen. Dre was convinced that Shawntay was bipolar and hoped she hadn't passed that shit on to his son.

Dre stepped inside the apartment. Crap was everywhere. Crap

was always everywhere. He didn't understand how anybody could function in a place like this.

"You ever think about cleanin' up this dump?"

Shawntay planted both hands on her broad hips. "You wanna hire me a maid?"

"Why you need a maid? You don't work."

The nice Shawntay who had greeted him seconds ago had disappeared, replaced by her psycho twin. "Don't come up in here startin' nothin', Dre."

Why do I even waste my time tryin' to talk to this crazy bitch?

"Little Dre, hurry up," he called into the back room.

Shawntay leaned against the wall and folded her arms, hoisting her breasts six inches higher. "Want me to hang out with y'all this weekend?" she asked with a purr. The nice Shawntay was back.

"Naw."

Shawntay puckered her lips and sulked. "Well, don't be bringin' him back late."

"After I pick him up from school tomorrow, we're goin' out to eat. I'll have him back by six. If we're runnin' late, I'll call you."

"Ain't no need to call," Shawntay snarled. "Just don't be late."

Dre started to respond, but knew that would only escalate the drama. He turned and pushed open the screen door. "Tell Little Dre I'm waitin' for him in the car."

CHAPTER 15

A ngela entered the small conference room and mentally took roll. Two members of the task force were missing. "Are Salina and Zack coming?" she asked, taking a seat at the table.

"Salina's on her way," Jon replied. "Said she has something big to report. As for Zack, let's just enjoy the fact that he's missing in action."

"Well, let's get started," Angela said. "I'd like everyone to report out on their individual assignments. You go first, Tyler. What did you find out about Live Now?"

Tyler opened a yellow folder. "Live Now is one of twenty DBAs operated by The Tustin Group. In the early '90s, The Tustin Group made a ton of money selling the policies of AIDS patients. When the new AIDS drugs came onto the scene and increased the life expectancy of people with HIV, they switched their focus to cancer victims and, more recently, the elderly. The founder and CEO of the Company, Tom Bellamy, used to be a commercial real estate broker. He started out in his twenties and was filthy rich by his thirties. He told one interviewer that he entered the viatical business because he got bored selling office buildings. The company posted a gross profit of fifty million dollars last year."

Jon whistled.

"You were also going to research some additional legal theories we should consider," Angela said. "Did you find anything helpful?"

Tyler glanced at his notes. "In addition to internet, mail and wire fraud, we should also consider—"

Zack noisily entered the room and took a seat at the far end of the table, although the rest of the team was gathered at the opposite end. "Sorry I'm late."

Angela refused to react to what she assumed was an attention-grabbing move. "Go ahead, Tyler."

When Tyler finished his presentation, Zack started pelting him with questions. "Did you read *U.S. v. Janson*?" he asked in a manner meant to intimidate.

Tyler looked embarrassed. "Uh . . . no."

"Why not? It's—"

"Hold up, Zack," Angela said, cutting him off. "I'm not concerned about nailing down specific legal authority right now." She turned to Tyler. "Good job."

Zack rolled his eyes just as Salina hurried into the conference room. "You absolutely won't believe this."

"Don't tell me," Zack said facetiously, "there's been another viatical murder."

"Nope," Salina said. "There've been *two* murders."

Angela gasped. "You're kidding.

"I wish." Salina took the open seat next to Angela. "And both of the victims just happen to be clients of Live Now who sold their policies a few weeks before they died."

Salina passed around copies of a memo to everyone at the table. "The first woman, Joanna Richardson, suffered from kidney disease. She was killed in a hit-and-run while taking a stroll in her Leimert Park neighborhood. Four days before that, an elderly woman, Mildred Matthews, died in a suspicious fire at her home in Compton. If you count Veronika Myers and her mother, that makes four deaths tied to Live Now. I'm sorry, but I don't think they were accidents. These Live Now guys may only be pressuring dying people in other states, but in California they're killing 'em."

"I knew it, I knew it!" Zack said, pumping his fist in the air. "This is the case I've been praying for."

"Don't get too excited," Angela said. "If we look into this, we'll have to team up with the D.A.'s Office."

Zack huffed. "Well, we just have to be careful about how much information we share. We don't want them to get all the credit when we crack this murder ring."

"We don't even know whether it is a murder ring yet. Let's just hope no one else is killed." Angela turned to Jon. "When you go undercover, I want you to be careful."

"I'll be fine. I'm a federal agent packing heat, remember?"

Angela smiled to herself. The Postal Inspection Service wasn't exactly the FBI.

"Salina, this is great work," Angela said. "Did you find out anything about the brokers who work for Live Now?"

Salina's face lit up. "If you love me now, you're really, really, really going to love me after you hear this."

"Spill it," Zack said anxiously.

"The broker who sold the policies of the people I just mentioned recently left the company. The guy who replaced him just got his license. If this company is as unscrupulous as it appears to be, they hired the right man for the job." Salina smiled. "When we bust their operation, his involvement is going to attract some big headlines."

"Just tell us what you found out," Zack said, sounding annoyed.

"First he's a lawyer," Salina said, smiling. "His name is Waverly Sloan."

"Yes!" Zack exclaimed. "It's always nice when we can put one of our own behind bars."

"That's not the best part," Salina continued. "I did some digging. He's not just a lawyer, he's a recently *disbarred* lawyer."

Zack and Jon responded at the same time. "Jackpot!"

PART TWO

It's All Good

CHAPTER 16

Waverly stood on the front porch of his magnificent new home in Palos Verdes Estates, watching the moving van back out of the driveway. His face glistened with pride.

In just over two months as a viatical broker, he'd earned enough money to render his financial problems a distant memory. His aggressive marketing efforts were so effective that terminally ill patients in need of cash began ringing his phone off the hook.

Two clients who had life expectancies of less than six months had died within days. The investors who purchased their policies, thrilled with the fast return on their investment, were clamoring to hand over even more money. An oncologist he'd given a finder's fee for referring a patient, even came on board as an investor. Waverly now had his own source of ready cash and didn't need to rely on investors from Live Now.

Deidra walked up behind him and circled her arms around his waist. "Admiring your kingdom?"

Waverly smiled. "You might say that."

Just a few weeks ago, he wasn't sure how long he'd be able to pay the mortgage on his townhouse and now he was living in a six-thousand-square-foot mansion. The doctor who had owned the house dropped dead of a heart attack, both underinsured and heavily in debt. His elderly wife was close to losing the place and just wanted out. Waverly gave her a few thousand dollars and worked out a deal to lease the house with an option to buy. Their townhouse in Culver City was now on the market.

Waverly followed Deidra back inside. The living room, an impressive circular expanse with a twenty-foot ceiling, was crowded with boxes and new furniture still encased in plastic. They had just returned from five days in Cabo, where they did nothing but lay on the beach, make love and shop.

Deidra headed for the kitchen to confer with the interior decorator, who was busy directing her team of helpers. Waverly opened the French doors and stepped out onto the veranda, which overlooked the crystal blue waters of the Palos Verdes coastline. He liked the sound of the ocean waves crashing against the rocks below. He still couldn't believe the turn his life had taken. Not only had he earned over a hundred grand in commissions from the sale of six policies, but there were another five deals set to be inked in the next day or so. On top of that, he'd actually been helping people. For once, all was right with his life.

"Knock, knock. May we come in?"

Waverly glanced back toward the living room just as his in-laws knocked on the open front door. He had sworn Deidra to secrecy about the house until today. Waverly wanted to see Leon's reaction for himself.

"Welcome," he said, returning to the living room and waving them inside.

Leon whistled and did a slow three-sixty turn. "This is quite a place. Business must be pretty darn good."

Waverly smiled. "I'm doing okay." He enjoyed moving just a couple of miles from his pompous father-in-law and buying a house that dwarfed his.

Leon walked over to the French doors and took in the ocean view. Leon had a view of his neighbor's backyard.

Deidra came bouncing into the room and rushed to hug her mother. "Don't you just love it?"

"It's beautiful!" her mother cooed, appearing genuinely happy for her daughter.

Leon stepped out onto the veranda. "This is really something." The compliment was not nearly as exuberant as his wife's. "This place had to cost you over two million."

"Close," Waverly said, not bothering to explain that he was essentially a renter.

The housekeeper appeared and asked Deidra what room she should start next.

"You have a housekeeper now?" Leon asked. "A few weeks ago, you couldn't afford a trip to Paris and now you've got a multimillion dollar house *and* a housekeeper? Did you hit the lottery and forget to tell us?"

"Leon, stop it," his wife, Myrtle, scolded.

Waverly would never understand how a man with so much could envy him for attaining the same, all to the benefit of his daughter. But in Leon's eyes, Waverly's increase in stature somehow lowered his. As usual, Deidra stepped in as peacemaker.

"C'mon, Daddy." She took her father by the arm. "Let me show you the rest of the house."

After dinner delivered by a nearby Italian restaurant, Leon cornered Waverly alone on the veranda.

"So tell me about the big case?"

Waverly folded his arms and grinned. "No big case, Leon. In fact, I'm no longer practicing law."

His father-in-law's face flushed with astonishment. "Really. Exactly what business *are* you in?"

"Insurance investments," he said.

"Really? Tell me more."

"I find people interested in investing in certain insurance products. As the broker, I earn a commission on every sale. The bulk of my clients are wealthy doctors with too much money on their hands."

"Interesting," Leon said eagerly. "Maybe I'd like to get in on it."

That was not a request Waverly was willing to entertain. He didn't want his father-in-law anywhere near his new cash cow. "Sorry, Leon, but I don't think it's a good idea to mix family and business. And anyway, you already have more money than you can spend."

"You can never have too much money," Leon said with a chuckle, shoving both hands deep into his pockets. "I'm serious, I'd like to—"

"Sorry, Leon. Can't help you." Waverly gave him a patronizing pat on the back, then pulled open the French doors. "Let's head back inside. I think we're having tiramisu for dessert."

CHAPTER 17

Angela browsed a rack of wedding gowns at the Dare to be a Diva bridal shop on Melrose, while waiting for her mother and sister to arrive. She looked up just as her sister entered the store.

"Dang, girl!" Jada grabbed both of Angela's hands and lifted them in the air so she could get a better view. "How much weight did you lose?"

Angela beamed with pride. "Seventeen pounds."

"Tyra Banks ain't got nothing on you!" She gave her sister a hug. "Finally, Mama can stop bugging you about losing weight for the wedding. Has she seen you yet?"

"Today'll be the first time."

Jada turned up her nose. "Knowing her, she'll still have something snotty to say. Just ignore her, okay?"

"I will," Angela promised. "As long as you do the same."

Jada laughed. "That's asking way too much."

Jada and their mother, Lola, bickered constantly. Their already strained relationship worsened after Jada flunked out of Yale, in large part, because she spent more time playing dorm hairstylist than studying English Lit. That was several years ago, but Lola Evans still hadn't forgiven her firstborn for selecting the Vidal Sassoon Academy over the Ivy League.

They took seats in a waiting area. "You really going through with this?" Jada asked.

Angela picked up a *Brides* magazine from the table. "Please don't start."

Despite her growing attraction to Dre, Angela had finally decided to honor her commitment to Cornell. They'd just spent a long weekend in Santa Barbara and actually had a wonderful time.

"You're not even excited about the wedding," Jada said.

"Yes, I am." Angela sounded more defensive than she meant to.

Jada smacked her lips. "I'll never understand how you can be such a barracuda in the courtroom and such a wuss when it comes to your personal life. You're only marrying Cornell because your clock is ticking. If you want a baby, then have one. It's not like you couldn't take care of it. You don't need a husband."

"I know that." *But that's not the way I want to do it.*

"The wedding is less than three months away," Jada continued, "and you're just getting around to ordering your dress. You don't want to marry Cornell, but you know Mama would have a hissy fit if you backed out. You need to stop letting her run your life."

Angela shifted in her seat. "She's not running my life."

Jada made an exasperated sound with her lips. "I couldn't believe you let Mama pick your wedding colors. Burgundy and grey? Ugh. You hate burgundy and I've never seen you in grey."

Before Angela could come up with a retort, Lola Evans floated into the shop in a cloud of rose-scented perfume. "How are my girls?" She bent to give each of them a big air kiss.

After hitting sixty, their mother lost her attraction to solid colors. Today she was wearing a silk blouse that was a neon mix of orange, brown and yellow. Her shoulder length hair was gathered on top of her head in a long ponytail.

Lola was barely seated before she pulled several bridal magazines from a big, orange purse. "I've found some beautiful gowns I want you to see." She opened a magazine to a page flagged with a Post-it Note. "What do you think?"

Every dress pictured on the two-page spread had a high neckline and way too much lace for Angela. Now that she was almost back into a size eight, she was looking forward to wearing something a little sexier.

"Well?" her mother said in anxious anticipation.

Angela hesitated.

"Look at her face, Mama," Jada interceded. "She hates them."

"Your sister does not need you to talk for her," Lola said, her tone snippy.

Angela silently gritted her teeth. *Yes, I do.* "They're beautiful, but I had my heart set on a strapless dress."

"Oh, no, no, no, no, no." Lola pressed her hand to her chest. "Not for an afternoon wedding. And honey, you don't have the arms for that style of dress."

"Don't have the arms?" Jada said, scrunching up her face. "Mama, have you even looked at her? Angela, stand up."

When Angela didn't move, Jada grabbed her wrist and pulled her to her feet.

Lola leaned back to take in her daughter's dramatic weight loss. "Oh, you lost some weight. You look nice, baby."

"*Nice?*" Jada said. "Is that all you have to say? She looks amazing. And I'm not aware of any book that says afternoon weddings and strapless gowns don't mix."

"I wasn't aware that you had picked up a book since you dropped out of Yale," Lola huffed.

Before Jada could snipe back, Angela flagged one of the bridal consultants. "We're ready to get started now."

"How is Cornell, honey?" her mother asked, as they walked back to the fitting room.

"Fine." Angela wasn't in the mood to hear her mother go on and on about how lucky she was to be marrying a man like Cornell.

"I guess he's certainly glad you finally lost weight." Her mother's words stung, but Angela didn't need to respond because Jada charged to her defense.

"Mama!" Jada nearly screamed. "I can't believe you said that to her."

As her mother and sister commenced another round, Angela checked out of the conversation. Jada was right. She wasn't excited about the wedding or about marrying Cornell. Would she feel differently if she had been engaged to Dre?

Her sister nudged her. "What in the world are you smiling at?"

"Nothing." Angela didn't even realize she'd been smiling.

Several feet away, her mother meandered along an aisle of hideous debutante dresses. "Come take a look at these, baby," Lola called out.

Jada shot Angela a look that challenged her to speak her mind.

Instead, Angela groaned and slogged her way over.

CHAPTER 18

The driver eased the black Crown Victoria into the driveway of Erickson's stately Hancock Park home. Relaxing in the backseat, he drank the last of his scotch, grimaced, and braced himself for another show.

After tipping the driver, Erickson climbed out and grabbed his carry-on bag. He had just returned from Washington where he'd undergone a grueling round of meetings and interviews. The job was his. He could feel it. Without that knowledge, he would not have had the strength to carry on with this charade.

Dropping his bag just inside the entryway, he found Corky waiting to greet him. "Hey there, boy!" Erickson reached down and massaged the dog's back. "I bet *you* missed me."

He started for the bedroom, but heard the sound of the television wafting from the family room and headed there first. As expected, his sister-in-law, Sophia, sat in front of the television set, glued to an episode of *Forensic Files*. She was addicted to true crime shows. Tales of murder and mayhem actually seemed to delight her.

"Welcome home." She managed to face him without taking her eyes off the television screen. Physically, his wife bore little resemblance to her older sister. Sophia's dark brown hair hung heavily down her back. She never wore makeup and her long bangs nearly covered her green eyes, which made her resemble some shaggy animal. It was completely understandable why she had never married.

"How's Claire feeling today?" Erickson asked.

This time, Sophia glanced away from the TV screen, but not for more than a couple of seconds. "Fine."

Erickson wanted to scream that Claire was not fine. Nothing around his house was fine.

He often wondered how much Claire had confided in Sophia. *Did she know about the DVD?* He was fairly certain that she did not. Appearances were important to Claire. She would not have shared his transgressions even with her only sister. And if Sophia had known, he would have sensed it. He'd never met anyone more transparent.

Erickson entered the bedroom, locking the door behind him. Except for a small lamp on the nightstand, the room was almost movie-theater dark and reeked of despair. Claire was watching *Desperate Housewives.* Her viewing habits were as atrocious as her sister's.

Claire's mood swings had been growing more and more severe. Erickson wondered what temperament he would face today.

"How are you feeling?" he asked, reluctant to test the waters.

"I'm fine," Claire replied, just above a whisper. He was thankful that the darkness prevented a clear view of her face.

Taking a seat on the edge of the bed, Erickson took her hand. She did not pull away, which he interpreted as a positive sign. He was increasingly at a loss for words in Claire's presence. It would have been nice to share his excitement about his trip to Washington. But he would not give his wife more ammunition to assassinate him with.

Everything was in place for the surgery. The payout from the policy—two hundred and fifty thousand dollars—had already been deposited into their bank account. Claire had been examined by a surgeon, who confirmed that she was a suitable candidate for the procedure. Scheduling the date was the only loose end.

Over the last few days, however, Claire had become non-committal whenever he brought up the subject.

Erickson awkwardly caressed her hand. He knew he should proceed slowly, but he did not have time for delays. He needed Claire's agreement to move forward with the procedure.

"Have you given any more thought to when you'd like to schedule the surgery?" He despised the spinelessness in his voice.

Claire laughed softly. "Couldn't you wait five minutes before you begin badgering me again?"

Badgering you? he wanted to scream. *I'm trying to save your god-damn life!*

"I don't understand." He stroked the back of her hand. Maybe she was just nervous. "The surgery is your best hope. It's our best hope."

"I've changed my mind," Claire announced, easing her hand from his. "It's a waste of money. We should just face reality. I'm going to die."

Yes, Erickson thought, *you are.* But he did not have the time to wait for some unknown date. The surgery was part of the plan and they had to stick to the plan.

"But the surgery was the whole reason we sold the insurance policy," he said.

"I said I don't want to do it," Claire snapped. "And please don't mention it to Sophia or Ashley. I don't want them getting their hopes up. I've been reading about the operation on the Internet. The odds of success are very low."

Erickson eyed the laptop sitting on the nightstand to her right.

"We spend all that money. I suffer for another few months, then I die. It's not worth it."

"But don't you think—"

"I said I don't want to do it!" Claire practically shouted. "So forget it."

Erickson had not anticipated this. He had no idea how it would impact Becker's plan.

"It's time for me to get my final wishes in order," Claire said. "I'll put everything in writing. I'd like to be cremated."

That surprised him, but Erickson didn't care one way or the other. In fact, it made things easier. If something went wrong, there'd be no body to examine.

With Claire's change of heart, getting his hands on that DVD was more important than ever. Though he'd never seen it, he did not doubt its existence. He had searched the house, numerous times, to no avail. It had to be here. Claire would not have trusted it in the hands of anyone else.

"What about the DVD?" he asked. "You said you were going to give it to me."

Claire had turned back to the television screen and did not appear to be listening to him. "No, I didn't. I said I would *think* about giving it to you. I've changed my mind about that, too."

Erickson wasn't sure he could control his temper. "I understand that you want to ruin me, but what if somebody found it? Is that what you want?"

Claire laughed. "I think the world should know who the chairman of Jankowski, Parkins really is."

Erickson wanted to snatch her by the neck and squeeze the life out of her right that very moment. "I'm tired of your games," he said, finally lashing out. "You probably made the whole thing up just to hold over my head." He got up to leave.

His words seemed to energize her. "You don't believe me? You think I made it up?"

She fumbled beneath the covers, retrieved the remote control and aimed it toward the DVD player underneath the television. "Take a look at this."

The television screen filled with Erickson's image. He was sitting at the desk in his study, staring at his computer monitor. Only his head and shoulders were visible above the back of his leather chair. He was wearing the bathrobe Claire had given him as an anniversary present three years ago.

A sick feeling churned in his gut and he felt blindingly dizzy. He had looked everywhere for the DVD except in the one most obvious place. Had it been there all along?

Panic ripped through him as he focused on the pornographic video he had been viewing in the privacy of his office. A hidden camera, which he quickly estimated had been posted on the bookshelf near the door, had caught him enjoying what he considered nothing more than a harmless pastime.

On the television screen, Erickson looked calm and relaxed as he backed away from the desk and turned sideways, providing a clear profile of his face. He opened his robe and began moaning as he gently stroked himself. His eyes were glued to the computer monitor on his desk which showed three, sun-starved girls lying on a thin cot in a room barren of other furniture. An accented voice, someplace off camera, instructed the girls in a foreign language. They slowly responded, awkwardly touching themselves in private places. All of the girls were Asian, likely Filipino, and no older than ten or twelve.

Erickson charged across the room and slammed his fist against the panel of the DVD player. It seemed to take forever for the disk to slide out of the machine. When it did, he grabbed it and cracked it in half. "Is this the only copy?" He was surprisingly calm.

"Perhaps," Claire said with a shrewd smile.

The thought of anyone else seeing the DVD caused a blast of terror to slice through him. The video painted him as some pervert, which he was not. He had never touched a child. Any child. Ever. His private fantasies were just that.

Erickson was not sure he could wait for Becker to carry out his plan. He needed to complete the process himself. Right this moment.

Instead, he stormed out of the room, grabbed his keys from a table in the hallway and headed for the front door. He needed to take a drive. A nice long one.

CHAPTER 19

Hey, little bruh, what's hap'nin'?"

Waverly frowned at the sound of his brother's voice. There were so many calls coming in from terminally ill people, he had developed a bad habit of not checking his caller ID before picking up.

"Hey, Quincy," Waverly said dryly.

"Don't worry, I'm not callin' to borrow any money, bruh. Just wanted to say hey."

That would be a first.

Having just signed up two new clients, it was turning out to be a good day. He was also enjoying his first week in his plush new office on Wilshire Boulevard. So he wasn't up for dealing with any nonsense from his brother.

Quincy rambled on about nothing in particular, taking way too long to get to the point. That told Waverly that whatever he wanted was major.

"Hey, man," Waverly said finally, "good talking to you, but I'm a working stiff. Gotta get back to work."

"What you doin' ain't work. You're livin' the high life."

Waverly hadn't told his brother much about his new business. Only that he was now helping wealthy people invest their money. But once Quincy heard about the move to Palos Verdes Estates, he only saw dollar signs.

"Since you brought it up," Quincy said tentatively, "I was just talkin' to a friend about your business."

Waverly pinched the bridge of his nose with his thumb and index finger. This was not going to be good.

Quincy seemed to be waiting for him to say something. When he realized that Waverly didn't plan to, he plunged ahead.

"Uh, one of my buddies knows a guy who knows a guy who'd like you to do some investin' for him."

"I'm not looking for any new investors, Quincy. Tell your friend thanks, but no thanks."

"C'mon, man. Just do me this favor. I already told 'em all about you."

"I'm curious, Quincy. Just what does your friend do for a living?"

"He's in business."

"What kind of business?"

"I'm not really sure. Import, export, I think."

"And what's his product?" Waverly asked. "Marijuana, crack, meth or all three?"

"Li'l bruh, I wouldn't get you hooked up with the wrong kind of people. I swear this guy is on the up-and-up."

"Sure he is. He's probably looking for somebody to launder his drug money. I'm not interested."

"C'mon, at least meet the dude," Quincy begged. "Then you can judge for yourself."

A meeting wasn't necessary. If the guy was even remotely associated with his brother, he was bad news. "I gotta get back to work. Good-bye, Quin—"

"Wait, don't hang up." The desperation level in Quincy's voice rose ten notches.

"You gotta help me out on this. They're kinda expectin' to talk to you. If they don't, they're gonna take it out on me."

Waverly lowered his head and exhaled. He should just hang up the phone. He was not about to risk his very lucrative career dealing with his brother's thug friends.

"I can't help you this time, Quincy."

"Can't you just talk to the guy? I can't go back and tell 'em you won't even speak to him. You can't dis' him like that. This dude is pretty high up."

"High up in what? Some drug cartel?"

"C'mon, bruh, just do me this one favor."

"Can't," Waverly said, then hung up.

He flipped open the calendar on his desk and saw that he only had one appointment left for the day. Waverly usually went to his clients' homes, but Jerry Billington had insisted on meeting Waverly at his office. Waverly wondered if that meant Billington hadn't told his family he planned to sell his insurance policy.

Pulling Billington's intake folder from his file cabinet, Waverly reviewed the information he'd taken down during a lengthy telephone conversation with the man. Divorced business executive with terminal lung cancer. Forty-three years old, father of two college-age kids. Six-month life expectancy. The next part made Waverly smile. Billington had a policy worth three hundred thousand dollars, which meant thirty grand for Waverly.

When Billington finally walked into his office, Waverly gave him a quick once-over. He lacked the dull gray pallor that Waverly had come to associate with terminal cancer. But the man had probably lost a great deal of weight. He was skinny enough to be blown away by a strong gust of wind.

Waverly offered him a seat and asked if he wanted coffee.

Billington declined.

"We've gone over most of your information on the telephone and I have your application here. All we need to do now is—"

"I'm not sure I understand how this all works," Billington interrupted. "Can you explain it to me again?" He spoke in a low, gravelly voice.

Most of his clients wanted money, not repeat explanations. But Waverly took the time to review the process again, step by step. When he was done, Billington scratched the crown of his head.

"I'm not really sure I should do this. My kids and grandkids could probably use the insurance money."

Waverly winced inside. He was already counting on the commission. But he had never been one to apply pressure tactics.

"This is an important decision, Mr. Billington. If you're not sure, we shouldn't proceed. Have you discussed this with your family?"

"No, I can't seem to find the right time to bring it up."

Waverly closed the folder. "I think you may want to do that."

A surprised look crossed Billington's face.

"Why don't I give you a few days to give it some thought?" Waverly continued. "You can call me back to reschedule our appointment after you've spoken with your family."

Billington seemed hesitant and started biting his nails. "What do *you* think I should do?"

"I'm sorry," Waverly said. "I really can't make that decision for you. If you're not sure you want to sell your policy, we shouldn't proceed."

The man just stared back at him and didn't say anything for a long while. "If I go through with it, how soon will I get the check?"

"It all depends on how fast we can get your medical records from your doctor."

"My doctor's a golfing buddy." Billington pulled out his wallet and handed Waverly a business card. "He promised me he would do what he could to get my records to you right away."

"I really think it's best if you talk this over with your family first," Waverly urged him.

Billington waved his hand in front of his face. "Never mind. I'll tell them. What's next?"

This time, Waverly hesitated. He didn't want any hassles after the guy died. It was always better if the family knew the deal up front.

"Our in-house doctors have to review your medical history," Waverly explained. "I'll see if I can give your case priority. If there aren't any glitches, I should be able to get a check to you a couple of weeks after the medical review is finished."

"So how much will I get?" Billington asked, his indecision now forgotten.

"As we discussed over the telephone, fifty percent of the face value of your policy. That's one hundred and fifty thousand dollars."

Billington grinned. "Who gets the rest once I'm dead?"

"There are some administrative fees that go to Live Now and the doctors who evaluate your medical records. My commission also has to be paid. The rest goes to whoever invests in your policy."

"And who's that?"

"I can't disclose that information. These policies are generally purchased through a trust."

"Sounds like somebody's going to hit it big when I kick the bucket. What's your take?"

"Ten percent," Waverly said slowly. He'd never had such an inquisitive client. Most people were just happy to have money coming their way.

"Why do you get so much?"

"That's the standard commission, Mr. Billington."

The man was asking way too many questions. "Like I said before, if you aren't certain about proceeding, we should hold off."

"No, no, I'm ready."

Waverly tried not to reveal how happy he was with Billington's final decision. "Okay, then. I'll request your medical records and call you in a few days with an update."

CHAPTER 20

J ust after ten, Dre drove into the darkened streets of L.A.'s Skid Row and parked his Volkswagen near 5th and Crocker Streets. He looked around, then got out to stretch his legs.

As he waited for his client to show up, he watched a bum peer out of a cardboard tent as two drunks stumbled by. He rarely made runs downtown anymore. Too risky. But Junior, a long-time client, was in a fix and Dre agreed to do him the favor.

He mentally calculated his take for the day. He had nine thousand in the pocket of his lightweight trench coat and was about to collect another six grand. The thought of the money empowered him. He was close, real close, to getting out.

Dre was also more than ready to take things further with Angela. He looked forward to hanging out with her after their cycling class, but just talking to a babe wasn't hittin' on nothing. Dre figured coming on too strong with a sistah like Angela would be a mistake. He had put it out there. She would have to make the next move.

Besides, Dre knew that if he wanted to pursue her as his woman, he would have to come correct. He hadn't exactly lied when she asked what he did for a living. He did buy and sell foreclosures. But could he really keep her from learning about his *other* gig? Even if he got out of the game, could she accept his past? Dre told himself she could. Angela was real people. He just hoped Mr. Fiancé kept doing whatever it was he was doing. Or *not* doing.

He heard movement from the rear and spun around. Junior was strutting toward him. Dre chuckled. Junior was a slightly built, dark-skinned man who walked with the exaggerated swagger of a heavyweight boxer. He probably weighed a buck twenty, if that.

They acknowledged each other with only a curt nod. Junior handed him a paper bag filled with cash and Dre passed him a larger bag containing product. There was no need for either of them to check the contents. They had it like that.

Dre jumped back into his Jetta and headed home. As he drove west on 5th Street, he rolled down the window and rested his elbow across the door. At the last minute he slowed, deciding not to speed through the yellow light at Los Angeles Street.

As he sang along with Seal's rendition of *It's a Man's World*, Dre imagined taking Angela out dancing and wondered if she could step. He tried to think of where they would go on their first date. He would search the Internet and find someplace special. Damn, how he wanted to get with her.

"Don't move, muthafucka!"

Dre felt the barrel of a gun pressed against his left temple and froze. "What the hell?"

Before he could react, a brick shattered the front passenger window, stinging his face with chards of glass. "Pull over. Now!" a second man shouted from his right. Dre saw rotting teeth and a skeletal body.

Too afraid to move, Dre quickly assessed that he was dealing with a couple of crack heads. These dudes wanted money and drugs, not a murder rap. But mistakes happen.

"Pull over, muthafucka!" yelled the man with the gun.

Dre's pulse quickened. "Look, dude—"

"Are you hard of hearin'?" The man bashed the side of his head with the butt of the gun.

Dre's head throbbed in pain. He thought about flooring it, but didn't want to risk getting shot. Too bad his .38 was out of reach in a secret compartment in the back. Trying to reason with his attackers would be a waste of time. He gently pressed the gas, jerking the car into the intersection. Both men jogged along with the car as a minivan darted around them, horns blaring.

"Pull over to the curb!" The gunman seemed overly agitated. "Hurry up!"

Dre did as instructed, steering the car through the intersection in a herky-jerky motion. When the Volkswagen eased over to the curb, the man on his right leaned in, grabbed the keys from the ignition and threw them to the ground.

Blood trailed down the side of Dre's face and his vision was blurry. While the gunman kept his weapon aimed at Dre's head, the other man ran around, opened the driver's door and yanked Dre from the car. The man frantically patted him down, eventually finding the wallet in his back pocket which contained close to two hundred bucks.

"What else you got?" he demanded. "You got any rocks?"

Dre didn't answer. He felt equal amounts of rage and fear.

"I bet he's got some rocks, too," barked the gunman, who was a foot taller than his accomplice and stank of urine. "Find 'em! Hurry up!"

The smaller man quickly ransacked the car, but found nothing. As he moved in to search Dre a second time, Dre kneed him in the groin and grabbed for the other man's gun. While the accomplice bent in pain, Dre wrestled for control of the weapon.

Dre almost had it when he felt a blow to his face. The smaller man had composed himself and was pummeling him with what felt like a steel pole. Dre let go of the gun as he fell back onto the hood of the car.

He felt his trench coat being ripped open as three wads of cash wrapped in rubber bands, fell to the ground.

Just as he was about to fade into unconsciousness, Dre heard a police siren and saw a flash of blue and red lights, two, maybe three blocks up the street. The men instantly darted off in opposite directions as a police cruiser pulled up behind Dre's Volkswagen. The cruiser's headlights lit up the area like a movie set.

Two officers stepped out with their guns drawn. "Put your hands up!" one of the officers yelled.

Dre quickly complied. Both cops looked nervous, which made Dre doubly nervous. He raised his hands even higher.

The officers gingerly walked closer.

"What's going on here?"

Dre struggled to catch his breath. "I was . . . I was just robbed."

"Do you have a weapon?"

"No," Dre said, still holding his hands over his head. "I just told you somebody robbed me."

One of the officers, a big, burly black man, told Dre to turn around and face the car, then roughly patted him down. Satisfied that he was unarmed, the officer directed him to sit on the curb, then began searching Dre's Volkswagen.

"What're you doing down here?" asked the white officer, who kept his hand on his weapon.

"I was stopped at the light and two dudes broke my window and stole my wallet. When they heard your siren . . ." he paused, his breathing still labored, "they ran off. You . . . you saved my life."

"Well, we weren't trying to save your life," the black officer yelled over his shoulder.

From his sitting position, Dre watched as the officer rummaged through his car. He prayed that the cop didn't discover his .38. The officer moved the seats backward and forward, then bent down to search underneath them. He tossed Dre's floor mats and empty duffel bag to the sidewalk. "You got any drugs in here?"

"Two crack heads just robbed me," Dre said, using the sleeve of his coat to wipe a trickle of blood from his face. "I'm the victim here. Why you treatin' me like a criminal?"

"Because you are," the black officer shot back. "We ran your plates."

It took about twenty minutes before he gave up the search. The contents of Dre's car were now sprawled along the sidewalk.

"Ain't nothing here," the black cop said to his partner. He looked at Dre with contempt. "You wanna file a police report?"

"Naw," Dre said.

The black officer ordered Dre to his feet, lifted his chin and examined his bruised face. "Just a few minor bruises. You don't need an ambulance, right?"

Dre pulled away. "Naw, I'm fine."

"Good answer."

The cops headed toward their cruiser. "Don't let us see you around here again," the white cop shouted from the window as they drove off.

Dre thought about responding, but wasn't stupid enough to give them an excuse to cart him off to jail. "Thanks for everything, officers," he muttered.

He walked over to the sidewalk and starting searching for his keys. This was a sign, Dre thought, as he picked up a floor mat. It was time for him to close up shop. Time to get out.

Now.

The next day, Dre was about to take the stairs to the cycling room when he saw Angela heading in his direction. He stopped and waited for her to catch up with him.

She was only inches away when Dre's battered face stopped her mid-stride. He had a long gash near his left temple and his right cheek was dotted with tiny red marks from the shards of glass.

"What happened to you?" Angela reached out and gently

pressed both hands to his cheeks. Her touch felt soft and warm on his face.

Angela's reflexive gesture of concern apparently surprised her as much as it did Dre. She self-consciously dropped her hands to her side.

He smiled and tried to play down his injuries. "Car accident. And it wasn't half as bad as it looks."

"When? You should've called me."

Dre cocked his head. "I would've, but I don't have your number."

Angela's lips curled into a smile. "Well, I guess we'll have to fix that."

They'd been *friends* for more than three months now and he knew little more about her than her name, profession and that she was about to marry some guy she didn't seem to be all that into. Dre wished he could feel her hands on his face again.

"I'm fine," he said. He took her hand and she let him. "Let's go work out."

When their cycling class ended, Dre walked over to her, wiping the sweat from his face with a towel. "I need to talk to you about something. You have time to grab some coffee?"

"Sure," Angela said. "You have a legal problem?"

"Yeah, I do." He folded his arms across his chest. "You. I'll be waitin' for you out front." He walked off without giving her a chance to respond.

They took a short walk to the Starbucks in the Howard Hughes Promenade up the street. As they stood in line to order, Angela kept glancing back over her shoulder.

"What's the matter?" Dre teased, as they took a seat near the window. "You worried about dude catchin' us together?"

Angela smiled, then hunched her shoulders, which told Dre that was exactly what was on her mind. The clerk called his name and Dre retrieved their iced drinks. He set them on the table, then wasted no time getting to the point.

"Sometimes I find it easier to just put my shi—excuse me—put my stuff on the table," Dre said. "So here goes. I definitely have feelings for you and I'm pretty sure you have feelings for me."

Angela used that precise moment to take a noisy sip of her drink.

"Am I right?"

"Maybe," she said coyly.

"What's up then? If you've got the hots for me, why you marryin' dude?"

Angela laughed heartily. "How did we get from my possibly having feelings for you to *the hots*?"

Dre leaned back in his seat and stroked his goatee. "I know what I know. And what I know is your personal situation ain't what it's supposed to be. Is there really a fiancé or do you just wear that big ass rock to keep brothas like me offa you?"

A smile touched her lips, but didn't linger. "No," she said, suddenly solemn. "There's really a fiancé."

"So what's the deal?" Dre challenged. "You don't seem all that excited about gettin' married. Is it some old guy? You marryin' dude 'cuz he got bank or something?"

Angela rolled her eyes. "No, I'm not marrying for money. He is older than me, though. A little more than ten years."

"Ain't the wedding comin' up?"

Angela responded with a labored sigh. "Yep. Ten weeks and four days to be exact. My mother just put the invitations in the mail."

Dre spread his hands. "Well, what's the deal? Talk to me."

Angela averted her eyes. "I guess I don't know the deal myself. I'm not exactly sure Cornell is the man I want to spend the rest of my life with." She fidgeted with the straw in her drink. "And getting to know you has certainly complicated things. But, unfortunately, the train has already left the station."

Lines of confusion filled Dre's forehead. "Sounds like you're about to marry some dude you're not sure you wanna be with 'cuz you're too embarrassed to call off the wedding. That's crazy."

"I agree," Angela said.

Dre was dying to lean across the table and kiss her. Instead, he took her right hand in his and squeezed it. When Angela squeezed back, Dre knew. He knew he would eventually have her.

"Well, what you plan to do about it?" he asked.

There was a long pause before Angela responded. "I don't know," she said weakly. "I really don't know."

CHAPTER 21

"What do you mean Claire's not having the surgery?"
Becker appeared to be as stunned as Erickson had been when Claire sprang the news on him.

"You heard me," Erickson said, flopping down into an upholstered chair in front of Becker's desk.

"But why?"

"I think she's given up," Erickson said.

"Has she given up on destroying you, too?" Becker asked.

"I doubt it."

Erickson still could not shake the images on the DVD that Claire had secretly recorded. An activity that had once brought him pleasure, now threatened him with not just embarrassment and financial ruin, but prison time. Simply being in possession of child pornography was a federal offense. He had taken tremendous precautions before downloading the video from the Internet, using an email address, computer and credit card that could not be linked to him. Ensuring the privacy of his study had been the one precaution he had stupidly failed to take.

Becker slowly rocked back and forth in his chair. "What about her sister, Sophia? Maybe she could convince her?"

"I doubt it. Once Claire makes up her mind about something, she can be pretty stubborn."

Becker tapped his pen on the desk. "This isn't good."

Erickson didn't exactly see it that way. "We don't really need her to have the surgery, do we?" He still had no idea how Becker planned to carry things out. Did he want Claire to have the surgery because he planned to sneak into her hospital room and inject her with some lethal drug?

"It would just be preferable if her death followed the surgery," Becker explained. "Like I said, no one would think you had a motive to kill her after trying to save her life."

Erickson wanted to laugh. *Yeah, I have a motive alright.* He just prayed no one ever found out what it was.

"Well, I can't convince her. So where do we go from here?"

Becker stood up and started pacing the short distance between the window and his desk.

"Let's proceed," he said. "If something were to go wrong, there's always the evidence that you wanted her to have the surgery. I can testify to that and so can her doctors and that viatical broker. You told him why you wanted the money, right?"

Erickson nodded.

Becker leaned his head from side to side, cracking his neck as he continued to pace. "Actually, I guess it's really not that big of a problem. Just means a minor change in plans on my end."

"There's something else you should know," Erickson said.

Becker abruptly stopped pacing.

"Unbeknownst to me," Erickson continued. "Claire made Ashley her sole beneficiary about six months ago."

"And you're just telling me this now!" Becker looked incredulous. "Someone could argue that you convinced Claire to sell the policy to get access to half of the insurance money when you really weren't entitled to any of it. I thought Ashley's grandparents left her a trust fund. I'm really surprised Claire did that."

That's because you have no idea what's going on in my household.

"Ashley only gets three grand a month from that trust," Erickson explained. "But it won't be a problem. I'll just give her the two-fifty. That will completely erase any financial motive."

Becker let that alternative settle in for a few seconds. "Good idea. Sophia and Ashley knew you were trying to convince Claire to have the surgery, right?"

"Unfortunately, no. Claire didn't want to get their hopes up, so she never told them she was even considering it. Anyway, I thought you said your plan was failsafe. Sounds like you're planning on someone pointing the finger at us." Erickson intentionally used the plural pronoun.

"That's not going to happen, but I always plan for the possibility that something could go wrong. That's why my clients pay me seven hundred dollars an hour," he boasted. Becker's hourly rate was as high as some senior partners. "I never let anything slip through the cracks."

Erickson smiled. He could not have a wiser co-conspirator. "How does this change our timeline?" *In other words, how fast can you get rid of her?*

"I think we can speed things up now. Quite a bit."

"May I ask how you—"

Becker held up a hand. "I really don't want you to have any of the details. Just let me protect you, okay? Once this is done, I don't want to discuss it again. Ever."

"That's fine, I just—"

"No, I mean it. When Claire's gone, she's gone. I'm not going to share any of the details. Before or after. Ever."

"I'm fine with that and I don't need specifics," Erickson pushed. "But can you give me some idea of how soon you plan to move forward?"

"Soon," Becker said. "Very soon."

"Her sister Sophia is usually around the house."

Becker paused. "That could be a problem, but I'll come up with something." He cracked his neck again. "One more thing. Claire hasn't contacted a lawyer or talked to anyone about filing for divorce, right?"

"No," Erickson replied. "Not that I'm aware of."

"Good. Keep it that way. Have you heard anything more from the White House?"

"Nothing definite. But based on the increasing frequency of the calls I'm getting, I'm definitely still in contention."

"Of course you are." Becker snapped his fingers. "I almost forgot. I have something for you." He opened a drawer to his left and pulled out a silver, framed photo. He handed it across the desk to Erickson.

The eight-by-ten portrait showed Becker, his wife, son and four daughters, dressed in blue jeans and white shirts, standing on the beach. There was a larger version of the same photograph on the credenza behind Becker's desk.

"You have a beautiful family," Erickson said, reciting the response he knew Becker both wanted and needed. "It's amazing. The twins are the spitting image of Staci."

Glowing with pride, Becker took a seat on the corner of his desk. "And my boy Garrett is turning out to be quite a handsome kid, if I do say so myself."

"How's he surviving with four sisters?"

"*Him?*" Becker chuckled. "How about me?" He folded his arms. "Make sure you keep me aware of your travel plans. Ideally, I'd like this to go down when you're out of town. Preferably, far away from the scene of the crime."

CHAPTER 22

Waverly backed into a stall in the underground garage of his office complex and climbed out of his brand new Lexus.

Business was going so well, he'd traded in his ancient BMW. Deidra begged for a new Lexus of her own, but Waverly denied the request. But only because he planned to surprise her with a Mercedes E-Class convertible for her birthday in three months. He couldn't wait to see Leon's face when she pulled up in *that*.

Waverly opened the back passenger door and was about to grab his briefcase when he felt the presence of someone or something nearby. He peered across the hood of the car, but saw nothing. He glanced back over his shoulder and his body became immobile.

In an empty stall just a few feet away, Waverly saw a human heap lying on the ground. He took a few steps forward, stopped, then ran over. "Christ, Quincy! What happened to you?"

Quincy tried to answer, but blood not words, spewed from his brother's bruised lips.

Waverly crouched down and placed two fingers in the crook of his brother's neck. He felt a strong pulse. Quincy's left eye was swollen shut and his face was a mass of black, red and purple bruises. Waverly lifted his shirt and was relieved to see no stab wounds or bullet holes. His face had taken the brunt of the beating.

"Quincy, what happened?"

Quincy moaned something indecipherable in response.

Waverly pulled out his BlackBerry to call for an ambulance, then suddenly slipped it back into his pocket. He would take Quincy to a hospital himself. He slid his arm underneath Quincy's neck and tried to help him up.

Quincy winced in pain.

"You have to help me," Waverly said. "C'mon, get up."

It took some effort, but Waverly managed to get Quincy to his feet. They stumbled the few steps to his car and Quincy fell across the backseat, splattering blood all over the immaculate cream interior. Waverly climbed into the driver's seat and started the car.

What had Quincy done now?

As they reached the garage exit, Waverly glanced at the attendant sitting in a small glass booth. She was reading a magazine and didn't even glance his way. He stuck his card key into a slot and waited for the gate to lift. Waverly didn't know whether to go left or right and tried to compose himself long enough to figure out the direction of the closest hospital.

He looked back at Quincy. "I'm taking you to the hospital, okay?"

"No," Quincy moaned. "I'm okay. No hospital."

"You need to see a doctor," Waverly insisted.

Quincy tried to sit up. "No!" he cried out. "They're gonna start askin' a lot of questions that I can't answer. Take me to your place. Please!"

Waverly was torn. Quincy needed medical attention, but his fear of going to the hospital meant he was probably involved in something illegal. Waverly needed to know what was going on first. At the next light, he cut off a UPS truck and headed down La Cienega toward the freeway.

By the time they pulled into his three-car garage, Quincy was able to exit the car with Waverly's help, but every step elicited a painful whimper. They were a few footsteps from the door that led from the garage to the kitchen when Waverly realized he had left the garage door up. He pressed a button to the right of the door. This scene was not something he wanted to explain to his new neighbors.

When they finally staggered inside, Deidra covered her mouth with both hands. "Oh, my God! What happened?"

"I wish I knew." Waverly deposited his brother into a chair at the kitchen table. "Go get some towels."

Deidra dashed down the hallway and returned in seconds.

She handed Waverly the towels, but did nothing else to help. "He can't stay here," Deidra said.

Waverly ignored her. He wiped the blood from his brother's face as best he could.

"Wet this for me, will you?" He hurled one of the towels at her.

Deidra did as asked, but the disapproval on her face only deepened.

Waverly examined his brother more closely. He'd taken an ugly beating, but his bruises didn't appear to be life threatening. Waverly helped him wash up, gave him a change of clothes and put him in one of their three guest bedrooms.

It was almost four hours before Quincy was finally awake, though one eye remained swollen shut.

Waverly gingerly sat down on the side of the bed. "Tell me what happened."

His brother started to whine. "I told you, man, you need to call that guy. Next time they're gonna kill me!"

Waverly took in a big gulp of air. "How much do you owe them?"

"Not a dime. I swear. They just want you to call 'em."

"How much?" Waverly demanded.

Quincy tried to turn away, but even the slightest shift in position seemed to cause him extensive pain.

Waverly raised both the volume and intensity of his voice. "How much, Quincy?"

"I don't owe anybody anything. They just wanna talk to you."

"About what?"

"I don't know. Your business, I guess."

Waverly pounded the wall above the headboard with his fist. "How would they possibly know about my business?"

He could imagine his brother sitting in some sleazy bar, bragging to some lowlife about his rich brother the insurance investor.

"I'm sorry," Quincy cried. "I didn't mean to get you into any trouble. I swear I didn't."

"You haven't gotten me into any trouble. You need to worry about what you've gotten yourself into."

"Just talk to the dude," Quincy begged. "Don't let them kill me. Whatever it is, just tell him you can't do it. Maybe he'll accept it from you."

They both knew that wasn't going to happen.

"He's gonna call you tonight." Quincy looked away. "At nine o'clock on your cell."

Waverly pounded the wall again. "What? Who's going to call me?"

"I don't know. I'm just tellin' you what they said before they messed me up."

"You gave them my number?"

"I had to!" Quincy started to cry. "You gotta at least talk to him. If you don't, they said they're comin' back to kill me *and* you."

CHAPTER 23

The day after Angela and Dre admitted their feelings for each other, Cornell asked Angela to meet him for lunch. Cornell usually ate lunch in his chambers, so the invitation surprised her. Maybe he sensed that her love for him was slipping away.

Angela stepped inside the Water Grill and walked up to the maitre d's stand. As the hostess led Angela to Cornell's table, she saw him glance down at his watch. Angela's chest tightened in anticipation of a reprimand.

Cornell rose and pulled out a chair for her. "You're late," he complained, as soon as the hostess was out of earshot.

Cornell was the ultimate time freak. But being eight minutes late wasn't enough to raise a stink over. He had already spoiled what Angela had hoped would be a pleasant lunch at one of her favorite restaurants.

"You have a cell phone. You could've called. You know I have to be back at court by one."

She started to tell him about the fender bender that tied up traffic on Grand, but decided to let it go. No excuse would be sufficient for Cornell. "Sorry," she mumbled.

"You look nice," he said gruffly, then reached over and squeezed her hand.

She thought about how much gentler Dre's touch felt. In many ways, Cornell had filled the void left by her father's passing.

Like her father, Cornell was strong, responsible, and intelligent. But in other ways, he was nothing like Samuel Evans. Her father had been an easygoing, affable man who'd always placed family first. No one other than Cornell would ever be first in Cornell's life.

The waiter appeared with a Diet Coke, which Cornell had apparently taken the liberty to order for her. Actually, she'd wanted a Sprite.

Angela wondered when they had lost their connection or whether there had never really been one.

Still holding her hand, Cornell took a sip of his iced tea. "You really do look great," he said. "Do you think you'll be able to keep the weight off this time?"

Angela eased her hand away and picked up her menu. "We'll see," she mumbled, more to herself than to Cornell.

She stared at the menu, but her mounting anger made the words an unreadable blur. The saddest thing about Cornell was that he had no idea he was being offensive. *Would he treat his children the same way?*

"How's everything at work?" he asked.

"Busy," Angela said, glad that the conversation had turned to something she wanted to talk about. She wished she could tell Cornell about the task force and their sting, but it was a confidential operation, one that could very well end up being a bust. When Jon sold his phony insurance policy through Waverly Sloan, the man hadn't pressured him at all. She hoped Sloan wasn't on to them. Angela was now considering having someone else pose as a terminally ill patient to see if Sloan treated them the same way.

Angela was about to tell Cornell about a new case she might be handling when he launched into a complaint about an attorney who spent ten minutes discussing the facts of a lower court decision that had been overruled. At least half of the attorneys who appeared in his courtroom, Cornell claimed, were lazy and incompetent.

"I wonder how the fools even passed the bar."

Angela tuned him out, her thoughts drifting to Dre.

"Angela? Did you hear me?" Cornell tapped her hand. "What did you decide?"

"Oh, excuse me." She picked up the menu. "I'll have the crab cakes."

"Where has your mind been lately? I asked if you decided on a dress yet. Since you were late, I ordered the white fish for you. I substituted spinach for the garlic mashed potatoes. It's the lowest calorie meal on the menu."

She wanted crab cakes, not white fish. She now planned to wolf down her food so she could get back to work.

"Tell me about your dress," Cornell prodded.

"I let my mother convince me to wear one of those big, poofy dresses with a mile-long train. You'd think she was the one getting married. But she never had a wedding, so I gave in. I really wanted to wear a strapless gown."

A waiter poured more tea into Cornell's glass and he added two packets of Splenda. "I don't think it's a good idea for you to go strapless. Your arms aren't toned enough."

A burst of heat inched up Angela's neck. What in the world was she thinking? She couldn't spend the rest of her life with this pompous, self-centered jerk. She slowly removed the napkin from her lap, balled it up and tossed it onto the table. "I'm not hungry anymore."

"Oh, c'mon, Angela. Since when did you become so sensitive? I was just trying to—"

She pushed back her chair and stood up.

"Angela!" Cornell said through clenched teeth. "Don't make a scene. Sit back down. Right now!"

The simple act of remaining on her feet in direct disregard of an order from the Honorable Cornell L. Waters, III, gave her the same sense of power she felt when she nailed a liar on the witness stand. As she stared down into his rage-contorted face, she knew there was no way she could or would marry him. She grabbed her purse from the table and calmly strolled out of the restaurant.

Angela picked up a Caesar salad from a sandwich shop near her office and ate at her desk. Hours later, stuck in traffic on the Santa Monica Freeway, she realized that she did not want to go home. Breaking off the engagement would not be easy.

She tried to reach her sister, but the call went to voicemail. She then thought about dropping in on one of her girlfriends or even her mother, but they'd take one look at her long face and sense that something was wrong. She couldn't handle being interrogated right now.

Before she knew it, Angela was pulling her Saab into the parking structure next to the Spectrum Club.

She scanned the rows of cars looking for Dre's white Volkswagen. There was no cycling class tonight, so she wasn't sure he'd be there. She was about to give up when she spotted his car wedged between two SUVs on the third level. She pulled into an empty space nearby and headed inside.

Dre was walking toward the exit just as Angela stepped inside. He smiled big when he saw her.

"Glad to see you," he said, his expression echoing his words. He leaned back and gave her an admiring once over. "Nice suit. You had to be the baddest lookin' attorney in court today."

She tried to laugh.

"You okay?"

Angela nodded.

"No, you're not." Dre squinted at her. "Bad day at the office?"

She nodded again.

"Where's your gym bag?"

Angela pretended as if she had forgotten it. "I guess I must've left it in the car."

"Damn, girl, it must've been a *really* bad day."

Angela faked another laugh. "I don't even know why I'm here."

"Wanna talk about it?" Dre asked. "Let's go get some coffee. My treat."

She smiled in response to his invitation. What she really wanted was to feel his arms around her.

"C'mon. I won't tell old dude if you don't. Follow me to my car so I can dump my bag."

Dre held the door open and they walked toward the parking structure. Angela kept the elevator door from closing while Dre jogged over to his car and tossed his duffel bag into the trunk. He made it back to the elevator, looked at Angela's long face and frowned.

"Damn, girl, why you lookin' so sad?" He waited for the elevator door to close, then flipped a red switch stopping it. "Tell me what's wrong." He pulled her into his arms.

Angela could not believe how wonderful it felt to finally be this close to him. She tried to keep it together, but could not prevent tears from welling in her eyes.

Dre reared back so that he could see her face. "You gotta tell me what's going on."

"I don't think I'm getting married," she finally sputtered through her tears.

Dre's face brightened. "I probably shouldn't say this, but I'm damn happy to hear that." He cradled her closer.

Angela wiped her eyes with the back of her hand and tried to compose herself. "Sorry for the meltdown."

Dre gazed down at her, then gently pressed his lips to hers. Angela welcomed his kiss and eagerly returned it.

"You have no idea how long I've been wantin' to do this," Dre whispered.

Angela looked up at him, circling her arms around his waist. "Probably not half as long as I've been wishing you would."

CHAPTER 24

"When were you going to tell me about your trip to Washington?"

Erickson was in the bathroom washing up for the evening when Claire posed the question. He felt his heart leap to his throat. *How could she possibly know?*

He glanced over his shoulder, surprised that he had not heard her come in. Since he'd moved into one of the guest bedrooms, he almost felt as if he was in a separate house. He should've locked the door.

Erickson reached for a button on the built-in CD/DVD player and turned down the volume of the *Les Misérables* soundtrack. "What's to tell? Just a bunch of boring meetings."

"Really?" Claire's arms were folded, her right shoulder angled against one side of the doorframe.

There was something ominous in the way she uttered that single word. An internal alarm put him on high alert.

Erickson took in Claire's reflection in the mirror. Except for the weight loss and her awful coloring, she almost looked like the old Claire. Her hair was swept back off her face by a headband and her simple outfit—black Capri pants and a white shirt—exhibited a casual elegance.

Erickson reached for a tube of toothpaste from the medicine cabinet and squeezed the green gel onto his toothbrush.

"What could be boring about a meeting at the White House?"

Erickson inadvertently missed his mouth and stabbed his chin with the toothbrush. He set it down, wiped the toothpaste from his face with a towel and turned to face her. Claire's smile told him that her knowledge definitely meant trouble.

"I'm upset that you didn't tell me," she said, feigning injury.

Erickson wondered exactly how much she knew, but didn't want to assume. He'd learned that as a young lawyer. Never assume. Always confirm.

"Tell you what?" He turned back to the mirror and resumed brushing his teeth.

"That you're being considered for a job in Washington."

Erickson tried to appear nonchalant. "I was asked to keep it confidential." He could not let her know how much the nomination meant to him. That would only embolden Claire to use it against him. "Anyway, I'm just one of several candidates. I doubt it's going to happen."

"Exactly what job is it?"

So she doesn't know. "I just said I was asked to keep it confidential." He doused his face with warm water, then reached for a towel. "How'd you find out?"

"I have my sources." Her smile was more cunning now.

"If there's a leak, it could be problematic. I'd like to know how you found out."

"I saw your resume and boarding pass in your briefcase and put two and two together."

Outrage threatened to stop his blood flow. "So you're going through my personal belongings now?"

Claire ignored the question. "If you're relocating to Washington, when did you plan to ask me how I felt about the move?"

Never. You'll be dead by the time I move. He didn't answer.

This time she chuckled. "Oh, I see. You figure I'll be dead by then."

Her prophetic statement made Erickson shiver.

"I'm sorry, but I can't handle this *woe is me* thing today. I didn't share anything with you because there's nothing to tell. Like I told you, nothing's definite yet."

He motioned to leave, but Claire remained in place, blocking the doorway, her eyes casting aspersions he tried to ignore.

"I don't know what job you're being considered for, but I wonder how they'd feel knowing they were about to hire a pedophile."

"That's absolutely absurd! Don't you ever say such a thing to me again!" Erickson pointed his finger inches from her nose. He'd never had the urge to strike a woman before and had to dig deep to restrain himself. "I've never touched a child and I never would."

Claire laughed. "You're amazing, but I guess that's why you're such an excellent lawyer. You see the truth as you want it to be, not as it is."

"No," he said, sneering at her. "I see the truth as the truth."

Erickson roughly brushed past her. His forehead pulsated with indignation as he entered the humongous walk-in closet, half of it stocked with Claire's winter clothes. Too bad he couldn't just set a match to her side of the room.

Every evening, Erickson carefully selected his attire for the next day. He browsed the extensive lineup of suits, then reached for a grey Versace. He turned to the tie rack and selected a burgundy tie with tiny white polka dots.

What did Claire's knowledge mean for his chances of winning the nomination? Would she go public with the DVD after his nomination was announced?

Erickson walked back into the bathroom and hung the suit and tie in the dressing area next to the shower. He could feel Claire watching him, but intentionally ignored her.

Time was up. If Becker wasn't going to move and move immediately, he would take care of the problem himself.

CHAPTER 25

Waverly locked himself in his study and stared at his Black-Berry. He wanted it to ring, but at the same time, he prayed that it would not.

Quincy had really screwed up this time.

He checked the BlackBerry's charge level for the third time, then glanced at the time display. Two more minutes.

Waverly's life had been going too perfectly to allow Quincy to screw it up. Maybe he could buy Quincy out of his trouble. His temples throbbed with apprehension. He was thinking too much. He would not know what this was all about until the guy called.

At exactly nine o'clock, the familiar chirp signaling a call filled the room. Waverly did not realize how stressed out he was until he noticed his hand trembling as he reached for the BlackBerry. He pressed a green button and placed it to his ear.

"You there, Mr. Sloan?"

"Just tell me what you want."

"We have a business proposition for you," said a voice with a slight Spanish accent.

"Exactly who is we?"

"We is me," the man said. "That's all you need to know for now."

"What's your name?"

"My friends call me Rico."

"What's your last name?"

"Don't have one. I'd like to become one of your investors. And I'd like to get started right away. I have some cash I want you to invest for me. I understand you get your clients a pretty nice rate of return."

Waverly struggled to sound undaunted. "How do you even know what I do?"

"You invest in dying people."

"And just how do you know that?"

"I'm a very knowledgeable guy," Rico said. "Anyway, like I said, I'd like to become one of your investors."

Waverly was baffled as to how the guy could know about his viatical business when Quincy didn't. "If you're really interested in investing, we could've done this at my office. Without having my brother nearly beaten to death. And I don't take cash payments."

Rico's voice lost its playfulness. "You do now."

"Is this dirty money you want me to invest? Drug money?"

"My money is just as clean as the dough you earn ripping off dying people."

"I don't rip off anybody and I'm not going to risk my business by laundering what is probably drug money. And anyway, I can't deposit the kind of cash it takes to buy these policies without flagging the IRS. You should know that."

"Your brother tells me you're a pretty wealthy guy. Big house in Palos Verdes Estates. New Lexus."

Waverly's face grew hot.

"Here's how we're going to do it," Rico said. "I'm going to have money, cash money, delivered to your office at regular intervals. I want you to purchase my policies in the name of Goldman Investments, Inc. You're going to front the payments from your own bank account. You can then deposit my cash into your account a little at a time so it stays under the radar. Just have Deidra use cash when she shops."

His use of Deidra's name jarred him. "How do you—I can't do that. I *won't* do it."

"Yes, you will because you're a smart guy."

Waverly tried to speak, but his lips refused to part.

"I just want you to do the same thing for me that you do for all your rich doctor friends. Find me some dying folks, preferably ones who're real close to kicking the bucket. Buy their policies and send me a check when they're dead."

"And if I refuse and go to the police?"

"You won't," Rico said. "You care about your screwed-up brother too much, and I suspect you love your wife even more. I'd hate to have to pay her a visit while she's all alone in that big old house in Palos Verdes Estates preparing dinner for you. Or maybe I could drop by that Pilates class she teaches. Give her a little taste of what your brother got."

The muscles along his neck and shoulders turned into tiny knots. *How did he* . . . "Don't threaten me and don't threaten my family."

"You'll receive a package tomorrow with my first investment of fifty grand. More will follow. I'll need you to send me all the pertinent information on the dying folks. I need to personally approve every policy you buy."

"It doesn't work that way. We don't disclose the identity of the insured, just the particulars of their situation."

"I'm sure you won't have a problem bending the rules for me in light of what's at stake. You'll find more specific instructions with the first package, including a power of attorney giving you the right to sign any necessary documents on behalf of Goldman Investments. Once these folks croak, I'll let you know where you can wire my money."

Waverly felt trapped. How long had this guy been working on this plan?

"I look forward to doing business with you, Mr. Sloan," Rico said, then hung up.

Waverly started to hyperventilate and struggled to fight off a crushing surge of panic. He wanted a drink, but needed his head on straight so that he could assess his options. But did he really have any? If he went to the police, they would look closely at him and eventually discover that he wasn't even supposed to have a viatical license. It was also unlikely that the police could protect him or his family from a guy like Rico. They could've easily killed Quincy. Next time it could be him or, God forbid, Deidra.

Waverly couldn't believe it. He had no choice.

CHAPTER 26

I t was close to eleven by the time Angela returned home. She and Dre had driven to Venice Beach and walked along the boardwalk, holding hands, not saying much. Angela made it clear that their relationship could not commence until she had officially broken off her engagement with Cornell. Dre said he understood and would be waiting for her whenever she was ready.

When she opened the front door of the condo, she spotted a box of long stemmed roses propped against the wall. Calla lilies, not roses, were her favorite flower. Cornell, however, preferred roses.

Angela grunted as she stepped over the box.

Cornell was sitting in the living room in the dark, the piano of Thelonius Monk playing softly in the background. She headed straight for the bedroom without acknowledging him.

Angela had just kicked off her pumps and was about to unbutton her blouse when Cornell entered the room. She suddenly felt uncomfortable undressing in front of him.

"Where have you been?" His voice was infused with accusation.

"Out."

"Where?"

"No place in particular."

Cornell took a step toward her. "What's going on with you, Angela? You weren't always so sensitive."

She spun around to face him. "And you weren't always so insensitive." She took off her earrings and placed them in a dish on the nightstand.

"Okay. I'm sorry. Did you see the flowers in the entryway?"

Angela reached up to take off her necklace. "Yeah, thanks."

"If you want to wear a strapless wedding dress, that's fine. I'm sure you'll look nice."

"Never mind, I don't want a strapless dress. As a matter of fact, I don't want to wear any kind of dress because I don't want to get married anymore." *There. It was out.*

Stepping around him, Angela walked into the bathroom. When she tried to close the door, Cornell propped it open with his foot.

"I said I'm sorry." The enlarged veins in his neck told her he was struggling to keep his anger in check. "You're overreacting."

Angela opened the medicine cabinet and reached for her toothbrush. Cornell watched, arms folded, as she brushed her teeth, washed her face and applied toner and moisturizer.

When she attempted to walk past him, Cornell reached out and embraced her. She did not reciprocate, her body rigid, her arms dangling at her sides.

"We need to talk," Angela said, finally pulling away from him.

Cornell grinned. "Now we finally agree on something."

Angela led the way to the living room and turned on the floor lamp near the window, flooding the room with light. Cornell sat down, rested his right ankle on the opposite knee and extended his arm along the back of the couch. Angela took the loveseat across from him.

"Tell me why you're acting like this," Cornell said. "Is this some PMS thing or something?"

"I don't think we should get married."

He chuckled. "You're just having pre-wedding jitters. You've been working too hard. Why don't we both take some time off and drive up to Santa Barbara again?"

"That's not going to change anything."

"Look, I'm going to do you a favor. I'm not going to take what you're saying seriously because you'll probably feel differently in the morning."

"I won't," Angela said. "And this has nothing to do with what you said to me in the restaurant. I've been feeling this way for a while. I've just been too much of a coward to tell you."

She could see from the dazed look on his face that her admission both surprised and alarmed him.

Cornell chuckled again, but this time, with a hard edge. "We've sent out two hundred invitations. It would be very embarrassing to call off the wedding. Embarrassing for both of us."

His response only confirmed that she was making the right decision. Cornell cared more about what people would think than about losing her.

"I'm not worried about being embarrassed," she said gently. "I just can't go through with it."

Cornell stood up and, for a second, she thought she saw his lower lip quiver. "Don't do this. I love you and I want to marry you."

He sat down next to her, taking both of her hands in his. It had been a long time since he'd been this gentle with her.

"I'm sorry if I haven't been very attentive lately. It's work. I've been under a lot of pressure. It'll get better. I promise."

He waited for her to say something and when she didn't, he put his arms around her.

"We have something special, Angela. Let's not ruin it. Don't make a final decision yet. Please."

Please was not a word Cornell used very often. "Okay," she finally said, resenting her inability to stand her ground with him. She was only delaying the inevitable.

Cornell kissed her softly on the lips, then left the room.

If she'd had more time to think things through, she would have come up with some kind of ruse to force *him* into calling off the wedding. Actually, she could use a few days to get things in order. First she needed to find an apartment. She'd start searching in the morning. And the sooner she got the wedding cancellation notices in the mail the better.

Angela turned out the lamp on the end table and stared into the darkness. Cornell was not going to easily accept her decision, which meant the next few days were going to be rough. But she could handle it.

Especially since she knew Dre would be waiting for her.

CHAPTER 27

After another stressful week of waiting for a call from the White House, Erickson decided to let off some steam by futzing around in his garden.

He spent a couple of hours pulling weeds, fertilizing the soil and removing dead leaves. His work complete, he was now stretched out on a lawn chair, enjoying a beer.

The screen door opened and Sophia stepped onto the patio. "I have some errands to run," she said. "Anything you need me to pick up while I'm out?"

Yeah, a little privacy. "No," he said curtly.

"Claire's a little down today," Sophia said. "She asked me to pick up some movies. You should spend some time with her. Maybe bring her out onto the patio. She always loved your garden."

"I'll do that," Erickson said, knowing that he would not.

Sophia walked over to a patch of white roses and leaned down to take a whiff. "How are you doing?" she asked, her back to him.

"I'm fine."

She turned to face him. "No, how are you really?"

"I'm fine, Sophia." His gruff tone demanded privacy.

"This isn't easy for any of us," she said.

"I never said it was."

Sophia seemed to be searching for more to say. Instead, she picked up his gardening gloves and headed into the house. "I'll drop these off in the laundry room."

Erickson thought about going to the country club for a game of tennis, but didn't have the energy. He desperately wanted to know when Becker would be moving forward with their plan. Becker had said he wanted Erickson out of town when he acted. Erickson would be leaving for a business meeting in Chicago in the morning. Maybe once he was gone . . .

Erickson was still obsessing about his wife's unforgivable betrayal. He would not allow Claire to destroy his life over what was really nothing more than an innocent hobby which harmed no one. His biggest worry was that Claire had another copy of the DVD. *What if Sophia or Ashley found it?*

That nagging fear prompted him to give the house one more search. First he looked in on Claire and found her sleeping. This time, he started with more obvious places. He looked through the kitchen drawers and cabinets, the pantry, even the washroom on the back porch.

Thirty minutes later, exhausted from the intensity of the effort, he gave up. He was just returning to the patio when the doorbell rang.

He opened the front door to find Becker with three of his four girls in tow.

"Kaylee had a soccer game not far from here," he said. "So I figured we'd drop by to say hello. I wanted you to see how big they're getting."

Each of the girls reached up to hug him. Erickson quietly shuddered, anxious to make the physical contact as brief as possible, but at the same time wishing he could prolong it. He had never explored his sexual fantasies beyond the computer screen. And he never would. Most men were not strong enough to control their sexual urges. He was not like most men. He was not some pervert.

"C'mon back," Erickson said, leading them out to the back-yard. "I was just relaxing outside."

"How's Claire?" Becker glanced over his shoulder toward the bedroom.

"No one's here," he said, assuming Becker's inquiry might be for the benefit of Sophia.

They talked about work while the girls bounced around the yard like fleas.

"I need to make a pit stop," Becker announced. "Then we'll be taking off."

Erickson watched in frustration as the girls came close to stepping on his azaleas. Finally, he couldn't take it anymore. "Hey, girls, come tell me about the game."

It felt like a lifetime before Becker returned to rescue him from the childish chatter. Once they'd left, he went into the family room and began pouring over a stack of documents he'd already begun studying about the inner workings of the Justice Department.

Erickson heard the front door open and looked up, expecting to see Sophia. His eyes met Ashley's instead. She glowered at him, then stomped off down the hallway to her mother's bedroom.

Seconds later, after he had just grabbed another beer from the refrigerator, he heard Ashley scream and tear out of the room. "Call nine-one-one. Mommy's not breathing!"

Erickson didn't move.

"I said Mommy's not breathing!" she screamed again.

For some reason, he still couldn't move. *Had Becker. . .*

Ashley stepped around him, snatched the phone from the kitchen counter and quickly dialed 911. "I need an ambulance! My mother's not breathing!"

Erickson remained motionless as Ashley recited the address. She slammed down the phone and rushed back to her mother's bedside.

When he heard the rattle of keys that signaled Sophia's return, Erickson finally seemed to snap out of his fog. He charged down the hallway and pulled open the front door before Sophia could retrieve her key from the lock. "Claire's not breathing!"

Sophia darted past him into the bedroom where Ashley stood over her mother, holding her hand. Tears rolled down her cheeks. Sophia moved her aside, felt for Claire's pulse, then hung her head.

"I don't understand," Sophia cried. "Except for feeling a little depressed this morning, she was fine. How can she be dead?" She reached out to comfort Ashley, who pushed her away and lashed out at Erickson.

"He did it!" she charged. "He killed her!"

Erickson reeled backward. "What? Are you crazy?"

"You wanted us to dump her in a hospice. And since we wouldn't, you killed her!"

Sophia tried to embrace her niece. "Calm down, Ashley. Please calm down."

Ashley pulled away and swung her fist toward Erickson, just missing his face as Sophia stepped between them.

"You're not going to get away with this!" Ashley shrieked. "I swear to God, you're not getting away with it!"

PART THREE

Nothing But the Truth

CHAPTER 28

Waverly parked his Lexus across two stalls at an Episcopal church on Slauson in Ladera Heights. He was there to speak to a support group for terminally ill patients and their families.

His presentations had dropped off after his business started to blossom, but with the recent influx of cash coming in from Rico, he needed to find more dying people than ever. Vincent had recently supplied him with a list of groups where he'd have a good shot at picking up some new clients. The church was first on the list.

Luckily, Waverly had established a solid network of oncologists, probate lawyers and ministers who regularly referred terminally ill people in need of financial help. Since his forced business arrangement with Rico, he had upped his finder's fee to thirteen hundred dollars for patients with a life expectancy of six months or less. The finder's fee was a pittance compared to all the money he was raking in.

After a few days, Waverly resigned himself to his situation with Rico. He had purchased three policies in the name of Goldman Investments and, so far, no glitches.

The meeting was just about to commence when Waverly walked in. There were about thirty people in the room, mostly female, evenly divided between blacks and whites. He gave the group leader brochures to pass around, took a seat and waited to be introduced.

Waverly looked across a narrow aisle to his left and saw an attractive young woman with sandy brown hair styled in a short, spiky cut. Her eyes were a vivid blue, but conveyed a heavy sadness. She smiled at him and Waverly acknowledged the greeting with a nod and return smile.

The group leader asked everyone to stand so that they could begin the meeting with a prayer. When she instructed them to hold hands, the woman reached across the aisle and took Waverly's hand. As the group leader prayed, Waverly glanced down at his hand entwined with the woman's, then up at the profile of her face. Her eyes were closed and she seemed to be mouthing her own private prayer. She did not look ill and Waverly hoped she was at the meeting for a family member, not herself. She couldn't be a day over twenty-five.

Following the prayer and a short introduction, Waverly was invited up to the podium. He began with a basic explanation of a viatical settlement and how it could help those in financial need. He did not anticipate any tough questions. The working-class groups always seemed to take him at his word. When he finished his presentation, he urged anyone who was interested to contact him at the number on the brochure.

Waverly had just stepped outside the room when he spotted the young woman who had taken his hand standing at the end of the hallway. She appeared to be waiting for him.

"Thanks for your presentation," she said.

"You're welcome."

"I'm Britney. Britney Hillard. I'd like to talk to you about a viati—" she looked down at the brochure as she struggled to pronounce the word.

"Viatical settlement," Waverly said, finishing for her.

Britney smiled shyly. "Yes, that. I have colon cancer. I just finished up my second round of radiation. I still have an insurance policy through my job. I brought a copy with me." She pulled an envelope from her purse and handed it to him.

Waverly knew right away that he probably couldn't help her. These days, colon cancer patients lived for years. If she was undergoing radiation rather than chemo, that meant she had a good chance for survival. He always found it difficult to tell people that he couldn't help them because they weren't dying fast enough. He could not bring himself to say those words to Britney.

He took the envelope. "Why don't we schedule an appointment?" He pulled his BlackBerry from his inside jacket pocket. "I'm fairly open this week."

"I never know how I'm going to feel from day to day," Britney said. "It's a miracle I had the energy to come to this meeting. Would you have a few minutes to talk with me right now?"

Waverly hesitated. He didn't want to waste the woman's time, or his own.

Britney gave him a pleading look. "There's a Sizzler across from the Fox Hills Mall. We can go there. My treat."

"Uh, okay. Sure."

Waverly reluctantly followed her out of the building. As he started up his car, a gloomy feeling engulfed him. He talked to sick and dying people on a regular basis and always managed to detach himself emotionally.

Something told him he was going to have a hard time doing that with Britney.

CHAPTER 29

Two things prompted a change in Dre's million-dollar plan. Getting ripped off and a call from Angela inviting him to dinner. That had to mean she had finally called off her engagement.

Dre was a little more than one hundred grand short of reaching his million-dollar goal, but he had grudgingly come to the conclusion that he had to find a safer way to get there. Most dudes were too stupid or too greedy to know when to quit. Dre saw the handwriting on the wall.

To move his plan forward, Dre set up a meeting with a buddy from his old neighborhood who owned a real estate investment firm. Willie Ross and Dre had been homeboys since fifth grade. Willie knew Dre's vocation and had been trying to convince him to get out of the game for years. Willie was the real estate broker Dre used to buy his foreclosures.

As Dre sat in the reception area of Willie's office at Crenshaw and Vernon, he wondered how his life would have turned out if he had taken the straight and narrow. It wasn't like he didn't have the smarts. But sometimes circumstances took you in a different direction.

Willie walked into the reception area and embraced him warmly. He was a stocky, muscular guy with a baby face.

"Nice suit," Dre said, a bit of wistfulness in his voice.

"Thanks, man. You know I love me some Armani. C'mon back."

Willie attended Southern University and spent a few years playing minor league baseball. When he realized that he wasn't going to make it to the pros, he married a real estate agent and started buying and selling fixer uppers. He eventually began soliciting investors to buy commercial property and was doing quite well for himself.

Dre followed him down a wide hallway to a small office that looked out over a strip mall.

"It's time," Dre said, before he was even seated. "I'm ready to go one hundred percent legit."

Willie grinned good-naturedly. "I'm glad to hear that. I've been worried about you, bruh. That's a crazy life you livin'. Few guys are smart enough to get out in time. Does that gash on the side of your head have anything to do with your decision?"

Dre absently touched his face. "Yeah, man. I got robbed the other night. The dudes got me for fifteen big ones. Cash money."

"Ouch," Willie said, making a face.

"Exactly." Dre hesitated. He felt like a lovesick schoolboy who couldn't contain what he was feeling. "And I also met this female."

"Okay, okay," Willie said, nodding and smiling. "I can see from the expression on your face that she must be something special."

"Definitely." Dre's smile stretched from ear to ear. "And if I'm goin' to step to her, my situation has to be straight."

"She doesn't know anything about your line of work?"

"Naw, man. And trip this, she's a lawyer."

Willie's eyebrows arched in surprise. "Dawg, you need to tell her your situation. That's not something she should find out in the street."

"I plan to. But when I tell her I'm out, I want to be completely out. That's why I'm here."

"You interested in picking up some more property?"

"Yeah, but instead of fixer uppers, let's look into some apartment buildings. I'm ready to be a landlord. Something small. Five, maybe ten units."

"Okay, I'll get to work on it. I assume you're still mostly in cash."

"Yeah. That a problem?"

"Naw. I'll work it out." Willie was legit. For the most part. "Where'd you meet this lady?"

"I was at the gym just mindin' my own business. She just couldn't resist my charm." Dre stroked his goatee. "And don't laugh when I tell you this, but I ain't even got with her yet and I still can't stop thinkin' about her."

"Damn, dawg, she's got your nose this wide open and you ain't even hit it yet? What you waiting for, bruh?"

"It's all about timing, man. I really want my situation to be right before I make my move."

"Is she special enough to put a ring on her finger?"

Dre cocked his head. "That's a possibility," he said, smiling.

Willie chuckled. "I never thought I'd see you go down for the count, bruh. But I'm happy you found yourself a good lady. I hope everything works out for you."

"It will," Dre said. "It will."

When Dre walked into Baja Cantina on Washington, he found Angela seated at the bar.

"Ain't this a little close to home?" he asked. Dre didn't know exactly where Angela lived, but Playa Vista wasn't that far away. "Ain't you worried about runnin' into dude?"

"Cornell hates Mexican food."

Dre was encouraged by her lack of concern. *Had she already kicked dude to the curb?*

They settled in at a table near the fire pit. After the waitress took their drink orders, they munched on chips and salsa and made small talk. On the drive over, Dre decided that he would be patient and wait for Angela to broach the subject of her wedding. Ten minutes in, he realized he couldn't hold out.

Dre pointed to her left hand. "Does that mean you made your decision?"

Angela was still wearing her engagement ring.

She smiled. "Yes and no. I'm still wearing the ring because I don't want people at work asking me a bunch of questions that I don't want to answer. But, yes, I made my decision."

Dre held his breath and waited.

"I told Cornell that I wanted to break off the engagement," she continued. "He basically told me I was being emotional and asked me to reconsider until we could talk about it."

"And what did you tell him?"

"I told him I would. But since then, he's been pretending like I never brought it up."

Dre tried to keep the disappointment off his face. "You're goin' through with it then?"

"Nope. I just need some time to get my ducks in a row. I can't up and leave without a plan."

"I see."

"Sounds like you don't believe me," Angela said.

Dre hung his arm over the back of his chair. "When people want out of a relationship, they get out. When they don't, they find excuses to stay."

Angela started to say something, then reached for her purse instead. "I have something to show you." She removed an envelope and handed it to him.

"What's this?"

"Just open it."

Dre pulled out several legal-size sheets of paper stapled together. It took him a few seconds, but when he finally realized that he was holding the lease papers for Angela's new apartment, a big grin spread across his face. "Okay, so you *are* serious."

"Yep, I think I am."

Angela's apartment was in Ladera Heights on Springpark Avenue. That was practically jogging distance from Dre's place.

Dre could not stop smiling. He refolded the papers and slid them into the envelope. He had just handed the envelope back, when he stopped her.

"Hold up. Let me see that again." He unfolded the papers and scanned the second page. "You don't move in until the first of the month. You gotta hang with dude until then? Is that gonna be cool?"

"I'm telling him this weekend, then I'm moving in with my sister until the first."

"Why you even gotta wait that long? Tell him tonight."

"I need to get some things in order first. It's only a few days and I'll be working late every night this week. I also want to start packing up some of my stuff. I'm sure Cornell won't even notice."

"You want me to be there when you tell him?"

Angela laughed. "Oh, that would go over real well."

"Well, I can at least help you move."

"No, thanks. My sister's going to help me. I don't have that much stuff anyway. Mostly clothes and odds and ends. All of the furniture is Cornell's. He made me sell most of my stuff when we decided to live together."

"You can crash with me if you want," Dre offered.

"Thanks, but I really don't want Cornell to think I'm breaking off our engagement because of another man."

"What about the wedding?" Dre asked. "Have you cancelled it yet?"

"Nope, but the cancellation announcements are all addressed and sitting in the trunk of my car."

"When you talk to dude, if he gets crazy, I want you to call me," Dre said. "I mean it."

"Oh, that's so sweet. What're you going to do? Come over and beat him up?"

"If I have to, yeah."

"How do you know he wouldn't beat you up?"

Dre laughed. "'Cuz everything you've said about the dude tells me he's a punk."

Angela grew serious. "Don't worry. Cornell would never do anything that might soil his stellar reputation. He just can't face letting me go."

"I can understand that. I wouldn't wanna let you go either." Dre reached across the table and took her hand. "It's been a while since you've lived alone. I think I should probably spend the first few nights with you. In case you get scared."

Angela smiled. "You're something else, you know that?" She picked up her menu. "What do you want to eat?"

Dre winked seductively. "You."

Angela peered at him from atop the menu. "Just a few more days," she said, her voice full of mischief, "and I'm all yours."

CHAPTER 30

Erickson had not seen Sophia or Ashley in the five days since the coroner's van pulled out of the driveway. Now that Claire was gone, they were no longer a family. Not that they ever really had been.

Sitting on the patio, enjoying his garden, he took a sip of scotch and pondered his situation. Things could not have worked out more perfectly. Claire's cause of death had been listed as pancreatic cancer. He didn't know how Becker had pulled it off, but the man was a master.

Erickson's only problem now was Ashley. She was running around telling anyone willing to listen that Erickson had murdered Claire. There didn't seem to be any way to stop her character assassination. What was he going to do? Call up all their friends and explain that his stepdaughter was a catty little bitch just like her mother?

No matter what, Erickson refused to hide or cower. He just prayed that the White House never got wind of Ashley's lies. Such allegations against the chairman of one of the nation's most well-regarded law firms would be a big news story. The same allegations against the next U.S. Attorney General would set off a media firestorm. He had considered eliciting Sophia's help in silencing Ashley, but wasn't sure he'd get it.

Erickson walked back inside to refresh his drink, reveling in the almost magical silence that now engulfed the home. He was alone in the world again and that suited him just fine. Erickson had not been in contact with what remained of his own family for years. He had a sister in Michigan and cousins he'd never been close to in Ohio. His escape to New York by way of NYU Law School had been his way out of the harsh Chicago winters and he had never looked back.

Without thinking it through, he picked up the telephone from the kitchen counter and called Sophia's cell.

The minute she picked up, he had second thoughts, but proceeded anyway. "It's Larry. How are you?"

"I've been better," Sophia said. "And you?"

"As well as can be expected under the circumstances." He cleared his throat and decided to skip the phony chitchat. "I'd like you to speak to Ashley and ask her to stop her preposterous allegations. If she wasn't family, I would have already stepped in to stop her."

"Ashley's taking her mother's death very hard."

"We all are. But her allegations are ridiculous."

Sophia did not reply.

When Erickson translated the meaning of her silence, he almost dropped his scotch. "You can't possibly believe what Ashley's been saying."

"Claire was doing fine when I left that morning," Sophia said coldly. "On top of that, I was as shocked as Ashley was to learn that Claire had sold her insurance policy. It seems strange that she hadn't mentioned it to either of us."

Erickson tried to rein in his burgeoning rage. "Like I told you, Claire sold that policy to pay for an experimental operation. She didn't tell you about it because she didn't want to raise your hopes unnecessarily. But later on, she changed her mind about going through with the procedure."

"If you say so."

Anger bubbled in Erickson's chest. "Exactly what are you insinuating?"

"I'm not *insinuating* anything," Sophia replied curtly. "I'm *saying* that I don't think there ever was an operation. Ashley was Claire's sole beneficiary. She thinks you convinced Claire to sell that insurance policy so you'd be able to keep the money. And so do I."

"Are you nuts? I offered to give it to Ashley, but she refused to take it. And anyway, I'm not exactly hurting for cash."

"As I understand it, some people can never have enough money. I think you knew Ashley wouldn't accept a dime from you."

"I'm telling you the truth!"

"I'm sorry, but I find it hard to believe that Claire would have wanted her only child to end up with nothing."

Erickson closed his eyes and pressed the phone closer to his ear. "Nothing? Ashley gets three grand a month from her grandparents' estate. Claire knew she'd be taken care of. Just do me a favor and talk to her. I can't afford to have her lies picked up by the media."

"I'll see what I can do." The bitterness in Sophia's voice told him she would do absolutely nothing to help him.

"I've relayed Claire's wishes regarding her services to the funeral home." Erickson was now anxious to end the call. "If you and Ashley would like to keep the ashes, I don't have a problem with that."

Sophia gasped. "Ashes? What ashes?"

"Claire wanted to be cremated. She didn't tell you?"

"No, she didn't. I—I can't believe she would've wanted to be cremated. She never shared that with me."

"She told me she planned to talk to you."

"Well, she didn't."

Erickson reached for his scotch glass. "Claire said she would write everything down, but she never got around to it."

Sophia paused for a prolonged beat. "I'm really having trouble with what you're telling me. Claire always said she—"

"I don't care what she told you. This is what she wanted," Erickson said, flustered. "I have to go now."

"I don't think Ashley's going to be happy about this."

"Why should I be concerned about whether Ashley's happy or not? She isn't concerned about destroying my reputation."

Erickson hung up without saying good-bye. He refilled his glass with scotch, then made his way to his study. With Claire out of the way, he could enjoy his personal pleasures without fear of discovery. He turned on his computer, took a seat and waited as it booted up. He now wisely restricted his viewing habits to websites featuring women who were of age, but looked much younger. Erickson had also checked every crevice of the room to ensure that there were no recording devices Claire had neglected to remove.

He was fairly confident now that there were no copies of the DVD. Like the things Claire had failed to share with Sophia and Ashley, his indiscretions were something she had wisely kept to herself.

Before he could get settled in, the phone rang. It was the director of the funeral home. "Mr. Erickson, I've just received a call halting your wife's cremation."

Erickson sat forward in his chair. "What? From who?"

"From your wife's daughter. Ashley Morgan."

"She doesn't have the authority to—"

"I'm sorry, but when these types of family disputes arise, we can't proceed until they've been resolved. She told us she's asking the authorities to perform an autopsy. In light of that, legally we can't proceed. I'm sure you understand."

No, he did not understand.

"I wish Ashley had talked to me," he said. "She's been under tremendous stress. But do what you have to do. I have no problem with postponing the cremation until we get this all straightened out."

Erickson hung up the telephone and hurled his drink across the room. The glass shattered, leaving a light stain on the white wall.

For months, it had been Claire he feared. But now Ashley had taken the baton and run with it. He could not let the White House get even a whiff of his family drama. Even a request for an autopsy could wreck his chances of getting the nomination.

Erickson still had no idea of Claire's true cause of death. He had honored his agreement with Becker to never broach the subject again. But he was racked with curiosity. Instead of heading for the bathroom during his visit, Becker had obviously slipped into Claire's room. Had he drugged her? If so, what would an autopsy reveal?

He snatched the phone to call Becker, then almost as quickly set it back on the desk. He did not want phone records to show that immediately after speaking to the funeral director, he had called his law partner. That could unnecessarily implicate Becker.

Erickson walked back into the kitchen to fix himself another drink. He chastised himself for sounding so alarmed when the funeral director called. A man who had nothing to hide wouldn't fear an autopsy. He would not make the same mistake again.

But he had to get Ashley under control. No matter what it took to make that happen.

CHAPTER 31

Nobody knew the down side of procrastination better than Waverly Sloan. Ignoring a problem, he knew, never helped. So why didn't he just pick up the telephone and tell Britney that he couldn't sell her policy?

He stared down at the documents spread across his desk. Britney had an eighty-thousand-dollar policy and the medical records her doctor provided showed that she had Stage 2 colon cancer, which meant her prognosis for a complete recovery was good. No one would want to buy her policy under those conditions. Making it even harder, she had a group policy from her company. If she got fired from her job, the premiums to maintain the policy would be expensive. The investor would have to take on that cost, too.

Waverly's BlackBerry chirped and when he saw Britney's number, he grimaced. He decided not to answer it, but on the fourth ring, he picked up anyway.

"How are you doing?" Britney asked.

Waverly could tell that she was trying to sound upbeat. "I'm fine. What about you?"

"Not too good." She spoke just above a whisper. "But I'll feel a lot better if you tell me you'll be able to sell my policy. Have you had a chance to go over my medical records? I missed work again today. I think my boss is about to fire me and I don't have much money saved up."

Waverly sighed. "Most of the investors I spoke to weren't interested in buying your policy," he lied. "You—"

"Why? Because I'm not dying fast enough?" She broke into a
sob. "If I lose my job, I don't know what I'm going to do. Disability isn't even enough to cover my rent. My only option is to go
back to St. Paul and move in with my sister."

"You didn't let me finish," Waverly said. "I found an investor." He rubbed his forehead in consternation. He would just buy
the damn policy himself. "But I could only get you thirty thousand."

Britney's sobs grew louder, but he could tell that she was crying tears of appreciation, not sadness.

"Thank you so much! I didn't know what I was going to do.
Thank you so much!"

Waverly felt like her white knight . . . until he hung up. He'd
let his emotions cause him to do something stupid again. His
viatical license expressly prevented him from investing in the
policy of a client. He could end up having his license revoked,
which was a foolish risk to take. But no more foolish than laundering Rico's dirty money.

He reached into the bottom drawer of his desk, pulled out his
flask and poured a shot of brandy into his coffee cup. A thought
came to him. He did have another option. He could use Rico's
money to purchase Britney's policy. He'd been funneling so many
policies through Goldman Investments that there was a good
chance Rico wouldn't examine it too closely.

Rico's calls inquiring about whether any of his policyholders
had died yet had reached an annoying level. Of the deals he'd
brokered for Goldman Investments, Inc., two of the clients died
within days, netting Rico more than thirty percent on both
investments. He'd even decided to use Rico's money to purchase
Jerry Billington's three-hundred-thousand-dollar policy.

Waverly pulled up Britney's file on his computer and did
something he prayed did not come back to haunt him. He

changed her doctor's diagnosis of *stage 2 colon cancer* to *stage 4*. On the line for life expectancy, he deleted the words *unpredictable at this time* and replaced them with *five months*.

A knock on his open door startled him.

"Hey, son-in-law." Leon Barrett was standing in the doorway of his office. Waverly was so surprised he could barely open his mouth. He wondered how Leon had gotten past the receptionist.

His father-in-law marched up to his desk and stuck out his hand. "I was in the neighborhood and decided to look you up."

Yeah, sure. Waverly shook his extended hand without getting up.

Leon's critical eyes surveyed the office. "Pretty nice digs." He peered over Waverly's shoulder at the L.A. skyline. "This place is twice as large as your other office. How much does the lease on a palace like this run?"

None of your damn business. Waverly chuckled. "Money and politics are two things I never talk about, especially with family. What brought you to this side of town?"

It took a second for Leon to come up with a response. "Just meeting a friend."

"Really?" Waverly's brows knitted together. "Who?"

The two most important men in Deidra's life stared each other down, their years of dislike and mistrust suddenly out in the open.

"An old business associate of mine." Leon sat down though Waverly hadn't invited him to. "Guy Robinson. I don't think you know him."

Waverly made a show of checking his watch. "I was in the process of preparing for a client meeting which starts in a few minutes. I'm sorry, but I can't shoot the breeze with you right now."

Leon refused to take the hint. "You know, I was asking Deidra about your new business and, to my surprise, she couldn't explain to me exactly what you do."

"You know Deidra," Waverly replied. "As long as the bills are paid and she can shop all day long, she's not really interested in hearing about the particulars of how I make a living."

"The way I see it, if you have to hide what you do from your wife, it can't be too above board." Leon got to his feet and pointed a finger in Waverly's direction. "But mark my words, son. The fast money always runs out."

Waverly wanted to tell Leon Barrett to kiss his ass. Instead, his eyes turned into slits and he smiled. "Like I was saying, I have a meeting."

"Deidra told us about you coming home with your brother all battered and bloody. I understand he still has that drug problem and a gambling habit, too. It would be a shame if you got all mixed up with that stuff. I certainly wouldn't want my daughter exposed to something like that."

"Neither would I." Waverly stood up, towering over his father-in-law. "I hate to be rude, Leon, but like I said, I have a meeting to prepare for."

CHAPTER 32

In less than three weeks after his first visit with Waverly Sloan, Jon drove back to Sloan's office and picked up the biggest check he had ever had the pleasure of holding in his nimble little fingers. One hundred and fifty thousand big ones.

Angela had instructed Jon to take photographs of the check, then head straight to the bank to deposit it into a special account set up by the Postal Inspection Service. He ambled out of Waverly's office like the dying man he was supposed to be. He wasn't sure he believed Salina's theory that Live Now was murdering its policyholders, but just in case someone was watching him, he didn't want to blow his cover.

He took his time driving to the bank, wanting to savor the feeling of having such a big check with his name on it. After making the deposit, Jon called Angela from the parking lot outside the bank.

"Just made the deposit."

"Great. Did you take pictures?"

"Yep. I'll email 'em to you when I get home."

"How did it feel to be loaded for a few hours?"

Jon chuckled. "I gave some serious thought to skipping town."

"Yeah, right. Any new information? Did he pressure you in any way?"

"Unfortunately, no," Jon said. "You still thinking about sending someone else in to see if they get the same treatment?"

"Definitely. The whole theory of our investigation falls apart unless you can save the day. Now go home and play sick."

"Yes, ma'am. Right away."

Jon pulled into the driveway of his two-bedroom home in San Pedro just as a light rain started to come down. By late evening, as he was watching his favorite sitcom, *Two and a Half Men*, he suddenly craved a beer. He peered out of his living room window. The rain was coming down pretty hard now. If anyone had been watching him, they'd probably knocked off for the evening. A quick beer run wasn't going to hurt anything.

He picked up his keys from the coffee table, slid his gun into the holster at his waist, and headed outside to his Camaro.

Jon roared along 25th Street until he reached a 7-Eleven about two miles away. He parked in front of the store and hopped out. He grabbed a six-pack from the coolers, handed his ATM card to the clerk and was in and out in less than five minutes.

He placed the beer on the floor behind the driver's seat and was about to close the door, when someone stuck what felt like a gun into his lower back.

He instinctively turned, but a raspy voice stopped him.

"Don't turn around," the voice ordered. The man quickly patted him down, then snatched Jon's revolver from his waist.

"Get in the driver's seat and do exactly what I tell you to do. If you don't, you're dead."

Jon stayed put as the rain began to dampen his clothes. He had hoped it was just some kid trying to rob him, but the voice belonged to a mature man. Probably older than him. "Hey, man, if you want my car or my wallet, just take it."

"What I want is you behind the wheel."

Jon still didn't move. He looked into the store where the clerk was stocking a shelf on the back wall. Not a single customer was inside. Jon caught a glimpse of his assailant's reflection in the store window. He was shorter than Jon, white and clean-shaven.

"I said, get in!" the man seethed, jamming the gun deeper into his back.

Jon finally complied, slowly opening the door and climbing in. Fear pounded his chest with the force of a gong. Then it hit him. Live Now *was* killing its clients and he was about to be the next victim.

"Just tell me what you want?" Jon could feel his heart beating at double its normal pace.

"We're going for a ride," the man said, opening the back door and positioning himself behind the driver's seat. "Make a right out of the lot and just keep driving."

As soon as he started up the car, Jon detected the scent of some chemical that he was unable to precisely pinpoint. His mind was frantically trying to figure out how he was going to get himself out of this situation.

A few miles up the road at Palos Verdes Drive East, the man directed him to make a U-turn.

"Pull over," he said, when they reached a turnout area past the Trump Golf Course. "And cut off the engine."

As Jon followed his captor's instructions, he looked off to his right. He could see very little, but knew it was at least a fifty-foot drop to the bottom of the embankment. Was the guy going to throw him off of it?

"Look, let's talk about this. What do you want? I can—"

Without warning, the man looped a damp towel across his face, snapping his head back against the headrest, restraining him. Jon tugged at the towel, but the man held it firmly in place. Jon finally recognized the smell. It was chloroform! He continued to fight for air, but realized he was about to lose consciousness.

The man loosened his grip and Jon slumped forward against the steering wheel.

He exited Jon's car as a second man, who had been following in a blue truck, joined him.

"You got it?" the first man asked, as the rain pelted his face.

"Yeah," his accomplice said. "Hurry up so we can get the hell out of here."

The accomplice, a small, bearded man, pulled something from his back pocket and handed it to the gunman, who bent down to attach it underneath the Camaro, near the gas tank. He then opened the car door, reached across Jon's limp body and turned on the engine. After looking around to ensure there were no witnesses, he called out to his partner. "Let's do this."

He turned the steering wheel to the right, and with his accomplice pushing from the rear, they steered the Camaro toward a section of the guardrail which they had removed earlier in the day. Together, they shoved the car off the cliff, then watched as it tumbled down the hill, landing nose first before bursting into a vibrant ball of orange, yellow and purple flames.

Job done, they walked calmly to the truck, hopped in and sped off.

CHAPTER 33

E rickson and Becker were enjoying dinner at Ruth's Chris Steakhouse in Beverly Hills, celebrating the flawless execution of their plan. But now they needed a strategy to deal with the collateral damage.

"We have to get Ashley under control," Erickson said, his face and voice heavy with worry.

Becker waved a hand in the air. "I'm not worried about Ashley. She was bluffing when she called the funeral home. I made some calls. There isn't going to be any autopsy. The coroner's office is busy enough with all the real crime in L.A. They're not looking for any extra work."

"God, I hope so."

"You don't have to hope," Becker said. "That was a nice memorial service you held for Claire on Saturday. Once this autopsy nonsense is behind us, you can proceed with the cremation and the rest of your life."

Erickson took a sip of his drink. "Ashley claims she contacted the D.A.'s Office, too."

Becker hunched his shoulders as if that threat was no big deal either. "Are you forgetting who you are? You're chairman of one of the most influential law firms in the world. You think somebody at the D.A.'s Office would be stupid enough to touch this? Unless Ashley can produce some hard evidence—and she can't—

no deputy D.A. with half a brain would risk his career going after you based on the ravings of an obviously emotionally distressed young woman."

What Becker had just said made sense. Erickson was worrying for nothing. "I guess I've just been having second thoughts about—"

Becker raised a stern hand. "I told you before, we're not going to talk about this." He aimed a finger across the table. "You had a problem and now the problem is gone. That's what you wanted, right?"

Erickson stabbed at his steak with his fork, then nodded.

"If you're having regrets, that's only natural. You *were* married to the woman for thirteen years. You just need to complete the grieving process, then move forward." Becker took a sip of ginger ale.

"You're right," he said. But he really wasn't grieving at all and certainly had no regrets about disposing of his problem. He was pleased, however, that even Becker was buying his depressed widower act. Actually, he already had his eye on Mandy Mankowski, a new temp in the real estate department.

"I had some great news I wanted to share with you," Becker said. "But I'm not sure you're in the mood for it."

Erickson glanced up, but didn't speak.

"Remember that list you're on?" Becker said with a wink. "I know for a fact that it's down to just two candidates and you're still the front-runner."

That news did indeed perk him up. "Who's my competition?"

"I wish I knew. I asked, but Wrigley wouldn't tell me. You don't get to be Chief of Staff with a pair of loose lips."

Erickson hoped the announcement came soon. Moving off to Washington and taking on the challenges of the Justice Department would help kick start his engine. Since getting the call from the President, his litigation practice almost seemed mundane.

Until his selection was announced, maybe he would use the time to focus on his personal life. As Attorney General, there would be receptions and parties and fundraisers to attend and he did not like flying solo. He needed a replacement for Claire and this time, he would make a much wiser choice. Children, or even the desire for them, would be the first disqualifier.

Since Claire's death, the single secretaries at the firm, and a few of the married ones, were suddenly much more friendly and flirtatious. But aggressiveness in a woman disgusted him.

Mandy, the temp, was quiet and shy, traits Erickson favored. She practically blushed when he greeted her as he walked past her cubicle on the way to his office every morning. He pegged her to be in her mid-twenties, maybe even early thirties. She was just a smidge above plain-looking, primarily because she never wore makeup and dressed on the conservative side. He was glad that she hadn't ruined her body by gluing a pair of cantaloupes to her chest. She was probably an A-cup, if that.

Erickson emptied his glass. "How much time is appropriate before a widower starts dating again?"

Becker grinned. "You got a prospect lined up already?"

"No, not really," he lied. "Just wondering about protocol."

"I say give it four or five months. And keep looking sad like you've been doing around the firm. People really feel sorry for you. When it's time, you'll have your pick of attractive, intelligent women from L.A. to D.C."

Erickson smiled and took a bite of his steak. He didn't want another attractive woman. Beautiful women had options. His new wife would have no alternatives beyond him. And Erickson most definitely did not want a woman with above-average intellect.

The next Mrs. Erickson would be one thing: completely controllable.

CHAPTER 34

Without question, delivering checks to his clients was the best part of Waverly's new gig. It gave him a chance to play Santa Claus year round.

Only hours after brightening Jerry Billington's day, Waverly met Britney at a coffee shop not far from the Sizzler where they'd talked the night after his presentation. When he handed over the check, she thanked him profusely, explaining that his timing couldn't have been better. She had just been fired for excessive absenteeism.

Her firing was not good news for another reason. The insurance premiums Rico would have to pay to maintain her policy would more than double. Waverly decided that he would worry about that when the time came.

The business part of their discussion had lasted less than twenty minutes, yet they had now been chatting for over an hour. Waverly sipped black coffee while Britney drank some strange concoction of caramel and soy milk.

Conversation came easily to them.

"You have a great job," Britney said. "You get to help people."

"I do like it," Waverly said. "I actually got a call this morning from an *L.A. Times* reporter who's doing a feature on the viatical industry. She wants to interview me. I haven't decided whether I'm going to do it."

"Why not? It should be good for business."

Actually, he could use the publicity. But he couldn't risk having the reporter dig into his background and find out that not only had he been disbarred, but that he'd gotten his viatical license illegally and was laundering drug money to boot. "We'll see."

A little voice in Waverly's head kept telling him to end the chitchat and go home to his wife. But something else kept him glued to the chair. It was ego-boosting to be in the presence of an attractive young woman, especially one who showered him with gratitude. He wanted to know more about her and she seemed willing and open to sharing.

"How'd your last radiation session go?"

Britney took a sip of her drink. "The doctor says I'm in remission now."

"That's great news," he said.

Her face grew melancholy and Waverly got the feeling that she wanted more than words of comfort. He repositioned himself in the small wooden chair and tried to plan his exit.

"I don't expect to be in remission forever," Britney said. "I know the cancer's probably going to kill me before I'm forty. My father died of colon cancer and he was only thirty-five."

"You're not going to die," Waverly said, trying to sound empathetic. This time, he leaned forward and gave her hand a quick squeeze. When he tried to pull away, Britney placed her other hand on top of his and held it there.

"It's my fault," she said, finally releasing him. "I never went in for checkups despite my family history."

Waverly had more questions, but held back. There was something in him that wanted to do more to help Britney than just hand her a check. She was a beautiful young woman who deserved to live a long, happy life. He dismissed her doom and gloom and figured she was just feeling sorry for herself.

"I guess the good part of all this is that I don't have any kids," she said. "It was pretty rough when my dad died."

"No special guy in your life?" Waverly asked.

She smiled. "Nope. I had just started dating this one guy when I found out about the cancer. It must've freaked him out. Haven't heard from him since."

"Well, if there's anything I can do to help, just ask."

"Thanks. You've already done more than enough."

"Any reason you don't want to go back to St. Paul?"

"I'd just be a burden to my sister. My mother and I haven't spoken in a couple of years."

"Do they even know about the cancer?"

"Nope. If they find out, they'll start pressuring me to move back home. I'll tell them, but only when I have to." She stared him directly in the eye. "Can I ask you something?"

Waverly was about to give his consent, but Britney didn't wait for it.

"How long have you been married?"

He really didn't want the conversation to go in that direction. "Going on two and a half years."

"So you're a newlywed," Britney said. "Still happily married?"

Waverly smiled. "Yes. Very."

"Your wife is really lucky to have a man like you."

In her own not-so-subtle way, Britney was coming on to him. A woman with her looks and body knew how to entice a man. But Waverly had never been much of a ladies' man. He had a good thing with Deidra and wasn't going to jeopardize it for a fling with a kid.

"Is it okay if I call you sometime?" Britney asked. "Just to talk."

Waverly hesitated, then responded with an uncertain smile. "Sure."

He stood up. "I have to get home."

Waverly walked Britney to her car, where she thanked him for the umpteenth time. Her good-bye hug lasted much too long.

As he climbed into his Lexus, Waverly scolded himself for staying as long as he had. He was giving the girl mixed signals. He hoped Britney didn't call.

If she did, he would befriend her from a distance, and that was it.

CHAPTER 35

Angela took the day off and spent most of it browsing furniture stores in Pasadena and West L.A. It was nearly seven when she finally returned home to do what she had to do. Cornell was in the den watching C-Span.

"Glad you're home," he said, when she walked in. "You didn't answer your cell. You feel like going out for dinner? I made reservations at Roy's for eight."

A wineglass and open bottle of Merlot sat on the coffee table in front of him. It was just like Cornell to make dinner plans without inquiring where she might like to eat.

"I already ate," Angela said. It annoyed her that Cornell was pretending as if their conversation about calling off the wedding had never happened.

"Cornell, we need to talk." She set her purse on the coffee table, turned off the television and took a seat next to him on the couch.

"You wouldn't believe my day yesterday," Cornell began, as if he hadn't heard her. "The appellate court remanded another one of my cases. The idiots must be letting their interns write the decisions. And then this guy blows the date for filing his opposition brief and had the audacity to get nasty with me when I refused to grant him an extension. Can you believe that? I'm the goddamn judge. I have the power to hold him in contempt and he comes into *my* courtroom acting like an arrogant son of a bitch. It took every ounce of energy I could muster not to climb off the bench and kick his ass."

Angela almost laughed. Cornell had probably never had a fight in his life.

"Did you hear me? I said we need to talk about the wedding."

"Yeah, I heard you. I figured I'd just leave the subject alone and wait for you to bring it up again. Are you done going through whatever hormonal stuff you were dealing with?"

Cornell's belittling attitude only strengthened her resolve. "You asked me to give my decision to call off the wedding some thought and I have. But nothing's changed. I can't marry you. I put the cancellation announcements in the mail a few minutes ago. I'm sorry."

His eyes narrowed and he didn't say anything for a long while. "What's his name?" he asked coolly.

"This has nothing to do with anybody else." Angela braced herself for an argument. "I just don't think we should get married. It's just not working for me."

"Not working for you?" His body stiffened. "What the hell does that mean?"

"I don't want to argue about it. I made my decision." Angela stood up.

Cornell charged off the couch and grabbed her arm. "Come back here. Do you realize what you're doing? Do you know how many women would love to be in your shoes? After all I've done for you, this is the thanks I get?"

Angela felt a brief wave of panic, but knew showing fear would only embolden him. She snatched her arm away.

"I'm sorry, Cornell. I'll be packing up my stuff tomorrow." She had anticipated that Cornell would not easily accept her decision. She had prepared an overnight bag, which was already in the trunk of her car. "I'm moving in with my sister. Tonight."

As she attempted to leave, Cornell grabbed her by the arm again.

"Don't you walk away from me!"

Angela calmly matched his irate gaze with one of her own. "Let go of my arm. You're hurting me."

His grip tightened. "Who the fuck do you think you are?"

"Somebody who doesn't want to be married to you and this is precisely the reason why. You're not a man, you're a bully. Now let go of my arm!"

It took another couple of seconds before Cornell roughly pushed her away. Angela swayed, then lost her footing and fell to the floor.

His bulging eyes held such hostility that, for a moment, she feared that he might kick her.

Angela crab-walked away from him, then awkwardly rose to her feet. "I was hoping we didn't have to go through any drama, but I should have expected this kind of childish behavior from you."

"I don't need you. If you want to go, then go." He plopped back down on the couch and picked up the remote.

Her heart beating wildly, Angela darted into the bedroom to retrieve her purse, then realized she'd left it on the coffee table in the den. When she walked back into the room, she found Cornell riffling through her purse.

"You had the nerve to rent an apartment?" He held up her lease papers. "Where is it?" He scanned the pages, searching for the address.

"None of your business," Angela shouted, snatching the papers and stuffing them into her purse.

She had almost made it to the front door when she felt Cornell's fingers grip the back of her neck. He pulled her body toward him, almost lifting her off her feet, then twirled her around and hurled her against the wall. An explosion of pain shot down her back.

"I want to know who you're fucking!" he yelled, gripping her forearms and pinning her to the wall. She could feel his fiery breath on her face.

Angela's brave façade evaporated. She did not recognize this man.

"Cornell, what are you doing?" she said, her voice trembling. "Please let me go."

He leaned in and roughly kissed her. Angela tried to wrestle away from him when the ringing of her BlackBerry halted his assault.

Cornell snatched Angela's purse from her shoulder and fished around until he found her BlackBerry. "Maybe it's your boyfriend calling," he scoffed. "Who is this?" he shouted into the phone.

Angela prayed that it wasn't Dre. She had promised to call him as soon as she finished breaking off things with Cornell. He'd probably become worried when she hadn't called.

Her chest heaved up and down as Cornell listened in silence for way too long. "Here," he said finally, jamming the BlackBerry into her chest.

Angela placed it to her ear. It was Jon's sister, Debbie. She lived in the Chicago area. "Jon's been in a car accident."

"What? I just talked to him a few hours ago."

"His car went off an embankment in Palos Verdes."

Angela closed her eyes and shuttered. "My God! Is he okay?"

"I don't know," Debbie said, clearly shaken. "They couldn't tell me much. I just booked a red-eye. I won't get there until morning. Before he passed out, Jon told the paramedics he needed to talk to you."

Angela immediately knew why. Jon's *accident* was not an accident. Live Now really *was* murdering its clients. "I'll head over now. Which hospital?"

When she hung up, Cornell was standing in front of the door, blocking her path. "Why do *you* have to go?" he snorted. "He's not your family."

"He's my friend. Now move!"

"We need to finish our conversation." Cornell, looking flustered now, wiped his palm down his face. "Look, I'm sorry I—"

"I don't want to hear anything you have to say," Angela shouted. "Just get the hell out of my way."

She reached around him, opened the door and rushed out.

Erickson knew it was nonsense, but he felt like a failure.

"Just cool out," Becker urged his friend. They were having lunch at the Jonathan Club. "It's not the end of the world."

Earlier that morning, Erickson had received a call from the White House, but not the one he had been expecting. President Bancroft had made his pick and it wasn't him. Marianna Cervantes, a prominent Latina lawyer from L.A. with strong political ties, would be the next U.S. Attorney General. The formal announcement would be made Monday morning.

"It's not like you're not still chairman of one of the most influential law firms in the world," Becker reminded him.

"Maybe it's for the best," Erickson said dejectedly, sipping his second scotch, even though it was barely noon. "With the nonsense Ashley's been spouting, it would have been quite an embarrassment to win the appointment and have the media jump on *that* story."

Becker picked up a piece of fried cod fish with his fingers. "Nobody's giving any credence to what Ashley's saying."

It puzzled Erickson that Becker was not more concerned about Ashley's slanderous rants. Becker was the one with everything on the line.

"Do you really think anybody would believe you murdered your wife when she was already dying?" Becker said. "If we're lucky, somebody'll do us a favor and have Ashley committed."

"I don't think we can just ignore her. She's starting to make noise about the insurance money, claiming I stole it from her."

Becker stopped chewing. "I thought you were going to give her the money?"

"I tried. She wouldn't accept it."

Becker broke off another piece of fish. "Well, there's nothing we can do about it now."

Erickson took a bite of his grilled salmon, but he only had an appetite for scotch. "Were you able to find out anything more about an autopsy supposedly being done?"

"It's not happening," Becker said. "Claire had cancer and that's the official cause of death."

Becker leaned forward and slapped him on the arm. "Cheer up. Maybe you should take some time off."

"Yeah? And do what? I'd be better off pouring myself into a nice contentious contract dispute."

"You've been practicing law for more than thirty years. When do you plan to retire?"

"Probably never," Erickson chuckled. "I'll be one of those lawyers who dies keeled over a brief."

Becker's face turned serious. "I think it's time for you to start thinking about a suitable successor. And when you do, can I assume that my name will be at the top of your list?"

Erickson hesitated. "There are more than a few partners at the firm who want my job."

"You didn't answer my question," Becker replied pointedly.

"Of course I'll be nominating you. But the decision isn't mine alone to make."

"True. But your recommendation would carry a lot of weight."

"Like I said, I'm not going anywhere for the time being."

Erickson could see the disillusionment on Becker's face and that surprised him.

"It doesn't sound like you think I deserve the job." There was a defensiveness in Becker's delivery.

Erickson smiled. "I think you'd make a great chairman."

Actually, he didn't believe Becker possessed the leadership traits required to run a law firm of the caliber of Jankowski, Parkins. He was a super-talented lawyer in terms of intellect, but he lacked people skills. He'd lorded over his staff like an army general and was far too inflexible. Even more troubling, his ethics, at times, were questionable. Becker also insisted on putting his family first. No true leader did that.

"Well, when you do decide to retire," Becker said, "I expect you to lobby hard for me as your replacement."

Erickson had trouble meeting his friend's demanding gaze. *Was this the quid pro quo? I kill your wife, you give me your job?*

"I've been extremely loyal to you," Becker continued, "and I expect the same loyalty in return."

CHAPTER 37

Waverly had gone back and forth trying to make up his mind about doing the interview with the *L.A. Times* reporter. He finally decided it wasn't worth the risk. He left the reporter a voicemail message with his decision, but the woman was as persistent as a busy signal and continued to call.

Waverly didn't realize just how persistent she was until he was sitting at the counter at the Pantry, his favorite place to order breakfast for lunch.

A thin redhead slid onto the stool next to him just as he was about to dig into a plate of scrambled eggs and fried ham. "How's it going, Mr. Sloan? I'm Jill Kerr." She waited a few seconds, as if to allow time for her name to register. "From *The Times*."

Waverly's mouth fell open. "So you're stalking me now?"

"Nope. I think this is what you call fate. The Pantry is a popular hangout for *Times* reporters. Running into you is a complete coincidence."

Waverly didn't believe her. "We've never met before. How'd you even know what I look like?"

"The Internet. There're quite a few pictures of you from your lawyer days. You haven't aged a bit."

"Thanks." Waverly picked up his knife, cut off a piece of ham and stuck it into his mouth. "But I still don't want to be interviewed."

"Why not?"

"I don't trust reporters," he said, still chewing.

"Well, you can trust me. This is a feature story, for God's sake. What are you afraid of?"

Jill Kerr's demeanor was too easygoing, which made Waverly wonder if she already knew things about him that he didn't want her to know. She had probably spent most of her life using her pen as a sword. Waverly didn't want to be the next interview subject she sliced to pieces.

"You're in a pretty interesting business," Kerr began, after ordering coffee.

"I told you I don't want to be interviewed."

"How about this?" she said. "The minute I ask a question you don't like, the interview's over."

Waverly told himself to just climb off the stool and walk out of the restaurant. Instead, he eyed his plate. Unfortunately, the food was too good to waste.

Jill took his silence as acquiescence and pulled a pen and notepad from her purse. "How'd you first learn about this business?"

Waverly reluctantly told her about meeting Vincent at a conference. "When he explained the viatical business to me, I knew it was something I wanted to get involved in. The humanitarian nature of the business appealed to me."

"How do you find your clients?"

"I do presentations for cancer support groups, hospices, churches, places like that." Waverly said. "But a lot of my business comes through word-of-mouth referrals. Most of my clients find me."

"How many policies do you sell a month?"

"I think that's one of those questions I don't like," Waverly said, then smiled. "We're done talking, right?"

Jill hurled a smile back at him. "Don't you miss the practice of law?"

Waverly grunted. "You're not a person of your word. That certainly tells me I shouldn't trust you." He took a sip of coffee.

"I only have a few more questions," she pleaded. "I just need a couple of good quotes to round out my story. Do you miss the practice of law?"

Waverly took his time chewing his ham. So far, she'd asked nothing that could cause him any real harm. "Don't miss it at all," he said, between bites. "It's not nearly as time consuming and you don't have to deal with contentious lawyers. In this business, everybody I work with is on the same team."

"Who buys these policies?"

"Insurance companies and individual investors, including a large number of doctors, mostly oncologists. They deal with death every day and don't see the business as gruesome. They understand that they're helping people."

"And making a killing in the process," Kerr added.

A red flag went up, but Waverly felt a strong need to defend his profession. "I wouldn't call it a killing," Waverly corrected her. "There are administrative costs involved. The broker only gets ten percent. We have to pay doctors to review the medical records, the viatical company takes a commission, and there are documents that have to be copied, notarized and mailed. All of that costs money as well."

Jill didn't seem convinced. "To some people, that might sound a little shady."

"I thought you said this was going to be a feature."

"It is," Kerr said.

"You sound more like an investigative journalist than a features writer."

Kerr smiled. "Thanks for the compliment. I used to be. I don't mean to ask tough questions. I just want to make sure I get the entire picture."

"When someone comes to me to sell their policy," Waverly said, "they usually have no other options, no other place to obtain funds."

Jill nodded as if she understood.

"We're able to hand them thousands of dollars in a few weeks," Waverly continued. "We're talking about people who don't have much time left. They can't wait months to take that trip around the world or to get the medical treatment they need. I even had one client who was days away from being evicted from the home she'd owned for nearly thirty years. All because she was too ill to work because of her cancer. She had no other option. She's still alive six months later and still in her home."

"I guess your investor isn't too happy about that."

Another red flag shot up. "Actually, he's just fine about it. She has a life expectancy of a year."

"Do you ever get complaints from family members who were expecting a big insurance payout after their loved one died, but found out someone else was the beneficiary?"

"Most people tell their families what they are about to do," Waverly explained. "I actually encourage my clients to do that. Many of them sell their polices with the blessing of those closest to them."

Kerr looked down at her notes. "Do you make more as a lawyer or a viatical broker?"

Waverly paused. "If you define the currency as caring, I make tons more in this profession."

"And if the currency is money?"

He didn't like the question. He took a few seconds to carefully craft his response. When he finally spoke, he intentionally slowed down so Kerr could get every word.

"I don't define my career in terms of money," Waverly said. "I define it in terms of hope. I'm giving hope to people who wouldn't otherwise have any."

CHAPTER 38

I t took Angela longer than it should have to reach the emergency room at Torrance Memorial Medical Center.

She was so traumatized by Cornell's assault and the stress of not knowing whether Jon was dead or alive, that she went the wrong way on Lomita Boulevard. She was blocks away from the hospital before she realized it.

Angela backtracked and finally made it to the emergency room. She told the attendant that she was Jon's step-sister so she'd be allowed in to see him. The nurse was about to object, but Angela gave her a look that dared her to dispute it.

She was only allowed to spend a few minutes with him in the emergency room. She found Jon's bed at the end of a long aisle. He was heavily sedated and half his face was covered in bandages. The other half was so bruised and swollen she barely recognized him. The nurse told her that Jon had been thrown from his car seconds before it blew up. It was a miracle that he survived the accident.

Jon liked to drive fast, but he'd never been reckless. Even though it had been raining earlier, she found it hard to believe that he would carelessly drive his cherished Camaro off the road. His injuries were not the result of an accident. Live Now really *was* killing its clients.

Jon's sister arrived later that morning. Around noontime, Jon had been moved into a private room. Debbie had just left to call other family members with an update on her brother's condition when he finally regained consciousness.

Jon's right eye fluttered open. When he saw Angela standing next to his bed, he smiled, or at least tried to.

"Can't say you look too great," Angela joked, "but you're going to make it." She reached out and gave his right hand, the only body part that didn't appear bruised, a gentle pat.

"By the way," she said, "I'm your sister in case anyone asks."

Jon tried to smile again, but only one corner of his mouth angled upward.

"I need to know how your car went off that cliff. Did your accident have anything to do with Live Now?"

Jon mumbled something indecipherable. Angela leaned closer, but still couldn't make out what he was saying. She pulled a pen from her purse, then looked around for a piece of paper. She saw a napkin on the nightstand.

"Can you write?" She placed the pen in his right hand. "Tell me what happened."

Jon gripped the pen unsteadily. His scribbles were just as impossible to interpret as his speech. She would have to try something else.

"I'm going to ask you some questions and I want you to blink once for *yes* and twice for *no*. Can you do that?" She wasn't sure this would work since Jon's one visible eye was badly swollen.

Jon mumbled what Angela hoped was his consent.

Angela felt her BlackBerry vibrate, having turned off the ringer earlier when she entered the emergency room. Assuming the call was from Jon's sister, she pulled it from the pocket of her jeans, anxious to give Debbie the news that her brother was awake.

When Angela saw Cornell's number on the caller ID display, she felt nothing but fury. She stepped away from the bed.

"What do you want?" she seethed.

"I'm sorry about how I reacted," Cornell said. "I don't know what got into me. I hope you're okay. And Jon, too. How's he doing?"

"Do you even care?"

"Look, I said I'm sorry. Do you want me to come down there?"

"No, you don't need to come down here," Angela spat. "If you were concerned about me or about Jon, you would've driven me down here last night."

"You never gave me a chance to offer."

"That's the problem, Cornell. There are some things—no, there are a lot of things—that I shouldn't have to ask. I have to go now."

"We need to finish our conversation."

"No, we don't. You and I are done. I said everything I needed to say last night, except this. If you ever put your hands on me again, you're going to jail."

"Look, you're being—"

Angela turned off the BlackBerry and stuffed it back into her pocket.

She turned back to Jon and saw an unmistakable smile grace his purple lips. He'd always joked that Cornell was too uptight for her.

"Oh, so now you can smile, huh? And, yes, you heard right. My engagement is off."

It was liberating just saying the words. Angela couldn't wait to introduce Jon to Dre. She knew the two of them would click.

Jon suddenly darted upward and clutched his throat. He seemed to be having a hard time breathing.

"What's the matter? Are you okay?"

Jon coughed up a spurt of blood.

Angela snatched open the door and ran into the hallway. "Somebody help!"

A Filipino nurse who was tending to a patient in the next room stopped what she was doing and rushed past Angela into

Jon's room. He was writhing all over the bed, desperately gasping for air.

"Code blue!" the nurse yelled, as she pressed a button on the wall above Jon's bed.

In seconds, Angela was pushed out of the way and it seemed as if every nurse and doctor on the floor had converged around Jon's bed. She heard metal clicking, machines beeping, and a rush of words she didn't understand.

Angela had no idea how long she had watched the scene. But she would never forget the moment—the exact moment—when all the activity stopped, seemingly at once. The Filipino nurse, her head barely visible above the cluster of medical personnel, turned back and looked at her with apologetic eyes.

"Call the code," said a male voice from somewhere in the midst of the huddle.

A woman in a white coat raised her left arm and checked her watch. "Time of death: one fifty-seven p.m."

CHAPTER 39

Erickson leaned against the kitchen counter, enjoying a Chopin piano concérto, watching Mandy scurry about. It was nice being with a woman who was so eager to please. She was exactly what he needed to soothe his bruised ego.

Mandy eyed his empty wineglass. "Oh, I see you need more Chardonnay." She set aside the salad she was preparing, wiped her hands on her apron and refilled his glass.

The firm's non-fraternization policy prevented liaisons between partners and secretaries—or partners and any other employee for that matter. For now their affair was a closely guarded secret. Becker was right. It would not look good for him to be dating so soon after his wife's death. But Erickson figured it would be months before his relationship with Mandy became public knowledge. By that time she would have traded her temporary workstation at Jankowski, Parkins for permanent residence in his Hancock Park home.

When she handed the glass back to him, he kissed her on the cheek. Any act of intimacy between them was always at his initiation. That was the first test that Mandy had passed with flying colors. She was never the aggressor and he liked that. He attributed the trait to her rural Midwestern upbringing. They didn't raise women like her in California.

Mandy had performed well on his other tests, too. She was a good conversationalist, but not a chatterbox. She was poised enough to host a dinner party and had a decent knowledge of literature and classical music. Most importantly, Mandy knew how to follow his lead. That was the mark of a good secretary and a great wife. She could use some help selecting more flattering attire, but that could be easily fixed with an appointment with a personal shopper at Bloomingdales.

Erickson reached for the dishtowel next to the stove and dropped it to the limestone floor just in front of his feet. Mandy glanced over at him, evidently confused by the move.

"Get on your knees," he quietly, but firmly ordered.

Without hesitation, Mandy knelt before him, cushioning her knees on the dishtowel. Without further instruction, she unlatched his belt, unzipped his trousers and took him into her mouth.

Erickson leaned against the cabinet and splayed his left hand on the countertop to balance himself as he drank in the pleasure of being inside her mouth. Within seconds of their first intimate encounter, he could tell that she was a novice at this task and that pleased him. It further pleased him that she was a fast study.

Yes, he thought, *I've chosen well.*

Erickson stroked her head, trying to contain his excitement as she expertly serviced him. He liked watching her mop of dark hair bobbing over his crotch. At work, Mandy kept her hair wrapped in a neat bun. On their first date, he'd been surprised to see that it cascaded down her back, almost to her buttocks.

He gripped a patch of her hair and twirled it around his fist, pulling tighter as he struggled to delay his approaching eruption. Mandy eked out a whimper of pain, which aroused him even more.

As she tried to pull away, Erickson held her head in place, forcing himself further down her throat, ignoring her gagging cries. He came in a final, forceful heave.

Mandy coughed for several seconds, wiped her mouth with the back of her hand and looked up at him with the eyes of a child.

Erickson brushed her hair away from her face. "Thank you," he said, helping her up. "You gave me exactly what I needed."

She smiled sweetly as Erickson buckled his pants. Mandy washed her face and hands at the kitchen sink, then resumed her dinner preparations.

Erickson left to take a leak, marching down the hallway with a self-satisfied smile.

When he finished in the bathroom and stepped back into the hallway, he heard voices and wondered why Mandy had turned off Chopin and turned on the television.

As he got closer, the sound of a familiar voice filled him with angst. He rushed into the kitchen where Ashley was hurling questions at a bewildered Mandy.

"You couldn't even wait for my mother's body to get cold," Ashley wailed when Erickson stepped back into the kitchen.

"You just can't come into my house uninvited!" Erickson yelled. "What are you doing here?"

"I came by to pick up my grandmother's belongings that mother kept in the backhouse. I called your office earlier this week and your secretary said you'd be out of town." She gave Mandy an accusatory once-over. "Are you his secretary?"

"Perhaps I should let you two handle this in private," Mandy said timidly. She took off her apron and scampered down the hallway.

"Does your new girlfriend know you're a murderer?" Ashley asked in a voice loud enough for the entire neighborhood to hear.

"Get out of my house!"

"You are such a scumbag. You couldn't wait for my mother to die so you could bring some tramp in here. She's half your age."

"I'm not putting up with your nonsense anymore. You don't

live here. Get the hell out and don't come back. I'll have your mother's things sent to you." He held out his hand. "Now give me my goddamn key."

Ashley threw the key on the counter and it slid to the floor. "I know you've been blocking my attempts to get an autopsy done, but it's going to happen. You're a murderer and you're going to get what you deserve. You just wait."

She ran down the hallway toward the front door and Erickson followed.

Ashley opened the door, stepped onto the porch and turned back to say something, but Erickson slammed the door in her face. He immediately turned the deadbolt and hooked the chain.

As he returned to the kitchen, hoping to salvage his evening, he made a mental note to call Sophia in the morning and demand her key as well.

Better yet, he would call a locksmith.

CHAPTER 40

Waverly was relaxing in his home theater, enjoying a movie with Deidra and her parents, when his BlackBerry vibrated, signaling a call. He waited until it stopped, then slipped it from his shirt pocket.

The caller ID flashed *private caller.*

"No message. Guess it wasn't that important." Waverly rocked back in his red velvet chair. The room had six rows of comfy, theater-style seats and could accommodate twenty-four. Deidra sat to Waverly's left. His in-laws, next to Deidra.

A minute later, the phone buzzed again. And again, Waverly ignored it.

"Looks like somebody's kind of anxious to get in touch with you," Leon said.

The third time it vibrated, which was about thirty seconds later, Waverly wished he had turned it off. This time he answered. "Waverly Sloan," he said, annoyed.

"Just calling to check on that big payout I've got coming."

Waverly stiffened at the sound of Rico's voice. Deidra turned to stare at him. The near darkness concealed her face, but he could tell she was upset by the interruption. Waverly stood, stepped into the hallway and leaned against the wall.

He didn't appreciate Rico interrupting his family time. "What big payout?"

"You owe me some money, amigo. Some big money."

"What are you talking about?"

"That Billington dude is dead, so I have three hundred grand coming to me. When can I expect my money?"

"Dead? How do you know—" Waverly did not want to follow through on the thought that flickered across his mind. "I haven't been notified that Billington died. How would *you* know that?"

"You think I'm going to let you give that guy one hundred and fifty grand of my money and not keep track of him?" Waverly noticed that Rico's accent had completely disappeared. "Trust me, he's dead. I read it in the papers. When do I get my money?"

"I'll check into it. This doesn't happen overnight."

"I don't expect it to happen overnight, but I do expect it to happen soon. I'll call you tomorrow to find out when you'll be wiring my money."

Waverly hated not having Rico's number. He knew nothing about the man and if he needed to track him down, he wouldn't know where to begin. He had already tried to trace where he was wiring the money, but only found out that it was an offshore account.

"I'll look into it and give you a call. Give me a number where I can reach you."

Rico chuckled. "You know the deal. I'll call you."

Waverly hung up. When he turned around, Leon was standing a few feet down the hallway, his arms folded across his chest.

"Is everything okay?" Leon asked.

"Yeah, no problem. Just an issue with an investor."

"You look pretty upset. What was that all about?"

None of your damn business. "The guy's pretty demanding, that's all." When Waverly decided to move into his in-law's neighborhood, he hadn't anticipated that they would spend more time at his house than their own.

Waverly walked past his father-in-law and returned to his seat next to Deidra. He tried to focus on the movie, but his mind kept wandering back to Rico's call. How did Rico know Billington was dead? A weird feeling told him something was wrong.

"Don't kill me," Waverly said to Deidra. "But there's some work I need to do."

Rico claimed he read about Billington's death in the newspapers. Waverly wanted to find out if that was actually the truth.

Deidra huffed. "The movie just started. Can't it wait?"

"I won't be long." He rose from the chair. "There's something I need to look up on the Internet."

"Anything I can do to help?" Leon asked.

No, you nosey bastard. "No, thanks," Waverly said, heading for the door. "I won't be long. Just enjoy the movie."

CHAPTER 41

D re stepped off the elevator onto the second floor of Angela's building carrying a bottle of red wine and a bouquet of calla lilies wrapped in cellophane. He glanced down at his groin and cringed. There was no way he could show up at Angela's door in his excited state.

Checking the numbers on the apartment doors, he scoped out Angela's place, then made a U-turn and walked in the opposite direction. He spotted an exit sign, opened a door leading to a stairwell and stepped inside. He kept the door open just a crack so he wouldn't lock himself out.

Dre rested his back against the wall and tried to think of something—anything—except the fact that if his luck held out, he was about to get buck wild with a woman he'd been fantasizing about for months. He was so excited that he'd probably blow the second he saw her naked.

Five minutes later with no change in his condition, Dre gave in to the fact that his Johnson had a mind of its own. As he made the short walk back down the hallway, he hoped Angela was in a better mood. Since the death of her coworker, nothing seemed to cheer her up. She'd basically kept him at bay for the past few days, not even showing up at the gym. Then, out of the blue, she had called, inviting him over for dinner.

Dre positioned the flowers at waist level, then rang the doorbell.

The door slowly swung open and there she was, standing in front of him in a short, frilly chiffon skirt, which showed off her long, beautiful legs. Her red stiletto heels were a serious turn on. Her T-strap top was low cut and barely able to contain her voluptuous breasts. *Nice.*

"Welcome," she said with a smile. "You're my first official houseguest."

"Don't move," Dre said, stepping across the threshold, closing the door behind him. "Just stand there and let me look at you."

Angela angled her head, put both hands on her hips and crossed one leg in front of the other.

Dre was smiling so hard, his cheeks hurt. *The good girls are always the freaks.*

"Dang, you look good, girl."

"Thank you, sir. And you're looking pretty nice yourself. Is that a new shirt?"

Actually, it was, but she wasn't supposed to know that. "Uh, naw. Just haven't worn it that much."

Dre sensed that Angela was just as nervous as he was. They stood there smiling at each other like two middle school students about to have their first slow dance. He wanted to bum rush her, but knew he couldn't treat her like a tramp. Playing it cool, however, would be hard.

"Are those for me?" Angela finally asked.

"Oh . . . uh . . . yeah." He handed her the flowers, but held onto the wine bottle.

Angela smiled and took a whiff of the flowers. "How'd you know I liked calla lilies?"

"I know a whole bunch of stuff about you," Dre said, grinning. "But I got *that* info from your assistant."

Angela's smile widened. "You definitely get some extra points for that. I'll go get a vase."

He watched her turn and walk toward the kitchen, seemingly adding a little swish to her step. The back view was just as magnificent as the front. *The girl's got major body. Cornell is a fuckin' idiot.*

Dre followed her, no longer embarrassed about his very noticeable boner. When she bent down to open a cabinet beneath the sink, positioning her gorgeous ass high in the air, Dre lost it.

When Angela stood back up, he was right there, almost on top of her. Dre placed the wine on the countertop, then took the flowers and vase and set them aside. He gripped both sides of her waist and softly kissed her as he backed her into the tight wall space between the refrigerator and cabinet. When his tongue traced Angela's lips, he felt her whole body shiver.

"You have no idea how happy I am to finally be with you," Dre mumbled.

"Is that right?" Angela moaned softly into his ear. "If we don't stop, our dinner's going to get cold."

"I'm sure you got a microwave."

Dre's hands slid underneath her soft skirt and he gripped her ass, pulling her to him. She gasped with pleasure when he eased his hand between her wet thighs.

While his lips roamed everywhere, her lips, her cheeks, her neck, her breasts, Angela unbuttoned his shirt and explored his body with her hands. Dre unbuckled his pants and let them fall to the floor as Angela's hands traveled down his body. Her fingers slipped into his boxers and grazed the tip of him, so lightly, so sensually that he almost screamed. They continued to squirm and thrash against each other, their kisses and moans and pants totally unrestrained.

Without warning, Angela's moans abruptly stopped. Dre felt her hand flat on his chest, pushing him away.

What the hell?

Angela was saying something, but Dre's head was all fogged up and she was panting so much he couldn't understand what she was saying.

"What's wrong?" Dre felt like he'd just been doused with ice water.

"Condom." Angela still found it difficult to speak. "Did you . . . did you bring condoms?"

Dre pressed his hand flat against the wall behind her, then dumped his forehead on her shoulder. "Uh . . . yeah," he said, "but I left 'em in the car."

Angela started to laugh and so did he. They stood there cracking up for several long minutes.

"Okay," Angela finally said, "let's eat dinner first, then we can pick up where we left off. I made chicken lasagna. And it's really good if I do say so myself."

Dre stepped back, awkwardly pulled up his pants and rebuckled his belt. He didn't bother to button his shirt. What he really wanted to do was run down to the car so they could finish what they had started. But he didn't want to appear desperate. If she could wait, so could he.

"Here." She thrust the wine bottle into his hand. "The corkscrew's in the drawer next to the dishwasher."

He opened the bottle as she took wineglasses from the cabinet. They finally sat down at a small table near the kitchen, facing each other.

Dre had not eaten since lunch, but he had no appetite. He put a forkful of lasagna into his mouth. "This is really good," he said, barely tasting it.

"Thanks," Angela said. "How was your day?"

"Fine. How was yours?"

"Not bad. I didn't have any court appearances today, but tomorrow I—"

"Hold up," Dre said, his frustration obvious. "I can't do this. I can't sit here and make small talk with you like this." He put down his fork and stood up. "I've waited way too long to be with you and if I have to wait another minute, my balls are going to explode. I'm going to my car. And when I get back, be ready."

Angela smiled and watched as Dre pulled his keys from his pocket. He was inches from the door when she called out to him.

"Hey," she said, "do me a favor."

What now? "Yeah?"

"Hurry up because I can hardly wait. Promise me you'll run all the way to the car and all the way back."

Dre grinned and grabbed the doorknob. "Baby, if I could fly there and back, I'd do it."

CHAPTER 42

Jon's funeral, like most, was both sad and uplifting. Several attorneys recounted funny stories about him, most involving his love of cars. Angela shared how he ribbed her about being on Weight Watchers and praised him as one of her favorite case agents.

Jon's death reenergized the Operation Buying Time task force. They had no evidence that Jon was the victim of foul play, but everyone on the team believed he was. They reported their suspicions to the D.A.'s Office, but didn't plan to sit on the sidelines. The murder of a federal agent in the line of duty was a federal offense, squarely within their jurisdiction. *They* would find Jon's killer.

A few days after Jon's funeral, Salina gave the team a detailed report which contained a list of fifty-three clients whose insurance policies Waverly Sloan had brokered. It surprised Angela that half of his clients were already dead and more than a third of those died only weeks after selling their policies. Ten of them suffered accidental deaths: six from car accidents, two in fires at their homes, one in a boating accident and one after being shot during a robbery.

Angela was glad that her other cases and the work on the task force kept her too busy to dwell on the state of her personal life. Her mother still wasn't speaking to her after learning that she'd called off the wedding. Her sister Jada, on the other hand, wanted to throw her a party. The first few days after she moved out, Cornell had called her almost every day insisting that they meet for dinner to talk. She finally stopped answering his calls and, to her relief, they abruptly stopped. At the moment, her relationship with Dre was the only thing in her life that felt right

Zack barged into her office without knocking. "Take a look at this." He slapped a piece of paper on her desk.

Angela picked it up. "What's this?"

"The second complaint filed with the Department of Insurance against Live Now. This woman claims her stepfather pressured her dying mother to sell her insurance policy, then killed her. And guess who brokered the deal?"

Angela grew excited. "Waverly Sloan?"

Zack nodded with glee.

Angela skimmed the complaint. "Is she alleging that Waverly Sloan was in cahoots with the stepfather?"

"Nope. Sloan's name is nowhere in there. According to the daughter, she was the sole beneficiary on the policy. Her stepfather got half the money she was supposed to get. If her mother hadn't sold the policy, he wouldn't have gotten a dime."

"How much?"

"Two-fifty. The face value of the policy was half a million."

"No wonder the daughter's so pissed."

Zack had an exuberant look on his face. "That's not the most interesting part. Guess who the stepfather is?"

"Zack, how would I know that?"

"True. You'd never guess in a million years. Okay, it's Lawrence Erickson."

Angela's forehead crinkled. "Who's he?"

"The chairman of Jankowski, Parkins, Gregorio & Hall."

Angela whistled. "The stepdaughter is accusing *him* of murder?"

"You got it."

"Is there anything to it?"

"I'm not sure. My L.A.P.D. contact says the daughter's a little whacko."

"How'd the wife die?"

"She had pancreatic cancer. The daughter's been demanding an autopsy. But, so far, there's no indication there's going to be one since she was under a doctor's care and presumably died from cancer." Zack's eyes gleamed. "Do you know what going after a rich, powerful guy like Erickson could mean for our careers?"

"Why don't we just focus on nailing Jon's killer rather than a headline, okay?"

"We can do both," Zack said. "By the way, I came up with the perfect name for my TV show. *The Zack Attack*. You like it?"

"Never mind that. Tell me more about Erickson's stepdaughter."

"Don't know much yet. Except that she apparently despises the guy."

"If that's the case," Angela said, "then I might question her motives more than his. What's Erickson's side of the story?"

"According to the daughter, Erickson claimed they sold the policy to pay for an experimental cancer treatment, but the wife decided not to do it. Neither the wife's sister nor the daughter knew anything about it."

Angela read the complaint more thoroughly this time, then picked up the telephone.

"Who are you calling?" Zack asked.

"I think we should interview the daughter," Angela said. "Since Waverly Sloan brokered her mother's policy as well as Jon's, she might have some information that could help us."

Three hours later, Angela and Zack were sitting at a sandwich shop a few blocks from their office waiting for Lawrence Erickson's stepdaughter to arrive.

A petite blonde with a jittery disposition entered the café and glanced around. Angela headed toward her. "Ashley?"

The woman acknowledged the greeting by walking over, but didn't speak. She was dressed like a college student: faded blue jeans, white ducktail shirt, large red shoulder bag. She looked much younger than twenty-four.

"I'm Angela Evans and this is Zack Hargrove." Angela led the way to their table. Ashley sat down across from them.

"Thanks for meeting us," Angela began. "We—"

"Is somebody going to charge that asshole with murder?" Ashley demanded.

Angela gave Zack a quizzical look. "Any investigation into your mother's death would be handled by the D.A.'s Office. We're with the U.S. Attorney's Office. We're looking into an insurance fraud scheme."

Ashley glared across the table. "Insurance fraud? But you said you wanted to talk to me about my mother's death."

"And we do," Angela said hurriedly. "We have some questions about your mother's decision to sell her insurance policy."

"She didn't make any decision. The asshole pressured her to do it so he could keep me from getting the insurance money."

"Are you referring to Lawrence Erickson?" Zack asked.

"Yes. The asshole. That's what I call him because that's what he is."

Angela wasn't sure what to think of the hostile young woman. "We understand that your mother sold her policy to undergo an experimental cancer treatment."

"Really? Then why didn't she have it? And why didn't she tell me or my aunt about it? You want to know why? Because the asshole made it up, that's why. Selling the policy was the only way for him to get his hands on that money."

It crossed Angela's mind that Ashley might be falsely accusing Erickson of murder to get back at him for cheating her out of the insurance. "Do you know anything about Waverly Sloan, the broker who sold your mother's policy?"

"I told you we knew nothing about her selling the policy until after she died. The asshole handled everything."

"Your mother would've had to sign paperwork authorizing the sale."

"And she probably did. The asshole could convince her to do anything."

Zack rested an elbow on the small table. "May I ask why you seem to have such animosity for your stepfather?"

"Because he's an asshole."

"Can you be a little more specific?"

"I hated the way he controlled my mother. She did whatever he wanted. She sent me away to boarding school because that was what *he* thought was best." Ashley slumped back in her chair. "I only got to come home for two weeks in the summer and a week at Christmas."

Angela understood now why the D.A.'s Office had not followed up on her allegations. This girl had issues.

"Do you know if your stepfather knew Waverly Sloan before he sold your mother's policy?"

"I wouldn't be surprised. Maybe they had a deal to kill her and split the money. The asshole knows lots of people. I wouldn't put something like that past him. You should look into that. My mother hasn't even been dead a month and he's already dating a woman half his age." Ashley paused as if she had suddenly remembered something important. "I need to tell you about something he did right after my mother died."

Both Zack and Angela leaned forward in anticipation. "He had the audacity to call me and ask me if I wanted the two-fifty. Can you believe that?"

There were two ways to look at that, Angela mused to herself. It was either the action of a guilty man or an innocent one.

"That's how I know he did it. He's trying to shut me up. But I told him to keep the money because he's going to need it to buy stuff at the prison commissary."

Angela and Zack asked a few more questions, then headed back to the office.

"What do you think?" Angela said to Zack, as they strolled up Spring Street. "Ashley didn't have a shred of evidence to support her allegations against Erickson."

Zack shrugged. "That doesn't mean he didn't kill his wife."

"True," Angela said. "There's somebody else I think we should talk to."

Zack turned to face her. "Who?"

"Waverly Sloan."

CHAPTER 43

"You won't believe this!" Erickson barreled into Becker's office.

"Believe what?" Becker looked up from his computer screen.

"I just got a call from the White House. Cervantes is out and I'm in!"

Becker shot out of his chair. "What? I thought Cervantes' Senate confirmation hearing was supposed to start tomorrow."

"It seems there was a legal matter she neglected to disclose. She pulled some strings to help her nephew beat a drunk driving charge two years ago. I'm taking a red-eye to Washington tonight. They're announcing me as the new nominee tomorrow morning."

Becker rounded his desk and hugged his friend. "This is absolutely terrific!"

"You still coming with me?" Erickson asked.

Becker paused. "Of course," he said slowly. "But there's something you need to know. You better have a seat." He walked over to close the door, then fell into the chair behind his desk.

Erickson was still on his feet. "What's going on?"

"Live Now and Waverly Sloan are under investigation for fraud."

Erickson drew a blank.

"Sloan was the broker who sold Claire's insurance policy and Live Now is the company he works for."

"Okay," Erickson said. "And why would that be of any concern to me?"

"There's a task force out of the U.S. Attorney's Office here in L.A. Two prosecutors—two pretty sharp prosecutors from what I understand—have been looking into the company, Waverly Sloan in particular. Live Now is linked to another company that's under investigation in three other states for fraud."

"You didn't check the guy out before you referred him?" There was incredulity in Erickson's voice.

Becker raised his hands in defense. "He was recommended by an excellent probate lawyer I've known for years. There was no reason to think he wasn't legit."

Erickson finally sat down. "Is there anything else?"

"They think he's involved in a scam to buy policies and kill off the clients before their time."

"What!" Erickson exploded. "I'll never be confirmed if I'm linked to a scandal like that. That buys right into Ashley's allegations. Is it true?"

"My contact hasn't confirmed it one way or the other. A case agent working with the two assistant U.S. attorneys was posing undercover as a terminally ill policyholder. Waverly Sloan brokered his policy. He died the same day he picked up his check in a suspicious car accident. The prosecutors think he was murdered."

"Is Sloan murdering his clients or not?" Erickson pressed.

"I don't know for sure yet."

"Well, you damn well better find out! I figured the only problem I'd have would be putting a lid on Ashley. But now this!"

"Just calm down. I'm doing everything in my power to keep this under wraps." He opened a side drawer and pulled out a folder. He took passport-size pictures from a folder. One showed a young white man, the other an attractive black woman.

"I was planning to share this with you later today. Zack Hargrove and Angela Evans are running the task force. It's called Operation Buying Time."

"Do they know Sloan brokered Claire's policy?"

"I'm not sure yet."

"If they don't already know, we need to find a way to keep them from making the connection."

"I'm way ahead of you. The sooner you get confirmed, the sooner we'll have the authority to shut down their task force," Becker said.

"That's certainly a bright idea," Erickson scoffed. "I don't want another Alberto Gonzales scandal the day after I take office. If we shut down their task force, they'll run straight to the media."

"Don't worry. I'll come up with something. Frankly, I think Sloan's involvement might actually work to our advantage."

"How could you possibly think that?"

Becker's phone rang. He pulled it out and smiled. "It's Kaylee, she—"

"That can wait," Erickson said sharply.

"No problem." Becker set the phone on his desk. "Think about it. If Sloan is running the kind of scam they think he is, regardless of what the autopsy shows, we might be able to pin Claire's death on him."

Regardless of what the autopsy shows? "Exactly what is the autopsy going to show? Exactly how did you—"

"We agreed never to talk about it again, remember?" Becker said sternly. "We got lucky. Let's just leave it at that."

Becker's words didn't make sense. *Got lucky? What in the hell did that mean?* "So the autopsy's not going to turn up anything?"

Becker's face now displayed more confusion than Erickson's. "Not unless you know something that I don't."

The two men bounced blank looks at each other.

Erickson wondered if he was missing something. It was almost as if Becker was using some secret language that Erickson hadn't quite mastered.

"The White House plans to move quickly with my confirmation," Erickson said. "It's imperative that we keep a wrap on all of this."

"I think we can," Becker said. "In the meantime, I'm going to personally talk to Ashley."

"That's a good idea." Erickson stood up. "We both have a lot to lose if you can't convince her to shut her trap."

A baffled look returned to Becker's face. "Trust me," he said, reassuringly. "I'll take care of everything."

CHAPTER 44

Waverly was at his desk reviewing a new application when the receptionist called to tell him he had two visitors who refused to give their names.

He thumbed through his desk calendar and saw nothing scheduled. He had no idea what was up, but headed to the reception area to find out.

"I think it's best if we speak in private," the woman said, pulling him off to the side, away from the receptionist's desk. "I'm Angela Evans and this is Zack Hargrove. We're with the U.S. Attorney's Office." She flashed her credentials and extended her hand. "We'd like to talk with you."

"About what?"

"Like I said, I think it would be best if we spoke in private. Why don't we go to your office?"

Waverly hesitated, then led the way back to his office.

"What can I do for you?" he asked, as soon as they were seated. He did not like the way the fair-haired prick in the fancy suit was boldly inspecting his office.

"We're conducting an investigation into a complaint about a viatical settlement agreement you brokered," Angela began. "The client was Claire Erickson."

Waverly began to fidget with a paper clip, but dropped it when Zack seemed to take notice.

"A complaint? About what?" Waverly wanted a drink, but now was not the time to pull his flask from his desk drawer.

"We think Ms. Erickson's death may have been premature," she continued.

Waverly chuckled. "I don't mean to sound crass, but all of my clients' deaths are premature. Claire Erickson had pancreatic cancer and a life expectancy of less than six months. That's the only reason I was able to sell her policy."

"You've brokered fifty-three policies in just a few months. More than half of those clients are already dead."

That number surprised him. He didn't keep a running count of his clients who died. "You seem to be missing the point," Waverly said. "That's pretty much the way it's supposed to work."

"But they died much sooner than their estimated life expectancy and way too many died as a result of accidents," Angela said.

Waverly tried not to squirm in his chair. "No one can predict life expectancy with any certainty," he replied. "And you could walk out of my office right now and get hit by a bus. Accidents happen."

"Is that something you and your investors can arrange?" Zack asked.

The hard-charging woman prosecutor was bad enough, but Waverly definitely didn't like her little sidekick. "Hold on a minute." He rocked back in his chair. "Sounds like you're accusing me of knocking off my clients. Do I need an attorney?"

"You tell us," Zack said.

"No," Waverly snapped, "*you* tell *me*. Are you here because you think I had something to do with Mrs. Erickson's death?"

Zack made a teepee with his fingers. "That's one possibility we're looking into."

Waverly felt his armpits dampen. At least they weren't asking about Jerry Billington. After Rico's call demanding his money, he had searched the Internet for word of Billington's death. When he found none, he feared Rico may have been responsible for killing him. How else would he have known about the accident? But Rico had no connection to Claire Erickson. Waverly had brokered her policy before Rico came on the scene.

Waverly calmly stood up. "This meeting is over. You apparently haven't done your homework. I'd have absolutely no motive for killing my clients. My fee comes off the top. It doesn't matter to me if they die tomorrow or a year from now. I don't make a dime more or a dime less."

Zack and Angela remained seated. "Maybe it enhances your clout with your investors when you can produce a faster return on their investment," Zack charged.

"This is crazy. You can't come in here and accuse me of something like this. Like I said, this meeting is over."

Angela finally rose. "Would you be willing to turn over your records to assist in our investigation?"

"There's nothing in my records that would either prove or disprove your ludicrous allegations. But no, you can't go through my records. Not without a search warrant. My files contain confidential medical information and my clients value their privacy."

"Can you tell us who purchased Mrs. Erickson's policy?" Angela asked.

"No, I can't." Waverly wanted them out of his office. "Am I officially under investigation?"

"No," Zack said. He'd still made no move to get up. "Not officially. We have one other client to ask you about. Jerry Billington."

Waverly audibly gulped.

"We understand that he died the same day he picked up his check from your office," Zack continued.

"Mr. Billington died in a car accident when his car went off a rain slicked street," Waverly replied. "Like I said, accidents happen every day."

"Just seems a little strange, if you ask me. He picks up his check and a few hours later he's dead." Zack finally stood up. "I wonder how that will play to a jury?"

Angela placed a hand on the doorknob. "We've instructed his insurance company to freeze the payout on the policy until we've completed our investigation."

"And that could be some time," Zack added.

Waverly felt his lungs expand. "Exactly how much time is *some time*?"

"Several months," said Angela.

"Maybe even years." Zack pulled an envelope from the inside pocket of his jacket and placed it on Waverly's desk. "Oh, by the way, here's an order freezing your bank accounts."

"My bank accounts! Why?"

"We suspect that they contain funds which are the proceeds of an illegal operation," Zack explained.

"It appears as if you two came here for the sole purpose of trying to intimidate me," Waverly charged. "Well, it's not going to work."

"No, Mr. Sloan, we just wanted to make you aware of our investigation."

"What you're doing isn't fair to me or my investors," Waverly said. "If there's going to be a problem with Mr. Billington's policy, we can just cancel the viatical settlement and have his estate return the money."

"Sorry, but it doesn't work like that," Angela replied.

Rico would kill him for sure. Waverly had promised him a payment in two weeks, simply to stop his increasing threats. "I gave Billington one hundred and fifty grand."

"If our investigation determines that your business is on the up and up, your investor will get what he's owed."

Waverly could not hide his alarm. "This is blackmail. You can't keep the money *and* block the payout!"

Angela finally pulled the door open. "I'm afraid we can."

PART FOUR

A Done Deal

I f nothing else, Waverly was certainly a creature of habit. When a problem cropped up that he couldn't resolve, he resorted to his typical M.O. He ignored it.

Two days after the visit from the two assistant U.S. attorneys, Waverly surprised Deidra with a trip to Maui. While Deidra shopped, he snorkeled and overdosed on shrimp, lobster and booze. During the eight days they were there, Waverly pretended as if his problems didn't exist. He even turned off his BlackBerry and didn't check his messages the entire trip.

It was just after six on Monday morning and Waverly sat on the veranda of his fabulous home, gazing out at the ocean, sipping coffee brewed by an expensive contraption set on a timer. It was finally time for Waverly to face his reality. Their last night in Maui, he dreamed that the two federal prosecutors showed up at LAX and carted him off to jail, while Deidra screamed expletives at him.

Waverly tried to apply logic to his situation. If his clients really were being murdered, there was no way he could be linked to their deaths because he hadn't killed anyone. In just a matter of months in the viatical business, he'd made over five hundred thousand dollars in commissions. Was the gravy train about to end?

Although the U.S. Attorney's Office had frozen his bank accounts, Waverly still had access to a large amount of cash. He had close to fifty thousand dollars hidden around the house, and almost as much stashed in safe-deposit boxes at three different banks under a different name. He could survive for several months, but only if they significantly downsized.

Waverly walked back inside and watched a few minutes of the local news on the small flat screen in the kitchen. He was relieved when he didn't see a story about the deaths of Claire Erickson or Jerry Billington. What did surprise him was the announcement that Lawrence Erickson had been confirmed as Attorney General of the United States. *What the hell?* The White House obviously didn't know those two prosecutors were looking into Claire Erickson's death.

Once the news finally registered, he began to view Erickson's appointment as a positive. The new Justice Department chief could not afford to be linked to a scandal like this. He was now one of the most powerful lawyers in the country and the boss of those two arrogant AUSAs. Erickson would squelch their investigation the second he got wind of it. He would have to if he wanted to keep his job.

Feeling hopeful for the first time in days, he headed for the front door to retrieve the morning paper. The minute he bent down to pick it up, the *L.A. Times'* headline blared out at him.

DISBARRED ATTORNEY GETS RICH OFF THE DYING.

Waverly stood there on the porch in his half-open, cashmere robe gazing at the newspaper in disbelief, his own smiling face staring back at him. *That bitch!* Jill Kerr had screwed him royally.

The article wasn't about the viatical business or about Live Now. The story was all about him. It went into extensive detail about the facts that led to his disbarment. The reporter basically painted him as a greedy, unethical crook. Why was everybody persecuting him for a legitimate business that actually helped people?

The paragraph stating that a number of his clients had died accidentally, shortly after selling their policies, upset him the most. While the reporter didn't say so, she insinuated that there may have been something suspicious about the circumstances of their deaths. She might as well have said *he* had murdered them.

Waverly walked back inside, shuddering with rage. He marched over to the telephone to call *The Times*. This was defamation and he was going to sue. Then he froze. Deidra would see this story. She would know he'd been disbarred.

Deidra sauntered up behind him. Waverly flinched.

"You okay?" she asked. "You look like you just saw a ghost."

He quickly tucked the newspaper underneath his arm. He leaned down to kiss her, glad to have a wife who never bothered with things like current affairs, politics or newspapers.

"I think I'd like some breakfast this morning. How about pancakes?" He needed to keep her busy.

"You got it," Deidra said. Until the excitement from their trip wore off, she'd do anything he asked. He'd let her spend so much money in Maui that she even treated him to a blowjob the night before they left. Maybe he should send her off shopping right now.

His in-laws! Leon Barrett would see the newspaper and would be calling any minute. Waverly rushed into the bedroom and took the phone off the hook. He found Deidra's cell phone on the nightstand, turned it off and slid it underneath the bed.

Walking back into the kitchen, Waverly pretended to be reading a message on his BlackBerry. "I can't believe I forgot about a meeting I have this morning. Never mind about making me those pancakes."

Ignoring Deidra's protests, he headed for the bedroom. He had to get out of the house right away. If Leon Barrett couldn't reach Deidra by phone to deliver the news, he'd drive over.

Waverly knew he was taking the cowardly way out, but he couldn't face his wife. Not now.

CHAPTER 46

Angela was reading *The Times* article about Waverly Sloan when Zack walked into her office.

"Why do you look like the unhappiest guy on earth?" Angela asked.

"Because I am," Zack replied. "Guess you haven't heard?"

"Heard what?"

"You should check your email more often. Operation Buying Time is about to be no more."

"What?" Angela turned to her computer, but Zack placed a piece of paper on her desk.

"I printed out a copy for you. Read it and weep." The email was from Roland Becker, the new Deputy U.S. Attorney General.

Angela quickly read it.

"He's shutting down several task forces nationwide," Zack said. "And ours is one of them."

"What? Erickson just got confirmed and this is his first priority? Why is he doing this?"

"Supposedly, lack of funding."

Angela's eyes met Zack's. "This is crap. That *L.A. Times* article about Waverly Sloan proves that we're on the right track, but somebody wants us off his trail. Are you thinking what I'm thinking?"

"I'm way ahead of you," Zack said. "I did some checking. Becker and Erickson were both partners at Jankowski, Parkins. Some people say they're closer than brothers. I think they know we're about to link Erickson to his wife's death and they can't let that happen. It would look strange if they only pulled the plug on our investigation. Becker is shutting down several others to make it look legit."

Angela read the email again. "Maybe we're reading too much into this. This email says it's only a temporary shutdown until Becker can conduct a review."

"I don't buy it," Zack said. "You'll note that the three other viatical investigations aren't on the list. What do you want to bet ours will be the only one getting the ax?"

The phone on Angela's desk rang. Zack waited as Angela took the call.

"Barnes wants to see both of us," Angela said, standing up and slipping into her jacket. "Right now." Todd Barnes was Chief of the Major Frauds Section.

"What does he want?"

"He didn't say. But it sounds urgent."

Angela followed Zack out of the door and down the hall to Barnes' office.

"Close the door," Barnes ordered, when they stepped inside, "and have a seat."

Barnes was overweight and wore wire-rimmed glasses and wrinkled plaid shirts. It always seemed as if his mind was someplace else. "I need you to prepare a memo summarizing the status of Operation Buying Time. I'm sure you saw that email from our new deputy AG. He's in town and wants to meet the two of you."

Angela and Zack traded glances. They'd never met with Justice Department brass at Becker's level before.

"When?" Angela asked. "And why?"

"Three o'clock in the twelfth floor conference room," Barnes said. "And he didn't tell me why. Make sure your memo really pumps up your operation. He'll probably use it as a basis for deciding whether to shut it down permanently."

"Is Becker meeting with anyone else while he's here?" Zack asked.

Barnes nodded. "He's also talking to three other teams."

"I really hope we don't get canned," Angela said. "I think we could be close to figuring out who killed Jon."

"I'm afraid your task force is probably first in line for the chopping block. The viatical investigations in the three other states already have enough evidence for indictments. The charges against The Tustin Group in those cases will still reach the people operating Live Now. Anything you get would be icing on the cake."

Angela and Zack had previously advised Barnes that they thought Waverly Sloan might be killing his clients, including Jon, but they had decided not to disclose Lawrence Erickson's connection to Sloan or their suspicions that he may've had something to do with his wife's death. They feared that an attorney with Erickson's kind of connections could easily find a way to squelch their investigation. Apparently, that was about to happen.

"Were you invited to the meeting?" Zack asked.

"Nope. I offered to tag along," Barnes said, "but I was politely told that wasn't necessary."

Zack and Angela left Barnes' office and finished the memo with time to spare. They waited in the conference room for nearly twenty minutes before Becker arrived.

"Sorry I'm late." Becker gave each of them a firm handshake. "It's been a busy few days. I've been meeting with AUSAs all over the country. Tomorrow I leave for Chicago." He took a seat on one side of the conference table with Zack and Angela facing him.

"Here's the memo you wanted." Zack slid the document across the table.

"Great." Becker took several minutes to read it. "First let me apologize. I know how much work you've put into this investigation and I hate to put a kibosh on it. But funds are tight. Why don't you tell me a little more about it?"

Normally, Zack would have jumped at an opportunity like this. He looked over at Angela and waited. Neither of them wanted to start. Something told Angela they were on target about Erickson. Becker was simply fishing around to find out how much they knew. Well, he wasn't going to reel in a big one today.

Angela finally responded. "As you know, federal indictments are forthcoming against Live Now's parent company in Las Vegas, Syracuse and Miami. We suspect that the same fraudulent activity going on in the other cities—pressuring dying policyholders to sell—is happening here."

Becker glanced down at their report again. "Have you found any evidence that the company is doing the same thing here?" The memo neglected to mention that Jon hadn't been pressured by Waverly Sloan.

"Our investigation is just beginning," Zack said, "but it's taken an unexpected turn. We lost our lead case agent. He died in a car accident, but we think he may've been murdered as a direct result of selling his phony insurance policy. And he's not the first victim."

"Really? Is the D.A.'s Office looking into his death?"

"Yes," Zack said. "And so are we."

Angela could tell from Becker's expression that they weren't scoring any points.

"What can you tell me about—" Becker paused to peruse the memo. "What's the company's name again?"

"Live Now," Zack offered.

"Yes. Have you found any admissible evidence that anyone connected with the company is actually knocking off their clients?"

"Not yet," Angela said. "We've been looking at one of their brokers."

Becker leaned his head to the left and cracked his neck. "I see that in your memo. Tell me more?"

"His name is Waverly Sloan."

"Got anything on him yet?"

Angela crossed and uncrossed her legs. "No, not yet." She didn't want to reveal that Waverly had in no way pressured Jon to sell his policy.

"Have you identified any other clients besides your case agent and the four people listed in your memo who you think died under suspicious circumstances?"

They had intentionally excluded Claire Erickson's name from the memo. When Angela didn't step up to the plate, Zack expertly avoided answering the question like the skilled politician he might one day become.

"The D.A.'s Office may have some additional victims. A high number of Waverly Sloan's clients died in accidents, rather than from their illnesses. Too many to dismiss as a coincidence."

"I understand that," Becker said. "But is there any hard evidence pointing to foul play?"

"We're still looking into it," Angela said.

Becker folded his arms. "As you know, we're under serious budget constraints. It sounds like the other jurisdictions already have enough to nail these guys on the fraud allegations. And if these deaths do turn out to be homicides, the D.A.'s Office can pursue them. We need to conserve the extremely limited resources we have."

"Does that mean our investigation is history?" Zack asked.

Becker smiled. "I haven't made a final decision yet. Give me a chance to speak with all the teams."

"How long will that take?" Angela pushed.

Becker shrugged noncommittally. "A few weeks at the most." He leaned forward and planted his forearms on the table. "For the time being, your operation is on hold. That means no further investigation. Thanks for meeting with me on such short notice."

Zack and Angela exited the conference room and walked somberly down a long hallway. They didn't speak until they were back behind closed doors in Angela's office.

"That was a bunch of bull," Zack said.

Angela nodded. "I would have to agree."

"Then I guess Operation Buying Time is a done deal."

"No way." Angela sat on the edge of her desk and folded her arms. "I'm determined to find out if Waverly Sloan and Live Now had anything to do with Jon's death. And if I have to do it on my own time, so be it."

CHAPTER 47

I'm in trouble. Big trouble."

Waverly peered across the table at Vincent, who responded with a cautious gape.

"I'm listening, man. I'm here. What's going on?"

After ducking out on Deidra and spending a couple of frantic hours at his office, Waverly asked Vincent to meet him for a drink.

Waverly decided to just put everything on the table. "I've been selling a few policies on the side."

Vincent looked utterly perplexed. "And why in the world would you do that?"

"I had no choice."

"We always have choices, man. You might not like them, but you definitely have them."

Vincent took a sip of his Coke. "Tell me exactly what's going on. You've been raking in mountains of dough. Why would you risk your license by doing something like that?"

Waverly stared down at his drink so he wouldn't have to meet Vincent's chastising gaze. He started with the day he found his brother in his office building garage, lying on the ground like a bloody rag doll. When he recounted his first call from Rico, he had hoped to see compassion in Vincent's eyes. But he only detected shock.

"Why didn't you call me then?" Vincent asked.

"For what? They threatened my wife. There was nothing you could do about it."

"And exactly what do you think I can do for you now?"

Waverly did not like the condemnation in Vincent's tone. But he was right. He wasn't sure why he'd called him. Probably because there was no one else he could call.

He hesitated, afraid that if he spoke what was in his head, it just might make it true. But he needed a sounding board.

"I think this guy Rico may have murdered one or more of the clients he bought policies on."

Vincent's body lurched backward and he gripped the edge of the table. "Man, that's a hell of an accusation. And if it's true, it puts you in a very bad place. It also puts me and Live Now in an equally bad place."

Waverly offered no response to his statement.

"What makes you think this guy is killing your clients?"

"He called me right after Jon Billington died, asking for his money. How would he even know the guy was dead if he didn't have anything to do with it?"

"You gave the guy the name of the policyholder?"

Waverly looked down at his hands. "I had to."

It took a while before Vincent asked another question. "You don't have any proof that this guy killed him, do you?"

"Sometimes you just know," Waverly said. "And a few days ago—" He paused, wondering if he should just keep this to himself. "Two prosecutors with the U.S. Attorney's Office dropped in on me."

"For what?"

"They asked me a bunch of questions about the policies I brokered. They insinuated that my clients were dying prematurely and that maybe I had something to do with it. Today's story in the *L.A. Times* certainly doesn't help."

"*L.A. Times?* What story?"

Waverly opened his briefcase, pulled out the newspaper and slapped it on the table in front of him. He waited while Vincent read it. The only good thing about it was that Jill Kerr had not mentioned Jerry Billington or Claire Erickson. If she'd had any information about his link to Erickson, Waverly figured she would have used it.

Twice, Vincent stopped reading and glanced up at him. He finally put the newspaper down and pushed his Coke aside. "I'm going to need something a little stronger than this." He hailed down the waitress and ordered a vodka twist.

"Live Now is mentioned all throughout this article. We need to contact Bellamy and Cartwright and let them know what's going on," Vincent said. "The fallout could seriously hurt the company. I'm surprised they haven't already called you. And when you do talk to them, just make sure you tell them I had nothing to do with this."

Waverly didn't know why he had expected any help from Vincent. "What should I do?" he asked, simply to kill the silence.

"I would've advised you to go to the police, but in light of this whole money laundering scam you're tied up in, you'd be asking for some guaranteed jail time. And by the way, if your bribe to the Department of Insurance comes to light, leave me out of it."

Waverly chuckled and lowered his head. Vincent fronted the money and paid the bribe, but now it was *his* bribe.

Vincent looked at him and Waverly read the lack of sympathy in his eyes. They communicated that greedy people got what they deserved.

But this wasn't about greed. He wouldn't be in this predicament if it hadn't been for the threat to his family. His actions were dictated by fear, not greed. There had been no other option.

But now he had to find one.

CHAPTER 48

Angela eyed the clock on the dashboard of her Saab. She was meeting Dre for drinks at The Dynasty Restaurant & Lounge in Inglewood and she was fifteen minutes late. She had to circle the block three times before finally spotting an open parking meter around the corner on Hillcrest.

When she stepped inside the club, she spotted Dre sitting at a table overlooking a small dance floor. He leaned over the railing and waved.

"You lookin' mighty fly," Dre said, checking out her legs when she reached his table.

"Sorry, I'm late," Angela apologized.

"Calm down, baby. You ain't late. Why you stressin'?" He stood up, kissed her on the lips, then pulled out the chair next to him.

Angela immediately relaxed. Cornell would've been lecturing her about the importance of time management by now. Dre just seemed happy to see her.

"What do you want to drink?" he asked.

"Apple martini."

"They make a bomb caramel apple martini here. Wanna try it?"

"Sure." Angela gazed around the club. "This is where you hang out, huh?"

"Yep. The music is slammin' and the fried chicken is better than my Mama's. But don't tell her."

Angela laughed and took the paper napkin underneath Dre's wineglass to wipe the lipstick mark she had left on his lips. A worried expression suddenly distorted Dre's face.

"Shit!" he said under his breath.

Angela looked over her shoulder in the direction of Dre's gaze, but couldn't see what or who he was staring at. "What's the matter?"

"Nothin'. Just somebody I really don't wanna see."

She could feel Dre's body grow taut and wondered what was going on. Before she could ask again, Angela saw what had attracted his attention.

A shapely, dark-skinned woman of medium height was prancing toward their table. The look on Dre's face had now changed from frustration to embarrassment.

The woman boldly pulled out a chair and took a seat across from them. "Hey, Dre, how you doin'?"

"Nobody invited you to sit down," Dre said.

"Don't worry," the woman said, "I ain't stayin'. I just came over to say hello."

She had a long, reddish-brown weave streaked with blonde. Her bangs were angled across her face, shielding her left eye. The woman's hoop earrings were the size of lunch meat and her sheer lace top left nothing to the imagination. A red, spandex skirt barely covered her gargantuan ass.

"Aren't you going to introduce me?" The woman looked Angela up and down.

Dre pursed his lips. "It's a weeknight. Why aren't you home with Little Dre?"

The woman put a hand on her hip and tossed a handful of her fake hair over her shoulder. "Oh, so you can hang out during the week, but I can't?"

"I asked you who's takin' care of my son?" Dre demanded.

"He's at my sister's, okay?" She gave Angela another appraising look. "Stop being rude and introduce me to your little friend."

"Angela, this is Shawntay. My son's mother. Good-bye, Shawntay."

"If I hadn't seen y'all lockin' lips a second ago, I woulda thought you were his lawyer or something. Is that how y'all hooked up?"

Dre shot up. "I need to talk to you outside."

Shawntay ignored him and directed the conversation to Angela.

"If y'all gon' be an item, you'll probably be hangin' out with my son. So we need to get to know each other."

"Oh, hell naw." Dre gripped Shawntay's upper arm. "C'mon. We need to step outside and talk."

"Why we can't talk in front of your little friend?"

"Don't make me cause a scene up in here," Dre threatened.

With Dre's help, Shawntay grudgingly rose from the chair.

"Do Ms. Prim and Proper know what you do?" Shawntay asked, as Dre dragged her away.

Angela watched them weave their way through the packed club and out of the door. She pretended not to notice the curious gazes from other people in the club who had watched Dre leave with Shawntay. It was another ten minutes before they returned and headed in opposite directions.

"Sorry about that," Dre said, sitting down again. His face still had a stern expression. "Now where were we?" He tried to take Angela's hand, but she locked her arms across her chest.

"What was that all about?" she asked.

"Nothin'. Absolutely nothin'."

"Excuse me? I think you owe me more of an explanation than that."

Dre exhaled. "Hey, I'm sorry. I just got a little baby mama drama going on." He leaned over and kissed her, but Angela did not reciprocate. "She's just tryin' to cause me problems, which she's pretty damn good at. I swear she's psycho."

"She's the mother of your son. She must not be too psycho."

"Shawntay was never my woman, okay? You have nothin' to be jealous about."

"Who said I was jealous? I'm not even sure I can compete. I see you like your women a little rough around the edges."

Dre appeared genuinely embarrassed. "Let's just call it a lapse in judgment on my part. She was just something to do."

"What did you do? Take her outside and scold her?"

"Basically. I kick her down with way more child support than she needs to take care of my son and I've also agreed to pay her rent until Dre either graduates from high school or comes to live with me. She knows I ain't about to stand for no ghetto girl crap."

A pout remained etched into Angela's face.

"C'mon, babe, forget about her." He kissed her on the neck.

Angela still wasn't satisfied. "What did she mean when she asked if I *know what you do*?" Angela mimicked Shawntay's voice.

Dre stiffened. "Uh, let's just say I wasn't always the goody two-shoes that I am today."

"Oh, so you used to be a bad boy?" she asked, finally in a playful mood again.

"You might say that." He kissed her again and this time, she kissed him back.

Just when Angela was beginning to relax, she followed Dre's gaze across the room. Shawntay was sitting at the bar shooting him a nasty look.

"Shawntay doesn't look too happy. Are you sure you two are really done?"

"Hell yeah. Ignore her ass. She's crazy."

"That's fine," Angela said, turning back to him. "As long as she doesn't get crazy with me."

CHAPTER 49

It was after nine o'clock at night and Waverly had just circled the block—his own block—for the third time.

He finally eased over to the curb several houses away. While he'd been running away from his problems all of his life, there was one person he had to face. His wife deserved better. She'd left three voicemail messages on his BlackBerry that he'd been too much of a coward to even listen to.

Waverly wished he'd kept a change of clothes at the office as he had in the old days when he never knew when a last minute court appearance might be necessary. His shirt was wrinkled and he reeked of sweat and brandy. This wasn't how he wanted to make his plea. Maybe he could slip in and clean himself up before facing Deidra.

He had no idea what he was going to say. He turned the key in the ignition and drove slowly toward the home that had brought him so much joy. When he was two houses away, he pounded the steering wheel in frustration.

"Damn!"

Leon Barrett's Lincoln was now parked out front. Waverly pulled into the driveway and turned off the engine, but did not get out. He wanted to have a private conversation with his wife, but her father's presence meant that would not be possible. He hoped her mother and sister weren't there, too.

Just as he climbed out of the car, the front door opened and Leon marched down the walkway as if this were his domain.

"I didn't think you'd show up this soon," Leon said, his hands gripping his waist. "You really surprised me."

Waverly walked past him as if he had not been standing there. Deidra's mother stood in the living room. She didn't say a word, but the castigation in her eyes didn't require verbalizing.

"Where's Deidra?" Waverly asked.

He followed Myrtle Barrett's eyes down the hallway.

Deidra was standing halfway out of the bedroom. She looked almost as frazzled as he was. Her hair was a mess, her eyes were red and she had a tattered tissue in her hand. He half hoped she would run into his arms, but she didn't move.

Leon marched in and blocked his view of Deidra. "Let's hear it. I can't imagine what you could say to account for all the lies. But let's hear what you have to say anyway."

Even at a distance, Waverly could see the hope in Deidra's eyes. She wanted him to say something to make this all disappear. But there were no words that would accomplish that.

"I want to talk to my wife," Waverly said. "Alone."

"We're not going anywhere. Whatever you have to say to Deidra, you can say to us, too. Though I doubt your lies will be worth listening to. You were disbarred and you never even told your wife? You're really a piece of work."

Waverly wanted to sling him out of the way, something he could probably accomplish with a simple sweep of his hand. "Leon, this is between me and my wife."

"Oh, the hell it is. I—"

"Daddy, can you please give us a minute." Deidra crept further into the hallway. "Just go in the family room, okay?"

Leon stood his ground, fixing Waverly with a hateful stare. Then he turned and stalked off. Deidra's mother followed.

Waverly hurried toward Deidra. He now regretted the long

length of the hallways. Two people didn't need a house this big. As he reached out for her, Deidra shrank away.

"You need to explain," she said, her lips quivering with either anger or sorrow, maybe both.

She stepped into the bedroom and Waverly rushed in behind her.

Deidra sat down on the edge of the bed and stared up at him looking very much like a scared child. "Is it true? Were you disbarred?"

Waverly wished there was some lawyerly explanation he could offer her. Something that wasn't exactly the truth, but was close enough to it. "Yes," he said.

"And you couldn't tell me?"

"I wanted to. But I didn't want to disappoint you."

"So you never planned to tell me?"

No, not if I could help it. "I couldn't face letting you down."

Deidra wiped a tear with the shredded tissue. Waverly had never seen her in such a distraught state before.

"And this new business of yours," she said derisively, "is it really making money off of dying people?"

"It's not the way that reporter made it sound. I'm really helping people. People who need money in their dying days." His explanation sounded too much like a pitch to an investor.

She stared up at him with disgust and, for the first time, he saw her father's daughter.

He was about to speak when Deidra stood up, her eyes boring into his. "Are you killing people? Is that how we're able to live in this house? Because you're killing people?"

"Hell no!" Waverly shouted as if a louder response might be more convincing. "That's a complete lie!"

"*The L.A. Times* isn't the *National Enquirer.* Why would the reporter say that then?"

"She didn't say it. She implied it."

"And it's not true?"

"No."

He tried to reach for her again, but she pushed him away. "We aren't going to lose this house are we?" She was suddenly dry-eyed and angry. "Do you have any idea how embarrassing this is for me? I'm never going to be able to face my friends again."

Now, Waverly grew pissed. "Yes, Deidra, it *is* always about you, isn't it?"

"Don't you dare put this on me!" she said angrily. "I want no part of this. I want you out of here. You have thirty minutes to pack your bags."

Waverly chuckled. "You watch too many Lifetime movies. You're not kicking me out of my own house. I pay the bills here, remember? You want to leave, fine. Just make sure you take your mama and daddy with you."

Waverly walked past her into the bathroom and turned on the shower.

Ten minutes later, feeling clean and refreshed, Waverly lay back in bed, his fingers hooked behind his head as Deidra stormed around the bedroom, throwing clothes into a suitcase. He thought about asking her not to go, but actually wanted to be alone.

Longing for a drink, he jumped up from the bed and walked into the family room. He ignored his in-laws sitting on the couch and grabbed a fifth of brandy from the shelf behind the bar and poured himself two shots.

Leon stalked up to him. "You're a disgrace. How dare you—"

"Deidra's packing," Waverly said, taking a swallow. "I'll tell her you're waiting for her in the car. Now get the fuck out of my house."

Leon's face darkened. The body language of both men signaled the approach of a physical altercation.

Myrtle grabbed her husband's forearm. "Leon, let's go wait in the car. They can work this out without our help."

Leon continued to sneer at Waverly for several seconds, his

fists balled at his sides. "C'mon, Myrtle," he said to his wife. "Didn't I tell you this guy was up to no good? I knew it the minute I laid eyes on him. But nobody ever listens to me."

He paraded out of the room, slamming the front door behind him.

Waverly finished the rest of his drink and refilled the glass. He heard Deidra coming out of the bedroom and went to meet her. She was pulling a large suitcase on rollers with one hand, while struggling to hold on to an overstuffed duffel bag with the other.

"You need help with that?" he asked, reaching for the duffel bag.

Deidra turned up her nose at him. "I can manage."

Waverly threw up his hands. "Okay, fine then."

He stepped aside and Deidra walked out of the front door without another word.

Peering out of the bay window, he watched as Deidra climbed into the backseat of her father's Lincoln. He felt a pang of regret for the pain and turmoil he had caused her and wondered if he'd be able to fix things between them.

As he headed back to the bar for another refill, he focused on the bright side. At least he hadn't wasted his money buying her that Benz.

CHAPTER 50

Angela lay in bed watching Dre sleep. She turned on her side, her head propped up by her hand and began gently twirling Dre's chest hairs between two fingers.

He opened his eyes, then smiled. "What time is it?"

"Almost seven."

Dre yawned. "How would you like it if you woke up and found *me* playin' with *your* chest?"

Angela laughed. "I might actually like it." She continued her exploration, tracing the outline of a tattoo near his left shoulder. "Does getting a tattoo hurt?"

"Naw," Dre said. "Not if you're a real man like me." He flexed his arms and made his pecs move up and down.

She laughed. "Show off." She fingered a faded symbol on his bicep. "What's this supposed to be?"

"An owl, but the guy screwed it up."

"Why an owl?"

"It symbolizes wisdom."

Angela ran her finger to the left side of his chest. "This one's an anchor, right?"

"Yeah," Dre said.

"And the symbolism?"

"It's important to keep your feet on the ground. No matter how good life gets or how screwed up things are, you have to stay anchored. Otherwise, circumstances can beat you down."

"Wow, you are so deep," she said facetiously.

"Thank you." Dre smiled. "I try to be."

"So who's L.D.?" She pointed to the letters stenciled on his upper right shoulder.

"Little Dre, my son." He turned on his side and faced her. "How many tattoos you got?" He lifted the blanket and started running his hands over her naked body.

"Stop it," Angela said, laughing. "I'm really ticklish." She squirmed away and climbed on top of him, sitting up.

"I don't have any tattoos, but I was thinking about putting your name right here." Angela pointed to her left breast.

"You always got jokes this early in the morning?"

"Yep."

Dre pulled her to him and kissed her. "I really like kickin' it with you."

"Ditto," Angela replied. "I feel like playing hooky today. Let's go see a movie."

"No way," Dre said. "You're not gonna blame me when you get fired."

"I have loads of vacation time. Let's just hang out today. What do you have planned?"

"I'm rehabbin' a property on Western. They're almost done with the kitchen. I want you to come over and check it out when it's finished. I'm hopin' I can put it on the market in another month." He gave her a pensive look.

"Got something on your mind?" Angela asked.

Dre's eyes held hers. "Yeah, I do."

"Okay," she said, surprised at his sudden seriousness. "I'm listening."

"There's a lot you don't know about me."

"Really? So tell me."

"I will," Dre said. "When the time is right."

"How come you can't just tell—"

A loud knock boomed from the living room.

Angela's face clouded. "Someone probably has the wrong apartment. The only person who knows I live here is my sister. And she never gets up this early."

The knock suddenly turned into pounding and whoever it was started leaning on the doorbell.

"Angela, open the door! We need to talk!"

Angela jumped out of bed and scrambled into her robe. "I don't believe this!"

"Is that the judge dude?" Dre asked, sitting up.

Angela cringed. "I'm afraid so."

Dre snatched his jeans from the chair next to the bed and stepped into them.

"No, Dre, just stay here. I don't want a scene. I'm not even going to open the door. Maybe he'll just go away."

They waited, but the pounding only grew louder.

"Angela, please open the door!" Cornell sobbed. "I need to talk to you. I love you." He was obviously drunk.

Dre zipped up his jeans. "You need to let me deal with dude."

"No!" Angela said. "I'll handle it." She stepped into her house shoes and tied her robe. "Please stay here. I don't want him to know I'm seeing anybody."

Dre started to protest, but Angela held up both hands. "Let me handle this my way, okay?"

Closing the bedroom door behind her, Angela marched into the living room. She had never told Dre that Cornell attacked her the night she broke off the engagement. Her sister had wanted to go back and confront him. Maybe if she had, Cornell would've gotten the message.

"What are you doing here, Cornell?" Angela said through the closed door.

"I need to talk to you," he cried. "Please open the door, Angela. I just want to talk to you."

"I'm not opening the door. Just leave!"

"Open the goddamn door!" Cornell kicked it hard, causing Angela to jump back in alarm.

"If you don't leave, I'm calling the police!" she yelled.

"You have to talk to me. You have to give me another chance. Please, I love you."

"I'll talk to you," Angela said. "But not here. Not now. Leave or I'm calling the police."

She peered through the peephole and could see that Cornell was red-eyed and unshaven, wearing a rumpled suit that looked as if he'd slept in it. He had the same crazed look in his eyes that she'd seen the night of Jon's accident. Even with Dre in the next room and a heavy wooden door between them, she did not feel safe.

Cornell kicked the door again and Angela thought she heard one of the hinges crack.

She took a step back and bumped into a bare-chested Dre. Before she could stop him, he reached over her shoulder and snatched open the door.

Shock, followed by rage, spread across Cornell's sullen face.

"Dude, you need to back off," Dre said. "She told you it's over. You need to step."

Cornell seemed paralyzed for several seconds, apparently shocked into speechlessness. He lost his balance and fell back against the hallway wall.

Dre waited a few seconds, then shut the door in his face.

Angela covered her mouth with both hands. "You shouldn't have done that. You just made everything worse. No telling what he's going to do now!"

"He ain't doin' shit 'cuz he's a punk."

"You don't know Cornell. He doesn't like to lose."

"Well, he's definitely lost you, so he just needs to get used to it."

"I really wish you hadn't done that," Angela cried. "This just creates a whole new set of problems."

Dre pulled her to him. "Babe, you don't have a thing to worry about. Just trust me. I got this."

CHAPTER 51

Becker took a few seconds to rehearse everything in his head before picking up the telephone. He hoped his call to Waverly Sloan turned out better than his attempt to talk some sense into Ashley. Becker couldn't believe it when the little brat hung up in his face.

When Sloan came on the line, Becker thought the man's voice might have been slurred. He did not want to converse with a drunk. He wanted Sloan fully cognizant of everything he was about to say.

"I'm calling on behalf of United States Attorney General Lawrence Erickson," he began. Becker did not plan to give his name, even if asked. He might have to later deny that the call ever took place.

"What? You got a complaint, too?" Waverly's speech was badly garbled.

Becker paused. "I'm not sure what you mean."

"Join the crowd. It's Jump on Waverly Sloan Day."

Becker was disappointed. The guy was bombed. The conversation would not go according to plan.

"I'm calling because Mr. Erickson is concerned that your activities could create some unwelcome fallout for him. When he hired you to broker his wife's insurance policy, he had no idea about your criminal activities. I understand that you're under investigation for fraud and, possibly, murder. The things we've been reading about you are quite troubling."

"Whatever."

"Mr. Sloan, you need to listen to me and listen to me very carefully. If you had anything to do with the death of Mr. Erickson's wife, you're going to pay."

Becker's words seemed to rally Waverly out of his drunken stupor.

"What did you say?" Waverly's voice sounded a little clearer now.

"I'm sure you heard me correctly."

A long patch of silence followed.

"Is everybody crazy? You think I killed Mrs. Erickson, too?"

Too? "And who else thinks you murdered her?"

"Two prosecutors from the U.S. Attorney's Office came to my office without even making an appointment. They implied that since I brokered Mrs. Erickson's policy, I had something to do with her death."

Damn! So Hargrove and Evans *had* made the link to Erickson. The fact that they'd withheld that information was quite problematic.

"And exactly how do they think you killed her?"

"Beats me."

"Sounds like you're in quite a bit of trouble," Becker said. "I suggest you go out and hire a good lawyer."

"What's wrong with everybody? That woman was dying. All of my clients were dying. I had no motive for killing her or anybody else."

"That *L.A. Times* article certainly implied otherwise. And I've heard other disturbing information about you."

"Like what?"

"I didn't call to answer your questions, Mr. Sloan. I called to deliver a message. You will not get away with this."

Becker hung up the telephone. His sole intent in making the

call was to put the fear of God into the man. But Becker wasn't sure he'd accomplished his goal. His initial research on Waverly Sloan made him an unlikely murderer. He was a small-time ambulance chaser who'd never made much of a splash in the legal profession. Early in his career, he had achieved a few victories at trial, but in recent years, Sloan had settled half of his cases and the rest were dismissed.

Though Becker was presenting a calm front for Erickson's sake, Ashley's accusations were slowly gaining traction. The fact that they could not be proven did not matter. If the media picked up the story—true or false—Erickson would be ruined. So far, only luck had kept the story out of the media.

Becker was trying to do everything in his power to keep a lid on the situation, but frankly, he no longer believed that he could.

CHAPTER 52

Angela was now paying for lounging in bed with Dre for two mornings in a row. It was after ten by the time she made it to work that morning. Now, eight hours later, she had little to show for her time.

Rocking back in her chair, she closed her eyes as a big smile lit up her face. Lately, she was spending way too much time daydreaming about Dre. It was nice being with someone who liked to laugh and didn't take life so seriously. He called her during the day just because and they made love morning and night.

Cornell had not called since his confrontation with Dre earlier in the week. Angela felt guilty for calling off the wedding and blamed herself for not ending it sooner. She really wished that Cornell hadn't found out that she was already seeing someone else. But there was nothing she could do about that now.

Angela turned off her computer and started packing up to go home. She leaned down and retrieved her purse from the bottom drawer of her desk. When she sat back up, the blood drained from her face.

Cornell was standing just inside the doorway, one hand behind his back.

Oh, my God! Her first thought was that Cornell was holding a gun behind his back. Then she remembered the metal detectors at the entrance of the building. He wouldn't have been able to sneak a gun inside the courthouse. But he could still have some other kind of weapon.

He stepped inside and closed the door behind him.

"I don't want to talk to you." Angela was scared out of her mind, but tried not to show it. "You need to leave. Now."

Cornell's eyes were red and he looked tired, but he didn't appear to be drunk. "What are you trying to do to me?"

Angela had a question of her own that required an answer. "Why are you holding your hand behind your back?"

He took several wide steps toward her.

"Remember this?" He held a colorful wooden carving high in the air. "I bought it for you on our trip to Kenya. You left a lot of stuff behind. Like that ring that I'm still making payments on. I figured you'd at least want this." He slammed down the carving on the corner of her desk.

The fact that Cornell did not have a weapon did nothing to reduce Angela's anxiety level. "Thanks, but I don't think you should be here. I was just about to leave."

"Good. I'll walk you to your car."

"No!" She caught herself. She had to play it cool. "You don't need to do that. Just leave, Cornell. Please."

"After more than three years together, we can't even have a civil conversation?"

"We can talk later." She had to get him out of her office. "I'll call you tomorrow."

"Oh, so now you'll call me? I've been calling you since you walked out on me, but you refused to pick up. Guess you've been too busy screwing that thug with all the tattoos."

Angela took a step closer to the phone. "If you don't leave, I'm calling security."

Cornell picked up the carving and crashed it down again. "What kind of head games are you trying to play with me, Angela? You embarrass me like this and expect me to just sit back and take it?"

Angela now saw that crazed look in Cornell's eyes again. If she could just make it to the hallway, she could alert someone.

"I'm not trying to embarrass you. Nobody knows why we cancelled the wedding. Just tell people whatever you want and I'll go along with it."

Cornell stepped around the desk, blocking her path. "You will not embarrass me."

Angela boldly stood her ground. "This is the last time I'm saying this. If you don't leave, I'm calling security."

Cornell chuckled. "You probably couldn't even find a security guard around this place. If I wanted to, I could strangle you before they got their lazy asses up here. Why are you so anxious to leave anyway? You have to run home and fuck that thug? Why are you lowering yourself with a guy like that?"

"I'm leaving."

When she attempted to walk around him, he made a fist and punched her in the jaw.

Angela stumbled and screamed out in pain. She made a dash for the telephone receiver, but Cornell snatched it from her and grabbed her by the neck with both hands.

"You bitch!" he yelled, as his fingers clamped around her neck. "You will not disrespect me!"

Angela tugged at his wrists and tried to scream, but no words came out. The harder she tried to pry his hands loose, the tighter he squeezed. She spotted the wood carving on the corner of the desk and scooped it up. She swung wildly, aiming for Cornell's head, but the sculpture slipped from her hand.

Fearing that she was about to die, she reached down, grabbed a handful of Cornell's crotch and squeezed as hard as she could.

Cornell yelped in pain and immediately released her neck, but Angela wasn't ready to let go. He doubled over and tried to speak, but the hold she had on his groin had effectively severed his vocal chords.

Angela finally released him and dashed for the door.

"You bitch!" he finally sputtered.

Angela reached the door just as it opened.

"What's going on in here?" It was one of the maintenance men, who had come to empty the trash. "Ma'am, are you okay?"

Angela touched her numb face, her body still trembling.

"Ma'am, did he hurt you? Is everything okay?"

Cornell quickly composed himself and smiled at the man, an older African-American. "Everything is just fine," Cornell said. "We just had a little lovers' quarrel. I'm Judge Cornell Waters. This is my fiancé." He pointed across the room. "There's a picture of us right there on her desk."

The man glanced at the photograph, then turned to Angela for confirmation. He gently gripped Angela's shoulder. "Are you okay, ma'am? Did he hurt you?"

Angela could not stop shaking. She stared into Cornell's cruel eyes. "No," she said. "I'm . . . I'm fine."

"I guess I'll be leaving, then," Cornell said, smiling at her. "I'll call you later tonight."

He walked out and the maintenance man started to leave as well.

"No, please wait!" Angela called after him. "Can you walk me downstairs?"

CHAPTER 53

The report that Becker had received about Angela Evans and Zack Hargrove pissed him off. Contrary to his directive, Operation Buying Time was still up and running—just off the clock. That news had necessitated an immediate return trip to the U.S. Attorney's Office in L.A.

That the two AUSAs were continuing to investigate Waverly Sloan was no real surprise. They were convinced that the death of their friend and case agent was no accident and they wanted someone to pay. Normally, Becker respected people who had principles and stood by them. These days, he didn't come across many people who were willing to risk their careers for something they believed in. If this had been a different case, their actions would have been admirable.

They had yet to uncover any information of significance. But the fact that they were still prying around and asking about Erickson was reason for concern. His contact at the D.A.'s Office reported that Angela Evans had been calling around trying to find out if an autopsy would be performed on Claire Erickson. Zack Hargrove had even tried to interview Claire's sister, Sophia. Thankfully, she had refused to speak to him. Not surprisingly, Ashley had met with both of them.

He glanced at his watch. Zack Hargrove was set to join him in the conference room at the Spring Street courthouse in another ten minutes. Becker was about to put a well-orchestrated plan into action. Divide and conquer was one of the most important rules of war. If you kept your enemies busy fighting each other, they wouldn't have the time or energy to focus on fighting you.

When Zack walked in, he displayed the outward appearance of a cool, collected young man. But Becker detected a jittery edge underneath his designer suit.

"This may come as a surprise to you, but I've been making some calls," Becker began. "Some calls about you." In situations like this, it was a mistake to waste time beating around the bush. It was best to go straight for the jugular. *Neutralize your attacker on the first stroke.* He'd learned that as a Navy SEAL.

Zack shifted in his seat.

"And the reports I got back contained words like relentless, bright, tenacious. Those are all the kinds of things you want in a prosecutor." He paused, noticing that Zack had immediately warmed to the praise. "But you also want someone who knows how to follow orders."

Becker watched as Zack laced his fingers. No doubt to hide his nervousness.

"From what I can tell, you fit all of those qualifications as well. That's why Erickson and I want you to join us in Washington. We want you on our team at the Justice Department."

It seemed to take a few seconds for his words to register.

"The job we have in mind is media liaison," Becker continued. "You'd be the Attorney General's primary contact with the media. The current person in that position isn't an attorney. I think that's a mistake. The Bancroft administration plans to take a strong stance on several controversial matters. I want someone who understands the law acting as our spokesperson. The job is going to take you out of the courtroom, but someone with your talent can hop back in whenever you choose with no problem. So how about it?"

Becker already knew the guy's answer. He'd heard that Zack was dying to be a talking head. This job was the perfect stepping stone.

"I'm really flattered," Zack finally uttered.

"Does that mean you're accepting the job?" Becker wanted to keep the pressure on. "You're my top candidate. As you know, the Department is still trying to regroup from the Harris scandal. I can't give you any time to mull it over. If you want the job, I need to know right now. And by the way, there's a significant increase in pay."

Zack flashed a camera-ready smile. "Of course I want it."

Becker stood up, walked around the conference table and extended his hand. "Welcome to the team."

He placed an arm around Zack's shoulders and escorted him to the elevator. "You're going to love it in Washington. It's an exciting city. Much more intellectual than L.A. Is there somebody special in your life?"

"No," Zack said, still tongue-tied.

"Well, you'll have your pick of nice young women in Washington."

As he watched the elevator doors close, a smile crept across Becker's face. "One down, one to go."

Zack Hargrove was an easy fix. Angela Evans would be a much more difficult case. Based on the reports he'd received, she was hardworking, ethical and damn sharp. She wouldn't be so quick to sell out.

If Becker couldn't get her off Erickson's trail the easy way, he'd just have to play hardball.

CHAPTER 54

Two days after the threatening call from Lawrence Erickson's henchman, Waverly decided that he couldn't just sit back and wait for his situation to resolve itself. He needed a plan.

Appealing to Vincent certainly hadn't done him any good. Vincent had seemed more concerned about making sure he wasn't dragged into Waverly's mess than offering any solutions.

Following the release of the *L.A. Times* story, Waverly had been ignoring the calls from Live Now. He finally decided that it was time to face them.

"Have a seat," said a stone-faced Cartwright, when Waverly walked into the spacious suite at the downtown Hilton Hotel. Since they didn't maintain an office in L.A., their meetings were always held in hotels.

"Coffee?" Cartwright asked tightly.

Waverly eyed the mini-bar. Actually, he wanted a drink. "Sure," he said, then walked over to a counter and poured himself a cup. "Is Bellamy joining us?"

Just then, Bellamy, entered the room toting two files under his right arm. The CEO's expression was even more grim than Cartwright's.

"We got a call from a federal prosecutor by the name of Angela Evans," Cartwright began, once they were seated. "It seems the U.S. Attorney's Office is investigating you, which means they're investigating us. And that's not something we're happy about. You need to tell us exactly what's going on."

"They seem to think that some of my clients," Waverly paused, "our clients, expired sooner than they should have. Which is crazy. Those folks were terminally ill. They were supposed to die."

"Are you saying this is some kind of witch hunt on the part of the U.S. Attorney's Office and there's nothing to it?"

"Precisely," Waverly replied. He wondered how much they knew. Vincent had agreed not to share any information with them about Rico, but Waverly didn't expect him to keep his word.

Bellamy slid a folder with Billington's name on it across the table. "This is one of the insureds that prosecutor asked us about. What's his story?"

"He died in a car accident."'

"Then why do they think you're responsible?" Bellamy asked.

"I have no idea."

Cartwright seemed anxious to resume control of the interrogation. "I understand you also put this company at risk by laundering drug money," he charged.

Damn that Vincent. "You've apparently talked to Vincent, so you know why I did what I did. I was placed in a situation where I had no other choice."

"Just how do you plan to fix this?" Bellamy asked.

"I need a little time to work some things out."

"We're not going to let your greed take this company down," Cartwright shouted. "We had nothing to do with any of this and that's exactly what we told the authorities."

"Calm down," Bellamy said to his partner. He turned back to Waverly. "I don't know what's going on and I don't really care, but you better fix it. And fast. If you need to cut yourself a deal, then do that. Just make sure this company doesn't get snared in your trap."

Waverly stood up. "I'll come up with something," he said, more to himself.

"There's probably no need to even say this," Cartwright added before Waverly reached the door, "but you no longer work for this company."

Waverly headed back to his car and had just put the key in the ignition when his BlackBerry chirped. He pulled it from his pocket, glanced at the display and saw that it was a blocked call. Rico.

He was about to ignore it, but was suddenly feeling bold, so he answered the call. "Hey, amigo."

"Where you been?" Rico's hostility seeped through the phone lines.

"Last minute vacation."

"That was a nice article in *The Times*."

"Glad you liked it."

"Looks like you're in quite a bit of trouble."

"Tell me something I don't know."

"Well, I'm calling to find out about my money," Rico said. "When do I get my three hundred grand?"

"It's going to take a little longer than I thought."

There was a long gap of silence. "And why is that?"

"The feds have instructed the insurance company not to pay out on the policy until the investigation into Billington's death is finished."

"And exactly what are the feds investigating?"

"I don't know. I was hoping you could tell me."

"Okay, then give me back the money I gave that guy, including the cut you got."

Waverly hung his head. "Billington cashed that check before he died. There's no way to get the money back."

"Then it looks like you're going to have to give me my money out of your own pocket."

"I wish I could," Waverly said, actually meaning it. If he could give Rico back every dime, he would. "They froze all my accounts. I don't have three hundred grand at my disposal."

"That's not my problem," Rico said. "I'm not in the business of charity work."

"Like I said, until this investigation—"

"No," Rico shouted. "It ain't like you said. It's like *I* say. You get me my money. I'm giving you one week. Otherwise, you or your brother or your wife, or maybe all three of you, will pay the price. And that's a promise."

Waverly held the BlackBerry to his ear for several more seconds before finally hanging up.

For some reason, he didn't feel the fear that Rico's threat was intended to generate. He was in so deep that he almost welcomed a threat against his life to put him out of his misery.

He pulled out of the parking stall and headed for the closest bar.

When life got rough, getting blasted always seemed like a great idea.

CHAPTER 55

Angela zoomed down the Harbor Freeway, intermittently sucking in long, deep gulps of air in an effort to calm herself. Her hands clenched the steering wheel so tightly, she finally had to let go so blood could start circulating again.

Her angst receded when she finally spotted her apartment building. As she drove into the underground garage, the angst returned. What if Cornell had followed her home? She pulled her Saab into her parking stall, but could not bring herself to turn off the engine. She double-checked the door locks, then surveyed the area. She didn't see anything suspicious, but was still too afraid to get out.

She put the car in reverse and drove to her sister's apartment in nearby Fox Hills.

When Jada opened the door, Angela crumpled into her arms.

"Oh, my God!" Jada screamed. "Why is your face swollen? What happened?"

"Cornell came to my office. He punched me in the face and tried to strangle me, but this maintenance guy—"

Before Angela could say more, the doorbell rang.

"That's probably Dre," Angela sniffed. "I asked him to meet me here."

Jada led Angela over to the couch, then went to the door. "You must be Dre," she said, giving him a once over. "I've been dying to meet the brother bad enough to steal my sister away from Cornell, but not under these circumstances."

Dre stepped inside. "Is Angela okay?"

Jada glanced over her shoulder in Angela's direction. "No, she's not."

Dre hurried over, but stopped when he was only inches away. He stared down at her bruised and bloated face, then pulled her into his arms.

"Dude put his hands on you?" There was disbelief in his voice.

Angela nodded and gripped him tighter.

"You need to call the police on his ass," Jada said. "Don't let him get away with it this time."

"*This time?*" Dre glanced at Jada, then turned back to Angela. "Dude put his hands on you before?"

"Yep." Jada handed Angela an ice pack. "The night she told him she was calling off the engagement."

"Why didn't you tell me?" Anger flooded Dre's face.

"Because this is *my* problem and I want to handle it *my* way."

"You call this handlin' it?" Dre was practically shouting.

Angela pulled away from him, sat back down on the couch and pressed the ice pack to her face. "Cornell is a judge. If I report him, his career will be over."

Jada threw up her hands. "That asshole tried to strangle you and you're concerned about his career? I'm calling the police right now."

"Screw the police," Dre said. "I'll handle it."

"No!" Angela said insistently. "I know you're both concerned about me, but let me try it my way first. I'm going to call Cornell's best friend. He'll talk to him. If that doesn't work, then I'll go to the police."

"Come here." Jada grabbed Angela's hand, pulled her up from the couch and led her down the hallway to the bathroom. She flipped on the light and positioned Angela in front of the mirror. "Take a look at your face."

Angela gasped. The severity of her bruises shocked her. The left side of her face was twice its normal size. A purple patch had already formed underneath her eye. She had several red welts on her neck. Dre stood in the doorway, steaming. Her eyes met his in the mirror. He was obviously upset that she hadn't confided in him.

Jada turned her around and hugged her. "Have you forgotten about all those domestic violence cases you handled when you were a D.A.? *If a man hits you once, he'll hit you again.* How many times did you tell me that?"

Angela brushed past both of them and went back to the living room.

"I have something I want to give you," Jada said. "I'll be right back." She dashed out of the apartment.

When Jada returned minutes later, she placed a small black pouch on the coffee table.

Angela stared at it. "What's that?"

"A Smith & Wesson thirty-eight," Jada said rather calmly. "If you're not going to report Cornell or even get a restraining order, you at least have to protect yourself."

"A gun! Are you nuts? When did you even get a gun?"

"I've had it for years. I keep it under the seat in my car. I take it with me into the shop every morning and I put it back every evening. Too many beauty shops in L.A. have gotten robbed. I'm not about to be a victim. And before you ask, yes, it's registered and I also took classes at the shooting range so I know how to use it. And I didn't tell you or Mama because I didn't want to hear any flack."

"Get that thing away from me," Angela cried. "If Cornell bothers me again, I promise I'll get a restraining order."

"Screw that," Dre said. "You need a gun *and* a restraining order."

Jada sat down next to Angela and took her hand. "Dre is right. How many women have you seen on the news who died holding restraining orders in their hands? A piece of paper won't stop a crazy man."

Angela defiantly shook her head. "No! I'm not going to—"

"You're a prosecutor," Jada said, cutting her off. "You could probably get permission to carry a concealed weapon."

"Not without explaining why I wanted it."

Dre reached down and squeezed Angela's shoulder. "I really think you should take the gun. Dude came at you twice already. No tellin' what he's going to do next."

Angela stared up at Dre, then turned to her sister. "It's not that simple! I can't just walk into court and walk out with a restraining order. Cornell will definitely fight it, which means he'll make counter accusations and create a whole lot of drama. I'd rather not escalate it to that level if I can help it. And it's not just a matter of Cornell being charged and kicked off the bench. The media will pick up the story because it involves a superior court judge and a federal prosecutor. I'd prefer not to have the particulars of my failed relationship highlighted on the local news. Just let me handle this my way. Cornell isn't himself right now. He just needs some time for the breakup to sink in."

"Well, it better sink in fast," Jada said. "Because if he brings his behind over here, he's gonna get a bullet in his ass."

"I want you to stay with me until this blows over," Dre said.

"No, I'm going to stay here. If Cornell thought I was living with you, that would really set him off."

This time Dre went off. "I don't give a shit about settin' him off! You can't let that dude run your life!"

Angela closed her eyes and pressed her palm to her forehead. "You guys have to let me do this my way. If Cornell's friend can't get him to back off, I promise I'll go to the police. But I'm not taking that gun."

CHAPTER 56

Becker raised his champagne glass high in the air. "Let me be the first to officially congratulate our esteemed chairman, Lawrence Adolphus Erickson, and wish him well. Give 'em hell in Washington, big guy!"

The conference room on the twenty-fifth floor of Jankowski, Parkins broke into loud applause. The belated going away party had been Becker's idea. The place was packed with lawyers, law firm clients and a few local politicians. Everybody in the room was now anxious to rub shoulders with a man who was on a first-name basis with the President of the United States.

Becker stepped aside so Erickson could take center stage. "Alright, alright," he said, gripping the microphone. "This is not a permanent good-bye. President Bancroft has just over three years left in his second term. So I'm only taking a short leave of absence. And mark my words, if I don't get my corner office back, I'm suing everybody in here."

The room vibrated with laughter.

"What my colleague here neglected to mention," Erickson continued, "is that I corralled him to come along with me. I'm really a novice in the world of politics so, thank God, I'll have Roland Becker watching my back. This is the most loyal guy I know. And the most ruthless. That's precisely the combination I'll need in Washington."

Erickson threw an arm around Becker's shoulders, which set off another long round of applause.

After Erickson thanked practically everyone in the firm, Becker found his way to the back of the room. He still had misgivings about the move to D.C. He wanted to run the firm, not be second-in-command at the Justice Department in a lame duck administration. But Erickson was right. When he returned from D.C., he'd be in an even better position to take over the firm because of his political connections.

Becker watched the long line of people waiting to personally congratulate Erickson. Since their arrival in Washington, it was much the same. All the attention was focused on Erickson. Being Deputy AG was almost like being an associate again. He was too old to be holding someone else's briefcase. But he had already accepted the job, so there was no backing out now.

"Why the sad face?" Tom Franklin, one of his law partners, sidled up beside him and slapped him on the back. "You having regrets about leaving us?"

Becker grinned. "Not at all. I'm pretty excited about the venture," he said, always willing to put on the right face.

"Man, who are you kidding?" Franklin raised his wineglass to his lips. "You aren't going to see any real action. Erickson's going to be front and center and you're going to be stuck in the background doing his paperwork. I couldn't believe you took the job. I heard you'll barely be making two hundred grand. I wish I had friends as loyal as you."

Becker didn't respond because he wasn't quite sure what to say. He mustered up a stiff smile and walked out of the room. He had just opened the door to the men's room when he heard words that stopped him in his tracks.

"Becker has no idea that Erickson is royally screwing him over." Becker knew the speaker's voice well. It was Max Ito, a senior associate who regularly worked on Becker's cases. "I heard that when the Management Committee met to discuss Erickson's successor, they wanted Becker, but Erickson told 'em he needed him in Washington."

"That's really messed up," the second man said. Becker did not recognize his voice. "Erickson acts like he can't take a piss without having Becker around to unzip his pants."

"Erickson actually told 'em to take Becker's name off the list," Ito continued. "Said he didn't have what it takes. Becker's spent the last twenty years kissing Erickson's ass. You'd think he'd support him. Can you believe that shit?"

The second man chuckled. "I can believe it. The moral of *that* story is, don't trust anybody around here with your career because everybody is out for themselves."

Becker took a step back, allowing the door to quietly close. He wobbled down the corridor, blinded by rage. He couldn't believe Erickson would betray him. Not after everything he'd risked for him.

Becker looked up to see the slightly intoxicated Attorney General approaching from the opposite end of the floor.

"Ready for a fun ride, old buddy?" Erickson asked, clutching him in a fatherly embrace. "We're going to make a great team in Washington."

Anger swirled deep in Becker's gut, but somehow he managed to summon up a phony smile. Erickson hugged him so close that Becker could almost taste the scotch on his breath.

"Yeah," Becker said, finally pulling away, "we're going to be quite a team."

CHAPTER 57

Waverly finally made the decision to call his former attorney. Maybe Mancuso could use her contacts to find out exactly what might be in store for him. Did the two prosecutors have any real evidence that his clients had been murdered or were they just trying to scare him?

Waverly arrived at Mancuso's swank office an hour after making the call. She sat there, statue-like in her pink sweater as Waverly recounted the details of what had led him into the viatical business. He even disclosed his forced business arrangement with Rico and Goldman Investments and the money laundering that followed. He left out the part about the bribe that got him his viatical license.

Mancuso actually whistled when he was done. "This sounds like something out of a movie."

"Well, maybe when this is all over you can negotiate the movie deal for me. Right now I need more than just legal advice. You have a reputation for having behind-the-scenes connections. I need you to use your resources to find out what's going on."

Mancuso was a rich lawyer precisely because she was a smart lawyer. Her first question was the most obvious one. "You were disbarred. How'd you get a viatical license?"

Waverly looked down at his hands and fingered his wedding ring. "We paid a bribe to somebody at the Department of Insurance."

Mancuso raised her eyes toward the ceiling. He thought she was about to start lecturing him and, if she did, he planned to get up and walk out.

"I'll see what I can find out," she said after a long silence. "But I'm not sure I can be of much help. You don't have anything to bargain with. Any deal I might be able to make would require you to lead the police to this Rico character, but you've never even met the guy."

Waverly began to wonder if reaching out to her had been a mistake. He didn't need someone to tell him he was screwed. He already knew that. At least this conversation, unlike the ones with Vincent and the Live Now executives, was protected by the attorney-client privilege.

"If I were you," Mancuso said, "I'd put a kibosh on brokering any more deals. The feds are probably watching you."

Tell me something I don't know.

"I'll make some calls," Mancuso said halfheartedly. "See what I can find out."

"Thanks." Waverly stood up.

"I'll need a retainer," she said.

Waverly sighed. "How much?"

"I'll cut you some slack since you're in a pinch. Thirty thousand should cover things for the time being."

That's what you call slack? Waverly pulled out his checkbook, wrote in the amount and handed it to her. Too bad it was going to bounce.

He drove home to his big empty house and headed straight for the liquor cabinet. Out of brandy, he turned to vodka. In no time, he'd fallen asleep on the couch in the family room.

When he woke up early the next morning, he realized that the five-thousand dollar couch their interior designer had picked out was not intended for sleeping. His back felt like he'd been lugging around a slab of cement.

Waverly sat up and clicked on a lamp. When he tried to check the time on his watch, it took several seconds for his eyes to focus. It was much earlier than he'd expected. Just after four in the morning. He looked around for the vodka bottle. He found it underneath the couch. Empty.

After lying around for another hour or so, some internal force kicked in that told him this situation could not be handled like the rest his life. This time, he would have to be the one to make things right.

Despite what many people thought, for the most part, the legal system worked. Sure, there were those occasional *60 Minutes* stories about some innocent guy who served half his life in prison for a crime he didn't commit. But those cases were the exception. Prisons were packed with people because they were guilty and that was exactly where they needed to be.

Waverly wasn't guilty of anything except wanting to protect his family. He certainly had nothing to do with the deaths of Claire Erickson or Jerry Billington or anybody else. He would go to the police and tell them that. Justice would prevail. Why was he even worrying? So what if he laundered a little money. He did it under duress. He would tell the police everything he knew about Rico and cut a deal that would keep him out of prison.

Waverly hobbled over to his kitchen drawer, found a notepad and pen, then shuffled back to the couch. He would analyze his situation like the real lawyer that he used to be. Screw Mancuso and her thirty-thousand-dollar retainer.

He drew a line down the middle of the page and wrote *pro* at the top of one column and *con* at the top of the other.

He started his analysis with the prosecution angle. It was always best to know where your opponent was coming from. In the worst case scenario, what were his crimes? Money laundering was the one crime that Waverly couldn't deny. He would have duress as a defense which might buy him some sympathy with a jury. No, there would be no jury. He could not, would not, put his life in the hands of twelve incompetent strangers with their own agendas and motivations.

If he couldn't cut a deal, he'd waive his right to a jury and take his chances with a judge.

Maybe he could keep himself out of prison by turning state's evidence against Rico and whoever else was involved. The most serious crime he might face would be accessory to murder if Rico had indeed killed Jerry Billington or anyone else. Another investor had purchased Claire Erickson's policy, so those prosecutors would not be able to connect Rico to her murder. If she even *was* murdered. A competent prosecutor, however, could easily use circumstantial evidence to make it appear that Rico and Waverly had been working together.

Waverly stared at the notepad, then tossed it onto the coffee table. This was a useless exercise. He wished he had something to drink. He would wait to hear what Mancuso found out, provided she wasn't too pissed off about his check bouncing. He just hoped she could help him cut a deal. They always wanted the big fish, not the little guy.

But Waverly also knew that prosecutors liked making examples out of lawyers. A lawyer gone bad deserved exactly what he got. The *L.A. Times* article proved that. They would make him the poster child for corrupt attorneys.

Waverly closed his eyes and tried to think. The ringing of his BlackBerry startled him. He pressed ignore and it stopped ringing. He did not want to hear another threat from Rico. Whether he produced the money or not, he was probably next on Rico's hit list.

In the meantime, he had to protect his family. He would call Quincy and tell him to disappear until all of this was over. First he needed to let Deidra know that her life was also in danger.

When Waverly dialed her cell phone, she picked up in a half-slumber.

"Deidra?" The cowardice in his voice was embarrassing even to him. He should just demand that she come home. She had taken an oath to stick with him for better or worse, richer or poorer. She owed him loyalty more than anything else. He'd done all of this, mistakes and all, for her.

"Deidra, are you there?"

"What do you want?"

Waverly did not sense the same bitterness he'd felt when she walked out, which gave him hope. "You okay?"

"I'm fine."

"Deidra, I—"

"I don't want to talk to you and I'm not coming home. So don't ask."

"I'm not asking you to come home," Waverly said. "I'm calling to tell you that you're not safe. Your parents either."

Deidra started to whimper. "I'm not going into hiding because of something you did."

"Listen to me. This is serious. Whoever is killing my clients might come after you and your parents to get back at me. Do you understand me? You can't stay in town."

Waverly heard a soft cry of alarm.

"I want all of you, including Rachel, to take a long vacation. Just for a few weeks until I can figure something out."

CHAPTER 58

Angela called in sick for three days after Cornell assaulted her. It took that long for her bruises to fade enough to conceal them with foundation.

Her second day back at work, Cornell sent three dozen long-stemmed roses to her office. When Angela read his note, it only enraged her.

> *There's no excuse for my behavior. I guess I just lost it. I'm Sorry. If you can forgive me, I'll find a way to forgive your betrayal. Let's just put this all behind us. Call me.*
>
> *Yours, Cornell.*

All day long, her coworkers kept coming into her office, admiring the flowers and asking if she and Cornell were getting back together. Tired of the inquiries, Angela finally dumped the flowers in a trash bin outside the cafeteria. When her assistant asked about them, she lied and said she put them in her car.

On her way home, Angela stopped off at the Starbucks in the Ladera Center. She was walking out with a Caramel Frappuccino when she spotted Cornell standing outside on the patio.

She froze in place, causing a woman to collide into her from behind, splashing Angela with her drink.

"Sorry," Angela said. The woman angrily stepped around her.

Cornell smiled, then waved.

The sight of him angered her as much as it frightened her, but she was not going to live in fear. She continued on her way, carefully surveying the area as she walked. Several people were seated on the patio outdoors. Two security guards stood in front of the adjacent TGI Friday's.

Angela intended to march right past Cornell to her car. When he started heading toward her, her stomach knotted up so fast she thought she might throw up.

"How're you doing, Angela?" Cornell began walking alongside her. "You have a couple of minutes to talk?"

Angela kept moving, letting her conduct communicate her response. She nervously glanced around the parking lot, thankful for the crowded environment. She could see that Cornell was completely sober, but that knowledge offered little comfort.

"Did you get my flowers?"

"Yes," she replied, "and I threw 'em in the trash."

"If that's the way you feel, fine. I just wanted to apologize to you in person about the other night at your office."

Angela regretted having parked so far away. "Fine. Now leave me alone."

"Why are you in such a hurry? You have to go meet that—"

Angela finally turned to face him, animosity spewing from her eyes. "Get the hell away from me and stay out of my business!" She walked faster, but Cornell easily kept pace.

"Angela, what are you doing? Why would you choose to be with a guy like that?"

Now he was really pissing her off. She wanted to throw her drink in his face. She whipped around and pointed a finger at him. "I'm done putting up with your craziness. Our relationship is over. Who I see is none of your damn business. And if you don't leave me alone, you'll never see a seat on the federal bench because your ass will be in jail."

Cornell laughed. "I always liked it when you got feisty. It

usually took a while for you to get revved up, but when you did, watch out." He smiled. "Just answer one question for me. Why would you risk your career over that thug? Why would you choose to be with a convicted felon?"

His words felt as jolting as the punch he'd delivered to her face. "What? What are you talking about?"

"I'm talking about your new boyfriend, Andre Lynell Thomas. The drug dealer."

A burst of heat stung her cheeks. "You're a liar!"

"Wait a minute . . ." Cornell's face lit up and he took a step backward. "You didn't know? You really didn't know that your new boyfriend is a drug dealer?"

Angela wanted to keep walking, but her feet refused to cooperate.

"When you get to work tomorrow, go look up his court file. Possession of a kilo of cocaine with intent to distribute. He was sentenced to two years, but managed to walk out in eight months thanks to prison overcrowding. Your ghetto boyfriend is in the drug trade."

Cornell had definitely lost his mind. How did he even know Dre's name? He had to be making this up. She continued toward her car, fighting the urge to run.

"I ran his plates," he called after her. "I'm surprised you didn't. Guess he didn't bother to tell you, huh?"

Angela finally reached her car and snatched open the door. "And how did you even know what kind of car he drives? Have you been following me?"

"No, not really. I happened to drive by your place one day and saw the two of you getting out of his car. A Volkswagen? C'mon, Angela. If you don't want to be with me, fine. But you can really do a lot better than a guy like that."

Cornell was still talking, but Angela had stopped listening. She climbed into her Saab and started it up. It took every ounce of willpower she could muster not to run his ass down.

When he was out of sight, she rolled down the window, desperate for air. *You really didn't know that your new boyfriend is a drug dealer?* Cornell was lying. He had to be.

Her BlackBerry rang. It was Dre. "I'm running late," he said. "I'll be over at seven-thirty instead of seven."

Angela willed her voice to sound normal. "Okay," was all she could manage. When she confronted Dre with Cornell's allegation, she wanted to be able to look him in the eye.

She was pulling into the underground garage of her apartment building when she remembered something that seemed to back up Cornell's claim.

The night they had met for drinks at The Dynasty, Dre seemed panic-stricken when his son's mother walked up to their table. Shawntay's words floated back to her. *Do Ms. Prim and Proper know what you do?*

A burning sensation swelled in her chest. *Have I really been that stupid?*

When Dre arrived an hour later and attempted to pull her into his arms, Angela backed away, out of his reach.

"I ran into Cornell today at Starbucks and—"

"If he messed with you again, I swear I'll kick his ass."

"No," Angela said. "He had some things to tell me. About you. Things I've been praying aren't true."

Dre did not flinch or otherwise alter the blank expression on his face. He also didn't utter a sound.

An innocent person, a person with nothing to hide would immediately have some questions of his own. *What are you talking about? What did he say?* But there were no questions from Dre. Only silence. She knew from personal experience that only the best criminals were that cool under fire.

"He said that you're a drug dealer. A convicted drug dealer."

Again, Dre did not open his mouth.

"Is that true?"

"Is he still followin' you?"

"I'd appreciate it if you would answer my question."

"If you're askin' me if I'm currently a drug dealer, the answer is no."

Angela folded her arms across her chest. "*Currently?* And if I asked if you were *previously* a drug dealer, would the answer be different?"

Dre's eyes bore deeply into hers and his jaw line tightened. "Yeah. It would."

Angela covered her mouth. "Oh, my God!"

He reached out for her, but she jerked away.

"I'm not proud of what I used to do," Dre said. "But it's not something I do anymore."

Angela did not want to hear his explanation. She wanted him to get out. But she could not find the words to tell him that through the shock.

"I'm sorry you had to find out from him. I should have told you myself."

Angela had a million questions, but they were all jumbled up inside her head. "So the real estate stuff was a lie?"

"No. I do flip foreclosures."

"How? You can't get a real estate license if you're a convicted felon."

"I never said I had one. You just assumed that. I have a buddy who does my deals for me."

"What about the college stuff? Was that a lie, too?"

"No, I really do have a degree from Long Beach State. I never lied to you, Angela. About anything."

"In my line of work, an omission can be just as misleading as a straight-out lie."

Dre could not meet her eyes.

"Do you understand what I do for a living? I'm not just a lawyer, I'm a federal prosecutor. I can't be dating a drug dealer."

"I just told you. I don't deal anymore."

"You're a bright guy, Dre. Of all the things you could possibly do, why in the world would you choose to deal drugs?"

"It's not that simple."

"Well, make it simple!" she screamed. "Tell me why some-body as smart as you are would choose to sell drugs? Did you sell drugs to kids, too?"

Dre shoved his hands into his pockets. "Maybe we should talk about this another time. When you're a little calmer. Why don't I just leave?"

Angela glared at him. "Yeah, why don't you?"

CHAPTER 59

B ecker had just returned home after two days of nonstop meetings in Washington. He was in the family room helping the twins with their math homework when his cell phone rang.

He glanced at the display. It was a call he'd been anxiously awaiting.

"Lia, how are you?"

Lia Green was Roland Becker's most reliable source for confidential information coming out of the Los Angeles District Attorney's Office. Becker had never practiced criminal law, but his corporate clients often needed his assistance with criminal matters. A teenage son picked up for drunk driving. A wife with an unexplainable penchant for shoplifting. A domestic violence allegation that needed to be quietly erased from the books. Often the best deals were cut long before the charges were ever filed.

Thanks to Lia, Becker was always able to place the right calls and negotiate the right deals.

"You wanted a heads up on any significant developments regarding Claire Erickson's death," she said. "Well, here goes."

"I'm listening," Becker said.

"Cancer didn't kill her."

Natalie had just written down a wrong answer and Natasha was trying to tell her she'd made a mistake. Becker wasn't sure he'd heard Lia correctly over the twins' bickering. "What did you say?"

"You heard me right," Lia said.

"Okay," Becker said slowly. "But if she didn't die from cancer, then what killed her?"

"She was drugged. The autopsy stated that she died of acute morphine intoxication."

Becker could not get his arms around this news. "Are you sure?"

"I saw the autopsy report with my own eyes. It was injected through a vein in her arm."

Becker didn't know what to say. He had assumed Ashley's allegations against Erickson were false. But now . . .

"This isn't going to be good news for your boss," Lia said. "Not with all the noise his stepdaughter's been making. This actually gives her claims some credibility."

"You've heard about Ashley's allegations?"

"Sure. Everybody around here has been hands off, thinking she was a little loopy. But now a lot of folks are salivating to get their hands on the case. It's not going to be pretty."

"Dad, can you tell Natasha that's wrong?" Natalie was tugging on his shirt.

"Not now," Becker said.

"But, Dad, I told her—"

"I said not now!"

Natalie's blue eyes expanded and Becker instantly regretted his outburst. He held the phone to his chest and gently caressed his daughter's shoulder. "Daddy has a problem at work. Just give me a minute."

Becker walked out to the patio, which overlooked the hills of South Pasadena, to continue the call. "I have to tell you, I'm in shock."

"I can tell that through the phone," Lia said.

"I know Lawrence Erickson better than anybody. He did not murder his wife."

"Well, somebody did because the amount of morphine in Claire Erickson's system was no accidental overdose."

Becker gathered a few more facts, then hung up. He sat quietly on the patio, his elbows on his knees, his chin resting on his fists. There was a light breeze that made it a perfect Southern California evening. He could hear the rustling of some animal in the distance.

He did not plan to relay this information to Erickson right away. That Claire had been drugged did not make sense. Maybe the two AUSAs were on to something and Waverly Sloan *was* killing his clients. But from everything Becker had learned about the guy, he didn't seem bright enough or shrewd enough to be part of such a scheme.

From the beginning, Erickson had been overly worried about the slow progress of their plan. *Had he grown impatient and killed Claire himself?* No. Erickson would not have done so without consulting with him first. Not with everything he had put on the line for him. But then again . . .

During their meeting in Becker's office after Erickson learned that his nomination was a go, Erickson had made some pretty confusing statements. It was almost as if Erickson had been under the impression that *Becker* had killed Claire. But she died before he could act. Becker had assumed, from natural causes. That was why he had told Erickson that they'd gotten lucky.

Becker wouldn't have been stupid enough to kill Claire with a traceable drug like morphine. As a Navy SEAL, he'd learned multiple techniques for cutting off the air supply with little chance of the true cause of death being picked up during an autopsy.

After dropping by Erickson's home with the girls that day, Becker had peeked in on Claire to say hello, but found her sleeping. Or was she already dead then? Erickson had been home alone with Claire that afternoon, which meant he'd had sufficient time to drug her. He had both opportunity and motive.

As Becker tried to erase the possibility from his mind, the conversation he'd overheard in the men's room rushed back to him. After learning that Erickson had not supported him for chairmanship of the firm, Becker was carefully and patiently plotting his revenge.

His friend and mentor had already double-crossed him once.

Had he actually done it twice?

CHAPTER 60

I'm going to tell you like it is," Mancuso said. "You're in quite a bit of trouble."

Waverly had scheduled another meeting to hear what Mancuso had learned from her inside connections. They were seated in a private room at the City Club where Mancuso was a member.

"The police think you're killing your clients," she said.

"I already know that," Waverly said irritably. "Do they have any evidence to support their claim?"

Mancuso squinted suspiciously. "I thought you said there wasn't any?"

"There isn't. But don't act like you haven't seen innocent people get railroaded. What do they have?"

"Nothing solid," Mancuso replied. "But the large number of your clients who kicked the bucket accidentally won't look like a coincidence to a jury."

"I want to make a deal," Waverly said.

"What do you have to deal with?"

"I could turn over the guy I think may be responsible."

Mancuso folded her arms. "You told me you don't even know who he is."

"I don't. I'll just have to figure something out. Maybe we can set up some kind of undercover sting or something. I can wear a wire."

"It's not that simple," Mancuso said, toying with her pink bracelet.

"What do you mean?"

"The D.A.'s Office won't put money into that kind of effort until you spill your guts. And that's not something I'd recommend that you do."

"Why not?"

"Because there are too many uncertainties. You could be left holding the bag."

"You're the dealmaker. Get me a deal."

"It doesn't happen with a snap of the fingers. And it definitely doesn't happen when my clients write me bad checks."

"I'll make good on it. I didn't know that the U.S. Attorney's Office had frozen my accounts when I was in your office the other day," he lied.

The skeptical look on Mancuso's face said she didn't believe him. "I want you to write down everything you can remember. Then we'll go over it and figure out our next steps."

"You have to get me a deal," Waverly pleaded. "I can't do time."

Mancuso tapped her pink pen on the table. "I'll see what I can do. In the interim, you need to figure out what you're going to use for collateral."

"Excuse me?"

"I don't work for free. I'm sure you can come up with something."

Waverly wanted to laugh. "Okay," he said, standing, "we'll figure it out at our next meeting." Since he had to conserve his limited funds, there wouldn't be another meeting.

He was a few miles from home when a frightening thought hit him. *Britney!* If somebody was actually killing his clients, then Britney was in danger. He pulled over and started fumbling through the papers in his briefcase until he found her telephone number. He had to warn her.

Waverly dialed her number, but her voicemail came on.

"This is Waverly. Waverly Sloan, I need to talk to you right away. Call me back as soon as you can. Please."

Waverly sounded much too panicked. If she had read that *L.A. Times* article, she'd be too afraid to call him back. He would never be able to forgive himself if something happened to her. He should at least go by her place to check on her.

He tried Britney's number again and this time, she picked up.

"I was calling to check on you," Waverly said, relieved to hear her voice.

"I read that newspaper story about you killing your clients!" Britney shouted into the telephone. "Stay away from me. If you come anywhere near me, I'm calling the police!"

CHAPTER 61

D re had not heard from Angela for two days. He was so concerned about Cornell coming after her again, that he had begun following her to make sure that he didn't.

He borrowed a buddy's 4Runner so she wouldn't spot him. He trailed her to work and back, and even followed Cornell for a few days. Maybe the dude had finally gotten the message.

Dre had tried to reach out to her, but his phone call and text message both went unanswered. Hell, he'd faced tougher situations than this before. Angela just needed some time to think things through. To realize that he was no longer the man he used to be. He had decided to change his life, in large part, because of her. He was not about to give up on being with her.

But Dre could not make that happen if Angela wouldn't even talk to him. He purchased a throwaway cell phone figuring that she might pick up if she didn't recognize the number.

He dialed her office. When she answered, he didn't waste any time. "Hey, it's me."

She remained silent.

"We need to talk. You asked me why I did what I did and I owe you an explanation. How about if I drop by your place tonight?"

Angela still didn't say anything and he waited. He construed it as a positive sign that she hadn't hung up in his face.

"Not my apartment," Angela said finally. "I'll meet you at Baja Cantina. I'm working late. It'll be close to eight before I can get there."

"Okay," Dre said, then hung up.

It was now 8:21 and he figured she wasn't coming. He took another swig of beer and was about to leave when he saw Angela enter the restaurant. She looked pretty jazzy in a black, double-breasted pantsuit. He couldn't help smiling. No woman had ever taken hold of his heart like this before.

She walked up to him at the bar. "Thought I wasn't coming, huh?"

He decided not to respond. At least she was in a playful mood.

"Let's go get a table." Angela turned and walked off.

Dre chuckled to himself as he followed after her. Women were such a trip when they knew they had you by the balls.

Angela avoided making eye contact until they had placed their food orders.

"Okay," she said, her head tilted, her arms folded against her chest, "let's hear it. Why does a smart, articulate, college-educated guy like yourself decide to become a drug dealer?" She fixed her lips into a pout.

"It's a long story," Dre said.

"I have the time if you do."

"Is this how you do your thing in court? Just pin 'em against the wall and fire questions at 'em."

"Pretty much."

He wasn't sure where to begin. But he knew he couldn't feed her any bullshit. The truth was, he didn't really have a satisfactory explanation. At least not one that would be acceptable to her.

"You probably can't tell," Dre said, "but I've always been a little hardcore."

"Oh, so your life of crime was genetic. Is that what you're telling me?"

"Stop givin' me attitude and hear me out." He took a sip of beer. "For most of my life, I was pretty average. Average in sports, average in school. Except I did okay with the ladies."

Dre smiled. Angela didn't.

"I made it through Long Beach State, but just barely. I only had a C average, but I got my degree and I'm proud of that. When I finished up and started lookin' for work, it was a joke. I'd interview with all these stuffed shirts. Didn't matter whether they were black or white. I was way too hood for their environment. I didn't even know how to dress. Definitely didn't speak the language. So I ended up gettin' the only job a brother could get, working security."

Angela seemed to be listening and that encouraged him.

"I spent most of my days sittin' in a guard booth reading. One day, this dude from my old neighborhood came up to me. I knew he was cracked out. He asked to borrow ten dollars. Said if I loaned it to him, he'd pay me back twenty bucks on the first of the month when he got his disability check. I didn't think he would, but I loaned him the money anyway. But he paid me back right on time. I ended up loanin' him money three more times and he paid me back every time. I made one hundred percent profit on every dollar I loaned him."

"Oh, I see," Angela said, with a cynical punch to her voice. "So you were a loan shark before you became a drug dealer?"

"Yeah, basically, I was." He could tell that his admission surprised her. "He told other people and everybody started comin' to me for loans. Ninety-nine percent of the time, ninety-nine percent of the people paid me back. One hundred percent on the dollar."

"Okay, so you loaned money to a bunch of crack heads so they could get high until their government checks came in. Great."

"If I didn't loan them the money, they would've done something illegal to get it."

"You're good with your hands. Getting a job at Home Depot never crossed your mind?"

"When I applied for jobs like that they told me I was overqualified. Lookin' back on it, I had too much attitude. I was too angry. I didn't know how to interview or even how to dress. Nobody was goin' to hire me."

The waitress set their food on the table, but Angela pushed hers aside. "Go ahead. I'm curious about how you went from loan shark to drug dealer."

Dre decided to ignore the sarcasm. "One of my regular customers came to me one day, said he knew a guy he could buy drugs from. Said since I had dough, if I fronted the cash, he would sell it for me and take a small cut. That's basically how I got started. And it just blossomed from there."

Dre could not interpret the expression on her face. He suspected she wanted a more sympathetic story. Alcoholic parents, foster care, juvenile hall. But he had none of that. His sister was a social worker and his brother, a pretty successful plumber. His father had been in and out of the picture during his younger days, but his mother worked as a legal secretary and provided a stable home life. His family was under the impression that following his short stint behind bars, he had traded the drug business for flipping houses full time.

Angela picked up her fork and stabbed at her enchilada. "You said you don't do it anymore. Was that the truth?"

"Yep."

"When did you stop?"

"A while ago."

"What's a while ago?"

"A few weeks."

"*A few weeks?*" Angela laughed. "This is unbelievable. So why'd you quit?"

"'Cuz I met you." Once again, his response caught her off guard. He just hoped it earned him some brownie points. "It was never a life I planned to be in for the long haul. And now I'm out. Completely."

The waitress returned and refilled their water glasses. "Anything else you wanna know?"

"No," Angela said softly. "Not at the moment."

Dre was glad that she had finally run out of questions. He picked up his beef taco and took a bite. "Cornell hasn't been hasslin' you anymore, has he?"

Angela chuckled dryly. "No, but he's been telling everybody that he broke off the engagement. He told one of my friends that I cheated on him so he had to put me out."

"What a punk move. That brother has some serious issues."

"That's certainly what my sister thinks."

"And you don't?"

"Yeah, Cornell has his issues," she said, looking him dead in the eye, "but don't we all."

Dre stared back at her, wishing he could reach across the table and kiss her. "Yeah," he said, "I guess we do."

CHAPTER 62

Erickson gazed at the huge seal on the wall across from his desk. He still couldn't believe it. He was the Attorney General of the United States of America.

His office wasn't nearly as plush as his corner suite at Jankowski, Parkins and his salary, not even half of what he earned as chairman of the firm. But the degree of influence he wielded and the pride he felt sitting at the helm of the U.S. Justice Department could not be equaled by anything he'd ever achieved in either his personal or professional life to date.

He had just returned to his office following a meeting with five Democratic congressmen when his assistant rushed in with an urgent message from Wrigley, the President's Chief of Staff. Erickson was wanted at the White House. Immediately. A driver had already been called and was waiting downstairs.

Erickson's mind raced with possibilities as the sedan zoomed along Pennsylvania Avenue toward the White House. Erickson presumed that the President needed his sage legal advice on some confidential, high-security issue. That thought heightened the sense of power he felt.

Once he reached the White House, instead of going to the Oval Office, Erickson was escorted into Wrigley's office. The Chief of Staff was speaking into a headset. He pointed Erickson to a seating area near the window. Wrigley paced back and forth as he conducted his call. Erickson picked up snatches of the conversation. It did not appear to be anything urgent.

Erickson was disappointed that he hadn't been summoned for a meeting with the President. He had only spoken with Bancroft twice since taking the job and only for a matter of minutes. It was Mark Wrigley who really ran the show at the White House.

Wrigley finally took off his headset. He walked over and sat down on a couch across from Erickson.

"I've received three calls today about you from various sources of mine in Los Angeles. What in the hell is going on with your stepdaughter?"

Wrigley's words landed like a punch Erickson hadn't seen coming. "What do you mean?"

"Don't fucking play me!" Wrigley yelled. "Your stepdaughter is running all over town accusing you of murdering your wife. Don't sit there and act like you don't know anything about it."

Erickson was not used to people talking to him in such a manner. Other than his father, no one spoke to him that way. Ever.

"My stepdaughter is an emotionally troubled young woman," Erickson tried to explain. "She—"

"I don't care about her mental state or yours. I only care about the impact of her allegations on this administration. Do you know how incompetent we're going to look if we have to go out and find yet another Attorney General?"

"You won't have to do that," Erickson assured him. "And there won't be any fallout for the President because I had nothing to do with my wife's death. Claire died of cancer and Ashley is just having trouble dealing with the loss."

"Then lock her up someplace until she *can* deal with it. As it stands now, her conduct has the potential to create problems for this administration. I'm not going to let that happen. Do you understand?"

"I do," Erickson said.

"And the next time I have to hear something this serious about you from somebody else, I'm not going to be very happy about it. If there's something going on in your personal life that could cause embarrassment for the President, I need to know about before anybody else. You got that?"

"I understand," Erickson said.

Wrigley stood up. "Then fix this. Now!" Wrigley stalked back over to his desk.

Erickson waited until he was in the security of his office before calling Becker.

"We have a problem," he said. "The White House has gotten wind of Ashley's allegations. I just got chewed out by Wrigley."

Becker groaned in exasperation. "I'll try to talk to her, but you know how volatile she can be."

"I'm not going to lose this job because of her defamatory theatrics!" Erickson said. "I want her silenced."

"And exactly how am I supposed to do that?" Becker asked.

"I don't care how you do it, just get it done," he shouted. "I told you weeks ago that Ashley's allegations were going to be a problem, but you said they were no big deal because no one would listen to her. Well, you were wrong. They're certainly a big deal now. My career and my reputation are on the line."

"I'll handle it," Becker said.

"Make sure you do," Erickson said, and slammed down the phone.

CHAPTER 63

Waverly pounded the steering wheel in frustration.
He had to find a way to convince Britney that her life
could be in danger. He thought about proceeding to her place
anyway, but that would only freak her out. He drove toward
home, racking his mind for a solution.

He pressed the remote on his sun visor and pulled his Lexus
into the garage. He felt like going for a long drive, but was too
mentally exhausted for such an excursion. He wouldn't have such
an option much longer. With money tight, his Lexus would be the
first thing to go.

As he closed the garage door and entered the house through
the kitchen, something stopped him the moment he stepped inside.
Someone else was there. He could sense their presence. Smell their
scent. Had Rico or one of his henchmen come after him?

Waverly stepped back into the garage, his legs unsteady. What
should he do? Call the police? And say what? *The guy I was laundering money for came to my house to kill me.*

He looked around, scanning the garage shelves in search of a
weapon. He spotted a hammer hanging on a hook and grabbed it.

Waverly cautiously stuck his head back into the kitchen. "Get
out of my house!" he yelled. "I have a gun." Until now, he
thought guns were dangerous weapons that could do more harm
than good. Now he wished he had one.

He waited, listening for movement. He finally took several more steps inside, each one filled with trepidation. He looked to his left into the family room and his mouth fell open.

Someone had left a message for him in red spray paint on the wall above the couch.

Get me my money. Deidra is next.

Furious, Waverly tore through the rest of the house, hammer in hand, peeking into rooms, opening doors, checking around corners. When he was certain that the intruder had gone, he pulled out his BlackBerry and dialed Deidra's cell phone.

"You have to call me back right away," he said. "I need to know that you're alright."

He wondered if Deidra had heeded his warning to leave town. He would not be able to relax until he knew she was okay. He waited thirty long, nerve-racking minutes. As much as he hated having to face Leon Barrett, he couldn't rest not knowing whether his wife was safe. He went back to the garage and started up his car.

It was only a two-mile drive to his in-laws' home. He screeched into the driveway and jumped out.

Leon Barrett opened the front door before he could ring the bell. "You're not wanted here," he said.

"I don't plan to stay. Where's Deidra? Is she okay?"

"Son, you're a disgrace. You know that? People like you give the law profession a bad name. You—"

"I didn't come here for a lecture, Leon," Waverly said, trying to keep his cool. "Where's Deidra?"

"She's not here."

"Is she okay?"

"You should've been thinking about that when you decided to start ripping off dying people. You—"

"I just need to make sure Deidra's okay," Waverly said. "Where is she?"

"I don't think she wants you to know that."

"Did she leave town like I asked?"

Leon's eyebrows fused together. "You asked her to leave town? What kind of stuff are you mixed up in, boy?"

Waverly was glad that Deidra hadn't shared his request with her father and wished he hadn't either. He stepped forward until his chest almost touched Leon's nose. "Just tell me whether she went away, damn it!"

Leon backed away. "She's at Martha's Vineyard with her mother and sister. Went there a few days ago."

Waverly's heart rate finally slowed a few beats. He turned and headed back to his car.

"I don't want to see you around here again," Leon shouted after him.

Waverly tuned out Leon's words, climbed into his Lexus and backed out of the driveway.

He was still worried about Britney's safety. For all he knew, Rico could be someplace right now plotting to kill her or any one of his clients. Thankfully, he had not made a personal connection with any of his other clients. Did that mean he didn't have an ethical obligation to let them know that their lives might be in danger? No. He needed to call every single one of them, not just Britney, and tell them they might be a target for murder. But how would that look to a jury of his peers?

"Shit!" He pounded the steering wheel again.

Waverly could not sit back and let something happen to Britney. He would just have to convince her that she was in danger and help her find a safe place to hide. He would figure out what to do about his other clients later.

He pulled over to the curb and popped open his briefcase. He looked up Britney's address and punched it into his navigation system.

Waverly was determined to make sure Britney was safe. Whether she wanted his protection or not.

CHAPTER 64

Angela found it next to impossible to concentrate at work. She had just walked out of a meeting, but couldn't remember half of what had been discussed.

She plopped down behind her desk and massaged the back of her neck. Her life had gone from bliss to anguish in a matter of days. At least Cornell had finally stopped calling. She assumed the conversation she'd had with his best friend, Rupert Byrdsong, had worked.

"I need you to talk to Cornell," Angela had begun. "He's basically been stalking me."

Rupert didn't say anything for a while. "Is it true?" he finally asked. "Are you dating a convicted drug dealer?" A partner at Byrdsong, Ivy, McNeil and Wyatt, Rupert was a major mover and shaker in L.A. Just the kind of guy Cornell liked to rub shoulders with. Angela and Cornell had frequently doubled-dated with Rupert and his wife.

"Whoever I'm dating is nobody's business," Angela snapped. "I just need you to convey a message to him because he doesn't seem to hear it when I tell him. The only reason I haven't reported him to the police is because I don't want to destroy his career. But if he ever comes near me again, I will."

"Cornell is pretty broken up," Rupert said. "He's not himself. Apparently you aren't either."

"I'm just fine. If you care about your friend, you'll deliver my message."

Angela's assistant walked in and handed her a package. Angela knew what was inside without even opening it. She waited until the door closed before pulling out Dre's file from his state court case.

She rifled through it until she found his rap sheet. There was only one arrest and one conviction. *California Health and Safety Code Section 11351.5, possession or purchase for sale of cocaine base.* At least he wasn't a career criminal.

So far, everything Dre had told her was the truth. There was even mention of his degree from Long Beach State. Angela closed her eyes and pressed two fingers to both of her temples. She couldn't believe she was actually trying to justify what Dre did, or used to do, for a living. But she couldn't deny how much she missed him and wanted him in her life.

She rested her head on her desk, cushioning it in the crook of her arm. When she looked up, Zack was standing over her desk.

"You okay?"

Zack's eyes surveyed her desk. Angela quickly closed Dre's file and slipped it back into the envelope.

"I'm fine," she said, trying to sound cheerful. "What's up?"

Zack looked uncomfortable and she knew why. She'd heard that he was moving to D.C. and taking a job on Erickson's staff. He was selling out and she was going to tell him as much.

"I'll just blurt it out," Zack finally said. "You need to know that there are a lot of rumors floating around the office."

"Rumors about what?"

"About you and Cornell."

Angela held up her ringless left hand and waved it back and forth. "Yes, my engagement is off. If that's all people have to talk about, so be it."

"It's not just that. A maintenance guy told one of the secretaries that Cornell attacked you in your office last week."

Angela stiffened. The man had been nice enough to escort her all the way to her car. He had also promised not to mention the incident to anyone.

"That's not true," she lied. "We had a disagreement and we both got a little loud. That was it."

"I just thought you should know. And there's something else—"

"Zack, I don't want to discuss Cornell with you or anybody else. Okay?" The people in her office were nothing but gossips. The lawyers were worse than the secretaries.

He ran his fingers through his hair. "Okay, but I just wanted to tell you that—"

"I said I don't want to know, Zack." Angela stood up and picked up her purse from the desk. "I don't mean to be rude, but I was just about to leave."

Shortly after seven, Angela pulled into the underground garage of her building, turned off the engine and removed the key. Her car was in the shop for a tune-up so she was driving her sister's Mazda.

Angela was always careful now to survey her surroundings before exiting the car. She noticed a young woman headed for the stairwell. Angela had just opened the door and planted her left foot on the ground when Cornell seemed to appear from nowhere.

She screamed and tried to close the door, but Cornell lunged forward, snatching it open.

"I just want to talk." Cornell gripped the door with his left hand and extended the palm of his right toward her. "Just relax. I'm not going to hurt you. I promise."

"We don't have a damn thing to talk about. You need to get it into your head that our relationship is over." She tried to close the door, but Cornell had a firm grasp.

As she stared up at him, she felt like a fool for ever feeling sorry for him. Jada was right. She should have called the police the first time he put his hands on her. She had prosecuted enough domestic violence cases to know better. Men who battered women were fueled by jealousy and insecurity. They lacked the ability to think or act rationally. To hell with Cornell's career. As soon as she made it to her apartment, she planned to call the cops. Tomorrow morning, she would get a restraining order.

"I took care of you for three years. Don't you at least owe me a few minutes of your time?"

"You didn't take of care me. I took care of myself." Angela immediately regretted her retort. It wasn't smart to risk angering him further.

Leaning sideways, she felt around on the floor. She couldn't remember whether her sister had taken the gun when Angela dropped her off at the beauty shop that morning. She prayed it was there. When she felt the soft velvet and the hard lump underneath, a torrent of relief followed. She slipped the .38 out of its pouch and into the pocket of her jacket.

"If you don't leave, I'm calling the police," she threatened, although her BlackBerry was out of reach, buried in her purse.

"The police? Really? Maybe you should call your drug dealer boyfriend instead."

Her right hand clutched the .38. Angela had never fired a gun before, but she was more than ready to learn on the job. Maybe it was better to just keep him talking until another car entered the garage. She looked past him to where the woman had been, but saw no one. *Where in the hell is the security guard?*

"C'mon," Cornell said. "Let's go up to your place so we can talk." He pulled the door open even wider.

The man was truly delusional if he thought he was getting anywhere near her apartment. "I already told you. I don't want to talk to you. Now leave me alone!"

Angela tugged hard on the door and almost closed it, but

Cornell pulled it open again. She was just about to lean on the horn when Cornell's demeanor abruptly changed.

"Okay, okay, don't overreact. If you want me to leave, I will." He let go of the door and took a step back. "Go on up to your apartment. I won't bother you."

Angela wasn't buying it. She put the key back in the ignition, but when she tried to close the car door, Cornell charged forward, reached over the window, grabbed her arm and snatched her from the car.

He shut the door, then backhanded her across the face. Blood splattered from her nose, spotting Cornell's grey suit.

"You bitch! Who do you think you are?"

Pinning her arms at her side, he banged her body against the hood of the car. He reeked of alcohol.

"Maybe you like it better when I act like a thug." He leaned in and roughly kissed her.

Angela swung her head from side to side and tried to pull away. When she screamed, Cornell fastened his hand around her neck. He squeezed for several seconds, then let go.

"I could kill you right now if I wanted to," he said. "And if you scream again, I will."

As hard as she tried, the fearless facade she so desperately wanted to maintain shattered. Tears welled in her eyes and rolled down her cheeks. She tried to retrieve the gun from her pocket, but Cornell had her right arm locked at her side.

"Oh, so now you want to cry. I bet you weren't crying when you were out cheating on me." He let go of her arm and backhanded her across the face again. Another gush of blood spewed from her nose.

"Does that thug fuck you better than me?"

She turned away as the right side of her face went numb. Cornell pulled her toward him, then slammed her back against the car again.

Excruciating pain radiated down her back, but the crazed look in his eyes frightened her far more than the blows to her body. The look told her that she would not leave the garage alive.

"Answer me, bitch! Who fucks you the best?"

"You," Angela finally sputtered.

When Cornell reared back to slap her again, Angela slid her right hand into her pocket and pulled out the gun. In one quick move, she jammed it into his stomach.

"Get away from me or I'll blow your goddamn guts out!" Angela screamed.

Cornell staggered sideways, his bravado gone. It took him only seconds though, to regain it. "I thought you were afraid of guns." He was laughing now. "Is that a present from that ex-con you're fucking?"

Angela took baby steps to her left, trying to make it back inside the car. Her hand was wobbling so violently she feared she might drop the gun. She reached behind her back with her left hand to open the door. She was about to climb inside when Cornell charged at her. He grabbed her wrist, forced the gun downward, and pulled her away from the car.

"You, bitch! How dare you pull a gun on me. I'll kill you!"

They were both wrestling for the gun when Angela felt a heavy weight on her back. A long arm reached over her shoulder and down between her and Cornell.

"I got it, Angela!" Dre yelled. "Let go!"

She heard Dre's voice, but was too paralyzed with fear to do anything except grip the gun tighter.

"Angela," Dre yelled, "let go!"

She tried to comply, but terror disabled her.

Suddenly, a gunshot echoed through the garage like a dozen firecrackers going off in a tunnel and time slowed. Cornell's eyes grew wide and both hands clutched his stomach. He lurched forward as his lanky body plunged to the pavement. Expletives continued to spew from his lips as an expanding circle of bright, red blood darkened his white shirt.

Angela looked down at the gun in her hand and began wailing. "Oh, my God! Oh, my God!"

Dre eased the weapon from her hand and set it on the hood of the car. He pulled her to him, encircling her with both arms.

A security guard rushed over. He stared down at Cornell lying in a pool of blood.

"What happened?" the man yelled, pulling out his useless baton.

"He was attackin' her," Dre said calmly. "I shot him. The gun's over there."

Angela stiffened. "What? No, I—"

Dre pressed her mouth to his chest, cutting her off. "Call an ambulance," he told the rent-a-cop, "and the police."

The man fumbled for the cell phone in his back pocket.

"Let me handle this," Dre whispered into Angela's ear. "When the police get here, just listen to everything I say and repeat it. Okay?"

"But you didn't shoot him. I—"

"No," Dre said firmly. "You got way more to lose than I do. This is straight up self-defense. Cornell was attackin' you. You've got the bruises to prove it. We all struggled for the gun. I had my hand on top of yours and *I* pulled the trigger, not *you*. That's the way this is goin' down."

Angela grew even more hysterical and almost slipped from Dre's grasp.

"Baby, you have to calm down." Dre buried his face in her hair and struggled to keep her from sliding to the ground. "Everything's goin' to be fine. I promise you, I got this."

PART FIVE

To The Rescue

Waverly stood a few feet away, behind a large post, watching Britney enter her apartment.

She was struggling to hold on to three plastic grocery bags and seemed to be having trouble finding the right key. On the third try, she let out a long sigh and turned the doorknob. The second she opened the door, Waverly ran in after her, closing the door behind him.

"Please don't kill me!" Britney shrieked, dropping her bags to the floor. She tried to dash down a hallway, but Waverly caught the end of her T-shirt, pulling her back toward him.

"Just calm down!" Waverly said, throwing an arm around her waist from behind. "I'm not going to hurt you."

"Let me go!" Britney struggled violently to escape, wildly swinging her arms and legs. Surprised by her strength, Waverly had to work hard to restrain her.

When he tried to cover her mouth with his hand, she bit him.

"Ow!" Waverly yelled. "Please stop and listen to me. I promise I'm not going to hurt you."

Britney continued to fling her arms like a windmill. Waverly finally lifted her high in the air. "I'll let you go, but only if you stop fighting me."

"I read that newspaper article about you murdering your clients!" Britney cried. "Please don't kill me!"

"That article never said I was murdering my clients," Waverly shouted, "because I'm not. But somebody else is. I'm only here to keep you from becoming the next victim."

The intensity of her movements slowed and she finally stopped struggling. Waverly could feel her chest heave up and down from the workout.

"If I let you go, are you going to cooperate?"

Britney nodded slowly.

Waverly put her back on the ground, but kept a firm grip around her waist.

"I just want to talk to you, okay?"

She nodded again and he finally released her. She turned to face him and he saw sheer fright in her eyes.

"We need to sit down and talk," Waverly said.

"In here." Britney shakily pointed toward a tiny living room. Just as Waverly took a step in that direction, Britney dashed down the hallway and Waverly took off after her. She reached the bathroom seconds ahead of him. She darted inside and tried to close the door, but Waverly managed to get an arm inside.

"Ow!" Waverly yelled, as Britney pressed against the door, trapping his arm. "You're going to break my arm!"

"Get out of my apartment!"

"Just listen to me," Waverly pleaded, his arm throbbing in pain. "Let me get my arm out of the door and I'll step back so you can close it. But I really need you to listen to me."

Waverly waited and Britney finally released her pressure on the bathroom door and he pulled his arm free. She quickly closed and locked the door.

"If you want the money back, I'll give it to you," she screeched through the door. "But please don't kill me!"

Now, Waverly had reason to be fearful. The neighbors were likely to call the police any minute if he didn't quiet her down. "I told you I'm not here to hurt you. I need you to listen to my story. I'm going to tell you everything. Things my wife doesn't even know. And when I'm done, you're going to have to trust me."

"No, wait!" Britney whimpered. "I have to tell you something first. Somebody just—"

"No," Waverly interrupted. "You can tell me later. I need you to listen to me first."

Waverly pressed his head against the door and began telling Britney his story. All of it. He started with being disbarred, then explained how he had landed in the viatical business. When he got to the part about his brother being beaten up and Rico threatening Deidra, he heard Britney gasp and hoped that meant she believed him.

"I didn't know somebody was killing my clients," he said through the door. "I swear I didn't. I'm only here because I was concerned that you might be next. You can't stay here. It's not safe. Do you understand? Do you believe me?"

After a long pause, he heard the click of the lock and Britney opened the door. "Thank you for caring about me." She threw her arms around him and pressed her face to his chest.

Waverly hoped she wasn't just humoring him until she had another opportunity to escape. "I have to tell you something," she said.

"You can tell me later. We have to get out of here because—"

"No, I have to tell you now!" Britney insisted. "Somebody just got shot downstairs!"

Waverly could feel her body quivering. "What? When?"

"Just now. In my garage."

"Please don't let them get me, too!"

"Tell me what happened."

"I had just left the garage and stepped into the stairwell with my groceries when I heard this couple arguing. I put down my groceries and cracked open the door to watch. The woman kept telling the guy to leave her alone, but he wouldn't. Then he grabbed her and hit her and started choking her. She pulled out a gun and told him she was going to shoot him and he backed away. I got scared and picked up my groceries. The next thing I heard was a gunshot."

Waverly rushed back down the hallway to the front of the apartment. He peered through a small slit in the curtains to the street below. Cop cars were everywhere. It didn't seem likely that the shooting had a connection to Rico, but Waverly wasn't taking any chances.

He turned back to Britney. "The police will probably be going door-to-door interviewing tenants and looking for witnesses. We need to get out of here. Is there a back way out?"

CHAPTER 66

D re sat in the back of a police cruiser, cradling Angela as she
bawled hysterically into his chest.

He felt like everything around him was spinning out of control and he couldn't make it stop. Within minutes of the shooting, cops with guns drawn flooded the garage. At first, they had talked in harsh, angry tones, ordering them both to put their hands up. They were roughly frisked and had questions thrown at them faster than they could respond.

But when Angela told them she was an assistant U.S. attorney, which an officer confirmed by pulling her credentials from her purse, everything changed. She actually knew one of the female cops from her stint as a deputy D.A. They went from accusing and condescending to deferential and concerned.

He would not have believed it if he had not seen it for himself. A judge lay on the ground with a bullet in his gut and Dre had confessed to shooting him. Yet, he was sitting in the back of a police cruiser, uncuffed, holding his woman and being treated like a victim, not a suspect. *Was this how the other half lived?*

The car door opened and a female officer stuck her head inside. "I'm Officer Dickson. How's she doing?"

"Not good," Dre said.

He had already explained that Cornell had been stalking Angela and had assaulted her twice. He told them that Angela and Cornell had been wrestling over the gun when he arrived on the scene and rushed to her aid. As the three of them struggled for control of the gun, it went off. Dre said he was pretty sure that he was the one who pulled the trigger.

Another cop approached and pulled Officer Dickson aside.

Dre desperately needed Angela to stop crying so they could get their stories straight.

"Angela, we need to—"

A male officer opened the driver's door and got behind the wheel while Officer Dickson rode shotgun. She looked back at them through a screen that stretched the width of the car. "We need you two to go down to the station so we can go over what happened, okay?"

Were they actually asking for permission? This shit was too weird. Dre nodded. "Sure."

As the cruiser drove away, Dre saw a coroner's van pull up, giving him the answer to the question he'd been too afraid to ask. This was now a murder case, which meant that he and Angela were murder suspects.

Dre held Angela closer. Her sobs had turned into dry hiccups and his shirt was soaking wet from her tears. He needed to hear her version of events. If their stories didn't match, that would present a major problem.

He grazed his cheek along the top of her head. When he looked up, his eyes met the driver's in the rearview mirror. The cop's gaze telegraphed malice and distrust. Now *this* was the kind of pig he was used to dealing with. Dre finally turned away and stared out of the window.

A half an hour later, they pulled into a police substation. The female officer pried Angela from Dre's arms and led her away. Dre was taken down a separate hallway and placed in an interrogation room that smelled badly of body odor. *Yeah, this was more like it.*

Dre had sat alone in the room for forty-five minutes before he started to get antsy. He figured they were questioning Angela first, which made him even more uptight.

When two detectives eventually entered the room, one black, one Asian, Dre immediately sensed that his special treatment had ended. He could see the cynicism in their macho body language. The black cop, a balding, heavyset guy, was carrying a thin manila folder.

Neither cop bothered to introduce himself. "Looks like you're picking in some pretty high cotton, my brother," the black cop began.

Dre wasn't sure what the guy was getting at, so he said nothing. When a cop—black or white—began an interrogation by addressing you as *brother*, you were no doubt in trouble.

"Are you and that prosecutor an item?"

"I didn't get your names," Dre said.

"Forgive us for being rude," the Asian cop cut in. He had badly scarred skin and spoke with a noticeable accent. Dre assumed he was Korean. "I'm Detective Martin Tao and this is my buddy, Detective Dwayne Martin. What's up with you and that prosecutor?"

Dre formed a teepee with his fingertips and rested his elbows on the table. "We're friends," he finally said.

"Close friends?" Detective Davis asked, taking a seat across from him.

"Yeah."

"How close?"

"Close," Dre said.

Detective Davis looked at his partner. "You know, we were just wondering. Do you think she's seen this?" He opened the folder and pulled out a stapled document. He dangled it between two fingers, waving it back and forth. "Does she know her *close* friend is a convicted drug dealer who should still be locked up, but caught a break because the state doesn't have enough prison space to hold all of its scum?"

Dre flexed his fingers. These clowns were straight out of some bad sitcom. "She knows."

Suspicious glances ricocheted between the two detectives. They had apparently assumed she didn't.

Detective Davis moved his chair closer to the table. "This really has nothing to do with the case, but I was just wondering." He paused and smiled up at his partner. "I've never had any prosecutor pussy. What's it like?"

Detective Tao burst out laughing, pressing his fist to his mouth.

Dre grew even more heated, but knew there was no place to safely channel his rage. The smart part of him wanted to try to reason with these bozos. Tell them there was no need for the disrespect. But instead, he decided to give back what he got.

"Actually, it's pretty nice." He smiled and stroked his goatee. "You outta try it some time. But I suspect you couldn't even pay a hooker to screw your fat ass. Don't cops have a weight requirement?"

Detective Davis charged across the table, stopping when his nose was only an inch from Dre's.

Dre never moved a muscle.

Detective Tao grabbed his partner by the shoulder and pulled him back into the chair.

"I read the account you gave at the scene," Detective Tao said, his mannerism more professional now. "Tell us what happened. How'd that judge end up dead?"

Dre knew he should ask for an attorney, but if he did, that would only make them think he had something to hide. That innocent until proven guilty bullshit was just that. He directed his attention solely to Detective Tao, leaving Detective Davis to seethe.

"Angela had broken up with him and he couldn't handle it. He attacked her in her office and—"

"When?"

"A week ago."

"Did she report it?"

"No?"

"Why not?"

He spread his hands, palms up. "He's a judge. She was concerned about messin' up his career."

"They break up because of you?"

"No."

"How'd you happen to come to her rescue?"

"After I found out he put his hands on her, I thought he might try something again, so I started followin' her. Watchin' out for her."

"Sounds like a pretty convenient plan to get the guy out of the way, if you ask me," said Detective Tao.

Dre wanted to pound the table, as well as the two detectives. "Why don't you stop wastin' my time and yours?"

"Was that your gun?" Detective Davis asked.

They were definitely messing with him now. They'd probably already run the serial number. "I'm an ex-con. I'm not allowed to carry a gun."

"Whose was it?"

Dre assumed it belonged to Angela's sister, but he wasn't giving up any info. "Don't know."

They peppered him with a few more questions, then abruptly walked out. They came back twenty minutes later and told him he could leave. For now. Dre concluded that his story must have matched Angela's.

He stood up. "Where can I find Angela?"

"She left," Detective Tao informed him. "Her sister picked her up thirty minutes ago."

A look of surprise blanketed Dre's face. He saved her life *and* took a rap for her and she left him hangin' without even a thank you?

"Guess you weren't as close as you thought, huh?" Detective Davis taunted. "You need bus fare?"

CHAPTER 67

Becker was not used to having people disrespect him, but Erickson's stepdaughter was a piece of work. Thank God he didn't have a kid like her. This was all Claire's fault. Loyalty was the first trait you taught your kids. Ashley had zilch.

Earlier that day, he had contacted Ashley by phone to ask if she might have some time to talk. She called him Erickson's lackey and hung up in his face. *Did she know who he was?*

He called back an hour later and she hung up as soon as she'd heard his voice. Now he had to get ugly, which was always tricky with a woman. They were emotional by nature, so you could never predict how they might respond.

Becker parked his Range Rover near Ashley's apartment building and waited for her to arrive home. He didn't have time for this crap, but this wasn't a job he could trust to anybody else. He finally saw Ashley pull up in her Hyundai and start looking for a parking space. Ashley circled the block, then parked at the far end of the street, several cars behind him.

As she climbed out of her car carrying two shopping bags, Becker gazed at her in his rearview mirror. She wasn't much to look at and he couldn't remember seeing her crack a smile even once. Claire should've gotten the girl some braces. That would have helped tremendously. According to Erickson, she'd never even had a date. Becker shook his head. Still a virgin at twenty-four. That alone probably accounted for most of her hostility.

Becker actually understood why Ashley despised her stepfather so much. He never would have shipped off one of his kids to some boarding school to be raised by strangers. Becker existed for his wife and kids. Sometimes, he just enjoyed watching his children at play, awed by the young lives that he had produced in his own image.

Some of his law partners thought he was insane for having so many kids, but Becker prided himself on his reproductive skills. He had wisely chosen a wife who not only felt the same way, but had the genes to match. He couldn't have put up with all that fertility testing crap some of his colleagues had to endure. He could look at Staci and she would end up pregnant. Real men could do that.

Just as Ashley walked past his SUV, Becker quietly opened the door. He had to be careful about how he approached her. Their conversation would be short and to the point. She was about thirty feet from the entrance to her building when he called out to her.

"Hello, Ashley," Becker said pleasantly. "I need a few minutes of your time."

She jerked around, startled by his presence. He walked up to her, stopping with only a couple yards between them.

"Get away from me or I'll scream." She took two steps backward as Becker moved closer.

Becker spread his hands. "Go for it. I'm not doing anything to you and anybody who hears you scream will be able to testify to that. Everybody thinks you're nuts anyway. That will confirm it."

She looked around as if to gauge how safe she was. The street was lined with cars, but there was no one else in sight.

"There's something I need you to know," Becker said. "You're not going to get away with defaming Larry. I want you to stop spreading your lies."

Her eyes spewed hatred, and Becker actually felt the loathing Erickson had been forced to endure.

"Get away from me! You're just Larry's paid gopher. Did he send you over here to threaten me?"

"He has no idea I'm here. This is all my doing. I'm not about to let my friend go down for a murder he didn't commit. If you weren't family, he would've already sued you for defamation."

"He's not my family," she hissed.

"Just back off, okay?"

Ashley laughed. "He murders my mother and then sends you over here to threaten me. Both of you are incredible. You're wasting your time. You don't scare me."

Becker could see that he didn't. She was a pretty feisty young woman.

"Did you know that the police think that broker who sold your mother's insurance policy may have had something to do with her death?"

"Larry killed my mother. You know it and I know it. That broker is just a convenient diversion."

After receiving the news about Claire's autopsy, Becker was still wrestling with the possibility that Ashley could be right.

"And just so you know," Ashley continued, "my next call is going to be to the *Washington Post*." She repositioned her grocery bags and stood toe-to-toe with him, as if daring him to touch her. He admired her moxie.

The standoff lasted a few more seconds, then Ashley turned on her heels and proceed to her apartment.

Becker felt a rush of intense satisfaction. The trip had gone extremely well. He knew that Ashley would do exactly what he asked her *not* to do and that was precisely the point of his trip. He hoped she did call the *Washington Post*. Her wild allegations on the front page of a national newspaper would prompt the White House to ask for Erickson's immediate resignation.

Erickson had screwed him out of the chairmanship of the firm and apparently double-crossed him in their plot to dispose of Claire. Becker was now determined to ruin him professionally.

The best part of it all was that he didn't have to do a thing except sit back and let Ashley run amuck.

Becker was about to climb back into his SUV when a thought hit him, stopping him cold. He stood stock-still, letting the idea percolate.

Ashley despised her stepfather and wanted to destroy him. Ashley discovered her mother's dead body. Ashley canceled the cremation and demanded an autopsy. Ashley had motive, means and opportunity. It made complete sense. Erickson had not killed Claire. Ashley killed her mother and was setting up Erickson to take the fall.

Becker actually smiled. The clever little cunt!

CHAPTER 68

Waverly and Britney managed to sneak down an alley in the back of her apartment without being spotted by the growing crowd of cops out front on Springpark Avenue. Waverly had parked a block away on Fairview, only because he couldn't find a closer spot. Now he was glad.

"We going to your house?" Britney asked, once they were seated inside his Lexus.

"No. It's not safe there." Waverly turned right onto La Cienega, not exactly sure where they were going.

"I guess we're on the run, huh?" Britney said.

Waverly turned and gave her a look. "This isn't some game."

Britney hunched her shoulders. "I'm just trying to keep the mood light, okay?"

Waverly kept his focus on the road.

"You have any decent music?" She leaned forward, popped open the glove compartment and rifled through it. "Where do you keep your CDs? You do have some, don't you?"

Waverly needed silence to think clearly. He wanted to tell her to shut up, but didn't want to hurt her feelings.

Britney spotted a compartment between the seats and opened it. She grabbed a stack of CDs and started flipping through them. "Yep, should've guessed it. Nothing but old school R&B. You're very predictable."

"Do you remember what I told you back at your place?" Waverly asked.

Britney nodded.

"Then what do you have to be so happy about? Someone is definitely trying to kill me and maybe you, too."

"Actually, I'm trying *not* to think about it." He noticed her knee bouncing up and down, which told him that maybe she really was rattled by everything that had happened.

Britney slipped in *The Best of Al Green* into the CD player and pulled a pack of gum from her purse. "Want some?"

"No, thanks."

"Have you figured out where we're going yet?"

"Yeah. You got a credit card?"

"I have several," Britney said with pride.

"We're going to the Marriott near the airport on Century. I need you to check in. For all I know, the police are looking for me. I can't risk using my credit cards. I'll make sure you get your money back. We just need a place to hide out until I can figure something out."

She lifted her eyebrows seductively and puckered her lips. "The Marriott, huh? One room or two?"

"One," Waverly said. "With double beds."

She feigned disappointment. "Does your wife know we're spending the night together?"

"I never said anything about spending the night together. I just need a place to chill for a minute. As soon as I put a plan together, we're splitting up. Is there someplace I can take you where you'll be safe?"

"The safest place for me to be is with you." She reached over and placed a hand on his thigh. "I think you could use my company. You seem a little tense."

This was a distraction he didn't need. "Cut it out."

Britney smiled at him. "Say that like you mean it."

Waverly grabbed her hand and tossed it back into her lap.

She smiled, then winked. "No big deal. We can finish up another time. When you're not busy driving."

Less than twenty minutes later, they pulled into the driveway of the Marriott and valet parked. As Britney registered, Waverly lingered in the lobby, scanning the place to ensure they weren't being watched. Once Britney had checked in, he met her at the elevators.

"We're on four," she said, pushing the elevator button. "Unfortunately, they were out of rooms with double beds, so we're stuck with a king. Something about a big convention in town." She gave him another wink as the elevator doors opened. They exited on the fourth floor and Waverly followed her down the hallway and into their room. He immediately locked the door, then fell onto the bed, exhausted.

Britney checked out the room, then started opening the drawers of the cabinet that held the TV. "I can't believe they don't even have a minibar. I'm calling room service. I need a drink."

"No alcohol," Waverly said. "We both need a clear head."

"Party pooper." She grabbed the TV remote and started channel surfing.

"Wait!" Waverly shot off the bed. "Go back to that last station."

"What?"

"That newscaster just said the name of that prosecutor who's after me. Go back. Hurry up!"

Britney switched back and they both zeroed in on the television screen.

"That's my apartment building!" Britney said, pointing.

A reporter live at the scene was recapping the shooting of Superior Court Judge Cornell Waters, III. A picture of Angela Evans and a mug shot of a man identified as Andre Thomas, filled the screen. When the report ended, Britney turned to Waverly, wide-eyed.

"That's the shooting I was telling you about! But that's not how it went down."

"What do you mean?"

"That prosecutor was the woman I saw pointing the gun at that judge. That other guy wasn't even there."

"Are you sure?"

"Hell yeah."

Waverly was trying to make sense of what Britney was saying.

"I'm telling you," Britney insisted, "that reporter got it wrong. That guy didn't shoot that judge. That lady attorney shot him."

CHAPTER 69

Still woozy from the sleeping pills her sister had forced her to take, Angela sat up in bed, startled by the unfamiliar surroundings. Distress set in and it took several seconds for her to realize that she was in her sister's apartment, in her sister's bed.

"You okay?"

Jada stood at the foot of the bed, her face heavy with worry.

Angela shut her eyes as the events of the previous night slowly flooded back to her. "What time is it?"

"Close to two."

"In the afternoon?"

Jada nodded.

"Please tell me I just had a very bad dream and that Cornell isn't dead."

Jada sat down next to her on the bed. "No," she said, "you weren't dreaming."

Angela started shivering and Jada wrapped her arms around her. "It's okay, Angela. It's going to be okay."

"No, it's not," she cried. "I can't believe it. I killed Cornell."

Jada pulled away. "What? You didn't kill Cornell. Dre shot Cornell. And, anyway, it was self-defense."

"That's not how it happened. I did it."

"According to the news reports, Dre told the police that he fired the gun."

Angela was sobbing uncontrollably now. "He's just trying to protect me. I can't let him do that."

"Do you understand what you're saying?" Jada asked in alarm.

"I'm telling you, Dre didn't shoot Cornell. I did."

Angela stood up, but felt lightheaded. She tried to take a step but tripped over her own feet. Jada rushed to catch her.

"You can't go anywhere right now," Jada said, helping her back to bed. "Anyway, Mama is on her way over. She's in hysterics. The news reports are saying Dre was your boyfriend. Cornell is dead, but all she wants to know is why her daughter is dating a drug dealer."

Angela held up a hand. "I can't deal with her right now. Call her and tell her I left."

"Gladly," Jada said. "And I know I shouldn't say this, but I'm glad that asshole is dead. If you hadn't been driving my car last night, you wouldn't have had my gun to protect yourself and you'd be the one dead, not Cornell."

"Please, Jada, don't. I can't handle—"

"And I'll tell you another thing, I know you're still trippin' because Dre used to deal, but in my book, he's way more of a man than Cornell ever was. Do you think Cornell would've taken the rap for you the way Dre did? Hell no. I'd much rather see you with Dre than Cornell."

Right now Angela wasn't interested in being with *anybody*. "I need to call my boss. I probably don't even have a job anymore." She spotted her purse on the nightstand and retrieved her Black-Berry. She was about to call the office, but suddenly remembered that she hadn't even bothered to thank Dre for saving her life.

"I need to talk to Dre first." When she looked at the call display, she saw four missed calls from him. She hit redial and waited as the phone rang.

"I'm so sorry," she cried at the sound of his voice.

"You don't have anything to be sorry about."

"I shot Cornell, but everybody thinks you did."

"Everybody thinks I did it because I did do it," he insisted.

"You don't have to do this, Dre. And I won't let you."

"You're not *lettin'* me do anything. I already told the police that I killed him. Please tell me you told them the same thing."

Angela tried to think. "I'm not sure what I told them. I was so out of it I can't even remember."

"Didn't they question you?"

"Yeah, but not very long. I was crying so much I could barely get any words out. I knew one of the detectives. I think he cut me some slack. But I'm going to have to tell my story eventually."

"Well, you're goin' to tell them that I pulled the trigger."

Angela was dizzy with confusion. She thought back to her first solo murder trial, a domestic violence case where the wife had shot her husband. The woman had insisted that she couldn't remember firing the gun. Angela destroyed her on the witness stand, ripping her story to shreds. Now she realized that the woman may have been telling the truth because her own recollection of what had happened the night before was nothing but a big haze.

"I need to see you," Dre said. "Can I come over?"

Angela wanted to see him, too, but she had to get her head on straight first. There was still the fact that he was a drug dealer and she did not want to be in love with a drug dealer. Even one who had saved her life.

"I don't know if that's a good idea. My mother's on her way over. And I need to talk to a lawyer."

"What for? You *are* a lawyer."

"There's a reason they say a lawyer who represents himself has a fool for a client. I need to get some legal advice and so do you."

Silence wafted from both ends of the phone.

"Are you still there?" Angela asked.

"Yeah, I'm here."

"I want to thank you again," Angela said. "How did you end up in the garage?"

"I didn't believe Cornell was going to back off," Dre said. "I'd been keepin' an eye on you."

"Well, I'm glad you were."

"But not glad enough to let me come over?"

"We're both in a lot of trouble."

"What trouble?" Dre said. "Dude got what he deserved."

Angela could not bring herself to share Dre or Jada's views on that point. At one time, she had loved Cornell and had planned to be his wife, to have his children. The image of his hands around her throat couldn't completely erase those memories. Angela closed her eyes and wished she could make this all go away.

"I really want to see you," Dre prodded.

I want to see you, too. "Just give me some time," Angela said. "I promise. I'll call you."

CHAPTER 70

E rickson sat on the balcony of his magnificent townhouse overlooking the Potomac, sipping an expensive scotch and enjoying the tranquility.

Becker's predictions had been right on target. The media had not picked up on Ashley's unfounded accusations and it appeared that they would not. He'd placed his faith in Becker and, as promised, his trusted friend had taken care of everything.

Since Becker didn't appear to be worried about the results of Claire's autopsy, Erickson saw no reason to be. Once the autopsy was released, everyone would know Ashley was a lunatic and this whole ordeal would be put to rest. Erickson planned to return home next week, pack up and never look back. The following weekend, Mandy would be flying in for a visit.

His cell phone rang and he glanced at the caller ID. It was a Los Angeles area code. He picked up.

"Hi, it's Bill Randolph." Randolph was a reporter for the *L.A. Times* Erickson had known for years. The journalist often called on Erickson for newsworthy quotes on controversial Supreme Court decisions. He was one of only a handful of reporters who had Erickson's personal cell phone number. "Congrats on the new job."

"Thanks. What can I do for you?" Erickson was always leery about talking to reporters, even the ones he liked.

"Can't say you're going to be happy to receive this call."

Erickson sat forward, put down his scotch and switched the phone from his left ear to his right. "And why is that?"

"There are rumors floating around about the results of your wife's autopsy."

Trepidation hit him like a brick to his skull. If Randolph was following up on a rumor, it was as good as fact. He was that kind of reporter. "And. . ."

"And it indicates foul play."

"Excuse me?"

"The autopsy report shows your wife died from an overdose of morphine."

Erickson was glad he was sitting down. "How could that be?"

"I suspect that's what the authorities are going to be asking you."

He trusted Randolph—to the extent you *could* trust a journalist—but he knew he could not say another word. "I think I need to cut this conversation short."

"Can we talk off the record?" Randolph asked.

There was no such thing as off the record. If you provided information to a reporter, you should anticipate that it would eventually make its way to print, no matter what promises were made. Even the best ones would sell you out in the hope of writing a story that might win them a Pulitzer.

"Tell me what else you know," Erickson said.

"The amount of morphine your wife had in her body could've killed a horse. Far in excess of what her doctor had prescribed."

Christ! Why in heaven was he hearing this from a reporter and not Becker? "This is very disturbing news," Erickson said. "I need to go."

"The drug was administered intravenously. The coroner is classifying her death as a homicide."

Erickson grabbed the scotch bottle and refilled his glass. He was now the husband of a murdered woman. In the eyes of the police, the husband was always at the top of the potential suspects' list. With the vicious lies Ashley was spreading, no one would believe his proclamations of innocence.

Randolph seemed to be giving him time for the news to sink in and he appreciated that.

"Any idea how the drug got into her system?" Randolph asked.

"No and, as I said, we need to cut this conversation short."

"Sounds like this is all a big surprise to you."

"Of course it is," Erickson said, his irritation obvious. "When are you planning to run this story?"

"I'm not sure yet."

"I'd appreciate a heads up before you do."

He hung up and cursed. How incredibly stupid he'd been to trust Roland Becker. There was no way he was going down for murder.

Especially one he didn't commit.

CHAPTER 71

It took some doing, but Waverly had finally convinced Angela Evans' assistant to call her cell and pass on his urgent message. He was now staring at his BlackBerry, willing it to ring.

"She'll call," Britney said.

Waverly sat at the foot of the bed, his back still aching from having slept in the chair all night. Britney was lying on her stomach near the headboard, obnoxiously smacking gum.

"I wish I could see that attorney's face when you tell her she's cold busted," Britney said.

Waverly wished he could, too. He stood up and headed for the bathroom. Angela Evans was the only card he had left to play. He hoped it was a winner.

He walked back into the room just as Britney was putting away her cell phone.

"I said no phone calls. Who were you talking to?"

"Just my friend Shana. Since my diagnosis, she's been checking on me every day. If she called and couldn't reach me, she'd flip out. I left her a message letting her know I'd met a new guy who was taking me away for the weekend." She winked.

"I told you I didn't want you calling anybody. So don't make another call. Somebody could be tracking you, too." As he said the words, he realized how much of a risk he was taking by using his own phone. But if Angela called, he'd have to answer.

"Okay, okay. Do you really think that prosecutor's going to agree to meet you?" she asked.

"I'm hoping."

"Do I get to tag along?"

"Nope. You're staying right here."

"I can be your lookout."

"No, thanks."

"Okay, whatever. I'm going to take a shower." Britney pranced over to the closet near the door and pulled out one of the terry-cloth bathrobes. "I love these hotel robes." She rubbed it against her face. "One day, I'm going to buy myself one."

Out of the corner of his eye, Waverly could see her lift her T-shirt over her head and unsnap her bra.

"Hey," she called over to him.

"What?" Waverly kept his eyes on the television screen.

"I'm talking to you."

Waverly yawned. "And I'm listening."

She hurled her bra across the room and it landed in his lap. Waverly finally turned to face her. Britney was still in her jeans, but was naked from the waist up. The girl just didn't get it. Halle Berry couldn't get a rise out of him right now.

"Sorry about that." She sauntered across the room, her firm breasts slightly bobbing with each step. "I was aiming for the bed." She bent toward him, though she didn't need to, and retrieved her bra from his lap. Her breasts nearly brushed his lips.

"You don't quit, do you?"

She smiled, slowly unzipped her jeans, stepped out of them and stood before him in nothing but a lacy pink thong.

"Last chance," she said, her shoulders erect, her belly button inches from his nose.

"Why don't you go take that shower?" Waverly said.

When she didn't move, he grabbed her arm and gently pulled her to the side. "You're blocking the TV."

The flash of anger in Britney's eyes was so intense that, for an instant, it unnerved him. She did an overly dramatic turn and stomped off to the bathroom.

Thirty-two minutes later, Waverly got the call he'd been praying for.

"This is Angela Evans. I'm returning your call." The woman had the same lofty tone as when she had barged into his office with the arrogant blonde prick.

"Thanks a lot," Waverly replied. "I wasn't sure you would actually call me back."

"Well, I'm calling. What can I do for you?"

"It's not what you can do for me," Waverly said. "It's what I can do for you."

"Excuse me?"

"I realize you've been through quite an ordeal in the last few hours, so I won't waste your time. I have someone who says that shooting in the garage of your apartment building didn't go down the way you and your boyfriend claim it did."

When Angela responded with a soft intake of breath, he knew Britney had it right.

"What's she saying?" Britney asked. She was seated next to him on the bed, bouncing up and down.

Waverly put a finger to his lips. "Are you there, Ms. Evans?"

"I have no idea what you're talking about," Angela said finally.

"Well, let me explain. I have a friend who lives in your apartment building. She was there when you pulled out that gun."

"And exactly what did she see?"

"I'll share more details when we get together."

"Who said we're getting together?"

"I did."

"I don't think that's a good idea. If you have information about the case, then you should take it to the police."

"Do you really want me to do that?" Waverly taunted. Prosecutors were natural born bluffers. She was probably stressing out on the other end of the phone.

"What is this? Some kind of extortion attempt?"

"Not at all, but I do want something from you," Waverly said.

"And why doesn't that surprise me?"

"All I want is for you to make sure I get a fair shot. I didn't murder anybody. I need you to help me prove that."

"You need to call the D.A.'s Office."

Waverly ignored the advice. "We need to talk. Face-to-face," he said. "Then I'll reveal the information I have about your fiancé's murder."

When Angela didn't answer, Waverly kept talking. "You need to trust me. I think it could be worth your while. You really don't want me and my witness to go to the police."

"How do I know this isn't some kind of scam?" Angela asked.

Waverly laughed. "You know my situation. I'm in no position to scam you or anybody else. I just want to convince you that I haven't done anything wrong."

"You could've done that when we came to your office the other day."

"Things are different now. I swear, I'll explain everything to you, but we have to talk in person. I want you to meet me at the Marriott Hotel. The one on the corner of Century and Airport Boulevard. There's a sports bar in there called Champions. Eight o'clock. I'll be waiting for you. And make sure you come alone."

The phone fell quiet. At least she was giving his proposal some consideration.

"Why there?" Angela finally asked.

"I'd just feel safer in a crowded, public place."

Again, Waverly gave her as much time as she needed to contemplate his request.

"Please come," he said, trying not to sound desperate. *You're my only hope.*

CHAPTER 72

When Dre saw Angela's number pop up on his cell phone, his spirits immediately lifted. He figured she was having second thoughts and wanted him to come over.

"Somebody was in the garage! They know that I shot Cornell, not you!"

"What?"

"Somebody saw the whole thing!"

"Who?"

"I don't know," Angela said. "He wouldn't tell me the person's name."

"Who's he?"

"Waverly Sloan. An attorney we were investigating in an insurance scam."

"I don't understand," Dre said. "How did he get mixed up in this?"

"I don't know. He claims he has a friend who lives in my apartment building. Says the friend saw everything."

"That's way too much of a coincidence. I don't buy it. What does he want? Did he ask you for money?"

"He wants me to meet him at the Marriott near the airport. He thinks I can help him with his case, but I can't."

"I don't think you should go," Dre said. "He may be settin' you up. For what, I don't know."

"What if he really does have a witness?"

"This is bullshit. We were all strugglin' for the gun. There was no way for anybody to tell who pulled the trigger."

"But what if—"

"But nothin'," Dre insisted. "This don't sound like it's on the up and up."

"I'm going," Angela said. "He told me to come alone."

"You damn sho' ain't goin' alone. I'm comin' with you."

"I can't keep dragging you into my craziness."

"Too late. I'm already up in it."

Dre heard another phone ring.

"Hold on," Angela said anxiously. "This might be him calling back. I made the mistake of calling him from my sister's line so he has this number. Let me call you back."

Angela grabbed the telephone receiver from the nightstand. "Hello."

"I was just calling to check on you." It was Zack.

"Oh, hi." Her voice fell flat. "I thought it was someone else."

"Sorry to disappoint you."

"No, I didn't mean it like that. Thanks for calling."

"Sounds like you might have the makings of a real legal thriller," Zack teased. "If I were you, I'd be taking lots of notes."

Angela laughed. "Zack, you're one in a million. Don't you ever forget that."

"Thanks," he said proudly. "Did the papers get it right? Are you really dating that guy?"

"I don't want to talk about this right now."

"Hey, I've been telling everybody around here that it's nonsense. I figured if I got it from the horse's mouth, I could squash the rumor mill."

"I appreciate your trying to look out for me, but I have far more important things than the office rumor mill to worry about right now."

"I bet you do. Anything I can do to help?"

Angela was about to say no and rush him off the phone, but reconsidered. "Can you email me a copy of that background memo Salina prepared on Waverly Sloan?"

Zack paused. "Why do you need that?"

Angela scrambled for a plausible explanation. "I'm still convinced that he's responsible for Jon's death. I'm not abandoning our investigation. Can you do it?"

A couple of beats passed. "Okay, sure."

She could tell that Zack didn't buy her story, but he took down her personal email address anyway.

"Just make sure you keep me in the loop," Zack said. "You've got the story of the year. I bet you're going to end up getting a book contract *and* a movie deal."

Dre called Angela back and finally convinced her that it wasn't safe for her to meet Waverly Sloan alone. A few reporters were milling around her apartment, so she arranged to pick him up in the parking lot of the nearby Ladera Center.

Dre spotted Angela's Saab as she drove down the aisle in front of the CVS store. He climbed out of his Volkswagen and waved her over.

"How you doin'?" Dre asked, as he settled into the passenger seat and hooked his seat belt.

"Pretty awful. What about you?"

"Not too bad considerin' I *could* be in jail for murder."

"That's my guy," Angela said, "always looking at the silver lining."

My guy. Dre almost smiled. He liked hearing her call him *her* guy, even though her words dripped with sarcasm.

The events of the past few days had obviously taken a lot out of her. She wore black slacks and a simple white blouse, with her hair pulled back in a loose bun. Her face was bare of makeup and dark circles surrounded her puffy eyes.

Dre sensed that Angela did not want to talk, so he didn't push it. He was just happy that she had relented and let him tag along. That meant she needed him. When she appeared to be heading in the direction of the 405 Freeway, he broke the silence.

"It'll be faster if you just stay on La Cienega, then make a right on Century," Dre offered.

No," she barked back at him. "It's better to take the freeway."

What was up with the attitude? "Okay, you're the driver."

"Yes, I am. So that's the way I'm going."

He cocked his head and stared at her. *All broads are crazy,* Dre thought. *Every last one of 'em.*

The silence made him antsy, so he reached out to turn on the radio.

"Don't do that," she said, practically yelling. "I can't think with music on."

Dre looked out of the window and stroked his goatee. He was only along for the ride to help her ass. He wasn't going to sit there and deal with her bitchiness.

"Can I ask you something?" He turned to face her. "Why you givin' me attitude?"

It took Angela a long time to respond and when she finally did, the harshness in her voice was gone.

"Didn't realize I was doing that. Sorry." A tear trickled down her cheek. "I got a call from Cornell's mother right before I left my apartment. She said some pretty nasty things to me. Of course, Cornell told her that *he* called off the wedding because *I* was screwing around with a drug dealer. The news reports played right into that."

Dre tried to think of something to say that would make her feel better, but came up empty. He wished he could say what he really felt. *The muthafucka got what he deserved.*

They were exiting the freeway on Century Boulevard now.

"The hotel is goin' to be up there on the right, before you get to Airport Boulevard." Dre pointed up ahead. "You need to slow up or you'll miss the driveway."

This time, Angela didn't bite his head off. She slowed and made a right turn, which took them up a short incline to the entrance of the hotel.

Angela drove toward the valet area. When the attendant approached, Dre hopped out and walked around to talk to him. Angela was puzzled when Dre pulled two twenty dollar bills from his wallet and handed them to the man.

"What was that for?" Angela asked, when Dre returned to the car.

"He's goin' to keep the car parked out here and leave the keys underneath the floor mat."

"Why?"

"We have no idea what's about to go down. I don't wanna have to wait for the car if we need to leave in a hurry."

"If you're trying to scare me, it's working."

"I'm tryin' to prepare you, not scare you. If this guy is actually killin' his clients, you could be in danger. You ready?"

"I guess so."

"We shouldn't walk in together since he told you to come alone. If you don't see him when you first walk in, just take a seat. He's probably someplace watchin' you."

Dre heard a low moan and saw fear on Angela's face. He wished he could kiss it away.

"Tell me what the dude looks like," Dre said.

Angela gave him a quick description of Waverly.

"The Lakers are playin' tonight, so the bar is likely to be packed," Dre pointed out. "That's a good thing."

Angela wrung her hands. "Where are you going to be?"

"Close," he said, fighting the urge to embrace her. "Don't worry. I'm not lettin' you out of my sight. Nothin's going to happen to you. I promise."

CHAPTER 73

I have some good news and some bad news," Becker said, when he reached Erickson by phone in Washington. "First the bad news. I need you to get back home. Tonight."

"What's going on?" Erickson asked. He explained that he had just left a luncheon at the French Embassy and was standing outside waiting for his driver.

"I just got word that the L.A.P.D. plans to serve a search warrant on your house early tomorrow morning."

A hushed string of swear words flew from Erickson's end of the phone. "So it's about to be over."

"Not necessarily," Becker replied, though he knew that it was.

"I don't need your platitudes. I'm only in this situation because of you!"

Becker remained silent. Just as he had anticipated, Erickson was behaving like a cornered rat. No one as weak as Lawrence Erickson deserved to be Attorney General of the United States, much less chairman of a firm like Jankowski, Parkins.

"Just calm down," he said to his friend.

"Don't tell me to calm down!" Erickson whispered. "I didn't kill Claire, but if they're serving a search warrant on my home, that means somebody thinks I did."

Becker ignored his temper tantrum. "They aren't going to find anything when they search your house, are they?" Becker asked.

"How can you ask me such a thing? And exactly when were you going to tell me that Claire's autopsy showed she died from a drug overdose!"

Now, Becker was ready to erupt. *Erickson knew about the morphine? But how? Unless . . .*

"And don't pretend as if you didn't know," Erickson said.

"Yes, I knew," Becker finally replied. "But how did *you* know?"

"A *Times* reporter called me a few hours ago."

"Why didn't you tell me about the call?" Becker asked suspiciously.

"Why didn't *you* tell me that you were stupid enough to kill Claire with a traceable drug?" Erickson shot back.

Becker's brain froze. "I didn't kill Claire."

"You were at my house with your daughters," Erickson sputtered. "You left to use the bathroom and minutes later, Claire was dead."

"I said I didn't kill Claire," Becker repeated sternly. "I told you I was only going to do it when you were out of town. And I wouldn't be stupid enough to inject her with a drug like morphine. That's what you've been thinking all this time? That *I* killed her?"

Becker began to sweat. Was this all an act on Erickson's part? The tale about *The Times* reporter sounded awful convenient. Maybe Erickson knew about the morphine because he administered it. Had Becker been wrong about Ashley? Had Erickson killed Claire with the intent to set *him* up to take the fall?

"If you didn't do it, then who did?" Erickson asked, bursting with impatience.

"Until I learned about the autopsy report, I thought she died from the cancer," Becker said. "Like I told you, I figured we just got lucky."

"That autopsy report certainly says otherwise," Erickson said. "Are you telling me you have no idea who killed her?"

Becker boldly decided to test the waters. "Perhaps you did."

"What? That's ridiculous!" Erickson snarled. "How could you even utter those words?"

"Hold on a minute." Becker yelled to his wife, then returned to the phone. "I don't have much time," he said hurriedly. "Kaylee has a soccer game."

"I think this discussion is a little more important than Kaylee's soccer game. Who did it, goddamn it? Was it Waverly Sloan?"

"No, it wasn't Sloan." Becker intentionally paused. "I think Ashley did it. Ashley killed her mother and she's framing you for the murder."

Becker could hear movement on the other end of the line and imagined Erickson stumbling off the curb. "What? Are you insane. She wouldn't kill her—"

"Think about it," Becker interrupted. "Ashley despised you for sending her away. She probably harbored similar feelings for her mother for letting it happen. Ashley discovered her mother's body. Ashley cancelled the cremation. Ashley demanded an autopsy. And now she's waging a campaign to pin the murder on you. What better way to get her revenge?"

Becker gave his boss several seconds to absorb the news.

"Do you know for sure?" Erickson finally asked.

"As sure as I can be," Becker said. Actually, he believed there was an equal chance that he was talking to Claire's killer.

"You said you had some good news and some bad news," Erickson said weakly. "What's the good news?"

"That AUSA who's been investigating Waverly Sloan and Live Now may be facing a murder charge herself."

"What?"

"Turn on the news when you get home," Becker said. "Believe it or not, Angela Evans was dating some drug dealer. One or both of them shot a judge she was planning to marry in a few weeks. I suspect she won't have much time now to work on linking you to Waverly Sloan."

CHAPTER 74

Angela stepped inside the Airport Marriott Hotel and scanned the lobby. Her eyes traveled from the registration desk, to the concierge and bellman stations, to the comfortable sitting areas.

A large neon sign to the right marked the entrance to the Champions Sports Bar. She walked inside, but loitered near the doorway. It wasn't as crowded as she had expected it would be.

It was a typical sports bar. Flat screen TVs hung from the ceiling. Colorful sports memorabilia papered the walls. Barstools and comfy booths dotted the room. Servers in black and white striped referee uniforms maneuvered through the semidarkness carrying trays of drinks and appetizers. She saw no sign of Waverly Sloan.

As Angela passed the bartender, a rotund Latino with a Fu Manchu mustache, he winked, which made her smile and helped lessen some of her anxiety. She selected a booth at the south end of the room because it gave her the best vantage point of the rest of the bar.

Angela slid into the booth and waited. Every few seconds, her eyes scoured the room for any sign of Waverly Sloan. She began to question whether he would actually show up. The man was suspected of killing his clients. Maybe this was some kind of trick. She tried hard to block out her unconstructive thoughts, but couldn't think of anything else to concentrate on.

When her nerves seemed ready to shatter, she saw Dre sitting at the far end of the bar nursing a drink. His presence instantly calmed her.

Angela pulled out her BlackBerry to look up Waverly's number just as he walked up to the table.

He sat down across from her. "Thanks for coming."

Angela wasted no time. "Okay, I'm here. What do you want?"

"Like I told you on the phone, I want you to hear my story. I didn't murder any of my clients. I just want a fair investigation."

"And like I told *you*, you should be talking to the police or the D.A.'s Office, not me."

"I need you to talk to them for me," Waverly said. "They'll believe you."

"I doubt there's much I can do to help you. I have my own troubles, remember? I'm only here because I'm curious about this witness you claim to have."

"I don't *claim* to have a witness. I actually have one."

"Where is he? Or is it a she?"

"Around," Waverly said.

Angela was much too exhausted for any antics. "I've been through hell in the last twenty-four hours. I don't have time for games."

"I'm not playing games," Waverly said. "My life and my career are on the line. Just like yours."

Angela stared directly into his eyes and Waverly stared right back. "If you really didn't kill your clients," she said, "that will come out in the end."

Waverly chuckled. "Oh, so you're telling me I should just believe in truth and justice for all? That innocent people don't get convicted? I'm a lawyer, remember?"

"For the most part, the system works."

"Well, I can't take a chance on it possibly not working for me. Someone's trying to set me up and they would probably prefer to have me dead."

Angela made a face. Guilty people always claimed they were set up. But she was here, so she might as well hear his story. "And exactly who would want to set you up?"

Waverly's eyes flickered around the room. "One of my investors."

"What's his name?"

Waverly cracked his knuckles. "Unfortunately, I don't have much information on him. All I know is that his name is Rico."

"You don't know his full name?" she asked, incredulous. "How could he be an investor if you don't even know his name?"

"I've never met him. He had me investing in the name of his corporation."

"Why?"

"Our deals were under the table, so to speak."

"*Under the table?* Does that mean you were laundering dirty money?"

"Basically."

"Drug money?"

Waverly was slow to answer. "I don't really know for sure. But probably."

"And you think this guy is killing your clients and setting you up to take the fall?"

"Yeah, I do."

Angela gave him a look that said she did not believe a word of his story. She leaned over the table. "Let me get this straight. Some bad guy"—she paused and made imaginary quotation marks in the air with her fingers—"is killing your terminally ill clients and blaming it on you. You don't know this *bad guy's* name or address or even what he looks like, even though you've been investing thousands of dollars for him. That's what you want me to tell the police? Why would anyone, not to mention the police, believe that story?"

Waverly leaned back in the booth. "I think my story is just as believable as the tale you've been spinning. Let's see what I can remember from the news reports. A smart, successful assistant U.S. attorney who graduated from Stanford Law School, dumps her judge-slash-fiancé only weeks before their wedding because she'd rather be with a convicted drug dealer. The judge isn't happy about the breakup and drops by her place to talk to her about it. The assistant U.S. attorney takes out a thirty-eight to shoot him, but her ex-con boyfriend comes running from out of nowhere and pulls the trigger for her. The attorney and the drug dealer claim it was self-defense. The judge can't tell his side of the story because he's dead." Waverly paused. "Why would anyone believe *that* story?"

Angela was fuming now. Waverly seemed to sense that and used the opportunity to continue pushing her buttons.

"My witness says your boyfriend was nowhere around when you pointed that gun at the judge. My witness also says the judge backed away the second you took it out. When you shoot some-one who's retreating, that's not self-defense. That's murder."

Angela's recollection was still hazy regarding exactly what had happened in the garage. But she wasn't about to admit that to Waverly. "I don't believe you even have a witness. If you did, they'd be here."

"Get away from me or I'll blow your goddamn guts out!" Do those words ring a bell?"

The room suddenly felt swelteringly hot. Those words—her words—took Angela right back to the garage. She could almost feel Cornell's hand around her neck.

"Oh, I have a witness alright," Waverly continued. "And I can see from the expression on your face that my friend must have quoted you correctly. You help me cut a deal and I guarantee you my witness will never surface."

Angela did not know how to respond. She needed to know everything his witness knew. "I want to talk to your witness," she said. "Is it a man or a woman?"

Waverly hesitated as if he was uncertain about giving up that information. "It's a woman."

"What's her name?"

"You don't need to know that right now."

"I'll need to talk to her before I agree to go any further. And I'm not saying I can actually help you." She paused. "But I'll try."

Waverly's entire body exhaled. "I'm not ready to produce her yet. But to prove to you that she really exists, I'll let you speak to her on the phone." He rose from the booth. "I need to make a run to the men's room first."

Angela watched Waverly walk away. Her hands were shaking so badly, she'd kept them hidden underneath the table during the entire conversation. She glanced toward the bar. Dre wasn't there. She inspected the rest of the room. *Where is he?*

She flinched when her BlackBerry vibrated. She grabbed it from the table. Dre had sent her a text.

Get car hav 2 go now!

Angela stared at the message, perplexed. She typed a quick reply.

Why?

Dre fired back.

Cant xplain jus do it!

CHAPTER 75

E rickson simmered with anger as he stood in his family room surveying the destruction caused by the L.A.P.D.'s rampage through his home. The entire house was in complete shambles and there was absolutely nothing he could do about it.

He had arrived home only minutes earlier, having decided that it was best that he not be present when the L.A.P.D. served the search warrant. It would not look good for the Attorney General of the United States to be pictured on the six o'clock news standing idly by while his home was ransacked by police.

His family room looked as if a herd of buffalo had thundered through it. The coffee tables and couches were turned on their sides. Lamps, pillows, magazines and books were scattered about the floor. In the adjacent kitchen, there was a broken dish on the countertop and an overturned trashcan on the floor. All of the cabinet doors were open and one was off its hinges.

The doorbell rang and Erickson hurried toward the entryway. He almost slipped in a pile of dirt spilled onto the floor from a potted plant that lay on its side.

He opened the door and Becker stepped inside.

"How are you?" Becker asked.

Erickson led the way inside. "I could be better."

A palpable level of distrust now existed between them.

When they got to the family room, Becker stopped and whistled. "Look at this place. This is obscene."

"I would have to agree." Erickson walked over to the bar in search of something to drink. He found a bottle of two hundred dollar scotch broken into several pieces, its contents having seeped into the carpet. He picked up an undamaged bottle of gin on the floor near the television and poured himself a drink.

"I would offer you a place to sit," Erickson said, "but things are a bit in disarray at the moment."

Becker set his briefcase on the center island in the kitchen which opened out into the family room. "Have you been watching the news?"

"Nope," Erickson said. "Figured it would be too painful. Did they find anything?" *Please tell me Claire didn't have a second copy of that DVD.*

"What's to find?" Becker asked.

"Nothing," Erickson replied, resenting the question. "Absolutely nothing. But if Ashley's trying to set me up as you claim, there's no telling what she could have planted."

"It's too soon for me to know anything. My contacts need a few days to nose around. Anyway, no one's saying you're a suspect. Just a person of interest."

Erickson laughed. "Isn't that just a nicer way of saying the same thing?"

Becker spread his hands in a gesture of acquiescence. "Have you talked to the White House yet?"

"No." Erickson took a sip of vodka. "But I assume they've been calling."

"You *assume?*"

"I turned off my phone. I would suspect Wrigley's been trying to reach me."

"Yes, he has," Becker confirmed. "When he couldn't reach you, he called me. He's pretty hot. You need to call him right away."

"I will."

"Where do we go from here?" Becker asked.

"That's certainly a strange question coming from you," Erickson said. "You've been the one calling all the shots. Now that everything's a disaster, you want me to take over?"

"This wasn't how I planned it."

"Is that so?" Erickson now suspected that this was exactly how Becker had planned it. How stupid he had been. "If Ashley killed Claire, I want her behind bars."

"I have a copy of today's *L.A. Times* if you'd like to see it." Becker removed the newspaper from his briefcase and handed it to him.

The bold headline splashed across the front page nearly floored him.

FOUL PLAY SUSPECTED IN DEATH OF AG'S WIFE.

Erickson's face grew agitated as he read the story. "All this innuendo is completely slanderous! They might as well say I killed her. How can they do this?"

He hurled the newspaper across the room. At this point, there was nothing he could say or do to salvage his reputation. Even if he was cleared, the media speculation would do almost as much damage as a conviction.

"It is what it is," Becker said.

"*It is what it is?* Is that all you have to say? This was *your* idea and *your* plan, yet *I'm* the one holding the bag."

"You didn't kill Claire," Becker said. "So you have nothing to worry about."

"Don't you dare humor me! You read that story! Some prosecutor with a bug up his ass would love to further his career by putting me behind bars. Just tell me what evidence you have against Ashley so I can get this thing over with."

Becker averted his eyes. "I wish I had some, but I don't."

Erickson felt like he'd just been slapped. "But you said she killed Claire."

"And I think she did. I'm just waiting for more information."

"*You think?* You fucking think? That isn't good enough. If I go down, you're going down with me!"

Becker calmly closed his briefcase. "Like I said, I'll take care of everything. I'll give you a call after I talk to my contact."

CHAPTER 76

Angela grabbed her purse from the table and walked briskly toward the entrance of the bar. It took every ounce of willpower she could muster not to break into a sprint. The bartender winked at her again, but she didn't take the time to acknowledge him.

Trying not to draw attention to herself, Angela zigzagged through the crowded hotel lobby. *What did Dre see?* She charged through the glass doors and trotted to her car. Dre's decision to keep the car parked out front had been a smart move.

She snatched open the door and retrieved the keys from underneath the floor mat. As she started up her Saab, she looked around, praying Dre was on his way out.

Her pulse raced as she waited. *Where is he?*

Angela heard the rapid fire of gunshots, and seconds later a rush of people poured out of the hotel. More gunshots followed as a large wall of glass came crashing down, spraying debris in every direction. Hotel guests scattered about like ants, wedging Angela's Saab between frantic, screaming people. She couldn't move the car an inch even if she wanted to.

A pounding on the passenger window made her jump.

"Open the door!" Dre yelled.

She fumbled with the electronic door locks until they finally clicked open. Dre swung the door open and jumped inside. "Let's get out of here!"

"I can't move! Not without running over somebody." Just then, a man climbed across the hood.

Keeping her foot on the brake, Angela gripped the steering wheel with both hands, terrified that she was going to run over someone.

Dre reached over and pressed the horn, causing people to flee, giving them room to slowly move forward. They made it through most of the crowd and were headed down the ramp toward the street when the back door opened and Waverly Sloan tumbled in, falling across the seat.

"Somebody's trying to kill me!"

"Man, we ain't tryin' to get caught up in your bullshit," Dre shouted.

"Just drive," Waverly exclaimed. "We have to get out of here!"

Angela finally made it to the end of the ramp and turned right onto Century Boulevard.

"We can't go this way," Dre said, as Angela passed the intersection at Airport Boulevard. "This leads straight into the airport. Make a U-turn."

Angela glanced to her left. Huge plants and palm trees lined the median dividing east and west traffic. "I can't. There's no place to turn!"

"Just drive across the median."

Angela was so rattled, she could barely keep her hands on the steering wheel. "I can't do that!"

"Yes, you can," Dre insisted. "Just do it."

Waverly raised his head from the backseat. "No! Just keep straight. There's no way they're going to start anything inside the airport. The airport police would have this place shut down in seconds. We'll be safer in there."

"Hell naw!" Dre yelled. "If anything goes down on airport property, the police are going to shoot first and ask questions later. We have to turn around."

Angela was trying to decide what to do when a bullet pierced the back window, spraying glass throughout the car. She instantly swerved the car to the left, crossed over the median and headed back in the opposite direction, eastbound on Century Boulevard. Car horns blared at them from every direction.

Another bullet struck the left side of the car.

"Oh, my God! They're going to kill us! I can't do this!"

"Yes, you can," Dre said. "Just keep your damn foot on the gas and drive like your life depended on it because right now it does."

Dre turned to look through what was left of the back window. "The shots came from that black Escalade."

Angela cut around a Honda and almost collided with a delivery truck as she raced through the intersection at Aviation against a red light.

"They're gettin' close," Dre said. "Floor it!"

Angela screamed when another bullet took out the mirror on the driver's side.

"Please, baby, don't freak out on me. You're doin' good. Just stay calm and keep drivin'."

The Saab charged through the intersection at La Cienega just as a big rig ambled in front of her.

"Oh, my God! We're going to crash. I can't stop!" Angela jerked the steering wheel to the right and somehow managed to whip the car clear of the truck.

A second later, a thunderous boom rocked the entire street.

Angela glanced at the rearview mirror. The Escalade had barreled into the cab of the big rig, setting off a chain reaction of crashes.

Dre pointed ahead. "Make a left on Inglewood, then another left four blocks up on Ninety-Sixth."

"Why are we—"

"I don't have time to explain," Dre said, cutting her off. "Just do it."

Angela did as instructed and eventually brought the car to a stop in the driveway of a small, pink house with a neat yard. "Park in the back on the grass," Dre ordered, "and don't ask me why."

Once they were parked. Dre opened the door and jumped out. "Stay here. I'll be right back."

He returned in seconds with a set of car keys in hand. "Let's go. I got us another ride."

Dre opened the garage and drove a white van several yards down the driveway. Angela and Waverly climbed inside, while Dre parked Angela's battered Saab in the garage and locked it.

This time Dre got behind the wheel. "Put your heads down," he said. "I'm sure the police are looking for us."

Though she kept her head down as instructed, Angela could tell that Dre was taking a series of side streets. The ride ended about twenty minutes later at an apartment building on La Brea.

Angela and Waverly quickly followed Dre up two flights of stairs. He opened the door and turned on the lights.

"Is this your apartment?" Angela asked.

"Yeah."

Angela examined the neat interior. She had to step over several stacks of books to get to the couch.

"This doesn't seem like a smart place for us to hide out," Waverly said. "The police are probably on their way here to arrest us right now."

"This place isn't rented in my name. No one's comin' here because no one knows I live here."

Angela gave Dre a judgmental look that he ignored.

Waverly sat down on one end of the couch, Angela on the other. Dre remained standing, his arms folded.

"Dude, you need to tell us exactly what the deal is," Dre said. "I don't appreciate you gettin' us mixed up in this bullshit. Tell us what's goin' on."

Waverly dumped his head in his hands. "I really wish I knew."

"Why'd you send that text telling me to get the car?" Angela said to Dre.

He pointed at Waverly. "When he got up to go to the bathroom, I saw two dudes trailin' him. I just had a bad vibe and figured we should leave."

Waverly looked at Angela as if for sympathy. But like Dre, all she wanted was an explanation.

"I swear," Waverly said, his voice cracking, "I have no idea what's going on or who was shooting at us."

CHAPTER 77

Zack wasn't stupid. He knew the deal. Becker only offered him the media liaison job to get him off Erickson's trail. That was exactly how life was supposed to work. *You scratch my back and I'll scratch yours.*

He rambled around his apartment, packing up for his move to Washington. Most of his furniture was already on its way there. The last few items he was now loading into boxes would be placed in storage.

Zack figured that he and Angela must have been close, real close, to discovering something that could bring down the U.S. Attorney General. The question was, was he willing to look the other way in exchange for a job that would give him the kind of exposure and media contacts that could surely hoist him to talking-head stardom? Based on the packing boxes stacked around his apartment, apparently so.

The way Zack saw it, it was a win-win situation for him. If Erickson survived, Zack would have a pretty cool job. If Erickson floundered and ended up facing murder charges, he would be smack dab in the middle of the action. His insider's account would be golden. If George Stephanopoulos could snag a book deal *and* his own TV show, so could he.

Zack had spent two days in Washington where he'd been treated like royalty. He had an impressive office in the Justice Department building on Pennsylvania Avenue, a staff of five and his own budget. Becker had even arranged a private tour of the White House.

Sure, he was selling out, but didn't everybody? Eventually.

Instead of emailing Angela that background memo on Waverly Sloan, Zack told her he didn't want to create an email trail and offered to deliver it. Her new boyfriend had just shot her fiancé and she was worried about bringing down Waverly Sloan? That did not compute. Angela wanted that memo for another reason and Zack was itching to find out what it was.

When Angela had opened the door at her sister's apartment, she looked bruised and haggard. But after all she'd been through, that was totally understandable. They had chatted awhile about his move to Washington.

"Don't you see what they're doing?" Angela said. "They're trying to get you out of the way."

"I'm aware of that," Zack replied. He wasn't an idiot.

"And you're going along with it?"

"If I'm part of the inner circle. I'll be in a better position to discover what's really going on."

"Yeah, right. Even if you find out anything, you're not going to act on it."

Angela was absolutely right. He was not going to bite the hand that was feeding him.

Zack had tried to hang around to talk to her, but sensed that Angela wanted him to leave.

"You sure you don't want to talk about what happened?" Zack pried.

"I'm sure," Angela said. "Actually, I'm pretty tired."

But not too tired to read that memo. Zack ignored her hint. If she wanted him to leave, she would have to come out and say so.

"When do you leave for Washington?" she asked.

"In four days. I'm pretty psyched. I have an apartment in Georgetown and it's costing me a bundle. I thought L.A. rents were sky high."

"Well, good luck."

It was almost as if she had said, *Well, good luck, you sellout.*

"I hate to be rude," Angela finally said, "but I'd really like to get some rest."

"Okay." Zack still didn't make a move. "When do you plan to get started reviewing that memo on Sloan?"

"I don't know. Maybe tomorrow."

"Well, if you come up with anything, give me a call."

"I'll be sure to do that." Angela gave him a pathetic hug good-bye, then escorted him to the door.

So far, Zack had received three calls from colleagues who were speculating that maybe Angela—and not her drug dealer boyfriend—had really killed the judge. Zack couldn't believe that a woman as smart as Angela would get mixed up with a guy like Andre Thomas. Even if she was cleared in her fiancé's shooting, her career as a federal prosecutor was probably over. An assistant U.S. attorney dating an ex-con drug dealer would raise judgment issues and a taint she wouldn't be able to shake.

Tipping off Becker that Angela was still investigating Live Now might earn him some loyalty points. But could he really betray Angela like that? He wanted to find Jon's killer as much as she did.

After packing his last box, Zack rewarded himself with a beer. Before he could pop it open, his cell phone rang. He glanced at the clock. It was after nine.

"Can you believe this?" It was Tommy Tolbert, another AUSA. "First she's involved in shooting that judge and now she's in the middle of a major shootout. Is she trying to destroy her career or what?"

"Are you talking about Angela? What's going on?"

"What rock have you been hiding under, dude?" Tommy said. "Turn on CNN. Angela was involved in a shootout near the airport."

Zack dashed into his bedroom, stumbling over a box on the

way. His flat screen TV still hung on the wall. The woman who was subletting his apartment had paid him a grand to leave it up. *Christ! Where was the remote?*

He spotted it atop a box in the corner, grabbed it and hit *power*. The TV was already on CNN. He watched Anderson Cooper day and night. If you wanted to stomp the competition, you had to study the competition.

Zack was mesmerized by the sequence of events captured by the hotel's surveillance cameras. Angela was caught on tape, smack dab in the middle of a shootout, complete with a hail of bullets, fleeing hotel guests, and her ex-con boyfriend.

"Holy smokes!" *Was that Waverly Sloan jumping into the backseat?* Zack hit *pause*, then *rewind*. TiVo was a godsend.

Zack couldn't believe it. It *was* Waverly Sloan.

"You watching?" Tommy asked excitedly.

"I'm watching, but I can't believe it."

"This is better than a Will Smith movie!"

"Yeah, and knowing Angela," Zack said wistfully, "she'll end up selling the movie rights for millions."

Zack had to find out exactly what Angela was up to. He had to find out because he wanted a piece of the action, too.

CHAPTER 78

The United Airlines plane had just touched down at Reagan National Airport when Erickson received Becker's call.

"Where are you?" Becker asked.

"Just landed. I'm getting off the plane now." He stepped around a groggy teenager to retrieve his bag from the overhead compartment.

Against Becker's advice, Erickson had insisted on returning to Washington to discuss his situation in person with President Bancroft's Chief of Staff. If Wrigley understood that Ashley was a spiteful young woman who was out to destroy him, he might see things differently. Becker disagreed with his decision and urged Erickson to just hand in his resignation. But he decided to do things his way for once. He would no longer put his trust in anything Roland Becker had to say.

"The police plan to pick Ashley up for questioning," Becker said.

The news made him feel hopeful. The sooner Ashley was charged, the sooner his reputation would be salvaged. "How do you know that?" Erickson asked.

"One of my contacts," Becker said.

As he thought about this possibility, Erickson realized that Ashley's possible arrest was a double-edged sword. If Ashley had indeed killed her mother and ultimately confessed, she would likely tell police about his indiscretions. But it would be his word against hers. Who would believe a murderer?

"Did you find out anything more about the search?" He was still worried about the possibility that Claire had left another copy of that DVD somewhere around the house. Having the police discover it would destroy him.

"My sources haven't heard anything yet."

Erickson's phone beeped, signaling another call. He looked at the caller ID and winced. "It's Wrigley. I need to take it."

Erickson braced himself for a verbal onslaught, then clicked over.

"Is there a reason that you haven't returned any of my fucking calls?" the Chief of Staff shouted into the telephone.

Erickson was off the plane now, strolling down the jet way, surrounded by other departing passengers. He glanced around to confirm that no one could overhear the conversation.

"You lied to me," Wrigley roared. "You said your wife died of cancer. Have you seen the papers? We don't need this crap!"

Erickson let him vent. "I just landed at National. I was hoping to meet with you today."

"Save the cab fare and use it for your return trip home," Wrigley shouted. "You're out."

"I understand your concerns," Erickson said, taking a seat in a deserted area near one of the departure gates. "But I'd at least like to give you my side of the story. My stepdaughter framed me. *She* killed her mother, not me."

"Jesus Christ! Is that your fucking defense? *My stepdaughter did it.* Do you know how ridiculous that sounds?"

"Ridiculous or not, it's the truth."

"Well, we don't need this shit. The President wants your resignation. Immediately."

Erickson did not want to resign. That would only make him look guilty. "I don't think that's a good idea. I'm going to be cleared."

"We don't have time for you to be cleared. We can't have our Attorney General facing murder charges. The President will look like a laughing stock."

"I still think you need to hear my story. You're going to be getting lots of media inquiries. You'll need to know exactly what—"

"I don't want to hear your goddamn story. I'll have one of my aides contact you later. In the meantime, you can either resign or we'll fire you. You have until seven o'clock tomorrow morning. If I don't have your resignation by then, the Press Secretary will make the announcement at her morning briefing that you've been fired."

Erickson stood there with the phone to his ear as Wrigley hung up. Ashley had finally done him in. Or had she?

The more he thought about it, this whole chain of events appeared to bear the markings of a well-crafted Roland Becker plot. His law partner had aspirations to run Jankowski, Parkins. Had he arranged this whole chain of events to get Erickson out of the way?

On more than a few occasions, he'd seen Becker set a trap for an opposing counsel, carefully leading him down one path, while Becker quietly tiptoed down a different one. By the time his opponent finally figured out he'd been played, it was too late to do anything about it.

Erickson was not about to go down for a murder he did not commit.

If Ashley killed Claire, he would make her pay. And if Becker did it, Erickson would make him pay double.

CHAPTER 79

I really don't mean to be rude," Dre said, "but we need to figure something out 'cuz I ain't lookin' for no permanent room-mates."

Dre, Waverly and Angela were sitting in the living room of Dre's apartment, still shell-shocked from their ordeal.

"Don't think we're glad to be here either," Waverly said. "So what do we do?"

"Why you askin' me?" Dre shot back. "This is your mess. *You* need to come up with a solution to *your* problem."

Angela was curled up on the couch. She hadn't spoken more than two words since they arrived. Cornell's shooting was well over twenty-four hours ago and now this. Dre feared Angela was close to an emotional breakdown.

"Don't take this the wrong way, Dre," Angela said stoically, "but you're probably in the best position to help us figure out what's going on."

"And how's that?" he asked. "You two are the attorneys, not me."

"Let's just say that because of your background and experience in the"—she paused—"real world, you have a better understanding of the mindset of the guys who're after Waverly than we do."

Dre chuckled. "Oh, I get it. You're sayin' because I'm a criminal—correction— former criminal, I'm more likely to understand how another criminal thinks. Is that it?"

"Exactly," Angela said without apology.

Dre considered her statement. "I should be offended, but I'm not." He sat down across from them. "I've only heard bits and pieces of your story," he said to Waverly. "Why don't you tell me the whole deal. Startin' from day one?"

Waverly wiped sweat from his forehead with the cuff of his shirt and slumped further down on the couch. He began by explaining why he was disbarred, admitting that he had improperly borrowed client funds. Then, he recounted how Vincent had introduced him to the viatical business.

"Hold up," Dre said, interrupting him. "Did you already know this guy?"

"Not really," Waverly said. "I met him at a conference."

"Somebody you don't know offers you some get rich quick scheme and it didn't raise any red flags?"

Waverly paused and took a deep breath. "Do you want me to continue or not?"

"Sorry, dude," Dre said with a shrug. "Go ahead."

Waverly explained how he researched the viatical industry on the Internet, then met with the executives of Live Now to further confirm that it was a legitimate business.

"And you didn't think it was strange that this company hired you as a broker? Even though you were disbarred?"

"Only Vincent knew I'd been disbarred and he told me he didn't plan to tell them."

Dre turned to Angela. "Dude's pullin' my leg, right?"

Angela looked sympathetically at Waverly. "No, I think he's for real."

"You need to check your paperwork, dude. You probably don't even have a real license."

"No," Angela said. "We checked. His license is legit."

Dre wasn't taking Angela's word for it. He turned to Waverly. "Is it?"

"Technically, no. I couldn't get a viatical license after being disbarred. We paid off somebody at the Department of Insurance."

Dre slowly swung his head from side to side. "I don't know much about the vi—whatever you call it, but I suspect they set you up from day one. That's the reason we were dodgin' bullets tonight. You should've known you were dealin' with crooks when they agreed to get you a phony license."

Waverly seemed genuinely confounded. "And exactly why would they set me up?"

"'Cuz they're doing something illegal, like killin' people to get their insurance money. If something goes wrong, they'll have somebody to take the fall. That somebody, my brother, is you." Dre shook his head again. "Dude, you got hoodwinked big time. Where you from? Iowa? You need to spend more time in the hood."

"Tell him about the stuff involving your brother," Angela urged Waverly.

Waverly rubbed his eyes as he spoke. When he finished recounting how he'd found his brother beaten to a pulp in the garage of his office building and how Rico had threatened to harm his wife, Dre stopped him.

"I would suspect that your brother didn't know all that much about your new business. Am I right?"

Waverly's lungs filled with air. "Uh . . . well, yeah. I never told him exactly what I did."

"Didn't you think it was strange that Rico knew what you did for a livin' when he supposedly found out about you through your brother, who didn't know?"

"I wondered about it, but he was threatening my family. I guess I wasn't thinking straight."

"Like I said, somebody most definitely set you up. We just need to find out who." Dre paused. "There's something else that bothers me."

Waverly grimaced. "And what's that?"

"You owe Rico three hundred grand. He might waste you *after* he gets his money back, but not before. That tells me that maybe somebody else was tryin' to take you out."

"Like who?" Angela asked.

"Like Vincent maybe. Or the cats at Live Now. They certainly have a lot to lose if this insurance scam is traced back to them. If you're dead and gone, they can just claim it was all your doin' and they knew nothin' about it. I really doubt you could've gotten your license under the table without the company knowin' about it. If they were on the up and up, they would've checked you out. Maybe they wanted a disbarred lawyer precisely because you'd be the most likely suspect if something went wrong."

Waverly leaned back and stared at the ceiling. "I'm an idiot."

Angela folded her arms. "Does that mean you think Rico might be connected to the folks at Live Now?"

"Maybe," Dre said. "I'd need a crystal ball to know that for sure."

Dre turned back to Waverly. "Let me ask you something. If you were makin' ten percent off of all those deals, you must've made a mint. Why didn't you just pay the dude back with your own money?"

"I couldn't." He pointed at Angela. "Because of her."

Before Dre could ask for an explanation, Angela volunteered one. "We froze his bank accounts. We think that whoever was killing his clients, may have had something to do with the death of one of our case agents. He was working undercover as a terminally ill policyholder as part of our sting operation. His car went off a cliff in rainy weather. But we don't think it was an accident."

Waverly sat up and moved to the edge of the couch. "Sting operation? Billington was part of an undercover operation? He wasn't dying?"

"Nope. He was also a good friend of mine, so I'm determined to find out how he died." Angela turned to Dre. "Thanks for the analysis. Actually, I'm quite impressed. I think it all makes sense. Now can you come up with a plan to get us out of this mess?"

"Probably," Dre said. "Let me give it some thought. In the meantime," he looked at Waverly, "here's some free advice for you, my brother: If it sounds too good to be true, it probably is."

Waverly slumped back against the couch again.

"Do you have any bottled water?" Angela asked.

"Yeah," Dre said. "There's a case of water on the floor next to the cabinet. You'll need to use some ice if you want it cold."

Angela made her way to the kitchen and retrieved a bottle of water. "Where do you keep your glasses?" She reached up to open one of the cabinet doors.

Dre made a mad dash toward her. But by the time he reached her, it was too late.

Angela stared up at the contents of the cabinet, then at Dre. "You lied," she said angrily. "You said you quit."

"I did quit."

"Then what's that?" She pointed up at the cabinet. "I'm not stupid. I know what it's for."

Waverly stepped into the kitchen to see what Angela was so upset about. An entire shelf was stocked with bright, yellow boxes of Arm & Hammer baking soda.

"Exactly what *is* it for?" Waverly asked.

Both Dre and Angela gave him a look that said they both thought he was a moron.

"I bought that stuff months ago," Dre said. "I just haven't had time to get rid of it yet."

"There must be enough baking soda up there to flood half of L.A. with crack."

"Look, if I said I quit, then I quit."

Angela just stared at him, looking more hurt than angry.

He reached over her head and closed the cabinet shut. "What I told you was the truth."

"I don't believe you. You're just—"

Dre raised his hand, palm out, trying to calm her down. "Angela, just let it go before . . ." His voice trailed off.

"Before what?" She placed a hand on her hip. "Are you going to hit me, too?"

Dre's face went slack. "Why would you even say some shit like that to me?"

"You didn't answer the question," Angela challenged.

"I don't need to answer your question because it's bullshit. I don't hit women and I don't owe you an explanation for what I've chosen to do with my life. So don't keep harpin' about what I *used* to do. You can either accept my explanation or not accept it. I don't give a fuck anymore."

Angela opened her mouth to speak, but instead pierced Dre with a look that told him his words had wounded her as much as her mistrust had wounded him. She calmly turned and walked out of the room. Seconds later, Dre heard the bedroom door open and slam shut.

Waverly scrunched up his face. "This is one messed up situation."

Dre pulled a chair from the kitchen table and fell into it. "You ain't never lied."

Waverly's BlackBerry chirped and he pulled it from his pocket.

"Damn!" he said, glancing down at the caller ID display. "I forgot about Britney!"

CHAPTER 80

"Who the hell is Britney?" Dre asked.

"One of my clients." Waverly pushed a green button on his BlackBerry. "She's the one who was in the garage and witnessed the shooting."

As soon as he clicked over, all he heard was yelling. "I can't believe you just left me here!" Britney screamed.

Waverly massaged his left temple. "Just calm down. I was going to call you. Are you okay?"

"I just woke up. You're all over the news. I saw everything on CNN. You have to come get me! What if they come after me, too?"

"Nobody's coming after you because nobody knows where you are."

"You don't know that!"

"Just calm down. I'm coming to get you."

Dre shot him a mystified look. "Man, are you crazy? You can't go nowhere. Until you figure out who's after you, walkin' out of here is suicide."

Waverly pressed the BlackBerry to his chest so Britney couldn't hear them. "I can't just leave her there. Her life is in danger, too. And now that you've explained how I've been duped, it's definitely my fault. I have to do something."

"Is this some chick you're screwin' on the side? If it is, we don't need the additional drama."

"No, of course not. She's practically a kid. I hid her away because I didn't want her to be my next client they took out."

"How come you're not worried about any of your other clients?"

"Look, she has colon cancer and she doesn't have any family in L.A. I got a little attached to her, okay?"

Dre tugged at his goatee. "Tell her you need some time to work something out."

"What?"

"Just tell her," Dre ordered impatiently. "I'll take care of it."

That answer wasn't good enough for Britney, who continued to scream into the phone. Waverly finally hung up after warning her not to leave the room and promising to call back in ten minutes."

Dre was already on his cell telling someone he had a job for them to do. "What does she look like?" he asked Waverly.

"Five-three, about a hundred and ten pounds, mid-twenties with short sandy brown hair." He paused. "And she's white."

Dre gave him a look.

"Nothing's going on between us," he said. "I swear."

Dre asked for Britney's cell phone number, repeated the information into the telephone, then hung up. "My buddy's goin' to pick her up, but I don't want you to call her back until he gets there and checks everything out. She could be part of a setup to get to you."

Waverly waved away that possibility. "She's just a scared kid, man."

Just over an hour later, a burly, muscle-bound guy delivered a red-eyed Britney to Dre's doorstep.

She ran over and threw her arms around Waverly's neck and hugged him. "I'm so glad to see you. I was so worried about you after seeing that shootout on TV."

By the way Dre was frowning, Waverly could tell exactly what he was thinking.

"This is Dre," Waverly said, taking Britney by the wrists and placing her arms at her sides. "This is his place."

"Hi, Dre." Britney's body language was way too flirty.

"What's going on in here?" Angela was standing in the doorway that separated the living room and the hallway. She looked Britney up and down. "Who's she?"

"Angela, this is Britney," Waverly said. "She's one of my clients. She's also the witness who saw the shooting."

"Hi, Angela," Britney said cheerfully.

Angela ignored her greeting. "How'd she get here?"

"Dre sent a friend to pick her up," Waverly said. "I couldn't just leave her at the hotel."

Angela didn't acknowledge Dre's presence in the room and directed her question to Waverly. "What possessed you to bring her here?"

"Because there was no place else for her to go. Her life's in danger, too."

"Well, she's in even more danger now." Angela studied Britney's face.

"It's okay," Britney said. "I wanted to come."

Angela raised her hand and pointed at Britney. "I recognize you. You were in the garage when I first drove in. You were carrying grocery bags out of the garage."

"Yep," Britney said. "That would be me."

"I'm actually glad you're here. Have a seat. I want to know everything you saw and heard in that garage."

Suddenly, Britney's cheerful demeanor vanished. They all sat down and focused their attention on her.

"It's okay." Waverly gave her shoulder a squeeze. "You can talk to them. They're going to help us."

Angela switched to prosecutor mode. "You told Waverly that I shot Cornell, not Dre. Is that right?"

Britney nodded, no longer talkative.

"How could you see who shot Cornell when all three of us were wrestling for the gun?" Angela asked.

"Uh . . . well, I didn't actually see that part." Britney ran her fingers through her hair. "I only saw when the guy slammed you against the car and you pulled out a gun and told him you were going to blow his guts out. That's when I got scared and closed the garage door. I grabbed my groceries and ran upstairs." Britney pointed at Dre. "I didn't see him there at all. I never told you that I *saw* the shooting. I only heard the gun go off as I was running up the stairs."

Angela looked at Waverly with ice in her eyes. "It sounds like you don't have any information that disputes our version of the shooting. Was this some kind of scam you were trying to pull?"

Waverly couldn't believe this was happening. He shot Britney a dirty look. "I didn't realize that she didn't actually see the shooting."

Dre whistled. "Man, you're a piece of work. Did you even ask her if she saw the whole thing?"

"Not really," Waverly said, clearly embarrassed. "I guess I just assumed she did."

Britney clasped her hands. "Sorry."

No one spoke for several seconds.

"Did you guys see yourself on the news?" Britney asked, her face full of excitement.

"Yeah," Angela said. "And we aren't happy about it. I know my mother and sister are someplace freakin' out. I just sent my sister a text message letting her know I'm okay."

Dre stood up. "We ain't goin' to solve anything tonight. Let's just get some sleep and put our heads together in the morning."

He disappeared down the hallway and returned with blankets. "Angela, you can have the bedroom. Britney, you take the love seat, and Waverly, you can use the couch. I'll make myself a pallet on the floor."

He handed a blanket to Britney, another one to Waverly, and dumped the others near the door. "Towels are in the hallway closet. I'm goin' to wash up."

CHAPTER 81

B ecker pulled up in front of Sophia's house in West L.A. and turned off the engine. He hoped this meeting was more successful than his earlier visit with Erickson.

When Becker dropped by to check on him, Erickson was a drunken mess. It looked as if he'd been wearing the same clothes for a week. He badly needed both a shower and a shave.

Becker had banged on the front door for a full five minutes before walking around to the back of the house and finding Erickson sitting on the patio, staring off into space. Becker could smell the stench of alcohol five feet away.

"Didn't you hear me knocking?" he asked, as he walked up and took a seat at the patio table. Becker glanced over Erickson's shoulder and into the family room. The place was still almost as much of a wreck as it had been after the police search.

"I don't think you need anything else to drink." He eyed the unopened scotch bottle on the table and spotted an empty one on the grass. "And you probably need to eat something."

Erickson finally turned to face him, but said nothing.

"I'm going to help you out of this," Becker vowed. "I promise."

"Sure you are."

Becker hated weakness. Especially in a man. If he was in Erickson's shoes, he wouldn't turn into a pissy-ass drunk. He'd fight to prove his innocence. This was his role model? After learning of Erickson's betrayal, he simply wanted enough devastation to befall him to boot him from his coveted position as Attorney General and, hopefully, from the chairmanship of the firm as well. By the time it was all over, though, Erickson would be both professionally and mentally destroyed.

"I'm on my way to Sophia's place to discuss my suspicions about Ashley," he said. "I want to find out exactly what Sophia knows before I go the police."

A string of saliva dripped from Erickson's chin. "Be careful," he slurred. "You go over there accusing Ashley, and Sophia will probably call the police on *you*."

Now, as he climbed out of his Range Rover, Becker thought about the news he had to deliver. Sophia would have a hard time accepting that her niece was guilty of murder. But Becker was now convinced that she was. There was simply no other possible suspect. He no longer believed that Erickson could have killed his wife. The man didn't have the guts. Neither did Waverly Sloan. He may have been killing his other clients, but Ashley, not Sloan, murdered Claire.

Becker glanced at his watch. He was right on time. At least Sophia had been civil when he called to suggest the meeting.

She opened the door only seconds after he knocked. Becker stepped inside the small comfortable home off Olympic Boulevard in a primarily Jewish neighborhood.

"I made coffee. Would you like some?" Sophia asked.

"Sure. I take it black."

Becker took a seat in the living room. She returned shortly with two steaming mugs and a tray of homemade cookies just out of the oven.

"Thanks for taking the time to meet with me." He reached for the mug and took a sip.

"I guess you're here to talk about Larry."

He set the mug back on the table. "In part."

"I understand that you don't think he murdered Claire."

"No, I don't," Becker replied. "Actually I know who killed her and I suspect you do, too."

Sophia settled back on the couch. "Ashley told me about your visit."

"Then you know that I think she drugged her mother."

"That's ridiculous," Sophia replied. "Did Larry put that nonsense in your head?"

"Ashley discovered her mother's body, so she had opportunity. And she definitely had motive. She despised Larry so much, I don't think it's too farfetched to assume that she'd like to send him to prison for the rest of his life. She set him up."

"That's supposition, not evidence," Sophia said. "Ashley loved her mother. She wouldn't have killed her."

"Her mother was dying. Frankly, I think she despised Claire as much as she did Larry. Her mother chose to be with him rather than her. A jury could easily be convinced that Ashley killed her mother to frame Erickson, knowing she was going to die anyway."

"From what I've seen of you lawyers, I'm sure you could convince anyone of anything."

Sophia was absolutely right about that. Becker took another sip of coffee.

"So why are you here?" Sophia asked. "Hopefully not to urge me to turn on my niece. Because that's not going to happen. I know for a fact that she didn't kill her mother."

For a second Becker's eyes met hers and he saw something evil in them. Was he wrong about Ashley? If Ashley didn't kill her mother, then Sophia was the only other person who would have had access to Claire. As the possibility settled in, he grew uncomfortable looking into the woman's menacing green eyes.

"If Ashley didn't kill Claire, then who did?" Becker asked uneasily.

"Larry killed Claire. He killed them both."

"Both?"

"Claire and Ashley." Sophia raised the coffee mug to her lips. "He killed their spirit. He was an awful stepfather and a domineering husband. Neither of them had much of a life after he entered the picture."

Becker was careful not to show his growing alarm. Was he looking at Claire's murderer? Did the jealous spinster sister take Claire's life?

"There are many things about the Erickson family that you don't know," Sophia said. "Things about Larry that you could never fathom. Awful things. Things Larry would never share with you, his closest friend, or anybody else."

Sophia sounded so mysterious that he almost didn't want to know.

Becker gripped his mug with both hands. "Perhaps you should share them with me."

A sarcastic smile graced her lips. "You idolize the man so much, I'm not sure you could handle it."

"I assure you that won't be a problem." He set the mug down on the antique coffee table that separated them. His mind was whirling with possibilities.

"Go ahead," Becker urged. "Tell me everything."

CHAPTER 82

Shortly after five the next morning, Dre opened his eyes to the sound of a low foghorn. It took a second before he realized the sound was Waverly's snoring.

He tried to sit up, but a sharp pain shot down his back. He did not intend to spend another night sleeping on the floor. He would just have to come up with some brilliant solution to get his uninvited guests out of his crib.

A rustling sound made him jump. In the near darkness, he could see Britney sitting on the love seat, digging around in her purse.

Just as she turned in his direction, Dre pretended to be asleep. He watched through slitted eyes as she tiptoed past him down the hallway and into the bathroom.

Dre gingerly got to his feet and stepped into the hallway. Britney was talking to someone on the phone, but Dre could not make out what she was saying.

When Dre heard her stop speaking, he rushed back to his pallet on the floor. Britney walked back into the living room as Dre pretended he was just waking up.

"Good morning, sleepyhead," Britney said cheerfully.

"Hey," Dre grumbled. *This girl is too damn happy to be a cancer patient.*

He stood up and walked into the kitchen. He opened a protein shake and took a sip. Dre pretended to look away, but he could see Britney slipping her cell phone back into her purse.

"Want me to cook us some breakfast?" Britney asked.

Dre looked at her like she was crazy. "This ain't no pajama party."

"I didn't say it was."

"But you actin' like it is."

"You're such a party pooper." Britney flopped down on the love seat.

Dre returned to the floor, but sat up with his back against the wall, facing her. "Who were you talkin' to in there?"

"In where?"

"In the bathroom. Just a minute ago."

"I wasn't talking to anybody." Britney locked her arms across her chest.

"I know what I heard."

Britney blinked in rapid succession. "You heard the phone, but I wasn't talking to anybody. I was just listening to my voice-mail messages."

"That's not what it sounded like to me. Who you gotta talk to this early in the morning?" he asked again.

"You need to get your ears checked. I had the speaker phone on. Maybe that's why you thought you heard me talking. I went in the bathroom so I wouldn't wake anybody up."

The girl is straight up lyin'.

"Who you expectin' a call from?"

"Nobody in particular." Britney pranced barefoot into the kitchen. "I'm hungry. Mind if I check out the fridge?"

"Yeah, help yourself."

"There's not much in here," Britney said, opening the refrigerator door and peering inside. "Want me to go get some groceries?"

"Nobody's leavin' here," Dre said firmly.

"Okay, fine." She took an apple from the vegetable bin.

Dre got up and went to the bathroom to take a piss. As he

washed his hands, he stared at his reflection in the mirror. He was thirty-six years old, lived in the hood all his life and slung drugs for the last eight years and had never once had a reason to shoot anybody or get shot at. Lo and behold, he hooks up with a lawyer and in less than forty-eight hours, he'd not only taken the rap for shooting a judge, but almost had his own lights put out in a high-speed chase. Only in L.A.

He could hear Britney banging around pots and pans in the kitchen. He had a bad vibe about the girl. And when the vibe was this strong, it was usually right.

Dre picked up his toothbrush, then suddenly set it on the sink and marched down the hallway to his bedroom. He knocked on the door and waited for Angela to give him the go-ahead before entering.

When he stepped inside, Angela was sitting up against the headboard, Yoga style, watching the television on the opposite wall. She was wearing one of his tank tops and she looked sexy as hell. He could see the outline of her nipples through the thin cotton fabric. Dre tried, but couldn't take his eyes off of her exposed thighs.

She obviously noticed him staring, but made no move to cover up.

"I took the liberty of borrowing a T-shirt from your drawer. Hope you don't mind."

"No problem."

"You wouldn't believe the things they're saying about us on the news," she said. "Someone supposedly saw the three of us trying to cross the border into Tijuana."

"You shouldn't stress yourself out watchin' that bullshit."

"You're probably right." Angela folded her arms as if to block his view of her chest. "So what can I do for you?"

Dre hated it when she gave him attitude, but decided to let it slide. He rested his back against the door. "I ain't feeling the white girl."

"And exactly what does that mean?"

"It means I got a bad vibe about her."

"What do you want me to do about it? You brought her here."

Dre almost smiled. Black women were so good at being bitchy. Angela was probably a killer in the courtroom. But she wasn't in court. She was in his crib. And he wasn't about to let her disrespect him.

"I thought we discussed this yesterday, but let's try it one more time. I don't appreciate you givin' me attitude when all I'm tryin' to do is help you. I came in here to hip you to the fact that homegirl ain't who she says she is. And if that's true, that could be a problem. For you, me, and that clown in there."

Angela's face softened. "And what exactly is your vibe based on?"

"She was just in the bathroom talkin' to somebody on her cell. When I asked her about it, she lied and said she was listenin' to her voicemail messages. And I ain't no doctor, but the girl don't look like a cancer patient to me."

"Waverly said she was in remission."

"Remission, my ass. She has to be the happiest, healthiest-lookin' cancer patient I've ever seen."

He could tell Angela was considering what he was saying. "What do you think is going on?"

Dre was glad that he finally had her interest. "I don't know. But since somebody apparently wants your friend in there dead, we can't afford to assume they wouldn't go as far as plantin' somebody like Britney to make sure it gets done."

"You watch too much TV," Angela said.

"Actually, I don't. It's like you said, I know criminals."

"Okay, then, we need to talk to Waverly."

"That's exactly what we shouldn't do. The dude ain't the sharpest knife in the drawer. He'll just screw everything up."

Angela uncrossed her legs and tucked them underneath her. "If you're right, she could've called somebody and told them where we are."

"Nope," Dre said. "She has no idea where she is. When my

boy Mossy brought her over last night, he blindfolded her."

"You're kidding."

"My boy don't play. He picked her up around the corner from the hotel so he could make sure they weren't being followed. The girl definitely wants to know where we are, though. She just asked me about going out for groceries, and last night, right before I turned out the lights, she asked me if I subscribed to any magazines."

Angela's face went blank. "You lost me."

"If you wanted a magazine to read, you'd ask me if I had any magazines. You wouldn't ask me if I *subscribed* to any magazines. She wants a magazine with my address on it so she can give it to whoever she's working with."

Once again, Angela seemed to be impressed with Dre's assessment of their situation.

"There's nothin' around here that has the address on it, not even my driver's license," Dre said. "I have a plan to set her up. If she bites, then we'll know we've got a problem."

"What kind of plan?"

"I'm goin' to—"

"Hey, Dre," Britney called from the front room, "your phone is ringing."

Dre left to retrieve his cell, then headed back to the bedroom, still holding the phone to his ear. He finished the call with a big smile on his face. "I'm sooooo good," Dre gloated.

"What's going on?" Angela asked.

"That was Mossy, the one who picked up Britney last night. He said he's been rackin' his brain all night trying to figure out where he knows her from. And this morning it finally clicked."

"What did he say?"

"The girl's a stripper," Dre said. "In Vegas."

Angela hopped off the bed.

"That means she's probably hooked up with some pretty shady people," Dre continued. "And it also means that happy Valley Girl act she's playin' is total bullshit."

CHAPTER 83

Waverly had a bad feeling the minute he woke up. Not that things could actually get any worse than they already were.

It started with the frantic call from his brother, Quincy, who'd seen the news reports. After calming him down, Waverly had to contend with the increasingly violent threats Rico was leaving on his voicemail. Then there was his throbbing headache from alcohol withdrawal. It was just his luck to be hiding out with a real-life drug dealer who didn't have a drop of alcohol in his place.

Everybody else in the apartment was already up and about. Dre and Angela were sitting at the kitchen table. Britney was watching MTV, rapping along with Snoop Dogg.

"I made scrambled eggs and toast," she said, turning back to face Waverly. "There wasn't any breakfast meat. Want me to fix you a plate?"

Waverly yawned. "Yeah, sure. That would be great."

"We're out of orange juice." Britney peered into the refrigerator. "Should I run out and stock up on groceries?" she asked Waverly. "It's not like anybody's looking for *me*."

Dre threw Angela a furtive look that Waverly wasn't able to decipher.

"I'll have one of my buddies drop off some food for us later on," Dre said. "In the meantime, nobody's leavin' here until it's safe for all of us to go. Waverly won't die if he doesn't have orange juice for breakfast."

Waverly went to the bathroom to wash up, changing into a pair of sweats and a T-shirt Dre had loaned him. When he exited, Dre and Angela were standing at the end of the hallway speaking in hushed voices. They abruptly stopped talking when he walked up.

"Is something going on that I don't know about?" he asked.

"What makes you think that?" Dre replied.

"I don't know. Just a feeling."

"We're just putting our heads together trying to figure out our next step," Angela said. "We can't stay here forever."

The three of them walked back into the living room.

"What are they saying about us on the news?" Angela asked.

"You don't even wanna know," Britney said. "You're all either dead, injured or on the run."

Angela's face grew distraught. "I can certainly kiss my career good-bye. We haven't exactly been cleared in Cornell's death. It doesn't look good that we're in hiding."

Britney got up to turn on the dishwasher, then picked up her purse from the kitchen table. "Mind if I use the bedroom to lie down awhile?" she asked Dre. "That couch killed my back."

"Go right ahead," Dre said.

Unless Waverly was imagining things, once again, Dre and Angela traded wary glances. "You two need to tell me what's going on," Waverly said.

"We will soon enough," Angela replied hesitantly. "For the time being, just trust us."

Britney came out of the bedroom less than ten minutes later.

"That was a quick nap," Dre said.

"I couldn't sleep." She stretched her arms wide. "I'd rather stay in here and hang out with you guys anyway."

They watched news coverage of the shootout and their escape

until it depressed them. Britney made the wise move to turn on a sitcom Waverly had never seen before.

Both Dre and Angela kept fidgeting and looking at each other. An hour later, when Dre's phone rang, both of them jumped at the same time. Dre grabbed the phone and walked into the bedroom to take the call.

There was an angry look on Dre's face when he returned. He nodded to Angela, then marched straight over to Britney's purse and dumped its contents on the floor.

"What are you doing?" she yelled, scrambling to grab her stuff. She reached for her metallic pink Nokia, but Dre kicked it across the room and Angela grabbed it.

"Give it back!" Britney shouted, then charged toward Angela.

Angela tossed the phone to Dre.

Waverly watched the whole scene, not sure what to do or say.

"Waverly, help me!" Britney yelled to him.

Waverly was too dumbfounded to react.

Britney tried to snatch the phone from Dre, but he held it high above his head, out of her reach.

"What do you need a phone for?" Dre asked. "Who do you have to call?"

"None of your business!"

"You're not gettin' it back," Dre said. "I need to see who you've been callin'. We know you set up my boy over here. So you need to back up."

Dre's words stopped her cold.

She planted her hands on her hips and pouted. "You must be smoking something."

Dre turned to Waverly. "I left a utility bill on the kitchen counter because I had a feeling your girl was workin' with somebody who's tryin' to get to you. Except they don't know where we are.

"The bill had my name on it, so she assumed it was for this place. She called somebody and gave 'em the address. But it was actually the bill for a foreclosure I'm fixin' up." He stared angrily at Britney. "A couple of your friends showed up there. They broke in, apparently lookin' for Waverly. But nobody was there because I knew what you were up to."

Britney's face colored and she took a step back.

Waverly felt nothing but rage. He walked up to Britney. "Is that true?"

"Of course not." She brushed her bangs from her forehead. "I don't know what he's talking about."

"I risked my life to try to save yours and you're trying to get me killed?"

Britney rolled her eyes. "Whatever."

Waverly snatched her by the arm, but before he could sling her across the room like he wanted to, Dre pried her arm free and pulled him away.

"Hold up, man. Just cool out. I got everything under control. Now that you know the deal, we can school you."

Waverly sat down, angry and embarrassed.

"Your cancer patient is a stripper. I suspect somebody put her up to this. I also suspect she doesn't have cancer. Is that right?"

"Screw you!" Britney shouted.

"That's more like it. Now you're actin' like the little hoochie that you really are."

Dre dragged her into the kitchen and forced her into one of the chairs. Britney kicked and screamed, but Waverly held her down while Dre wrapped an extension cord around her upper body, tying her to the chair. Waverly and Dre then picked up the chair and carried Britney to the middle of the living room.

"We're tired of playin' games with you," Dre said. "You need to tell us exactly what's goin' on."

"This is kidnapping!" Britney yelled.

Dre was about to stuff a dishtowel into her mouth, when Angela stopped him.

"She's right," Angela said. "So far, we haven't done anything illegal except break the speed limit and run for our lives. If we hold her here against her will, that would be kidnapping. I can't be a part of that."

Dre let the dishtowel fall to the floor. "If you're tellin' me you want me to let her go, then fine. But that will put all of our lives at risk. The way I see it, we don't have much of a choice. We need to know what's goin' down and she's the only one who can tell us."

Angela closed her eyes, seemingly torn.

"I'm with Dre," Waverly said. "We need to make her talk."

"Go ahead. I've probably already been fired anyway." She fell onto the couch. "When all of this is over, maybe they'll let all four of us share the same jail cell."

CHAPTER 84

Just as Erickson had not expected the man he trusted most in the world to betray him, he also had not expected to lose two careers.

After being forced to resign as Attorney General, his law firm partners dealt him another blow. Instead of allowing him to return to his post as chairman of Jankowski, Parkins, an emergency vote of the Management Committee stripped him of the job. The Committee also requested that he take a leave of absence until the situation surrounding his wife's death had been resolved. Overnight, he had gone from a Washington power broker to a pariah.

He should have known that Becker had his own motives when he so eagerly suggested murdering Claire. Erickson had been too preoccupied with his own rise to success to realize that Becker wanted the chairmanship of the firm and would do anything to get it.

He glanced at his watch. Nolan Flanagan would be arriving soon. Flanagan was a long-time friend and noted criminal defense attorney. Fearing that he could ultimately be charged with Claire's murder, Erickson had asked him to come over to discuss representing him.

When Flanagan arrived, Erickson showed him to the backyard where they sat on the patio to talk.

"I've been reading quite a bit about your wife's death in the papers," Flanagan said. "It's not pretty." He had dark unruly hair and a thick mustache. When he wasn't standing before a jury, he was usually dressed in corduroys and a sports coat.

"First things first," Erickson said. "What's your hourly rate?"

Flanagan waved him off. "I'm here as a friend, Larry. We can talk about money later."

Erickson no longer believed in friendship. He would never again trust another living soul.

"No," Erickson insisted, "I want to make absolutely sure our communications are protected by the attorney-client privilege. We're going to do this by the book. What's your rate?"

"Five hundred," Flanagan said reluctantly.

Erickson picked up his checkbook and scribbled out a check for fifteen hundred dollars. He tore it out and slid it across the table. "I suspect three hours should do it for today. We can work out a more formal arrangement later."

Leaning back in his lawn chair, Erickson looked past his friend out into his garden. "What I'm about to disclose is definitely going to shock you. But I'm going to tell you everything because you need to have the full picture if you're going to properly represent me."

Erickson planned to reveal all, with one exception. He would never tell anyone about his affinity for kiddie porn.

Flanagan held up a hand. "If you killed your wife, I don't want to know."

Erickson understood. An attorney could not intentionally put on evidence that he knew was false. But if he didn't know for sure, he had free reign.

"I did not kill my wife." Erickson looked him squarely in the eyes. "And that's the honest truth."

He began by explaining Becker's suggestion that they kill Claire to keep her from ruining his chances to become Attorney General.

"You were willing to kill your wife to get that job?" Flanagan asked, not hiding his amazement.

"She was already dying," Erickson said coldly. "Anyway, it was Becker's idea, not mine. He even agreed to commit the murder himself."

Flanagan gripped both arms of his chair. "And why would he do that for you?"

Erickson wished he'd taken the time to ask himself the same question weeks ago. "At the time, I assumed he did it out of loyalty."

"That's an awful lot of loyalty. I don't know anyone loyal enough to commit murder for me."

"He had another reason," Erickson said. "I just didn't realize it at the time, but Becker wanted the chairmanship of the firm. He wanted me to get the AG job simply to clear the way for him to step into my shoes. He was always reluctant about becoming my deputy. After I got the job, I think he set out to personally destroy me."

"So Becker killed your wife?"

"No, my stepdaughter, Ashley, killed Claire."

"Forgive me," Flanagan said, leaning over the patio table, "but I think I need a stiff drink."

Erickson returned from the kitchen with two bottles of beer. "Unfortunately," he said with a wry smile, "I've consumed all the hard liquor in the house."

He continued with his story and when he was done, Flanagan spent thirty minutes peppering him with questions.

"Tell me something," Flanagan said. "Why does Ashley hate you so much?"

Erickson absently tapped the beer bottle with his index finger. "She was quite a handful when Claire and I got married. She resented my being in their lives. Claire couldn't control her so we decided to send her off to boarding school. Ashley, however, blames me for that decision."

"What evidence do you have that Ashley killed her mother?"

"None, really."

"Then it's possible Becker actually did it?"

Erickson shrugged. "Anything's possible."

He could almost see the wheels turning in Flanagan's head. The best criminal attorneys didn't care about guilt or innocence. For them, the intellectual challenge came from winning an unwinnable case.

"From a defense perspective," Flanagan said, "it's easier to prove reasonable doubt when there's another plausible suspect to point the finger at."

"Well, we have at least two. Both Becker and Ashley have strong motives."

"If we point a finger at Becker as the murderer," Flanagan continued, "the plot to kill Claire will no doubt come to light. That would make you an accessory."

Flanagan stopped and took a long pull on his beer. "For your sake, let's hope Ashley did kill her mother. If she didn't and Becker goes down for murder, you could, too."

CHAPTER 85

D re knew that it wouldn't take long for Britney to fold.
Depriving her of food and water for three hours and
twenty-two minutes was all it took.

Angela and Waverly were sitting in front of the TV eating a
pepperoni pizza delivered by Domino's when Britney started
pleading. "You can't just let me starve."

Dre looked over at her. "Yes, we can."

"I need to go to the bathroom!"

"Guess you'll have to hold it until you tell us what we want to
know."

"I already told you, I don't know anything!"

Both Angela and Waverly had begun to think that maybe she
didn't, but Dre wasn't buying her denials. "I think you do," he
repeatedly challenged her.

It went back and forth like that until the pizza was almost
gone. Britney finally started talking once they untied her and gave
a slice of pizza and a bathroom break.

"How did you end up at that church meeting where you met
me?" Waverly asked.

"My boyfriend told me to go."

"Who's your boyfriend?"

"His name's Ricardo. Ricardo Montoya."

"Why'd he want you to go?"

"He runs this scam, okay? I don't have cancer. The medical records I gave you were fakes. But even if they had been real, I wasn't sick enough to qualify for one of those policies. Ricardo figured you would buy my sob story and sell my policy anyway. And you did."

"I helped you because I felt sorry for you," Waverly said. "You're the only client I ever did that for." From the look on his face, the betrayal still hadn't sunk in.

Britney smiled. "Guess that makes me a pretty good actress, huh?"

"How can we get in contact with Ricardo?" Dre asked.

"His number's in my phone. He's the one I gave the address to."

"Where does he live?" Dre asked.

"He lives in Vegas. When he comes to L.A., he usually stays at my place."

"What's Ricardo's line of work?"

"He's a dealer. Primarily meth, occasionally crack. Can I have something to drink?"

"Not until we're done," Dre said. "So was Ricardo killin' Waverly's clients after he bought their policies?"

"I don't know anything about killing anybody. I swear." For the first time, there was something earnest about her denial. "I've never known Ricardo to do anything violent. When I told him about that *L.A. Times* article, he said he couldn't believe Waverly was killing his clients."

"You're lyin'," Dre said, growing frustrated.

"I'm telling you all I know is that he helped a lot of people get insurance. Then he hired some doctor to fake their medical records and sent them to Waverly to sell their policies. Whatever money they got from selling the policy, Ricardo took half. You should probably let me call him. He's going to think something's up if I don't."

"So let him," Waverly said bitterly. He paced back and forth across the living room.

"What do you know about this guy named Rico?" Dre asked.

"He's so gullible," Britney said. "There ain't no Rico."

Waverly stopped pacing. "What do you mean?"

"Ricardo made all those calls."

Waverly's face cracked with embarrassment. "What does Ricardo look like?" he asked.

"Dark hair, kinda cute. I only date cute guys."

"What else?" Angela asked.

"Give me some soda and I'll show you a picture of him."

"Now, we're getting somewhere," Waverly said. "You have a picture of him? Where is it? Is it in your phone?"

"I'm not telling you where it is until you give me something to drink."

"Let's check." Waverly grabbed Britney's cell phone and started pushing buttons.

"It's not in my phone," she said calmly. "It's on the Internet. I'm dying of thirst. Give me some soda and I'll show it to you."

Angela gave Britney a can of Coke and she took several sips.

"Okay," Dre said, "now show us the picture."

"It's on my Facebook page," she said.

Dre's laptop was sitting on the coffee table. He brought up the Facebook home page. "What's your email address and password?"

"*BootyliciousBritney* at yahoo dot com. My password is *TooHot*."

"I'm not goin' to say a word." Dre pulled up the page and turned the computer around so she could see the screen. Britney had 732 Facebook friends. "Which one is he?"

"It's the third picture down. The one of the two of us together on the beach. He's in the orange swim trunks."

Dre handed the laptop to Waverly. "Do you recognize him?"

"Son of a bitch!" Waverly exclaimed.

"You know him?" Dre asked.

"Yeah, I know him." Waverly plopped onto the couch. "That's the guy who got me into the viatical business. That's Vincent."

CHAPTER 86

Zack had been sitting in his office sulking for most of the morning. He'd only come into work to clean out his desk and say his good-byes. Literally seconds after he got everything all packed up, he received a curt call from the Justice Department Personnel Office in D.C. His media liaison job was over before it started. Erickson was out and so was he.

When he started ranting about who was going to refund his deposit on the Georgetown apartment and pay to ship his furniture back to L.A., the guy hung up on him. The same thing happened when he tried to back out of the deal with the woman who was subletting his apartment. At least Barnes let him rescind his resignation.

His cell phone rang and he grudgingly answered.

"Zack, this is Angela. I need your help."

He sprang forward in his chair. "Have you lost your mind? Where are you? You know your career is shot, right?"

He opened one of the boxes he had just taped shut and pulled out a legal pad. He wished he had a tape recorder so he could record the conversation. The story of a federal prosecutor on the run with her drug dealer-lover following the murder of a judge was the perfect plot for a blockbuster. Maybe he would get his big story after all.

"At the moment," Angela said, "I'm more worried about staying alive than where I'll be working next week. I really thought long and hard before calling you, Zack. But I need somebody I can trust. I hope I don't regret making this call."

Was Angela about to confess to something? "Of course you can trust me," he said, trying to contain his excitement. "What's going on?"

"I'm close to closing in on Jon's killer. I think his death is definitely linked to Live Now."

Zack jotted down Angela's words as fast as she was speaking them. He was about to be part of the takedown of a murder ring that preyed on the dying. This might not get him his own TV show, but it could mean a six-figure book deal. He was almost hyperventilating, but managed to keep writing.

"I have some extremely confidential information that I need you to check out," Angela said, "but Salina's the only person I want you to discuss this with. She's a whiz on the Internet. But with everything going on with me, I figured she'd be too afraid of losing her job if I asked her to do the research for me. Can you ask her to do it without saying it's for me?"

Maybe. "Tell me what's going on first."

"I need you to run a sheet on a *Vincent Rivera* and a *Ricardo Montoya*. Also try *Ricardo Rivera* and *Vincent Montoya*. Try the first name *Rico*, too. Then I need to find out if a company called Goldman Investments, Inc., has any connection to Live Now, The Tustin Group or any of its affiliated companies."

"What's Goldman Investments?"

"A company Waverly Sloan was laundering drug money through."

"Whoaaa! How'd you find that out?"

"He's here with me right now, spilling his guts. If I can confirm a link between the companies, then I think we can prove that Live Now and its executives are connected to the deaths of Waverly's clients."

"Holy cow!" Zack said.

"What about Lawrence Erickson's wife. Did they kill her too?"

"We're still working on that. So can you do it?"

Zack sidestepped the question. "Where are you?"

"I'm in hiding. I can't tell you any more than that. You saw the news. Somebody is trying to kill Waverly, and maybe me, too. Will you help me?"

"Sure," he said.

"And remember, this is just between us. Don't tell Salina the information is for me and don't bring anybody else in on this."

He wasn't stupid. "Of course."

"I also have some telephone numbers I need you to look up." She gave him four numbers retrieved from Britney's cell. "I need to know as much as possible about the people connected to the numbers."

"Whose numbers are these?" Zack asked.

"That's what I want *you* to tell *me*."

"It may not be easy to keep all of this under the radar."

"I'm sure you can do it, Zack."

Angela's next words absolutely made his day. "When this is all said and done, it's going to be a huge story. I might not have a job, but I will definitely have a book deal and maybe even a screenplay to sell. If you want to be part of it, I really need your help."

Zack could almost see the hotel shootout scene on the big screen. The studio would probably want big-name actors. Brad Pitt would play him and that black guy from *The Unit* would make a decent Waverly character. Maybe Beyoncé or Jennifer Hudson could play Angela.

"I'm with you," Zack said excitedly. "Give me a couple of hours and I'll let you know what I find out."

CHAPTER 87

Erickson had just finished showering and changed into his gardening clothes when he heard a knock at the door. As he approached, the pounding grew louder.

"I'm coming!" he yelled. He wondered who it could be.

Mandy had just left to get a change of clothes. He felt lucky to have her. She was the only positive thing in his life right now. Later tonight, he planned to ask her to move in.

Erickson reached for the doorknob, but something made him peer through the peephole first. He saw two police officers and at least three men with TV cameras propped on their shoulders. A police cruiser was parked in the driveway and two more were double parked in front of the house.

Erickson's fists reflexively clenched. *This can't be happening. Are they actually going to arrest me?* This was such a travesty. He could only imagine what the neighbors were thinking.

He jerked the door open. "What do you want?"

"Mr. Erickson, we have a warrant for your arrest for the murder of Claire Erickson."

Before he could react, a uniformed officer stepped forward, pulled him outside, hurled him around and cuffed him.

"This is outrageous!" Erickson screamed. "What are you doing? I didn't kill my wife. I'm going to sue every last one of you!"

The officer pressed Erickson's face against the hard brick wall of his porch.

"Do you know who I am?" Erickson yelled. "You can't treat me like this!"

The officer swung him around and the photographers rushed forward, zeroing in with their cameras.

A flash of fear raced down his spine. He needed to call Becker. No! What was he thinking? Becker had probably set up this disgraceful scene. Erickson needed his attorney, Nolan Flanagan.

He tried to calm himself. Resisting arrest would not do him any good. "Who's in charge here?" Erickson asked.

"I am." Detective Davis stepped forward and introduced himself.

"You don't have to do this," he appealed to the detective. "I would've come down to the station voluntarily. Why don't you let me call my lawyer?"

"So it's special treatment you want. Is that it?" the detective replied.

Actually, yes. I do want special treatment. I was the Attorney General of the United States, for Christ's sake. "I just need someone to call my lawyer, Nolan Flanagan. Can one of you guys please do that for me?"

Detective Davis gave him a skeptical look. "Sorry, but you'll have to wait until you get down to the station."

Erickson looked over his shoulder and saw Becker approaching. Had he come to help or cause more harm? Maybe Becker could at least talk them into taking the handcuffs off. "That's my law partner coming up the driveway," he said to the detective. "Please let him through."

As Becker weaved his way toward him, Erickson could see his neighbors rubbernecking in clumps along the street.

"Becker," Erickson called out in desperation. "Please make them stop this madness. Tell them I didn't kill Claire! Tell them how Ashley set me up!"

Becker had almost reached him when an officer tried to block his path. Detective Davis ordered the officer to step aside and let Becker through.

"Could you give me a few minutes alone with him?" Becker asked. "I'm his law partner. I need to talk to him away from the cameras."

Detective Davis hesitated, then instructed two officers to escort Becker and Erickson inside the house.

"The cuffs stay on and we're going to be just a few feet away," the detective said, entering the spacious foyer and closing the door behind him. "You have five minutes."

"That's fine," Becker said. "I won't need that long."

The officers moved a few feet away to give them privacy.

Becker walked up to Erickson, his face less than an inch away. "You deserve to rot in prison," he whispered angrily. "I can't believe that I made you Kaylee's godfather. You goddamn pervert!"

Oh no! He knows! "I have no idea what you're talking about," Erickson stuttered.

"I just had a long conversation with Sophia," Becker continued. "I finally understand why Ashley hates you so much."

Erickson started to quiver. "You can't believe Ashley's lies. She's trying to destroy me."

"You're the liar!" Becker nailed Erickson with a solid punch to his left cheek that sent him crashing into the wall. The two officers rushed over and pulled Becker away.

"You sick fuck!" Becker yelled.

Erickson hung his head. His horrible secret was out. But that did not mean he had killed his wife. Nolan Flanagan would get him off.

"Becker," Erickson sobbed, "you must tell them the truth. Please!"

"I'd be glad to." Becker turned to Detective Davis. "Our ex-Attorney General killed his wife because she threatened to expose his penchant for child porn." Becker attempted to reach into the pocket of his jacket, but the officers restrained him.

"Don't worry," Becker said. "I don't have a weapon, but I do have evidence that proves he's a pedophile. I was about to hand you a DVD I have in my pocket."

Erickson's eyes widened. "How can you do this? You know I didn't kill Claire! You're framing me! You wanted me out of the way so you could take over the firm."

"I thought you said your stepdaughter framed you?" Detective Davis replied. He removed the DVD from Becker's pocket. "Now, *this* guy is the one who supposedly set you up? You need to get your story straight."

"Please don't do this to me!" Erickson cried out to Becker. "I won't survive in prison."

"We found traces of morphine on your gardening gloves that we picked up during the search of your house," Detective Davis said. "I suppose somebody planted the gloves, too?"

"Gloves? That's impossible? I'm being framed!" Erickson screamed. "I didn't kill my wife! I swear!"

"I hope you never see daylight again," Becker hissed. "Get him out of here."

An officer took the sobbing Erickson by the arm and led him back outside and through the crowd of police, media and spectators.

"You're going to make a lot of new friends in lockup," the cop said, as he stuffed Erickson into the back of the police cruiser. "They love perverts like you."

CHAPTER 88

Their interrogation of Britney lasted three hours and led Waverly to only one conclusion. He had no chance of the police believing his story unless he could turn over Vincent or Ricardo or Rico or whoever he was.

Waverly, Dre and Angela were huddled in Dre's bedroom, trying to plan their next move. Britney remained tied to a chair in the living room. Dre stepped into the hallway every few minutes or so to make sure she stayed put.

Angela's call to her colleague Zack, paid off in minutes, rather than hours. There was indeed a link between Live Now and Goldman Investments, Inc., the company Rico had instructed Waverly to purchase the policies for. After checking Ricardo's aliases, they found four criminal convictions. Two for check fraud, one for larceny and one for assault with a deadly weapon.

"We have to smoke Rico out," Dre said. "And the only way I know to do that is to convince him that he has a shot at you *and* his money."

"Oh, that's a great idea," Waverly said. "Using me as bait will probably mean I'll get a bullet to the head."

"That won't happen," Dre said. "I have some guys who can provide protection."

Angela sat down on the edge of the bed. "Exactly what are you suggesting, Dre?"

"Based on what Britney told us, this whole thing is a scam run by Ricardo-slash-Vincent, probably with the knowledge of Live Now."

Angela looked up at him. "What you do mean?"

"At first I was thinkin' that this Rico dude just wanted his money back. But if there is no Rico, just Vincent, he'd have a reason to want you dead. All of this stuff leads straight back to him and he can't afford to let that happen. But if you're dead, it would be easy to pin everything on you."

"Are you saying he doesn't care about getting his money back?" Angela asked.

"No, I'm sayin' he might let the money ride if it means he doesn't have to take a rap for murderin' a bunch of dying people."

"That makes sense," Waverly said. "It's not really about the money. With all the policies Rico bought, he's a long way from being in the hole."

"Yep," Dre said, nodding. "The dude definitely wants you out of the way. I guess we're goin' to have to use Britney to lead him to us."

"How?" Angela asked.

Dre paused to think. "By makin' Rico believe he's goin' to get to Waverly *and* his money."

"I'm not following you," Waverly said.

"Rico doesn't know that we know that he's Vincent. The next time he calls you, answer the phone and propose some kind of exchange. Tell him you have somebody else, namely Britney, who's goin' to deliver the money."

"He's not going to buy that," Angela said. "He's going to assume Britney talked to us."

"You may be right," Dre said. "That's why we're goin' to let him demand that Waverly show up. But you're takin' Britney with you."

"Show up and do what?" Waverly asked. "Get my head shot off?"

"I got your back," Dre said. "I'll call in my boys."

"No," Angela said, standing up. "This has gotten way out of hand. If we're going to do something like this, we need to have the police involved. Ricardo or Vincent or whoever he is probably won't be coming alone and neither should we."

"The L.A.P.D. will just screw everything up," Dre said. "I know some guys we can trust."

"No," Angela repeated. "Everything is already a mess. We need to call in the police. First let's figure out what we're doing with Britney." She turned to Waverly. "We need to convince her to play along. The next time Rico calls, you're going to tell him you have his money. Then we'll have Britney call him. She has to act like she's secretly making the call. She can tell him she wasn't able to call earlier because we've been watching her too closely. She has to convince him that we don't know anything."

"I'm sure he's pretty pissed about not findin' you at that address Britney gave him," Dre said to Waverly.

"She can just tell him she made a mistake," Angela continued. "That she didn't notice that Dre's name wasn't on that utility bill."

Sweat beads dotted Waverly's forehead. "Don't you think he'll sense a setup?"

"Not if we can convince Britney that it's not," Angela said. "I get the feeling that she's really afraid of the guy. There's no way she wants him to find out that she folded and told us everything. I think she'll play along if she thinks this is all going to lead to a happy ending."

"Wait a minute," Waverly said. "We'll have to make her think we actually have some money to turn over."

"I can help with that part," Dre said quietly.

"We're not talking about small change," Waverly said. "This guy is expecting me to hand over three hundred thousand dollars. In cash."

Dre hesitated, then opened his closet and removed a section

of the wall which hid a large, steel safe. He opened it to reveal stacks upon stacks of bills wrapped in rubber bands.

Angela rubbed the back of her neck and looked away.

"You're willing to give up three hundred grand for me?" Waverly asked, flabbergasted.

"Hell naw," Dre said, as he relocked the safe. "I'm willin' to *pretend* to give it away. We're goin' to stuff a bunch of bills into a duffel bag and show it to Britney so she can tell Ricardo, or whoever, that she actually saw the money. And when she's not lookin' we're switchin' bags. No way that money is walkin' out of this apartment."

"Sounds like we have a plan then," Waverly said.

Angela pulled out her BlackBerry.

"Who are you callin'?" Dre asked.

"My friend Zack," she replied. "I'm not one hundred percent sure we can trust him. But we'll just have to chance it."

CHAPTER 89

Britney was not at all excited about her role in the money exchange.

"Why did I have to come?" she protested. "Why couldn't you just do it by yourself?"

She was sitting in the passenger seat of Dre's borrowed van as they neared Kenneth Hahn State Park. Waverly was behind the wheel. Dre's friend Mossy had picked Angela and Dre up earlier. They were already stationed someplace in the park out of sight.

"What are you afraid of?" Waverly asked, as he turned off La Cienega and into the park. "Rico's your boyfriend. You think he's going to shoot you?"

"Of course not." Britney locked her arms across her chest and pouted. "Ricardo wouldn't hurt me. But if something crazy goes down, I don't wanna get hit by any stray bullets."

"There's not going to be any shooting," Waverly assured her, though he wasn't exactly sure about that. "You're going to hand over the money and then we're getting out of here. Unless, of course, you want to stay with your boyfriend."

"Uh . . . no," Britney said. "I . . . I'd rather go back with you."

"Really? You don't want to go back home with your boyfriend? I thought you said Rico never hurt anybody."

Britney huffed and looked out of the window.

When Waverly had finally spoken to Rico by phone, he told him he had the money and would give it to him in exchange for his life. Rico agreed and suggested that Waverly make the delivery after dark in the parking lot of the Baldwin Hills Crenshaw Plaza. Waverly vetoed that setting, insisting on a daylight drop off in an area that was far less congested. Waverly didn't want to run the risk of innocent people getting hurt just in case a shooting did break out.

Dre was the one who suggested Kenneth Hahn State Park. Located in Baldwin Hills, it was one of the most scenic parks in L.A., equipped with a Japanese garden, fishing lake, four playgrounds and more than one hundred picnic tables. The walking trails provided a view of the Pacific Ocean to the west and the Hollywood sign to the north.

It was early afternoon on a Monday and the park was nearly deserted. Waverly stopped at the entrance to pay the parking fee. He glanced around, hoping to spot a uniformed officer. Angela had turned to her colleague Zack, who called in law enforcement to set a trap for Rico.

As it turned out, Baldwin Hills was an unincorporated area manned by the L.A. County Sheriff's Department, not the L.A.P.D. Waverly prayed that dozens of gun-toting sheriff's deputies were hidden around the park, their trigger fingers ready to fire. He looked around for a sign of Rico and was happy that he couldn't find one.

As he slowly drove the van down into the park, then up a steep incline, Waverly felt increasingly skittish. Angela had assured him that they would be under close watch, but he had little faith that this delivery would take place without any glitches. He simply didn't have that kind of luck.

When he got to the top of the hill, he spotted Mossy sitting in his car at the end of a dirt path. He wondered if Angela and Dre had gotten out of the car or were hiding in the back seat.

Rico had instructed him to park at the top of the hill near the covered picnic tables. When he finally reached the area, Waverly took in the amazing view. He never even knew this park existed. He could actually see the downtown L.A. skyline.

His BlackBerry chirped and Waverly jumped high enough to hit the ceiling. He knew who was calling.

"Glad you're on time," Rico said, when Waverly answered.

"Where are you?" Waverly anxiously glanced around. He still had not cut off the engine.

"Around," Rico said.

Waverly tried to keep his voice level. "How do you want to do this?"

"Get out of the van with the money," Rico ordered.

"No way. Your girl—" Waverly caught himself. He couldn't let Rico know that Britney had exposed him. "Like I told you on the phone, my friend Britney's bringing you the money."

Rico chuckled. "Why would you use a woman to do a man's job?"

"If you want the money, she's bringing it to you. Otherwise, we're out of here." Waverly was still looking around trying to figure out where Rico was hiding. *And where in the hell are the sheriff's deputies?* He saw a few people milling around. He prayed they were plainclothes cops.

"Fine. Let's do this," Rico said. "Tell her to drop the money in the doorway of the men's restroom. Then go back to the car."

Waverly shuddered with relief. Britney would be back in the van before Rico realized that the duffel bag only held a few dollars piled on top of shredded newspaper. Even though Britney had put Waverly's life on the line, he was still worried about hers.

"Where are you?" Waverly asked again.

"Around, like I said the first time," Rico repeated. "I have a clear view of every move you make. So don't try to be a hero and do anything stupid."

Waverly hung up and gave Britney her instructions.

She just sat there hugging herself. "I'm scared."

"This guy is your boyfriend. What do you have to be scared of?"

"When I was watching the news reports, I recognized that black Escalade that was chasing you out of the hotel. It belonged to one of Rico's friends. He never goes anywhere without him. He's probably here, too."

"And you're just now telling me this?"

Britney looked genuinely sorry.

Waverly was too scared and too exhausted to be angry at her. "Look, I'm sure he's not going to hurt you. We have to get this over with. Here's the money." He pulled Dre's duffel bag from the backseat and dropped it into her lap.

After sitting there for a few more seconds, Britney stuffed the bag under her left arm and threw open the van door.

As she climbed out, Waverly finally spotted a figure in a thick patch of bushes about twenty feet away. He prayed it was an undercover sheriff's deputy.

Waverly watched as Britney timidly inched toward the men's restroom several yards away. When she got within a few feet of the open doorway, she tossed the bag inside and began running back toward the van.

"Watch out!" Angela yelled from some unknown position to Waverly's rear. "He's got a gun!"

Britney was just a few feet from the van when Waverly saw the man he knew as Vincent step out from behind a bush and take aim at Britney. Before he knew it, Waverly had thrown open the van door and dashed toward her.

Suddenly, he heard gunfire and bullets seemed to be flying in all directions. Vincent and his cohort were shooting it out with the sheriff's deputies. Waverly hooked his arm around Britney's waist and tried to run back to the van. But Britney was screaming and clinging to his body, making it impossible for him to make any real progress.

Waverly had just reached out to open the car door when the

first bullet hit him in the leg. Half a second later, he felt the sting of a second bullet pierce his chest.

As Britney slipped from his arms, everything went black.

.

CHAPTER 90

B ecker was so repulsed by the revelations about his long-time friend and mentor, that he was not sure he could bring himself to face the man. But in the end, he agreed to Erickson's request for a meeting.

Sitting in a special meeting room at the county jail, Becker's face hardened in disgust as he waited for Erickson to be brought in.

When the door finally opened and Erickson stepped inside, the image before him rendered Becker speechless. After only forty-eight hours behind bars, Erickson had transformed into a haggard old man. His eyes were ringed with dark circles, his face was pale and unshaven and he stank of body odor.

The prosecutor had successfully fought Erickson's request for bail, knowing that he had the financial resources to disappear and never be seen again. Becker did not think Erickson would survive this ordeal.

Erickson shuffled forward and took a seat at a small metal table across from Becker.

Becker waited for the guard to leave the room before speaking. "You asked me to come and I'm here," he said. "I don't have a lot of time so let's get this over with."

"I need your help," Erickson pleaded. "You know I'm innocent. You have to tell the police. I've tried to tell them about

404 Pamela Samuels Young

Ashley, but they won't listen. They'll listen to you. I won't make it in here."

"You're not getting out of here because this is where you deserve to be." Becker smirked. "You're going away for a long, long time."

"But I'm innocent! You know I didn't kill Claire!"

"You need to pay for what you did to Ashley."

"Ashley's a liar! I never touched her!"

Becker leaned across the table, enraged. "Just because you never touched her, you think that makes what you did okay?"

Erickson shrank away from him.

"Answer my question," Becker demanded. "Making a twelve-year-old child pose for pornographic pictures is okay? What did you do? Sell them on the Internet to other perverts? Every time I think about the fact that I made you Kaylee's godfather, it makes me sick to my stomach." Becker reached across the table and backhanded him.

Erickson's whole body whipped sideways from the force of the blow. "I'm sorry for what I did," he sobbed, "but please don't let Ashley get away with this. You have to tell the police she set me up."

"I'm not telling the police anything," Becker said calmly. "And anyway, it turns out that I was wrong. Ashley didn't kill Claire."

Erickson abruptly stopped crying. "What? How do you know that?"

"I know."

"But . . . if it wasn't Ashley, then who?"

Becker smiled stiffly.

"Wait a minute." Shock darkened Erickson's face. "So it was you?"

"You deserve exactly what you're going to get for stealing Ashley's innocence"—he paused—"and for betraying me."

"What? I never betrayed you."

"The Management Committee was considering me as your replacement for chairman of the firm. But you told them to take my name off the list."

Erickson's mouth gaped open, but no words followed. "I needed you in Washington. I—"

"Save the lies," Becker said. "I don't want to hear it."

Erickson wiped his face on the sleeve of his prison jumpsuit. "So it *was* you. You set me up!"

"No," Becker said. "I already told you. I didn't do it. But I wish I had."

Erickson seemed disoriented. Then his eyes filled with a knowing light. "How stupid of me! It was Sophia. She had a run of the house. She could've easily killed Claire."

Becker smiled. "No, it wasn't Sophia either."

"But you already said it wasn't Waverly Sloan. Who else could have done it?"

"You were set up, but it wasn't Ashley, it wasn't Sophia, and it wasn't me or Waverly Sloan." Becker paused in anticipation of Erickson's reaction to the shocker he was about to disclose. "Your wife framed you."

Deep ridges of bewilderment creased Erickson's forehead. "What? That doesn't make sense."

Becker leered across the table at him. "Actually, it makes complete sense."

"But I don't understand. Why would she—"

"The day before she died, Claire mailed that DVD to Sophia, along with a letter explaining her entire plan. When Claire planted that camera in your office and found out about your sick little hobby, she realized that what Ashley had told her about you years ago was true. She was consumed with guilt for sending her daughter away at your urging, rather than believe that you were forcing her to pose naked.

"Over a series of weeks, she began hoarding the morphine she got from her doctor. After planting traces of it on your gardening

gloves, she injected herself with a disposable syringe. She was quite
meticulous. She calculated exactly how much time she would have
to flush everything down the toilet and return to bed before
slipping into unconsciousness. What you did to Ashley was despic-
able. Claire was determined to make you pay, and apparently, that's
about to happen."

"You have to tell the police what you know!" Erickson wailed.
"Sophia has to give that letter to the police!"

"Claire instructed Sophia to burn it and that's exactly what she
did. And don't look for me to help you. As far as I'm concerned,
we never had this conversation. Anyway, no one would believe
this story coming from you. They have you on camera, remember? You have no defense to the child pornography charges and
you'd sound like a lunatic claiming Claire injected herself."

Becker leaned back in his chair and chuckled.

"You're actually lucky. Claire didn't want Ashley to be the
center of an embarrassing child porn case. She asked Sophia not
to ever reveal what you did to Ashley. Sophia was actually hesitant
about turning over the DVD to the police, but I convinced her to
give it to me. That DVD and the morphine found on your
gardening gloves are more than enough to send you away for
life."

Becker enjoyed the look of horror on Erickson's face. He
stood up as Erickson's sobs grew louder.

"Wait, please don't leave!" he pleaded. "You have to tell the
police the truth!"

"No, I don't. You deserve everything you're about to get."
Becker started walking toward the door.

"I never thought your wife was all that bright, but she definitely pulled one over on you. She planned everything out months
in advance and waited until her doctor told her she only had a few
weeks to live."

"Claire knew she was close to dying?"

"Yes. And that's when she moved forward with her plan. Her

decision to go along with selling the insurance policy and backing out of the surgery were all part of the setup. So was telling you she wanted to be cremated, but neglecting to share her wishes with Ashley or Sophia. She even consulted with a divorce attorney and told him she feared you might try to kill her. That testimony alone would probably nail you." Becker paused and smiled.

"Claire crafted a perfect plan and understood exactly how it would play out after her death." Becker smiled. "She anticipated that you would be charged with her murder and that Ashley would eventually recover the money you got from that insurance policy. And it looks like she was right. We both underestimated her. She was a brilliant woman. Ruthlessly brilliant."

Becker opened the door and called for the guard. "You destroyed Ashley's life and now you're going to pay with yours. I hope you get the needle."

When the guard reappeared, Becker stepped out of the room and completely tuned out the cries of his broken mentor.

EPILOGUE

Dre had just stepped off an elevator at Cedars-Sinai Medical Center when Angela called his name from the other end of the corridor. His face broke into a smile as he waited for her to reach him.

They had not spoken in the week that had passed since the shootout in the park. Angela had kept her distance and Dre reluctantly let her.

Angela was carrying a large bouquet in a white vase. Dre held a bottle in a brown paper bag.

Angela chuckled and pointed. "You can't bring wine in here."

"Why not?"

"Because it's a hospital."

"If I was stuck up in here, this is exactly what I'd want." Dre pulled the bottle from the bag to reveal not wine, but sparkling apple cider.

They both laughed.

"How've you been?" Dre asked.

"Okay," Angela replied. "And you?"

"I'm makin' it. You need help with that?" Dre asked, referring to the vase. "How about if we trade?" He took the flowers and gave Angela the bottle of cider.

"I think I'll put this in here." Angela stuffed the bottle into her oversize purse. "Wouldn't want somebody to think I was bringing banned substances into a hospital. I'm still a lawyer, you know."

"So everything's cool with your job?"

"Not exactly. I'm currently on a leave of absence trying to work out the terms of my resignation. It looks like I'll get to keep my license and won't have to face any charges before the State Bar."

"Why would you? We were both cleared in Cornell's shooting," Dre said.

"Let's just say there were some judgment issues involved."

"'Cuz of me?" Dre asked.

"Yes and no, but don't worry about it. I'll manage. Believe it or not, I'm thinking about opening up my own practice and doing some criminal defense work."

"Cool. With just the people I know, I could keep you supplied with clients for years to come."

Angela laughed softly. "So what've *you* been up to?"

"Not much. Workin' out, scoping out some new property. Other than that, just tryin' to play life by the rules."

"That's good to hear."

Dre hesitated. "Good enough for us to start kickin' it again?"

He could see from her face that Angela had not expected the question. Or maybe she had, but didn't welcome it.

"I've missed you, Angela," Dre said, plunging ahead. "A lot. I'd really dig it if we could hang out sometime. Completely on your terms. Doesn't have to be anything heavy. We could just catch a movie or something."

Dre waited for her to respond. When she didn't, he wanted to kick himself. *No sweat. At least I put it out there.* He wasn't about to start crying and slobbering all over himself like that weak ass Cornell. He made the effort and now he would walk away with both of his balls securely intact.

"Let's go make this special delivery," he said. "I'm not exactly sure where the room is."

Angela pointed down the hallway. "I think it's the fourth room on the right."

They silently walked down the corridor, a journey that seemed to take forever from Dre's perspective. Just as they were about to enter Waverly's room, Angela placed a hand on Dre's forearm.

"So much has happened to me in the last few weeks that sometimes I feel like I don't know up from down," Angela said. "But in answer to your question, yeah, I would definitely like to catch a movie sometime."

Dre nodded, then smiled, struggling to play it cool. He so wanted to pull her into his arms. Instead, he held the door open so Angela could enter first.

"You two look awful darn happy," Waverly said, when they stepped inside.

Dre and Angela eyed each other, then seemed to simultaneously blush.

"You must be Deidra." Angela extended her hand to a woman sitting in a chair next to Waverly's bed. Dre walked across the room and set the flowers on the window ledge.

"And you two must be my husband's partners in crime," Deidra replied. "I read the whole scary story in the newspaper. Thanks for delivering my husband back to me in one piece."

"No problem," Dre said.

The media reports gave Waverly most of the credit for helping to crack a dangerous murder ring that preyed on the terminally ill. Waverly actually came off looking like a hero. Dre figured that was the only reason Deidra was at his bedside.

"How you doin', my man?" Dre asked.

Waverly grinned broadly. "Just lucky to be alive."

He escaped with a shattered knee and a bullet wound to the chest. There were serious internal injuries, but his prognosis for a full recovery was great. Britney survived without a scratch and her boyfriend Ricardo was sitting behind bars. Thanks to the deal Britney cut for herself, he was going away for a long, long time.

Video cameras posted outside the 7-Eleven where Jon was kidnapped led police to one of his killers. The man later confessed to attaching a homemade bomb to Jon's car before sending it off the cliff. He also told police that he was paid by Ricardo to beat up Waverly's brother Quincy, and murder several other people, among them, Veronika Myers, her mother, and Joanna Richardson.

Information supplied by the hit man also linked the two Live Now executives to the murder scheme. The U.S. Attorney's Offices in Las Vegas, Syracuse and Miami were now reexamining their cases to determine if there had also been a high number of accidental deaths among the viatical patients in their states. The hit man's accomplice was still on the run.

Waverly had his own legal challenges to face. Fortunately for him, a murder charge would not be one of them. In exchange for his testimony, the prosecution agreed to cut him a deal that would keep him out of jail for money laundering, bribery and falsification of his viatical license.

Lawrence Erickson's indictment for his wife's murder made national headlines. A sanitized version of the video showing the former U.S. Attorney General watching child porn had somehow made its way to YouTube. The divorce attorney Claire had consulted before she died told *Good Morning America* that she was terrified that her husband was going to kill her before the cancer did. Prosecutors were convinced that they had a strong case for conviction.

Whenever Waverly moved an inch, Deidra bounced out of her chair and rushed to comfort him. "You okay, honey?"

In just the few minutes that Dre had spent in the woman's presence, he felt a bad vibe. If half of what Waverly had told him about his wife was true, he should definitely send her ass packing. He glanced over at Angela and smiled. But then again, once a woman got under your skin, there was really very little you could do about it.

Waverly pointed up at the television screen. "Hey, Angela, isn't that your coworker?"

They all turned their attention to the television screen. "Yep," Angela said, "that's Zack the Hack in all his glory."

Zack was sitting across from Bill O'Reilly. His navy suit looked fabulous against the royal blue of the Fox news set. Zack described with great emotion how he was instrumental in bringing down a deadly ring that victimized the dying. If he hadn't called in law enforcement, Zack explained, many more lives would have been lost.

"Homeboy is really trippin'," Dre said, when the interview was over. "You'd think he orchestrated the whole operation and rescued everybody single-handedly. He wasn't even there."

Angela chuckled. "You have to know Zack to truly appreciate him. He was on the *Today Show* this morning and is doing *Larry King Live* later tonight."

"Doesn't it piss you off that he's claiming all the glory?" Waverly asked.

"No, not really. I owe him a big favor for coming forward with that information about Cornell. If he hadn't, Dre and I still might be facing a long, drawn out investigation."

The D.A.'s Office officially ruled that Dre acted in self-defense in Cornell's shooting and quickly closed the investigation into his death, in large part because of information provided by Zack.

Unbeknownst to Angela, there had been two prior cases of sexual misconduct alleged against her ex-fiancé. The first victim was a court reporter who claimed Cornell became belligerent and refused to let her out of his chambers when she rejected his sexual advances. The other incident, which occurred only three months before Cornell began dating Angela, was far more serious. A summer clerk from Loyola Law School claimed that Cornell forced himself on her in his chambers.

Both women reported the incidents to their superiors, but no investigation followed. The Chief Judge, who should have initiated an internal investigation, covered up the reports. Cornell's only punishment was being assigned to a less prestigious courtroom.

There were rumors of other victims who were too afraid to make charges against a sitting superior court judge. Neither the court nor the D.A.'s Office wanted the public to know how the Old Boy's Network had protected one of its own. Rather than risk having the information come out during a highly publicized trial, they buried it.

Waverly directed everyone's attention to the television screen again. "Turn it up. There's some breaking news about Lawrence Erickson."

Angela and Dre simultaneously turned around as Deidra grabbed the remote. They all listened as CNN anchorman T.J. Holmes reported that former U.S. Attorney General Lawrence Erickson had hung himself in his jail cell.

"Oh, no!" Angela cupped her hand over her mouth. "I thought he was under suicide watch?"

"Unfortunately, he's not the first guy to off himself on suicide watch," Dre said. "He was a pedophile. The cops probably didn't take watchin' him too seriously."

A heavy cloud of sadness seemed to descend upon the room. They continued to listen until the CNN anchor began to rehash Erickson's ties to Waverly through his wife's viatical settlement. Dre picked up the remote and turned off the television.

"When are you gettin' out of here?" Dre asked, hoping to lighten the mood.

"In a couple of days, I hope."

"I want you both to come over to the house for dinner," Deidra said cheerfully.

Waverly gave her an anxious look. "I'm not too sure how much longer we're going to even be in that house."

Deidra toyed with her diamond bracelet. She clearly wasn't pleased to hear that news.

She daintily swept her bangs from her face. "Well, maybe we can all go out to a nice restaurant."

"Sure thing," Dre said. He figured Deidra would soon be long gone if Waverly couldn't come up with a suitable replacement gig.

After visiting for close to an hour, Dre and Angela left the room together. When they reached the elevators, Angela pointed down the hallway.

"Hold on a minute. I'm thirsty. There's a vending machine near the stairwell."

Instead of waiting, Dre followed behind her. He thought it was a good sign that she asked him to wait. Dre felt like he should say or do something, but he wasn't sure what signals, if any, Angela was sending him. Sometimes she was so damn hard to read. He'd wait for her to make the next move.

Angela stopped in front of the vending machine and started fishing around in her purse. "I don't believe this," she said, throwing up her hands. "I must've left my wallet at home."

"Don't worry about it." Dre flashed a dimpled smile and pulled a handful of change from his pocket. "I got this."

AUTHOR'S NOTE

Until just a couple of years ago, I had never heard of the viatical industry. I happened to be at a party chatting with a guy who mentioned that he was a viatical broker. When he explained more, my writer-brain immediately kicked into over-drive. I asked lots of questions and, almost immediately, the idea for this book began to take shape. By the time all my questions were answered, I knew the viatical industry would one day make a great backdrop for a mystery novel.

My research for this book included devouring dozens of arti-cles, books, websites and legal cases dealing with the viatical industry. Along the way, I came across many shocking tales of fraud and abuse. I also learned, however, that viatical settlements serve a legitimate need, as they can be a tremendous source of hope for terminally ill patients in desperate need of financial help.

For those folks in the viatical industry who are reading this book, I confess to intentionally taking a few liberties with the real-life process purely for entertainment value. Please don't hold that against me.

For more information about viatical settlements, you can find a wealth of information on the Internet. You can also contact your state insurance regulator for specific rules governing viatical settlements in your state.

ACKNOWLEDGEMENTS

Whew! Four down and many, many more to go. As always, I have a ton of people to thank.

First, my husband, Rick, who never (well, rarely) gives me grief when I keep the lights burning until the wee hours of the morning while writing in a corner of our bedroom. I couldn't do this without you constantly pumping me up. Mama Pearl and Daddy John, big props to both of you. Your excitement each time I publish a new book, makes me equally excited. To my newest writer-friend, *New York Times* best-selling author Sheldon Siegel. Thanks for the wonderful blurb on the cover of this book.

To the multitude of friends and relatives who critiqued the early drafts of this novel, as always, your feedback was invaluable. A big thanks to Diana Glasgow, Yolanda Oliver, Doris Brown, Melissa Carr-Reynolds, Jerry Samuels, Donny Wilson, James White (you were right about that chapter!), Olivia Smith, Bill Covington, Jerome Norris, Marsha Silady, Donna Lowry, Ellen Farrell, Debbie Diffendal, Ann Adame, Jewelle Johnson (a busy law firm partner I can *always* count on), Cynthia Hebron (thanks for the prayers), Kenneth Stokes, Diane Mackin (thanks for the book club questions), Karey Keenan (thanks for the proofreading), Virginia Gonzales, Geneva O'Keith, Cheryl Mason, Kelly-Ann Henry, Sheryel Davis, Pamela Goree Dancy, Paul Ullom (my seventh grade math teacher and self-appointed publicist), Charles Zacharie,

Waverly Crenshaw, and Bookalicious Book Club members Arlene L. Walker, Judi Johnson, Terri Doyle, Denise Walker, Saba McKinley, Nitta Richard, Kamillah Clayton, Claudette Knight, Helen Jingles, Raunda Jones, and Makeda Covington. Thanks also to my writing group, the Write Sisters, who saw this book in its early stages and helped me put the pieces together, Adrienne Byers, Nefertiti Austin and Jane Howard-Martin.

I'd also like to thank those experts who freely shared their knowledge and expertise: pharmacist Colleen Carraway Higgs, R.N. Selma Seale, State Bar attorney Margaret Warren, criminal defense attorney Colin Bowen, an ethical, caring, viatical broker who shall remain nameless, and former assistant U.S. attorneys turned big-time law firm partners, Duane Lyons of Quinn Emanuel Urquhart Oliver & Hedges, LLP, and Carolyn Kubota of O'Melveny & Myers, LLP. Thanks for answering my many questions.

A heartfelt thanks to those friends whose encouragement and support keep me fired up: Russana Rowles, Sara Finney-Johnson, Felicia Henderson and Monique Brandon (who all bought boxes of my books and handed them out to everybody they know), Karen Copeland (thanks for being my unpaid publicist, manager, motivator and road dog), Shirley Henderson (one of my biggest cheerleaders), Carol Rosborough (thanks for all the pub at the Post Office!), Shanita Williamson (thanks for hosting me in Boston), my homies Bettie Lewis, Olivia Smith (thanks for the prayers), Merverllyn Vaughn, Sharlene Moore, Stephanie Winlock, Marcia Drake, Cecelia Dickerson (thanks for running me all over Atlanta!), Donna Lowry (thanks for always being there), Roosevelt Womble (who sold enough of my books to open his own bookstore), and three new friends who happen to share my name, Pam Nelson (thanks for your encouragement), Pamela J. Broussard (thanks for the great publicity), and Pamela Goree Dancy (thanks for sending me that incredibly uplifting email when I needed it most).

Without a doubt, when this tough publishing business brought me down, my book club sisters always lifted me right back up. I have so enjoyed our lively discussions about my books via telephone and in person and you also fed me quite well. Thanks to each and every one of you: **Atlanta, GA**: Imani Literary Group, Literary Diversions Book Club, Georgia Association of Black Women Attorneys Book Club, Circle of Friends Book Club, RAWSISTAZ Literary Group, Mothers with Open Minds Book Club, Diamond Sisters Circle Book Club; **Houston, TX**: Cush City Book Club, Just An Opinion Book Club, Go On Girl! Book Club, Cover 2 Cover Book Club, Kismet Book Club; **Jackson, MS**: Conversations Book Club; **Kansas City, MO**: Mahogany Sisters Book Club; **Las Vegas, NV**: Las Vegas African-American Authors Book Club; **Nashville, TN**: No Stress Book Club; **New York, NY**: Sugar and Spice Book Club; **Phoenix, AZ:** Circle of Sisters Book Club; **Seattle, WA**: In the Company of My Sisters Book Club; **St. Louis, MO**: Just Us Book Club; **Southern California**: Wealth Book Club, Pearls: A Woman's Place to Read, Free Spirits Book Club, Bookalicious Book Club, Women with Vision Book Club, Nubian Sisters Literary Book Club, Blessed Brown Girls Book Club, Something to Talk About Book Club, Nubian Queens Literary Book Club, Barnes & Noble Mystery Book Club, It's Our Time Book Club, Essence of Books Book Club, Kindred Spirits Book Club, African Violet Book Club, The Desert Readers of Color Book Club, Chapters Book Club, So Raw Book Club, Jazzy Lady's Book Club, Wise Women of the Word Book Club, Sisterfriends Book Club, Sisters Untitled Book Club, Real Ladies Book Club, Hooked on Books Book Club, Ladies of Color Turning Pages, Sisterhood Literary Book Club, Sistahood Book Club, Tabahani Book Club, Tri-State Books and More Book Club, Nia Book Club, Phenomenal Women Book Club, My Friends Book Club, Hollypark Book Club, Circle of Friends Book Club, Bright and Breezy Book Club; **Northern California**: And We Do Too Read Book Club, Turning Pages Book Club, Underground Bookstore Book Club, Sistahs on the Reading Edge Book Club; **Washington, D.C. area**: Sistas Speak Literature Book Club, Umoja Book Club, The Divas Book Club, The Reading Circle of Friends, The Fannie Robinson Black Authors Discussion Group, Literate Ladies Book Club, Turning Pages Book Club, Divas Book Club, Sisters Book Club of Richmond, Virginia and Circle of Friends in Upper Marlboro. Please forgive me if I missed anyone!

A special thank you to the book club of book clubs, Black Expressions Book Club. Thank you Editor-in-Chief Carol Mackey for selecting my third novel, *Murder on the Down Low*, as an Editor's Pick. Finally, to Ruth Bridges of Literary Sisters, I love your wonderful retreats. Can't wait to come back!

A super special thanks to my talented team: publicist extraordinaire Ella Curry, President of EDC Creations Media, book cover designer Keith Saunders of Marion Designs, book layout designer Kimberly Martin of Self-Pub.net, graphic designers Lisa Zachery of Papered Wonders and Trenton Chappell, website designer Ikenna Igwe of Team Future Design Works, Bill Ralph and Keith Bauer at Malloy, Inc., and Susan Sewall, Cynthia Murphy and the rest of the team at the Independent Publishers Group. Thanks for the great job you all do.

To my fans, thanks for reading my books and sending me all those encouraging email messages. Stay tuned . . . there's much more to come!

DISCUSSION QUESTIONS FOR *BUYING TIME*

1. Do you think viatical settlements are appropriate investments?
2. What role, if any, did Angela's family dynamics play in her choices in men?
3. What leads some people to strive to attain power regardless of the cost?
4. Are men who marry gold-digging women like Deidra sucked in solely by physical attraction or something more?
5. Do you believe there is a perception that professional women are less likely to become victims of domestic violence than other women?
6. Why do you think Claire chose not to report Erickson to the police?
7. Did you agree/disagree with Jada's advice that Angela should have a baby without a husband?
8. If you were writing a sequel to *Buying Time*, what would happen with the relationship between Angela and Dre?
9. Which character in *Buying Time* did you like the most?
10. What did you like/dislike about *Buying Time*?

ABOUT THE AUTHOR

Pamela Samuels Young is a practicing attorney and bestselling author of the legal thrillers, *Every Reasonable Doubt, In Firm Pursuit, Murder on the Down Low,* and *Buying Time.*

In addition to writing legal thrillers and working as an in-house attorney for a major corporation, Pamela is the fiction writing expert for BizyMoms.com and is on the Board of Directors of the Southern California Chapter of Mystery Writers of America. The former journalist and Compton native is a graduate of USC, Northwestern University and UC Berkeley's Boalt Hall School of Law. She is married and lives in the Los Angela area.

To schedule Pamela for a speaking engagement or book club meeting, visit her website at www.pamelasamuelsyoung.com.

31901050211897